Melody of the Fates

Book One of
A Symphony of Two Keys

by
Matt Hofferth

Published by Hofferth Books LLC
Print Edition
Copyright © 2012 Matthew Hofferth
ISBN: 0983627711
ISBN-13: 978-0983627715

My Muses

For my mother, who always urged me to play my own song.
And for Mrs. Joll, who picked up on these notes before anyone else.

Tasher Nation Map

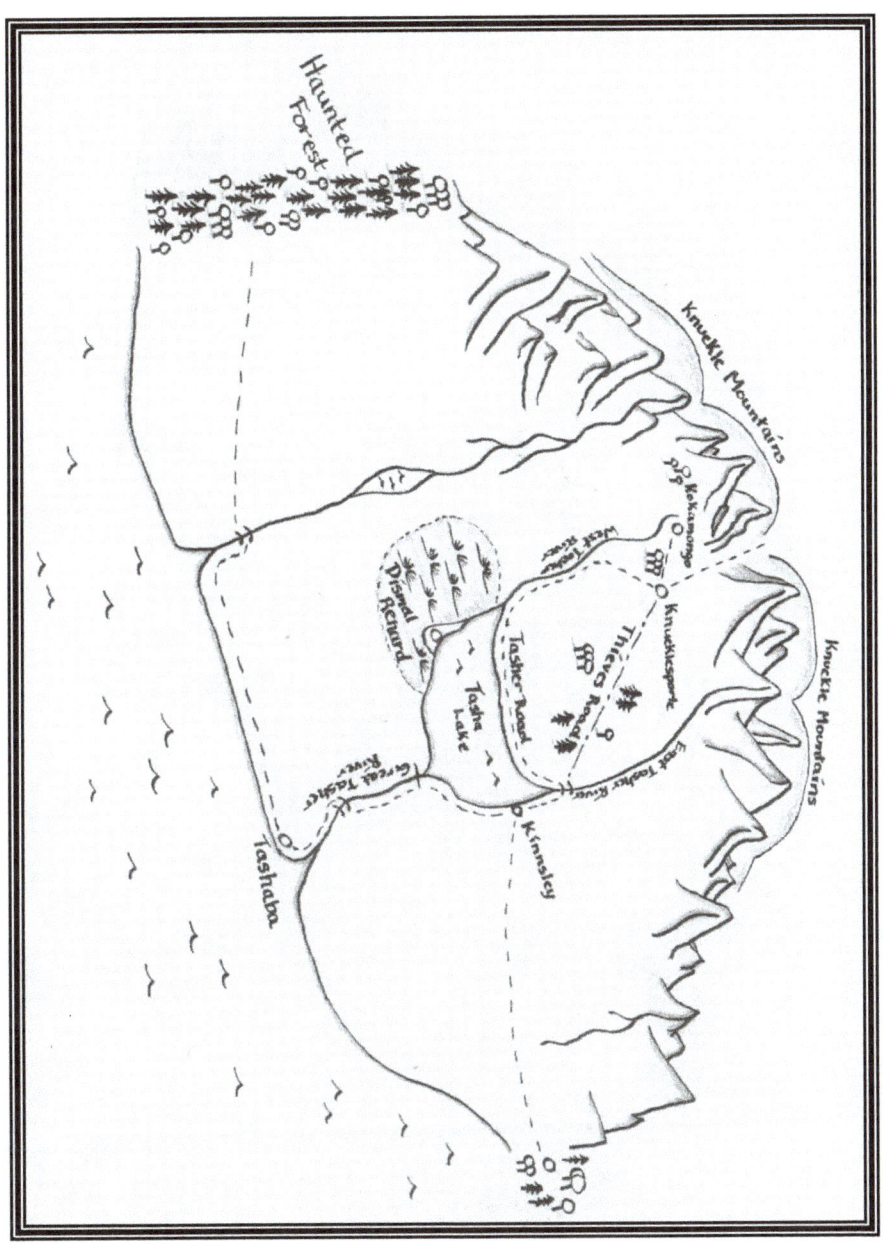

Melody of Fates

◊ Prologue

The clip-clomp of horse's hooves on wooden planks was subdued by a thick blanket of fog that crept silently up the river, tucking the lowlands in for the night. Stout stone supports fell away beneath sturdy planking, disappearing into the haze, and sloshing sounds spoke of swiftly moving water below. A lone man on a shaggy brown horse appeared out of the swirling dampness on the far bank of the Great Tasher River, leaving the impressive bridge behind. Rynel Swift paused for a moment. He reached up to slide his cowl back, revealing wise brown eyes in a youthful face.

Thick, stone walls solidified in the distance, with taller guard towers at evenly spaced intervals. Bulbous domes loomed over and behind the walls, vague evidence of the great city of Tashaba huddling beneath the fog. Ghost ships dotted the mighty river that ran along the east side of the city, sliding silently in and out of the busy harbor, the fuzzy lights of torches their only guide in the fading light of the day.

As Rynel approached from the north, he was relieved to see that the heavy wooden gates still stood open at this hour. The fog had rolled up the river from the nearby sea, obscuring even the sun, which made it difficult to tell the time. He had been afraid that his tardiness might necessitate entry by less desirable means. Rynel pulled his horse to a stop before the gate and dismounted, bending over ostensibly to adjust his turned down leather boots. While making a show of tucking his wide pants back into the tops of the footwear, he eyed the entrance warily. A torch burned fitfully on either side of the opening, and four heavily armored guards were in evidence, two at each side, long spears propped nearby.

The men lounged against the wall, rarely giving any of the passersby more than a glance or courteous nod. War had not seen these lands for some time, and the men were obviously unaccustomed to the need for vigilance. Pedestrians trudged in and out of the capital city, going about their business at the end of the day. Farmers led empty wagons back out to the surrounding homesteads, and travelers hurried in to try to get a spot at an inn before the gates were closed for the night.

The mundane scene comforted Rynel. He doubted the spies of the Grand Warlord had infiltrated Tashaba yet, but one could never be too careful. It had been quite some time since he'd been abroad, and he had hoped not too much had changed in the land he now called home. Still, as he reflected on it, it wasn't as if he had a choice. Recent events had urged him into action. The Ecclesiate needed to know what he knew. They needed to be prepared.

Standing up, Rynel adjusted the short, curved sword at his waist, tightening a belt that had loosened a bit from a long time spent in the saddle. He brushed off his dark leather vest, and straightened the cuffs of the shirt that stuck out from underneath, covering his arms. Finally, he ran a hand through curly black hair and picked up the reins of the horse, leading it toward the gate.

The guards nodded at him as he passed through, just another traveler looking for a room for the night; perhaps passage on a boat in the morning. Nothing to get excited about. Rynel returned the gesture, and then immediately turned his eyes to sweep the scene before him. A wide, stone-paved avenue opened up before him, clogged with wagons, horses, and people. Braziers burned brightly atop pillars, burning off some of the fog and making it easier to see in the city than it had been outside her walls. Small, dark alleys ran off to the right and left periodically, and the canvas awnings of street-side shops jutted out of the smooth walls of tall, sandstone buildings. Hawkers cried their wares, hoping to make a few final sales before the sun set, and dirty children darted through the crowds, earning stern looks. It was the usual bustle of a thriving Tasher city.

As Rynel made his way further down the avenue, the throngs thinned. Though he was anxious to get to his destination, he moved forward at a steady, unconcerned pace. The brightly painted wooden signs of the taverns called to him, but Rynel ignored them. He had more pressing business, though turning down the chance for a quick drink pained him. It had been a long, long time since he'd been in a tavern, but the man who was expecting him would not be found in one of the questionable establishments that Rynel preferred.

Soon, the awnings disappeared altogether to be replaced by ornate, white marble columns and wide, deep-set entryways. *Government buildings,* Rynel thought. He was nearing the heart of the city. The enormous dome of the Summit loomed ahead, squatting on thick columns and lording over the surrounding buildings, its uppermost reaches obscured by the fog. Beneath the dome was where the Ecclesiate met, and in front, there was a large rectangular plaza. The open area was one of many in the majestic city, but this particular plaza was known to be where the members of the Ecclesiate chose to mingle at the close of the day. True to form, it was quite crowded at this hour. Regular folk mixed with portly, red-robed men in matching hats. They were Eclectics, voting members of the Ecclesiate, and they milled around the various brightly lit monuments and fountains that dotted the plaza, conversing about issues of seemingly vast import.

Rynel despised most of these men. They were soft and had never held a sword. They preferred to talk about problems instead of solving them. Most had never even set foot outside the city. What did they know of the people they led?

He quickly found the man he was looking for in a group of garishly robed Eclectics that were gesturing animatedly and quite involved in their conversation. Rynel suppressed a grin as he watched. His friend had removed his red hat, revealing a bald pate, and was attempting to dominate the conversation. *Typical*, he thought.

Unnoticed, Rynel found a bench that faced the group and sat down to observe. His horse drank of its own accord out of the fountain that splashed next to him, earning him dirty looks from some of the nearby men. The bald man continued to gesticulate wildly, practically yelling at the group around him, some of whom had begun to nod in approval. Eventually, though, things began to wind down, and when he finished, he looked up at the bloodstained late evening fog and swept the plaza with his eyes worriedly. He soon found Rynel on the bench and excused himself from the conversation, waddling quickly across the square.

"Master Swift!" the man cried as he approached, a big grin breaking out on his lightly wrinkled face. "I received your message."

"Eclectic Marcko," Rynel said, standing and offering his hand.

Marcko enveloped him in a hug instead. "It has been too long," the man said, releasing him and still smiling. They stared at each other for a long moment before the man noticed the slurping horse. "Ah yes, I forget how tedious the journey can be," he said. "Come, come. Let's get you settled with a drink."

Rynel nodded and allowed himself to be led from the plaza. They didn't have far to go before Marcko turned and strode between a few columns and into a house. All members of the Ecclesiate were given residences near the Summit for when the council was in session. Many never left. Marcko, however, made it a point to visit the mountain villages he represented several times each year, which made him the closest thing Rynel had to a voice.

A servant took the reins from Rynel's hands and led his horse away while a second servant relieved him of his bags. Thus unburdened, the two men retired to an opulent room with walls lined by leather-bound books and a lit fireplace dominating one wall. Marcko settled his bulk into a cushioned chair before the fire and motioned Rynel to take the one across from him. A third servant shuffled in with a tray bearing two tumblers and a glass decanter filled with an amber liquid. The young woman set it on a table next to Marcko and retreated, leaving them alone.

Marcko poured two drinks and handed one to his friend. Rynel took a sip, and then sank back contentedly into his chair as a familiar warmth blossomed down in his belly. *Nothing like a stiff drink after a long trek.*

"A fine rum," Rynel nodded toward his glass.

Marcko raised his drink in response, "Only the best after such an arduous journey. To you, my friend."

Rynel returned the gesture and took another swig. A comfortable silence settled between the two men. The bald man might love to hear himself talk at the Summit, but he also appreciated time spent in leisure. *If only this were a simple social call*, Rynel thought, ruefully. Time was, however, of the essence. Rynel sat up straighter and fixed the Eclectic with a serious stare.

"Vral has learned the location of the Oracle. He will not simply sit on the information," Rynel said into the silence. "I will not allow it to fall into his hands."

Marcko froze with his tumbler halfway to his lips, frowning, "Those are dangerous words."

"Yet, they must be said," Rynel pointed out.

Marcko nodded thoughtfully and took a sip. After a moment he asked, "What do you need from me?"

Rynel set his glass on the wooden table beside him and leaned forward, "Allow me to speak at the Summit. The Ecclesiate must be warned. The Oracle must be protected, and the borders must be shored up. We have no idea how or where he will strike, but we know he *will*." He stroked a chin rough with stubble. "Also, we need to find out how he's getting his information. A spy, perhaps."

"That's not as easy as it may sound," Marcko replied. "There are many who wouldn't heed the word of a simple northern villager, and I know you can't reveal your sources. The Archon Basileus will fight us every step of the way." Marcko cursed. "Sometimes, I believe that man is in bed with the enemy."

"Then I'll show what I am," Rynel answered confidently. "Even Alexzandar would listen to me then."

"Foolish!" Marcko countered. "You know that is outlawed. It would be playing right into his hands. You would be jailed, or worse."

"If that's what it takes...."

Silence settled again after the exchange. Rynel would not back down, and he knew Marcko realized it. Once Rynel Swift had set his mind upon a course of action, he would see it through, no matter what.

Curiosity eventually got the best of Marcko, "I have to ask, what's in it for you? These are not your people."

Rynel looked down at his hands, folded on his lap, "I did nothing once before. I will not make the same mistake again. I will not see more power fall into *his* hands."

Marcko nodded absently, but Rynel could tell he was already calculating the politics in his head. An audience at the Summit was no simple matter. Favors would need to be called on just to get him in the door, and even more to be sure the right ears heard Rynel's plea.

"When?" Marcko asked.

"Tomorrow, if possible," Rynel replied. They would gain nothing by stalling.

Marcko drained the rest of his drink in one large gulp. "Then it appears I have a busy night ahead of me."

Rynel watched as his friend stood and left the room. Alone, he grabbed his glass and downed its contents. *How best to get their attention? Perhaps, if I sing light. That usually impresses people.* The empty room held no answers for him as he stared into the fire. Setting the tumbler back down, he reached for the decanter.

He was pouring himself another glass when the soft sound of a crashing cymbal jarred him so much that he spilled a bit of the liquid. Brushing himself off, he set the drinking implements aside and stood. The cymbal sounded again.

Not here, not yet, he thought.

The young servant reappeared, crossing the room silently to retrieve the glasses and decanter. She curtsied respectfully to Rynel, and then turned to leave. The cymbal sounded a third time.

"Wait," Rynel called to the woman. She turned and regarded him with curious eyes. "Do you hear that?"

"Hear what, sir?" she asked, cocking her head.

"Cymbals, do you hear cymbals?" Rynel pressed, still quite unable to trust his senses.

She smiled prettily and curtsied again, "I'm sorry, sir, but I do not." She turned and scurried out of the room, the hint of a concerned look on her face.

Rynel paused, his mind reeling. *Dare I get even more involved?* After a brief moment of indecision, he walked swiftly out of the room and exited the house. *Who else is there?*

Darkness had fallen completely, the only light on the street coming from torches burning in the entryway to each building. The fog that plagued the day still clung to the shadows, pulled by invisible strings across the pathways and up the stone walls.

Rynel stood back behind the columns and cleared his mind. Calling on a few tricks he learned a long time ago, he cocked his head and focused on the sound. With a nod, he started off back toward the plaza. From there, he walked quickly along the curvature of the Summit. At every intersection, he paused for a moment, letting the sound guide him. The quality of it told him a few things, chief among them that a servant of Vral was in the city. Perhaps, he'd already found their spy. Rynel knew as well as anyone the shortage of ability among the Tashers, but this exhibited lack of care was pure arrogance. One should always take care that you're not overheard. *There's always a bigger lizard*, he mused.

A dark alley, almost indiscernible in the dim light, snuck off from the main street to Rynel's right. He actually passed the opening once before doubling back to enter it. The sound was definitely coming from here. He paused before continuing on and moving quickly despite the dark, unconcerned with any potential obstacles or hidden assailants.

Near the end of the alley, Rynel found himself standing outside a dingy wood door. It was most likely the servant's entrance to another of the Eclectic's houses. Quietly, he tried the handle, but the door would not budge. It was locked. There was a keyhole on this side of the door, probably accessed with a servant's key, which Rynel obviously did not have.

He put his hand flat on the door frame. There was a soft glow, and a few seconds later the mechanism opened with an audible click. He eased open the door and slipped inside. Traces of light washed down a narrow stairway to his left. Rynel guessed that the servants used it as a back access to the second floor, so he climbed, following both light and sound now. At the top was a closed door, the entryway to the upper chambers, a glow bleeding beneath.

There was no lock on this door, and Rynel pushed it open to reveal a long hallway with doors on either side. Large candles burned in sconces on the wall, illuminating a richly patterned carpet and several paintings on the walls. Rynel crept down the hallway, taking care to make as little noise as possible. He hadn't gone far before he happened upon an open door. Tapestries adorned the walls inside and leather upholstered chairs sat spaced around the room. It was not completely unlike Marcko's library, except lacking books and with a bit more ostentation. On the floor, a man kneeled before a grand, heavily gilded fireplace. A roaring inferno raged within the impressive feature. It didn't give off enough heat, however, and thus seemed unnatural, as if the fire were more than simply a fire.

The man on the floor was the source of the clangor. The cymbals were clearly coming from him. What's more, he was talking to his fireplace, or, more accurately, the strange fire within.

"But my Lord, it is *protected*," the man was saying. "I cannot puzzle out how to bypass its guards."

"Do not waste my time and patience," the fire answered in a gravelly voice that Rynel recognized instantly. "At any time I can reach out with a Hand, and you know the price of failure. I *will* have that shard, one way or another."

Rynel stepped into the room. "Sending others to do your dirty work as usual, Vral?" he asked casually.

The man on the floor spun around, "Who are you? What are you doing in my house?"

Rynel ignored him, focused on the fire.

"So you *are* in Tashaba, Rynel," the flame crackled. "Such a logical choice. I am surprised you did not turn up before now." If the revelation elicited any emotion, the voice did not betray it.

"Yes, well," Rynel answered flippantly, "we can't all be as logical as you."

"A pity," Vral's voice in the fireplace said simply. "Kill him," he ordered.

"Yes, my Lord," the man on the floor replied. "Gladly."

Rynel narrowed his eyes, preparing to face the man in front of him. It swiftly became evident that the lackey was not well trained. There was no elegance to his attacks from the start. He simply lobbed a ball of fire across the room. Rynel responded by calmly holding up a hand, and the flames winked out. The man tried several other elements–charged air, rock, even water–and got the same results. Recognizing that he would not be able to touch Rynel from a distance with conjurations, the man pulled out a small knife, held it up, and flames began to dance along its surface. He flung it with a quick flick of the wrist, fire trailing behind as it rocketed across the room. Rynel didn't even appear to move this time, yet the knife shifted course in the air and passed harmlessly to his right. It lodged itself in a tapestry on the wall, twanging loudly. The fire jumped quickly to the cloth and began climbing up the wall.

Rynel grinned wickedly, drawing his sword. He calmly closed the distance between them. The man responded by wheeling and snatching up the poker from the fireplace. He held it in front of him, fear contorting his features. As Rynel approached, the man backed up. They traded step for step until the man backed into the wall next to the still roaring fire. There he began to quiver, holding the poker in front of him defensively.

"No, please, don't kill me," the man pled. "I know things. I can help you."

"I don't think so," Rynel answered.

The man raised the heavy metal poker to meet his opponent's blade as Rynel sliced downward. As expected, the blade cut cleanly through the solid steel of the poker like a hot knife through butter. Rynel's second slash was through the man's neck, with much the same effect. A hollow thud sounded as the severed head hit the floor, followed by a short staccato of limbs as the body followed suit.

"How... expected," Vral's voice rasped. Then flames died down to a more natural level.

"Nice seeing you, too," Rynel scowled toward the fire that was now just a fire.

Behind him, a woman screamed, startling him. Rynel spun around, searching for the source of the sound. A rather pretty blonde stood in the doorway, horror written plainly on her face as she stared at the blood pooling around the body on the floor. Rynel wiped the spatter off of his face and attempted what he hoped was a winning smile.

"Murderer! Guards!" she screeched, fleeing the room in terror.

"Great," Rynel sighed as black smoke began to fill the room. "Marcko's not going to like this...."

◊ **Chapter One**

Grand, snowy peaks stretch toward a cloudless sky. Where the sun touches the crusted white powder, it glistens as if imbedded with countless jewels. The light sweeps downward as the sun rises, illuminating the jagged gray rock where the snow ends. Stone gives way to a sparse tree line, and the golden rays touch the tips of evergreens as they continue their journey along the valley floor and to the plains beyond.

In among the trees, many treacherous leagues below, a tiny village lay sleeping. Two dozen wooden houses with thatched roofs sit in the darkness, shaded from the encroaching sun by the thickly clustered trees of the nearby forest. A small clearing surrounds a spring that bubbles forth from the dense rock to spill into a small pond. From the pond, the clear, cold water follows a straight path downward and through the middle of the village. Once past the village, the liquid diamonds are tossed over a cliff to sparkle in the sun as they make their way down the steep slopes.

At the base of the valley, the stream reappears from beneath the trees as an ever-widening rivulet that continues in a blue ribbon off to the distant plains. Eventually, as the sun continues to peek over the mountaintops, the spray from a larger waterfall below is kissed by the light and forms a rainbow, crowning the valley for a moment in splendor. Soon, the last vestiges of darkness will be chased away, but for now the world exists in that unreal, yet beautiful space between sleep and wakefulness.

The silence and serenity are unappreciated by Vraika, however. Sleep is a luxury for the weak. It is wasted time. It is for this reason and no other that Vraika rises early. Beauty. Peace. They are but passing fancies of a soft world.

Thin wisps of snow swirl around Vraika's feet as he stands framed by a rocky corridor hewn between the two tallest peaks of the Knuckle Mountains. The chilled air invades his nostrils and cracks like a whip across his bare arms. Vraika wears only a sleeveless black tunic, leaving his heavily marked skin exposed to the elements. He does not shiver. He stands like a dark statue carved from stone as the wind whistles around him and back through the narrow pass, making the crags seem to moan.

As the morning matures, small tufts of smoke rise from the woods far below, signs of civilization. The Tashers. Vraika's jaw clenches in anger. The Tashers have lived too long, too comfortably in this hospitable land. They will be swept before him and pushed off into the sea. They will break like un-tempered steel. They will be crushed like brittle bones. Such are the wishes of the Grand Warlord. Such are the wishes of the Fates. And Vraika serves.

A small dribble of blood escapes from the corner of Vraika's mouth where tooth has unknowingly pierced lip, and slides slowly to his chin. Raising one arm, he eyes the black steel bracer fastened to his left wrist with reverence. A crystalline, obsidian shard is embedded on the top, surrounded by a thin line of polished gold. It pulses faintly in anticipation of the coming carnage. His Focus. The source of his strength. Vraika fears it will be of little use in the upcoming battles, though. The Tashers have long been without a valid leader. They will make easy prey for his warriors. His strength will break them, and assimilate those found worthy. True leadership requires strength.

With a hand, Vraika wipes the droplet on his chin and stares at his red-stained palm. The Tashers. They have drawn first blood. They shall drown in it before he is through.

Vraika's eyes darken and begin to swell in time with the shard as they sweep the land below, searching like a bird of prey for his first target. A smoky cloud of darkness falls from his shoulders like a cape and pools around his feet. The narrow, recently unsealed mountain pass has led the Legion through the towering crags to an old, forgotten road that leads down to the plain. Off to one side, out of the way, Vraika fixates on the small village huddled near the spring. There is no obvious value in razing the village, but it contains Tashers. They have drawn his blood. They must be broken.

Burning black eyes lock onto the village. His invasion begins here, now.

~ + ~

"Mother," Werim yelled.

No answer.

"Mother," Werim yelled again, louder this time.

Still no answer.

"Renee!" Werim screamed, his voice cracking.

"What?" came the irritated reply from inside the house.

"Mom?" Werim queried once more, bursting through the front door and skidding to a halt just across the threshold. "*Whew,* I thought you had left already."

Across the room, a slim, red-haired woman straightened from the pot she had been crouched over. She calmly wiped her hands on her apron and fixed her eldest son with a level, green eyed stare. "Aye, 'tis me. And just where would I be going, hmm?" Her voice trailed off into the pleasant thrum of household noise. Fire crackling, stew bubbling; the general din of housework.

Strangely, the wooden spoon continued to spin in the pot, unnoticed, while emitting a faint, almost indiscernible glow.

Werim normally found his mother's unique, lilting accent comforting, but being the target of the stare, he soon began to squirm. To buy time, he ran one dirty hand through his curly black hair, tousling it further. Halfway through the motion, he pulled the hand back and fixed hazel eyes on grimy palms. He would have to wash tonight, his mother would see to that. He hated washing. Carrying buckets of water, heating it, pouring it in the big, brass tub. It was backbreaking labor, and for what? To get clean? He would be dirty again the next day. Why couldn't he just stay dirty?

"Um, I don't know," Werim admitted. "I guess I just thought maybe you'd gone away."

"*Hmpf,*" his mother snorted in reply. She reached a slender hand up and tucked a wisp of hair behind her ear before turning back to the pot. Casually, her hand found the spoon and continued stirring.

Werim blinked for a moment, his brain stumbling on the self-stirring spoon, but the delicious smells of cooking and pleasant hum of activity quickly chased the oddity from his mind. It was obviously a stew. The aroma of meat, vegetables, potatoes, and broth filled the small house. Werim's mouth watered in anticipation. He'd had nothing but a loaf of bread, stolen while the baker's back was turned, since lunch. It had been tasty, warm and fresh, but it was no match for mother's stew.

A loud thump startled them both as Werim's sister, Sharee, burst into the room. Her straight, auburn hair was cut short like her brother's. It barely reached the bottom of her ears and was slightly mussed from an apparent mad dash back to the house. Green eyes like her mother's quickly took in the scene. She was wearing the same tan pants and white, long-sleeved woolen shirt as her brother, though hers was markedly whiter. Both children were of similar height, and though the curves of early womanhood were beginning to differentiate brother from sister, they had yet to take a firm hold in Sharee. Lanky and awkward, the two could have been twins, though Werim claimed the title of eldest.

"Werim stole a loaf of bread!" Sharee announced.

The tattling was only a recent affectation. Growing up, Sharee had idolized her brother, thinking he could do no wrong. It reflected in her dress and mannerisms, but a recent jealousy caused her to be harsher on her brother than was strictly necessary. It wasn't Werim's fault he was older, and thus had reached his sixteenth year months sooner than she. Still, if he was now an adult in the eyes of the village, then he should begin to act like an adult. It was a view Sharee shared with her mother.

Standing aright from the pot once again and smoothing her apron, mother fixed son with another glare. The spoon continued to spin. Sharee was too intent on her brother's suffering to notice, and Werim's eyes had found the floor. He might be a good liar around the other village youths, but he could not for the life of him lie to his mother.

"Werim," she began in a serious tone, "you'll be going back to the baker's tomorrow to make this right, hmm? I think several hours o' sweeping floors should suffice, but be sure Roland is satisfied."

"But, Mom," Werim protested.

"No *buts*, Werim. What would your father say, hmm?" she asked, shaking her head.

"I'd ask him, but he's not here," Werim mumbled.

A frown creased his mother's face, but she said only, "What was that?"

"Nothing, Mom," Werim covered. "I'll make it right tomorrow. Promise."

"Good. Since that's settled, you can go get some water and wash up before dinner. 'Tis almost ready now," their mother said, turning back to the pot and snatching up the spoon. As Werim turned toward the kitchen to fetch the water buckets, Sharee attempted to slink in the opposite direction. Without looking, their mother added, "Both o' you."

"But, Mom," Sharee protested.

"Ah!" their mother snapped, raising the wooden spoon. The room had suddenly gone silent. "If you're going to dress like a lad and get into mischief like a lad, then you'll do the chores o' a lad, too."

Sharee crossed her arms and stomped a foot, "But I didn't steal the bread."

Their mother turned her head slightly and raised an eyebrow, "And you didn't stop him either."

A pout firmly ensconced on her face, Sharee redirected toward the kitchen where Werim waited with his tongue out.

~ + ~

After dinner, Sharee found herself washing dishes while Werim trudged in and out of the house with buckets of water. Her mother was in the living room, seated in front of the fire keeping one eye on the two of them and the other eye on a bit of wood she was carving. For as long as Sharee could remember, her mother and father had sold small, wooden trinkets out of their home. The town had a proper carpenter, but the villagers appeared to enjoy the intricate figurines. It didn't generate a lot of coin, but Sharee could never remember wanting for much of anything.

Her mother hummed an exotic tune as she worked, the notes building up swiftly only to float down like falling leaves. The enchanting hymn wafted into the kitchen. It was soothing, yet lively and for some reason reminded Sharee of the woods that she often played in with her brother and his friends. There weren't any other girls of Sharee's age in the village, so she'd always stuck with the boys on their adventures. Besides, she felt at home among the trees. The solid trunks, the soft moss, the shady canopies. They reminded her of home for some reason that she could never quite explain.

Soon enough, Sharee had finished the dishes and put them away in the wooden cupboards that ran the length of the kitchen. Joining her mother in the living room, she sat down and enjoyed the fire crackling in the hearth, punctuating her mother's notes. Strangely, the piece of wood in her hands almost seemed to glow and twist under her deft ministrations, and no shavings dropped to her lap. Sharee hardly paid attention as she stared into the flames and imagined the long, orange tongues were giant trees swaying to her mother's tune. She thought she could almost hear wood pipes in accompaniment with surprisingly intricate little trills on top of the melody. Small sprightly sparks danced around, rising up to disappear in the smoke as it traveled up and was sucked out by the river stone chimney.

Werim crashed in through the door and destroyed the mood, a wooden staff with two dripping pails hanging across his neck. He grunted as the containers swayed dangerously close to spilling and caught his balance. Hefting the staff, he trudged over to set it all down near the fire. Lifting the wooden handle of the steaming cauldron off its hook, he carefully lugged the heavy pot toward the stairs. Loud thuds reverberated off of each step as his made his way up.

Sharee's mother looked up from her carving to watch her son. Turning toward her daughter she said, "If he'd do it a pail at a time like I told him, it wouldn't be such a struggle."

Sharee rolled her eyes, "He never wants to do things your way, Mom."

Her mother chuckled, "Just like his father."

"I heard that," Werim yelled from upstairs.

The accusation was met with silence.

"When's Dad coming back?" Sharee asked hesitantly.

A concerned look crossed her mother's face for just a moment before she had a chance to suppress it. "When he's done what he set out t'do, he'll be back."

Sharee scrunched her face in confusion, "What is he doing, though?"

"Yeah, just what *is* he doing?" Werim added, appearing at the bottom of the stairs.

There was an uncomfortable silence as the children fixed their mother with penetrating stares of their own. Their father had been gone for almost a year now, and they each remembered the strange circumstances under which he had left.

One morning, he had simply announced that he was going to visit the soldiers camped near the capital city of Tashaba. He was quite vague on his reasoning and mentioned only that he had business with the general there. Their father had never been away on business before, and it was unlikely he was off to sell wood carvings to the Army. Still, their mother hadn't questioned it, so they hadn't either. The oddity deepened when it became apparent that the errand was not going to be a quick journey. Weeks turned to months, and with each passing day worry appeared to gnaw more hungrily at their mother.

"Your father may not look it," their mother replied finally, looking up, "but there are a great many things he knows about which the two o' you haven't the thinnest branch o' an idea. Even great generals need counsel on occasion."

"Will he be back in time for my nameday?" Sharee asked. She was only a month away from her sixteenth year, and she was anxious to catch up to her brother, if only for a few short months.

A shaken head was the reply, "I don't think so, honey. The capital is quite a journey, and he had a big job to do."

"Oh," Sharee responded. What else was she to say? Of course it was a disappointment, but there was no need to make her mother feel worse than she already did.

Werim went over and laid a hand on his sister's shoulder. "It's only another day," he said. After all, his sixteenth nameday celebration had been the first one their father had missed, a scant two days after he'd left. "We can have an extra celebration when he gets home."

"I know, but it's my sixteenth," Sharee whined. "He won't get to see me open my gift."

"Oh, he already knows what you'll be getting, dear," their mother's eyes twinkled. "You should be able to show it to him soon enough, and be better for the time."

Sharee took the bait. "What is it, Mom?" she asked breathlessly.

"Ah," their mother held up a finger, "you'll know on your day and not one minute before. Now go wash up and get ready for bed."

"I hope it's as neat as Werim's was," Sharee admitted, rising.

Werim laughed, "Fat chance. Besides, you can't even lift mine."

Sharee didn't reply, but shoved Werim roughly as she sprinted upstairs.

It took Werim a moment before lurching to follow her. "Oh, no you don't!" he yelled. "I just lugged all that water up there. I am *not* getting the cold turn again." Loud thumps sounded as Werim took the stairs two at a time.

The sound of a struggle echoed back down the stairs, brother and sister obviously fighting over the bathroom. "Mom," Sharee yelled.

"Werim, let your sister go first."

There was a muffled retort and a slamming door as Werim went to their shared room to wait. Their mother returned her attentions to her work. Her humming once more filled the house, and as Sharee relaxed in the warm water, she swore she could almost see faces taking shape on the wooden walls.

◊ Chapter Two

Another month came and went with no word from Tashaba. Werim was beginning to think his father might be dead, that he might never come back. After all, there were plenty of dangers out there in the world, even if his mother dismissed them all as tall tales.

He shut the heavy wooden door to the front of his family's house and gazed up at the bedroom window. The house was the only two story structure in the small village, and had wooden shingles to boot. Most of the other houses were much smaller with thatch roofing. Furthermore, four tall trees grew at the corners of the house where the slope of the shingles turned upward, making it appear as if the unique roof had been draped across a rope tied between four living supports. All in all, the house resembled a large, rectangular tent, pitched between the trees and made out of a strangely pliable wood. Werim had never before reflected on how odd this was. It was the only house he'd ever known. Recent musings about his father, however, had rendered him especially pensive.

Perhaps dad had been traveling with a company that was attacked, Werim thought as he started off across the village. Few travelers visited Kokamongo, but those that did often brought tales of constant war to the north. The Tasher Nation was relatively peaceful, but it was said that other lands weren't nearly so fortunate. Savages raged beyond the mountains, and strange religious fanatics held the lands on the northern border. As a result, foreigners were often looked at askance, as if their mere presence would somehow disrupt the equilibrium. Werim didn't know much about other lands and his parents didn't talk about it when he was around. He'd been known to eavesdrop on occasion, however, and would often catch the end of strange conversations about some Grand Warlord and his two hands. Didn't most people have two hands? It was all incomprehensible to Werim, but it put his parents on edge, and that was a rarity. Anything that could rile them had to be bad. Still, trouble stayed out of Tasher lands for the most part, and that was all there was to it. It was hard enough to coax a living from the mountains without worrying about foreign wars.

Werim hopped over the small stream that ran through the middle of the village, lost in thoughts about his father and war. A spring just to the northwest produced the cool, clear water and it ran straight through the village to where it spilled off a cliff overlooking the valley. Perhaps two dozen houses lined the bubbling stream with a winery, mill, workshop, and smithy on the outskirts. Small vineyards surrounded the spring, and ice wine provided the village with its major source of trade. Grapes harvested just after the first freeze produced a sweet flavor that was considered a luxurious treat further down the mountain and in the plains beyond.

Werim's house was nestled near the mountain pines on the western edge of the village, away from most of the other structures. The sparring ground on the east side of the stream was his destination. It was close to a dirt path that ran down the mountain and joined up with the broken, cobblestone road that ran the length of the valley. It was said that the road once served as a highway through the mountains to the lands beyond, but that many years ago a great earthquake had sealed the pass.

Further down, along the road, rivulets joined the main stream as it meandered down the slope so that by the time the road left the valley, a roaring river crashed onto the plains at its side. Up this high, though, the water was easy enough to leap without making a splash. Werim had heard tales of the great bridges that spanned the torrent on the plains, but he had yet to see them with his own eyes. Other kids his age sometimes traveled with their parents to one of the villages further down the mountain, but rarely did anyone travel so far as the plains. His own family never left the village, except for his father's recent departure. He often thought it was strange that they never went anywhere–that they had no family or friends to visit–but it was hard to miss what you never knew.

A cool breeze ruffled Werim's hair and sent a chill skittering along his spine. The crisp scent carried reminders that winter would be upon them soon, and winter in the mountains was no picnic. There would be no travelers until spring. Not even his father.

Maybe he went south into the Haunted Forest, never to be heard from again. That was another tale travelers favored, and Werim had caught mention of the forest in his parents' conversations, too, always in hushed tones. It was popular knowledge that no man who ventured into the dense forest returned to tell of what lay beneath the cursed boughs. Most travelers spoke of the trees hesitantly, and Werim caught his mother wearing a disapproving frown on more than one occasion when that particular rumor was given voice. She didn't seem to appreciate the grandiose tales of spirits in the woods.

All in all, it was hard for Werim to get a sense of what was really going on in the world, even before his father had left to get caught up in it. He had to admit that the tales of great heroes and bloody battles interested him, excited him even. Then, there were the trills of fear that raced up his spine when he heard about the tree spirits that roamed the forest, preying on anyone unfortunate enough to get too close. Or the knots that turned his stomach when someone described the way the savages beyond the mountains cannibalized the dead, building great fires to roast the bodies of their defeated foes for dinner. Werim suspected that many of the traveler's tales were just that, stories invented for entertainment and to scare children, but something about them tugged at him. It didn't help that neither of his parents ever wanted to answer his questions. They would always say that he'd find out soon enough, and that he shouldn't rush to complicate his life with the problems of others.

"Werim," A voice called.

Werim broke from his musings and looked up to find a mop of blond hair jogging across the sparring ground toward him, two sticks in hand. He couldn't help but break into a smile. Montgumbo, or Bud as he would tell anyone to call him–he hated his name–was Werim's best friend in the village. Bud was the same age as Werim, but much broader in the chest and arms. He even had the beginnings of a beard poking through on his chin and upper lip.

"Hey, Bud," Werim waved. "Is there anyone out here teaching today?"

Even as he asked, his eyes found the yard in front of him deserted. The sparring ground was really only a dirt circle on the outskirts of the village, the turf torn up from the young men who used it to hone their swordsmanship. Occasionally, one of the men from the village would stop by and offer some lessons, but recently, most were too busy; it was nearly harvest time.

Werim had witnessed his father giving instruction using a wooden staff, and the rapt attention of the other men had lent the critiques a great deal of weight. In light of that, Werim wanted to be proficient for his father's return, whenever that might be. He wanted his dad to be proud. Living up to the expectations of his family was going to be difficult with less than a year of practice to his name.

Werim, like all the other boys of the village, had received his sword on the eve of his sixteenth year. Before that, he hadn't been allowed to spar, being a child. Now, though, he and Bud were out almost every day, hoping to pick up what they could. Some of the younger men stopped by on their way to and from the fields, offering the boys a few helpful words, but it wasn't like the instruction Werim wished he could have gotten from his father.

"Nope, just us," Bud replied. He tossed one of the sticks in his hand at Werim, and the two headed out onto the yard.

They assumed positions across from each other. Bud held his stick up at the ready. Werim began to raise his as well.

"C'mon, Werim," Bud frowned. "Forms first. You're always supposed to start with forms. We can spar after."

Werim groaned but stepped up beside Bud and faced out. Both youths raised their sticks in unison. They began the routine of forms, flowing fluidly from one stance to the next. It was a delicate dance, and Werim was more graceful than Bud, but not by much.

Sweat glistened on their faces by the time they were done. Bud put one end of his stick into the ground at his side and leaned on it, catching his breath. Werim, however, was still dancing on the balls of his feet, twirling his stick menacingly. He was ready to spar. He was always ready to spar.

"You're just going to beat me again," Bud announced between breaths. "You've got longer arms. It's not fair."

"Maybe, but you're stronger," Werim pointed out.

"Just means I tire quicker," Bud answered.

"Here," Werim said, breaking his stick in half on his knee. "I'll go with a shorter stick this time. You usually use a longer sword anyways, so it'll be more real."

Bud perked up. "Fine, you're on."

The two youths faced each other this time. Bud leveled his longer sword at Werim, who bounced eagerly with a half sword in hand. He tossed the other half to the edge of the ring nonchalantly.

They began to circle one another, waiting on the other to make the first move. Bud stepped side to side in smooth motions, his muscles taut, ready to counter a strike. Werim flitted in and out, trying to coax his opponent into action. With the shorter sword, he knew he had to get Bud to swing before he could try to go in for a touch.

Eventually, though, Werim's patience ran out. He danced in too close, and Bud took a hack at his legs. Werim saw it coming, but was too slow to react to his friend's speedy strength. The stick caught him in the back of the knees and sent him sprawling to the ground.

"Protect your legs," Bud repeated one of their lessons. "You can't fight without your legs beneath you."

"Right, right," Werim answered, waving him off. "Again."

Werim leaped back to his feet and faced his friend again. Once more, they circled each other like animals sniffing, searching for a weakness. Werim went in close again, but this time leapt into the air, anticipating Bud's leg swipe. He easily touched Bud on the shoulder before landing.

Bud sighed, "Ah, you know me too well."

"You always do the same move when it hits," Werim observed.

Bud shrugged, "Stick with what works, I say."

"You could always, you know, just *try* to switch it up," Werim pointed out.

Again Bud just shrugged. "Let's go get our swords."

"Why, you want another go? For real this time?" Werim asked hopefully.

"And get in trouble again?" Bud responded. "No, thanks. If I come back with another scratch on my arm, mum'll tan my hide."

Werim pouted, "Come on, Bud, where's your sense of adventure?"

"Waiting until there's a real fight, like it's supposed to," Bud said.

"There'll never be a real fight up here," Werim whined. "Nothing like that ever happens this far from everything."

"Then I'll get very good at mending sacks," Bud offered. "Let's go."

Werim tossed his stick, end over end, at Bud. Its rounded tip struck the bigger boy in the chest, eliciting a grunt. In anger, Bud threw down his sword and ran at Werim, tackling him roughly. They rolled around for a bit, each struggling to get the upper hand before Bud finally ended up on top. He sat there for a moment, then got to his feet and offered Werim a hand.

"You ready now?" Bud asked calmly.

Werim swatted the hand aside and hopped up on his own. He glared at his friend, and then they both burst out laughing. Werim may win at sparring, but Bud could still outmuscle him.

"Yeah, let's go, you big oaf," Werim teased.

Bud retorted, "You throw like your sister."

They set off for the south end of the village where the smithy was located. The problem with live sparring was that you inevitably got a few notches in your blade. And a few scratches on your body. Parents generally frowned on the young adults coming home with wounds.

As Werim walked back through the village alongside his friend, he tried to appear as if on an errand, walking with presumed purpose. Bud's mother was the village seamstress, so he didn't have to sit around and learn her trade in the same way that Werim didn't have to help carve figurines. In that respect, the pair was a source of envy among the other boys in the village, who were pressed into service daily by their parents. Still, if caught lounging around, they were not immune to being sent to fetch this or that as a favor, something both of their mothers would encourage them to do. Werim's blisters were still healing from a month of sweeping bakery floors. He wasn't in a hurry to pick up more chores.

An absent father was another thing the two youths shared. Bud's father had run off when Bud was very young. At least Werim had gotten to know his father. Another bit of worry knotted itself in his bowels at the reminder. Maybe ignorance was bliss. Bud never seemed to have stomach cramps.

They found the stream and turned to walk alongside it. The village was quiet during the day, as most of the men were out tending the vineyards. Women could be seen sweeping out doorways, hanging clothes to dry, or just generally minding the other chores of a household. A strong smell wafted from the tannery as they passed the Peau house, and the boys paused to wave at Andree, another boy their age, who was busy beating a stretched hide with a large paddle. A glare from his mother in the doorway put both boys' heads down, and sent them quickly away. Andree frowned and beat all the harder.

The dual chimneys of the bakery crowned a house on the far side of the stream, the aroma of fresh bread enticing both boys to consider another small theft as they passed by, even if it meant another month of sweeping. Several young girls came out of the store with packages in their hands, giggling at the two boys and running back upstream.

The distant ping of hammer on anvil began to fall on their ears as they neared the smithy. They could see the top of the building behind the wooden houses sitting along the stream, its large chimney pouring black smoke. Scrontle Marteau, the blacksmith, was obviously working on something. Werim followed Bud away from the stream and in between two houses, ducking under a line of laundry and hurrying across the dirt path toward the large, stone building.

The smithy was the one structure that was made more of river rock than wood in the village. The peals of the hammer were much louder here, interrupted every now and then by a whooshing sound as the bellows were worked to fan the forge. Two huge, steel doors barred entrance to the structure, and the boys stepped up the stone stairs to stand before them.

A large iron ring was held in a loop to the doors, and Werim reached up, pulling the ring back and letting it fall with a loud clank. He repeated the sound twice more and then hesitated when the sounds of metalwork dropped off. They were replaced by heavy footsteps as the blacksmith approached the door.

The heavy doors were balanced on well-oiled pinions, and they flew apart as the burly blacksmith yanked them open to peer down at the two boys. He was a huge bear of a man with dark, curly hair that covered him like fur. Silver tinged the hair at his temples and brown, almost golden eyes bored into the boys before a wide smile cracked across his sweaty face.

"Master Suppe! Master Swift! Good to see you," he boomed. "Come in, come in." He turned and motioned them across the threshold.

"Hey Scrontle," the boys responded in unison, smiling broadly. Most of the adults in the village still treated them like children, but not the blacksmith. He had started using the honorific *master* for them the same day he'd finished their swords, and they had begun calling him by his first name. It was sort of an inside joke between the three of them.

"Master Suppe," Scrontle rumbled, "have you spoken to your mother about my offer?" Several days prior, he had approached Bud about possibly taking up an apprenticeship at the smithy.

Scrontle's wife had died during childbirth long before either of the boys had been born, but the result left him without an heir to his business. The village would need a new blacksmith eventually, and Bud was the logical choice. He was easily the strongest in the village and wasn't likely to take up needlepoint anytime soon. Plus, both boys had a good working knowledge of the forge already. Before they'd been allowed on the sparring field, they had frequented the smithy to help work the bellows and watch the implements being made. Though a majority of the work was farming implements, the occasional sword was worth the effort in their minds.

Werim figured that if Bud turned down the apprenticeship, it would be offered to him next. As much as he enjoyed watching the swords being made, he didn't think the blistering heat or the heavy physical labor were worth it. Watching and working were two different things entirely. When it was your job, you had to do it every day and not just when the mood struck. Werim wasn't so sure that part appealed to him. In fact, he wasn't very sure *what* he wanted to do. What did his father do, for that matter? When he wasn't out possibly getting himself killed, that is.

"I'll reach my seventeenth year in a couple of weeks," Bud replied. "Mum says that she'll sup with you after the celebration." Which was one way of saying the offer would be accepted. Most deals in the village were made over a light supper of wine, bread, and cheese in the evening.

Scrontle clapped his hand together loudly, "Very good! I s'pose you two are here for your swords, then?"

Both boys nodded, and the big blacksmith turned and lumbered through the hallway toward the forge at the back of the building. The air inside was markedly warmer than it had been outside, and Werim quickly joined Bud in rolling up his sleeves. Apart from the heat, a fine black powder coated everything in the house. Working the forge was a messy business, and the lack of wife or apprentice showed. Werim's shoulders ached as he realized this visit would likely necessitate another bath.

They stepped through a doorway and into the hottest room of the building, the smell of burning charcoal assaulting their nostrils. A huge stone fireplace dominated one wall of the room with the bellows off to the side. In the middle of the room sat a dusty black anvil with neat racks of tools arrayed around it. Several buckets of water were placed near the work areas, and a gleaming rack of finished equipment rested along another wall. Scrontle thumped over and grabbed two swords from the display and brought them back to a work bench near the door.

He set down Bud's large, two-handed sword first and leaned over it. The blade was long and straight with a simple two-pronged guard at the hilt.

"You'll see I got all the nicks out of the blade, and even cleaned up the inscription a bit for ya's," he said, gesturing.

Near the base of the blade, it read: *Styx.* Bud had named the blade after the fabled black river in the underworld that, as the child's tale had it, connected the sun to the moon. If you walked in the light, it was said to ferry you to golden spires and green pastures. If your path was one of darkness, then you were delivered to the realm of the spirits. Thus, children were warned to walk in the light lest the ferryman catch them unprepared.

"I have to admit I was sorta stumped to see it all notched up like that," Scrontle continued. He put one large, grimy paw to his chin, stroking sooty smudges that appeared to have sunk in over the years. "I mean, this here is some good steel," he finished, flicking one finger against the flat side of the blade and leaned back to view it skeptically as if he thought it would revert to its notched state right then and there.

The three sat looking at the sword for a moment before Bud grunted and grabbed it off the bench, throwing the leather strap over his shoulder so that the blade hung down his back. Scrontle shook his head and laid Werim's blade on the table. Once more they all leaned in.

"And yours, Master Swift, well, it's the darndest thing," he began, eyeing the smooth blade suspiciously. "Well, I know you said you's was fighting, but I swear I couldn't find a nick or notch on the thing. What's more, I was going to clean up your inscription too, so I threw it in the heat to soften up. I musta left it in there for a whole afternoon, and it never changed, not one bit. Burn me if it didn't! I even worked the bellows for a good half hour to make sure the fire was hot enough. Worked up quite a sweat, I did." He stood and backed away from the table, still fixing a wary eye on the blade. "If I hadn't made the thing, I would have accused you of using some kinda cursed metal or something."

Scrontle rubbed his chin again and began mumbling. "Maybe I let some extra ore spill in when I made it. But no, no, Bud's was out of the same batch..." he trailed off. When he noticed the eyes of the other two on him, he stood straighter and wiped his hands off nervously. "Well, in any case, there it is. Good as new."

Werim hastily snatched up his sword. It was about half the size of Bud's, curved and slightly wider at the top than the bottom with a rounded guard that wrapped around the hilt. His father had given special instructions to Scrontle, desiring the strange style for some unknown reason. Werim ran one finger across the inscription: *Scythe*. The same name as the legendary sword wielded by the gatekeeper of the spirit realm. It gleamed menacingly in the orange glow of the furnace, and Werim shivered despite the heat. Had he cursed the blade by naming it so? He quickly pushed the childish thought from his mind and hung the blade from his belt loop. Curses were no more real than the black river.

"Thanks, Scrontle," Werim announced and started to turn to leave. He nearly pushed Bud out the door.

"Yeah, thanks!" Bud echoed.

"Wait a minute!" Scrontle boomed before they got too far. Both boys turned around with quizzical looks. The big blacksmith held up a finger and stomped over to another work bench nearer the anvil. He scooped up the small, dirty cloth sack that was sitting there and walked back over to Werim.

"Here, your ma wanted these made," Scrontle said, fingering the knotted twine that closed the sack. "And tell her if what she gave me really works, well then I'll owe her a hundred more!"

Werim took the sack and frowned at it. "What did she give you?" he asked.

"Nevermind that," he said, waving his meaty hands and turning back to the forge. "You two hurry along now before I put you's to work."

Bud pulled the heavy metal doors shut behind them as they exited the smithy. The air seemed to hold an extra chill after the relative heat they'd just left, and both boys quickly pulled their sleeves back down. Werim eyed the sun where it was starting to sink into the valley, elongating their shadows.

He turned to Bud. "Mom's going to kill me if I don't make it home for dinner."

"Yeah, me too," Bud nodded.

They both began walking quickly back toward the stream. Reaching it, they turned and followed it north. They paused near the bakery, where the two would have to part to head to their respective houses.

"Sharee's nameday is tomorrow, right?" Bud asked, hesitantly.

"Yeah, you should come by," Werim said. "There's bound to be some good eating." He smiled mischievously.

Bud returned the grin after a slight pause, "Yeah, just what I was thinking." He cast a wave over his shoulder as he strolled off through the houses toward his own.

Werim sauntered over to the bakery and looked longingly through the window in front. He could almost taste the celebration food already. Namedays were fun even without a father, he decided. Casting one last look at the orange sky, he turned and ran like the wind for his house.

◊ Chapter Three

Night shrouds the valley. The icy winds of the mountain pass have degraded to a less biting breeze this close to the tree line. The column of Legionnaires snakes back up the forgotten road, men and beasts disappearing around a bend in the rocky corridor. It is taking longer than expected to traverse the treacherous path down from the pass. Vraika is not pleased.

"Warlord Vraika," a gruff voice utters, "the last of the Landshas be comin' troo da corridor now."

Vraika glances toward his second in command, Admiral Lugar Tyniente. Dark eyes stare back out of a scarred face. Lugar does not flinch under the unsettling gaze of the Warlord. It would take more than that to ruffle the weathered man. He is a seasoned veteran, with the ash under his skin to prove it. Standing among the Legion is paid for in blood; the returns recorded on the body.

There are very few Legionnaires that Vraika respects. After all, he is their Warlord, raised by Blood Rite. All are beneath him. Yet, Lugar had grown up with Vraika's older brother. Some might expect the man to be favored, but Vraika paid no heed to the tenuous ties of family. Destiny makes no room for such weakness. Respect, for him, is just another form of caution, and Vraika is painfully aware how high the Fates regard that particular path. His respect for Lugar runs only so deep as the markings beneath the Admiral's skin.

"I will give you one day to prepare the men. We attack 'ere the second rising of the sun. They best be ready, Lugar, or it be your bones on the fire," Vraika growls back in a deep bass.

"Aye, sir, they will be," Lugar responds. He opens his mouth as if to comment further, but then it reluctantly falls closed. Bushy, slate gray hair covers his head and runs down the sides of his jaw line, leaving his chin bare and emphasizing his blockish head. A particularly nasty scar mars the left side of his face, a remnant of a blade that barely missed removing one of his dark brown eyes. Lugar is obviously not one to shy away from a fight, though he has exuded reluctance for days.

"Is there a problem, Admiral?" Vraika asks.

The older man grimaces, "There be nothing of value in this village. Why not just send a few good men to be offerin' parlay?"

Vraika pauses for a moment, considering the suggestion. In the midst of his musings, he becomes aware of what he is doing, and his irritation ignites. He should not have to explain himself to this frail, old man. Lugar is not the Warlord. Vraika is the Warlord, and the Fates show no mercy. They grant no parlay.

Letting his anger flare, Vraika reflexively reaches inside himself and strikes the gong in the back of his mind. The enigmatic cymbal has always been there, his visualization, for as long as he cares to remember. To Vraika, striking it is as easy and natural as withdrawing the sword belted at his waist. The grand sound of the gong fills him, reverberating through his body. It feels as if his very bones should be vibrating, though he remains still as a stone.

His second in command does not react to the sound he cannot hear, though the tone continues to ring in Vraika's head. As it settles into a pleasant pulsing, the Warlord senses a nearby echo providing a faint counterpoint to his own humming. The source of the resonance is the black bracer he wears on his wrist. It always is. The crystal fragment embedded in the steel calls to him, and with a simple thought, he directs his noise to envelope the shard, harmonizing the two. A shudder courses through his body as the vibration amplifies. He feels as if the air around him should be humming, the rocks shaking in fear, though the only outward sign is a pulsing darkness coming from the crystal that is mirrored in his eyes.

Lugar, oblivious to the sound, sees the change in his leader's eyes, and takes a step back. Fear does not cross his features, but he immediately realizes he has said too much. His jaw clenches in anticipation of pain.

Do not do this, a voice familiar to Vraika skitters across his mind. The Grand Warlord had warned him about the voices in the shards.

Go away, Vraika thinks back at the voice furiously, staring at his second in command, unwilling to let his weakness show.

This is not a tragedy, but an atrocity, the voice responds calmly.

The resonances falter for a moment as Vraika's focus is thrown. The swelling darkness appears to flicker in his eyes like a dark, dying flame.

You. Are. Not. Real! Vraika screams in his brain, taking care to keep his face calm. Vral has promised that one day the voice will be silenced. When Vraika is strong enough, the Grand Warlord will teach him. The Fates have sounded.

He abruptly severs his contact with the crystal, jerking his vibration away from the stone's pulsing promises. The darkness in both eyes and shard winks out, but Vraika still feels the original noise coursing through him. It seems calm and contained when compared to the cacophony he had just held. Still, it is sufficient. He once more focuses on his second in command, but he cannot banish lingering echoes of the voice from his mind.

Lugar recognizes the opportunity. "I go to ready the Legion, by your order, Warlord," he intones officially, bowing his head and striking fist to breast before turning smartly on his heels and striding away from his Warlord.

Vraika stands rooted in place, seething. As his thoughts once more settle to a calm drone, tendrils of doubt worm their way into his brain. Perhaps there is merit to Lugar's suggestion. The old man has never shied away from a fight, nor has he ever attempted to rise above his station. He cannot hear the Song. As such, he would always be second in command, and he accepts that. Perhaps he questions not out of a desire for power, but out of his honor-bound duty as High Admiral in the Baraban Legion. Still, what is there besides power?

"Do not trust that one," a voice whispers near Vraika's ear like water falling on heated rock. "He seeks to cast doubt on your competency."

Vraika turns slowly to look at the diminutive figure behind him, silencing the noise in his mind. Bir Larse, Emissary of the Grand Warlord, is a short, sniveling young man–just a boy really–with pale skin and deep, blood-red hair. He can hear the Song, and the resonance is plain this close. Had Vraika been listening, he might have been forewarned of the boy's approach. Bir's narrow, yellow eyes seem to glint in the darkness and cast a menacing air about him that has nothing to do with his stature. Skinny to the point of emaciation, his stringy hair hangs limply to his shoulders. Young though he may be, he is the mouthpiece of the Grand Warlord. When he speaks, it is as if the Grand Warlord himself speaks.

"Besides," Bir continues in a raspy voice, screwing up his eyes as if he could see into the back of his skull, "the Grand Warlord was quite clear on this. Yes, yes he was." The Emmissary brings up one dirty finger and lays it alongside his nose. "Only the children are to be taken, the rest are to be ground to ash. Any children that can listen are to be brought to the Grand Warlord; the rest, you may use as you see fit."

"I know the command, Emissary," Vraika states with annoyance. "It was given to *me*. It be mine to carry out."

"I only advise," Bir hisses, shrugging. "Those who seek to contradict the Grand Warlord's wishes..." he trails off, spreading his thin arms wide.

"Do not be thinkin' of overstepping your station," Vraika rumbles. "Leave the Legion to me, Larse. One day, then we strike. We will be on the plains 'ere the first corpse is fully consumed."

"As the Warlord commands," snivels Bir, fading back into the darkness of the night.

~ + ~

Sharee awoke with a start. Thin morning light seeped through the window and cast a dim glow about the room. Werim was still snoring lightly in the other bed directly across from her, the gentle rumbling sound coming at slow, measured intervals. For a moment, Sharee flirted with the idea of regaining sleep. She pushed her face back down into her pillow and grunted softly. Her hair had transferred some of its clean, soapy scent to the fabric during the night, and she inhaled the pleasant aroma with a deep breath. She sighed. Excitement bubbled too close to the surface of her mind for her to give sleep a second go.

Throwing back her blankets, she sat up and tucked her legs beneath her. She carefully hid her bare knees under the large, roomy shirt she had worn to sleep. It was one of her father's. Most girls her age donned a long chemise for bed, and she had one in her wooden drawers along the wall, but lately she had taken to wearing the shirts she had worn as a child. Even if they didn't fall as far past her hips as they used to, the shirts were comforting.

Bouncing a bit on the bed, she ran her hands through her hair, testing for tangles. It would need to be cut soon; it was starting to get long. Part of her wanted to let it go, to see what it looked like. Her hair had always been short though, and she dreaded that her mother might try to put ribbons in it if it was long like some of the other, younger girls in the village. The last thing she needed was to look any younger. After all, today was the day she was to become an adult. It was finally her nameday.

A smile crept to her lips at the thought. She couldn't wait to see what her gift was. Her brother had gotten a sword. Maybe she would get a sword too, or at least a dagger. Something she would have to train to use. More likely she'd be given a new dress or a pretty hairbrush to try to entice her to be more like the other girls. The smile turned to a frown. Her mother wouldn't be *that* mean, would she?

The thought couldn't stick for long in her head though, and she let it evaporate to make more room for eager anticipation. Even if her gifts turned out to be duds, there would be good food. Her mom had gotten only the best foods for Werim's nameday, and she guessed the same would be done for her. She could almost taste the fresh sweetcakes and plump grape tarts. She might even be allowed a small glass of ice wine, a rare treat indeed.

Apart from the eating, there would be games. She loved playing Squares. Her mother made the best carved tokens, and Sharee was particularly good at the game. She could beat Werim three games to none easily. He just didn't have the proper patience, and Sharee enjoyed anything she could hold over her brother, however briefly. He was always so competitive, and it was up to her to not let him get too big of a head.

Best of all, she could go climb the trees in the woods and not even have to worry about getting dirty. For once, her mother couldn't chide her for being just the slightest bit messy when Werim was always such a slob. It was her nameday, after all. She could do whatever she wanted!

Sharee bounced over to her drawers and rummaged through to find some suitable clothes for the day. She almost settled on one of her dresses, but shut that drawer resolutely. Any other celebration, her mother would require her to wear a dress, but not today. She picked out her long black pants and a green long sleeved shirt. The pants fit her a bit snugly, but they were comfortable, and the shirt was nice without being too ostentatious. There was only a small amount of embroidery down the front.

Silent feet slid across the room, and Sharee slipped soundlessly through the door into the hallway. The wash room sat just a few steps to the left, but Sharee knew she would have to cross the creaky floorboard to get there. Did every house have that one, annoying creaky floorboard, or was it just hers? There was never a way around it without making a noise. Maybe if she put her foot here, and there.

Creeaaak!

Sharee froze, holding her breath. She counted a full ten seconds in her head. *One Folish kitten, two Folish kittens....* The house remained silent, and she released the pent up breath in a quiet hiss. After a short pause to calm her swiftly beating heart, she hopped lightly from the creaky board and in front of the wash room door. Ironically, the quicker motion made less noise. She glared back at the board accusingly.

It was not so much that she was afraid of waking anyone else up, she just wanted the opportunity to explore around the house on her own. Perhaps she would be able to get a sneak peak at her gift. Otherwise, her mother would likely make her wait until the evening, just to teach her patience, or some other silly life lesson.

Sharee scrutinized her reflection in the mirror hung on the wall of the wash room, bouncing up on her toes to try to view her entire body. She found her brush near the pitcher where she'd left it the night before and ran it through her hair a few times, enjoying the familiar feeling of the nighttime snarls being combed out. The big, brass tub against the far wall was empty now, but a small pitcher sat on top of the wooden cabinets in the room and held clean water. Sharee used the water and some soda powder she found in the drawers to rinse out her mouth. Smiling at the mirror, she smoothed out her clothes and, satisfied, exited the wash room.

The wooden stairs took her down to the lower level, where she was surprised to find her mother seated at the round wooden dinner table with two cloth-wrapped packages in front of her, staring intently into the fireplace. Sharee paused quietly at the foot of the stairs, thinking her mother had yet to sense her presence. A steaming mug of tea sat next to the parcels on the table, and her mother absently took a sip.

"Good mornin', m'little redbud," Sharee's mother said, lowering the cup without looking toward the stairs. "You're rising early, hmm?"

Sharee was startled for a moment. For sure, she hadn't made any noise. Had she? *Stupid board.* "I was too excited to sleep," she replied.

Her mother nodded, "An' so you should be. 'Tis a big day for you." She gestured toward the packages.

Sharee's eyes went wide. Those were *her* gifts. And here she thought she was going have to wait. In a trance, she crossed the room and sat down next to her mother, eyes still fixed on the lumpy forms on the table.

"Are those... *mine*?" Sharee asked hesitantly, not trusting her fortune.

Her mother chuckled and fixed her daughter with mirth-filled eyes. "Aye. That is, if you're ready for 'em."

Sharee nodded solemnly, "Of course I am. But... what are they?"

Her mother stood in one fluid motion and swept the bundles into her arms. She turned toward the front door. "Come with me," she answered.

Sharee jumped to her feet and followed on her mother's heels. The heavy wooden front door swung quietly shut behind them. Sharee had to stop herself from bouncing anxiously on her toes as her mother took a slow, deep breath of the morning air, then turned and headed away from the village.

The back of their house was all but swallowed by the mountain pines, growing right up to and around the back wall. The trees were tall and skinny, with plenty of space to allow for easy passage between. Sharee followed her mother awkwardly, trying hard not to trip on any of the exposed roots or moss-covered rocks. Her mother seemed to glide through the forest, a ghost among the trees in the morning mist. Sharee hoped someday she could match her mother's grace.

Curiously, she noted that her mother was not wearing her normal apron over a simple dress. She actually was dressed quite similarly to Sharee, tight pants and a long sleeved shirt. Her garments, however, were shades of green and appeared almost like leaves wrapped around her form. Sharee had never seen her mother wear the strange clothes before, and it only served to amplify her anticipation.

Deeper and deeper into the woods they went, daughter following excitedly after mother. Despite the questions racing through her mind, Sharee kept her silence. For no particular reason, she felt as if it would be somehow wrong to disturb the still morning air. There was a sense of solemnity to what they were about, and Sharee didn't want to ruin it, though she couldn't for the life of her discern why.

Soon, they had gone far enough that Sharee lost her sense of direction. She thought she could point vaguely in the direction of home, but they were beyond the parts of the woods where she and Werim would feel comfortable at play. Strangely, instead of feeling apprehensive about it, Sharee found herself exhilarated. It felt as if she were leagues away from her home, instead of just a short walk. She imagined she could feel the breath of the leaves around her; the clean, crisp smell of greenery and life, as the woods celebrated her nameday with her. The majestic trees bowed to them as they passed, shaking their boughs in adoration of the two women dancing among their roots. There was an extra liveliness to the forest that she had never noticed before. The mysterious energy pervaded her being, growing her excitement and causing her to quiver in anticipation.

It was assuredly all in her imagination, yet she still found it serendipitous when a clearing opened up before them, a single shaft of light spearing down through the mist to illuminate two moss covered rocks situated in the middle. Her mother walked across the clearing and sat on the first rock. Without hesitation, Sharee sat on the second one facing her mother. The packages rested on her mother's knees between them.

"Where I grew up," her mother began, "Namedays were celebrated much differently than they are here." She stared down at the lumpy forms on her lap, placing one delicate hand on them almost reverently.

"You mean you didn't grow up in Kokamongo?" Sharee asked curiously. She'd never given much thought to her parents' origins.

Her mother chuckled, "No. I didn't at that, child." She brushed a strand of red hair behind her ear and looked at her daughter with compassion in her eyes. "There are so many things t'tell you, to prepare you for. I don't even know where t'start," she trailed off, shaking her head.

There was a deep-seated forlornness in her mother's mood. Sharee didn't know what to say. Her mother was always so strong, so collected. It was unlike her to show much emotion, especially uncertainty and sadness. She was the very foundation of their family. Sharee loved her father, but he was emotional, impulsive even. It was her mother that always saw clearly to the heart of matters, her mother who was the shoulder to cry on; the calm in the storm. If her mother didn't know where to start, what could Sharee even hope to offer?

The sadness etched on her mother's face broke Sharee's heart, so she offered what she had. She reached out a hand and laid it on top of her mother's in silence. The two stared at each other for a long moment. Mother brushed daughter's cheek with a hand, pride and love eliciting tears in the corners of her eyes.

"Well, canno' move the forest," her mother said suddenly. "Can only plant new trees."

Sharee frowned in confusion. Her mother simply pulled back the cloth covering the first, larger package, revealing a long, smooth piece of wood, a slightly shorter strand of some sort of cord, and a quiver bristling with white arrows. The fletching on each arrow was a matching pristine white, while the quiver was darker with intricate carvings of vines that made it look almost woven. Sharee gasped; they were beautiful. And, what's more, they were *hers*.

"Where I come from," her mother said in a much stronger voice, "a hair brush is a poor gift indeed." She smiled warmly at her daughter, and then nodded encouragement for Sharee to pick them up.

Sharee cradled the gift in her hands, unsure of what to do next. After a moment, her mother showed her how to secure the quiver properly so that an arrow was an easy reach over the shoulder. The bow was strung and unstrung several times so that Sharee saw how it worked. Her mother watched as she withdrew her first arrow, running a hand along the solid wooden shaft all the way to the gleaming metal tip at the end. The arrowhead grew seamlessly out of the wood and was razor sharp.

Hesitantly, Sharee notched arrow to string. The weapon seemed as excited as she was when she brought it up and pulled back, surprised at how hard it was to bring the fletching all the way to her ear as instructed. Instead of feeling awkward, though, the position felt almost natural. Picking a tree at the edge of the clearing, she aimed and fired. The arrow buried itself into the ground several feet short and to the left of the tree. Her mother laughed and Sharee blushed.

"You'll get the hang of it soon enough," her mother assured her.

The next several hours passed by in what felt like mere minutes to Sharee. Her mother diligently taught her everything she needed to know about her gift, from simple care–*Take care o' your bow and it'll take care o' you!*–to the intricacies of archery form–*Keep your eye down the shaft, don' just be shootin' from the hip now!*–to the use of an unstrung bow as a simple means of defense. They had exhausted the two dozen or so arrows in the quiver and retrieved them several times before Sharee began hitting the tree with any sort of consistency. Despite her initial doubts, she began to find that she did, indeed, have an aptitude for the bow. Something about it resonated deep within her. She was far from consistent, her shots straying wide as often as flying true to what she was aiming at, but she felt like if she practiced at it, she'd be passable in no time.

The sun had climbed high in the sky before they sat down to take a rest. Sharee found that her arms were exhausted. She didn't think she could pull the bow back one more time if her life depended on it. Dutifully, she unstrung her weapon and put the string in a small compartment hidden in the bottom of her quiver.

"You keep track of that bow now. It's one o' a kind," her mother ordered. "Any other bow would be breakin' on you eventually, but not this one. I made it 'specially for you. Strongest stuff there is." She smiled proudly.

Sharee ran one hand along the unstrung bow fondly, and then propped it up against the rock. There was no way she'd let the thing out of her sight. Her mother needn't worry about that. Another thing occurred to the Sharee just then.

"Did you do this with your mother?" she asked.

Her mother smiled back, "Aye. And she kept on me 'till I was perfect. I got blisters somethin' awful," she sighed. "But, oh, the thrill o' the hunt!"

"Are you going to take me hunting?" Sharee asked.

"Of course! Jus' not today," she replied, glancing up at the sky. "We've spent too long as 'tis."

Sharee frowned, but her mom was right. Werim probably wondered where they were, and other folks from the village might be stopping by to offer a word or two. It was just so rare that her mom shared something of her past. Sharee wished she could halt time and live in the moment.

"There is one more thing I've yet to give you," her mother said solemnly. "'Tis perhaps the most important." She gestured to the second gift.

Sharee picked up the smaller bundle. It became immediately clear that underneath the cloth was a solid box that was perhaps as long as her forearm and half again as wide. She turned the package around in her hands a few times before unwrapping it. An intricately carved wooden container evidenced itself. It was a deep burgundy wood, something Sharee had never seen before, and the carvings were of familiar and unfamiliar faces. Her father, brother, and mother were there, along with several other men and women whom she'd never seen, though they appeared strangely familiar.

On the very top, in the center, was an extremely detailed depiction of perhaps the most majestic tree Sharee had ever seen. The trunk was wide and strong, with huge roots that propped it up off the ground so that it appeared to be floating. The branches were thick and strong, sweeping up to the air in smooth curves. If any tree of the forest could be said to resemble a castle, it would undoubtedly be this one. Each leaf had two shoots with five points on each shoot, so that they looked like thousands of little hands reaching up to the sky.

In awe, Sharee brushed her hand over the palatial tree. To her surprise, the box gave a pleasant warble, and the top flipped open. Sharee gasped at the two things she saw inside.

The first was a breathtaking amulet with two golden leaves that looked like they could have been plucked from the tree on the lid. In between the two leaves rested a faceted amber gemstone, as large as a robin's egg, glittering in the sunlight. The entire pendant hung from a green cord that appeared to have no clasp, yet would never fit over Sharee's head.

Below it laid a simple looking belt knife that took up the entire length of the box. The powdered white blade was in the shape of a single, long water lily petal, shooting straight out of a wooden handle that was the same deep red of the box. There were two holes where fingers could be slid through in the dark wood at the top before it thinned out to form the rest of the hilt. There were thorny, vine-like carvings in the wood, providing a grip of sorts, but otherwise the implement was unadorned.

Sharee carefully removed the amulet and held it up. Its center appeared to ignite and burn warmly in the sunlight as she stared into the clear yellow of the stone. Not knowing what to do with a necklace that did not seem to fit, she looped the cord over her wrist and returned her attention to the box. She removed the knife next, and was surprised by how light it felt. It did not seem to be made of steel. Her fingers slid easily into the holes and the handle fit comfortably in her right hand. Like the bow, the knife had a strange sort of resonance with her.

"This next part, 'tis goin' to hurt a bit," her mother said with a mischievous grin. "But I assure you, 'tis part of a ceremony I remember well from m'own youth."

Sharee looked at her mother questioningly. All she got in return was a slender hand held out. Sharee started to pass the knife to her mother, but at a shaken head and a pointed glance, she set the amulet in her mother's upturned palm. Her mother brought her other hand to hover over the gem and closed her eyes.

A faint trilling sound tickled Sharee's ear, but she paid it no mind as her mother began to hum a strange, mournful tune. To her astonishment, the amulet began to glow in her mother's hands. The air around it felt alive with energy, and Sharee thought she could hear the song her mother hummed, accompanied by pipes. It was a sad melody, tugging gently at the strings of Sharee's heart and nearly bringing a tear to her eye. The notes moved and flowed like a breeze through the trees, and Sharee found herself swaying in time with her mother.

As the music began to swell both in volume and tempo, her mother reached out and took hold of her free hand. A shiver traveled up her arm at the unexpectedly warm touch. Sharee allowed her fingers to be splayed, facing upwards, above the glowing amulet. The hand with the knife was guided until the cool blade was aligned with one of the wrinkles on her palm. Then her mother opened her eyes and brought her hand back on top of the collection in the middle. She had stopped humming, but the music continued on.

"You will need t'draw blood," her mother instructed, nodding toward the blade on her palm.

Sharee took a deep breath, and then drew the blade across her skin. She bit her tongue against the burning sensation of her shallow cut, and watched as the blood pooled up. Soon enough, a solid red line traversed her palm.

"Touch your blade to the blood."

Sharee complied, touching tip to edge of palm. She gasped as the blood appeared to slide up onto the white blade, running in spidery, red streaks up to the hilt. She jerked the blade away, holding it closer to her face to examine it, more out of curiosity than fear. The mournful tune had taken on a more ominous tone. Her hand dropped to her side, where it continued to bleed.

"Hold the blade here, steady now," her mother cautioned, indicating the region below her hand and above the amulet.

Sharee did as she was told. Her mother brought the hand holding the glowing gem up to the blade and touched the top of the stone to the blade. The red streaks appeared to be drawn off of the blade. Sharee watched in wonder as her blood was taken into the heart of the stone, forming small red veins throughout. There was a crescendo in her mind as the blade returned to a solid white.

"Blade t'blood," her mother intoned. "Blood t'blade. Blood t'blood, as one."

The melody stopped as her mother said the last word. Silence claimed the clearing once more. Sharee realized something special had just taken place, but she wasn't sure what, exactly, it was. She had heard tales of mystical happenings before, but had always dismissed them as flights of fancy. Yet here she was, her mother holding a necklace that now contained *her* blood. She had so many questions; she didn't even know where to start.

"The bow, 'tis a good gift," her mother observed. "This amulet, however, 'tis your *inheritance*."

Sharee was startled when she noticed that the cord of the necklace had been severed, her mother held one frayed end in each hand. Sharee leaned in to let it be tied on. Her mother's arms wrapped the cord around her neck, and then remained there, motionless. Sharee found herself staring into her mother's bright green eyes.

"I cannot tie this for you, daughter," her mother stated.

Sharee began to reach behind her, but something in her mother's eyes stopped her.

"I don't understand," Sharee admitted.

"You are special, Sharee," her mother smiled warmly. "Just now, you heard the music, no? You heard the Song?" When Sharee's eyes widened in astonishment, her mother nodded and continued, "You are a muse then, as expected."

"What does that mean?" Sharee asked.

"Everything and everyone has a Song, daughter, just not everyone can hear it," her mother explained cryptically. "Listen to your spirit, play your Song."

Sharee closed her eyes uncertainly. She wasn't sure what she was supposed to hear or do. There were thoughts and questions bouncing around in her head, but none of them made any kind of coherent sound. What was her mother even talking about? Maybe there was a mistake, maybe she wasn't what her mother thought. After all, her mother had been the one humming. That had nothing to do with her. There had been the humming, and those pipes.

The pipes! Where had those come from? Now that Sharee thought about it, she remembered several instances where she could have sworn she heard pipes. Not just today either, but other times too, usually when her mother was working or when she was just about to drift off to sleep. The more she thought about those strange pipes, the more they took shape in the back of her mind. Except they didn't look like pipes. No, what she saw was... a harp. She could count twenty-nine strings on a small, ornately gilded frame. It was a harp fit for royal court, something she remembered enjoying in descriptions from bedtime stories.

Still, there was no melody. Though she could now see an instrument in her head, it didn't produce any noise that she could hear, and it didn't explain the pipes. She tried to remember the sound she'd heard from earlier, but the harder she tried, the more she focused on the harp. Indeed, it seemed to Sharee as if she should be able to reach out and pluck it. So she did.

The sound of the string being plucked startled her. In fact, it startled her so badly that the noise was immediately choked off, and her mind was once again mute. She cast a questioning look toward her mother, who nodded encouragingly. She plucked the string again. This time, she let the sound ring. It flooded every corner of her mind with a crystal clear note, resonating in her bones. She closed her eyes and let herself be filled.

As the noise began to fade, Sharee heard an answering note on the pipes she had heard before. This time, she recognized that it had not originated in her head. No, the pipes sounded like they came from her mother. Sharee opened her eyes and found her mother smiling even wider.

"Listen," her mother ordered, holding up a finger and forestalling any questions.

Once more, Sharee heard the pipes, except that instead of a single note, this time the sound was woven into a simple melody. Her mother played it for her twice, and then nodded in her direction. Sharee focused on the harp, and began plucking the strings she thought would produce the correct notes. Astonishingly, it worked.

"A natural!" her mother clapped. "That one is for Knitting. Try singing it for the ends o' the cord."

Sharee obeyed, playing the melody and aiming the sound where she felt her mother's hands on the back of her neck. After the short tune was completed, her mother dropped her hands and the amulet stayed put. Sharee reached a hand back and felt a solid cord again.

"Are there more?" Sharee asked excitedly. "Songs, I mean?"

Her mother chuckled, "Of course. A Song for everything and in everything, a Song. Muses exist t'inspire creation, Sharee. It is what we do."

"Teach me another!" Sharee begged. "Please!"

"Ah, I see I have inspired a desire to learn." Mother put arm around daughter. "There'll be time enough for learning later," her mother said. "For now, we'd best be gettin' back t'the house. Werim will be wondering where we've got off to."

Together they gathered the gifts, and left the clearing.

◇ Chapter Four

"Where did you go this morning?" Werim asked as he settled under the blankets of his bed.

Sharee grinned to herself, remembering. Her special gifts were tucked safely under her bed, still covered by cloth. For some reason, she didn't really feel like sharing them with anyone just yet. When she'd arrived home, she changed, taking her necklace off and putting it in the box with her knife. Then, she'd wrapped the box up with the bow and arrows and stowed them. Maybe when she got better with the bow, she'd show her brother. She knew the first thing he'd want to do is try it out. She really didn't know what to say about the mysterious necklace.

"Just for a walk," she answered.

Darkness pressed at the window to their room. Sharee yawned. It had been a long day. In an endless stream, people from the village stopped by one after the other. Her mother cooked a lot of food, and each family brought a dish as well, so there had been plenty to go around. Sharee's stomach still felt close to bursting.

"Did you see what Bud's mom brought you?" Werim asked.

Sharee grimaced, "It *is* a pretty dress."

Her brother snickered.

Sharee also received a leather belt from the Peaus, a white apron from the Boulangs, and a new hairbrush from Scrontle. The big blacksmith had fashioned the heavy iron handle himself. It was hardly a dainty item, but he had been rather proud of the gift. At least he hadn't given her pots and pans.

"Werim?" Sharee started, breaking the silence that had fallen over the room. She continued when she heard a grunt, "Do you ever wonder where our parents came from?"

"What do you mean?" Werim asked sleepily.

"Well, they can't always have lived in Kokamongo," Sharee explained.

Werim's head popped up from the shadows of his pillows. "Why not?"

Sharee shrugged, "They're just... different. They don't fit in here. They don't talk the same as everyone else, for one thing."

"Geeze, 'Ree," Werim groaned, lying back down. "Everyone's different. Scrontle talks funny too, when you think about it, and he's definitely been here a long time. I mean, everyone knows him."

"Maybe," Sharee relented, "but did you see what Mom was wearing today?"

"A dress and an apron, same as every day," Werim replied.

"No, no," Sharee corrected, shaking her head. "Didn't you see what she was wearing when we came back from our... walk?"

Werim's head popped up again. Sharee could barely make out his scrunched up face in the dim light. "No, I guess I didn't look," he admitted. "Why? Did she forget the apron?"

Sharee scowled at her brother, "Remember the night before Dad left? That strange man that showed up at our house?"

Werim waved a hand, "Sure, sure. What's that got to do with anything?"

"Remember what he was wearing?" Sharee asked.

"You mean that ugly green shirt? Looked like it was made of leaves or something?"

Sharee nodded. "Mom was wearing a shirt like that this morning."

There was silence again as they both let the thought sink in. Then Werim said, "You think maybe they took it from that guy?"

"What? Like robbed him?" Sharee asked incredulously.

Werim shrugged, "I don't know, maybe they bought it or something."

"I don't think what she was wearing today would have fit that man," Sharee pointed out. She remembered the manly frame of the visitor. A shirt of his would have looked awkward on her mother, and the shirt she'd worn had appeared custom tailored.

"Still doesn't prove anything," Werim observed after a moment. "It could have been a gift."

"From who, Werim?" Sharee prodded.

Werim had no answer. Their parents didn't entertain often, and they certainly would have remembered had a visitor given such a gift. Still, that didn't mean it hadn't happened when neither of them were around.

"You still haven't told me what Mom gave you today," Werim reminded his sister.

Reaching down, Sharee found the solid wooden box wrapped in cloth under her bed. She took it out and set it on top of her chest. Then, she glanced over at her brother, stuck out her tongue, and rolled over, clutching the box. She enjoyed holding the secret over him too much to give it away just yet. He would find out soon enough, and when he did, he would be jealous. Sharee smiled to herself in the darkness. It had been a pretty good nameday.

As sleep began to encroach upon her thoughts, a faint melody from wooden pipes tickled her ears from the house below. Only half awake, she found the harp in her head and idly began mimicking the tune. One of her hands snaked under the cloth and found the smooth wood of the box beneath. She rubbed her fingers along the crack between lid and bottom, and a contented sigh escaped her lips as the music from below snuck up on its inevitable conclusion. *I wonder what this Song is for*, Sharee thought, but as the last note was plucked, sleep invaded with renewed force and fully claimed its hold on her.

~ + ~

Werim's eyes flew open in the dark room. For a moment he remained still, staring at the ceiling. His mind searched for what had jolted him awake, but couldn't summon anything. Turning over, he propped himself to see through the room's single window. The sky outside presented the faintest tinge of morning light. It was just before dawn. What was he doing up so early?

Then he heard it again, a strange sound like a gong being struck in the distance. It was faint, but distinct. The first strike was what had awakened him, and now it sounded again, ringing out until it faded in the background. With each strike it seemed to almost grow upon itself, as if building to an eventual crescendo. *What in blazes is going on?*

Werim swung his feet over the side of the bed and sat up, rubbing the sleep out of his eyes. His sister still breathed deeply in the bed across the room. Evidently the sound had not roused her. Then again, she'd always been the heavier sleeper. Werim stood and turned. He took one step, then stubbed his toe and fell back into the bed, hissing loudly. Glaring at the bed post, he called it a few choice names before rising tenderly to his feet once more.

Werim clomped across the room to the hallway. As he headed for the washroom, he strained his ears to see if he could still hear the sound. He thought he could just barely make it out, humming in the distance. A sudden, loud creak from the floor sent him jumping up in the air.

Stupid board, he thought, trying to calm his swiftly beating heart.

In the washroom, Werim's reflection stared back at him out of the mirror. His curly hair was slightly mussed and hazel eyes a bit sleepy still. The pitcher of water stood nearby, and he poured a bit into his mouth. His mother would yell at him if she caught him drinking from the pitcher, but he was pretty sure she wasn't awake yet.

The ominous gong crashed again, startling Werim and causing him to spit his mouthful of water into the mirror. *How could no one else in the house hear that?* The sound rang on, and

Werim stared blankly at the streaks running slowly down the smooth surface. He would have to clean that before his mother saw, otherwise he'd definitely get the rough end of the stick.

A dark green towel hung on a peg nearby. Werim snatched the fluffy cloth, using it to wipe away the liquid. When he was finished, the surface was still covered with streaks. Werim frowned. He poured some water on the towel, and used the dampened portion to wipe at the streaks. The moisture made it a little better, but not much. Giving up, he put the towel back on the peg. It would have to do.

Back in the hallway, Werim attempted to avoid the traitorous board by placing his feet on either side of the offending location so they were wedged against the wall. Having successfully navigated into the position, he discovered that the hallway was a bit wider than expected. The result left him a bit uncomfortable, unbalanced, and unsure if he could lift a leg in order to take another step. Leaning to one side, he placed a hand flat against the wall and lifted his left foot, wedging himself upward. He hovered over the middle of the floor for a moment before he began to slowly stretch his leg forward. The board was not going to scream at him this time.

Just as he was about to place his foot on the floor, the mysterious gong banged in his ear. As with previous soundings, the strike was significantly louder. It was so jarring that he lost his balance, wobbled backward, and fell squarely on his butt. There was a loud creak as he hit the floor, made worse by the knocks of his flailing limbs against the wall.

"What in blazes is going on o' there?" his mother hollered from her room.

Blast. He was caught. There was nothing for it now but to trudge back down the hallway and face the music.

He opened the door quietly and ducked inside as if minimizing his entrance noise somehow made up for the crash in the hall. His mother was sitting up in bed, a book on her lap and a candle burning beside her. She had apparently been up already. At the sight of her eldest son sneaking into the room, she merely raised an eyebrow. Werim was about to make a lame excuse covering his fall, but the gong sounded again. Was it his imagination or were the strikes coming more rapidly, too?

"Do you hear that?" he asked of his mother.

"Hear what?" she retorted. "Hear you flailin' around like a willow in a windstorm?"

The gong sounded again. It wasn't even waiting until the old sound faded now.

"*That*," Werim tried to explain. "The gong."

At the mention of the instrument, his mother's eyes got wide. "You hear a gong?" she pressed. "Are you certain?"

"Yes," Werim replied. It sounded again as if to punctuate his statement. "It's starting to speed up now."

In fact, now that the crashes were closer together, it almost sounded like there were several distinct tones. The rhythm of the resonance pulsed against his ears and, as Werim listened, he thought he could make out not one cymbal, but several distinct brassy sounds.

His mother stood and cocked her head to one side. After a moment, she found it. Her eyes narrowed a bit further with each subsequent beat, and her face grew cloudier until it seemed a tempest was inevitable. Werim wasn't sure what about the sound should make her so angry, but he wasn't brave enough to ask either. *Oh man, I'm in for it now*, he thought.

Surprisingly, instead of thundering at him, she said simply and calmly, "Go and wake your sister." When he hesitated for a moment, she added forcefully, "Now!"

Werim ran back down the hallway, ignoring the creaking board and bursting into the bedroom. Each step was punctuated by a gong burst. They were definitely getting more rapid now, becoming more of a continuous march than solitary strikes.

"'Ree," he shouted. "Wake up!"

"What? Who?" she mumbled, jolting awake and scanning the room, blankets held close around her. She locked eyes with her brother. "Geeze, Werim, what are you–?"

"Mom told me to wake you," he interrupted. The gongs were really picking up speed now. "Don't you hear that?"

"Hear wha–," she began, cocking her head in a mirror image of her mother, and then choked off the words. "What *is* that?"

"Gongs," Werim declared. "Lots of gongs."

Sharee shook her head, "Yes, I get that, but who is banging on a bunch of gongs randomly?"

Werim eyed her quizzically. "It's not random," he stated. "You can hear a very clear pattern. And it's getting faster, like it's building to something. I don't know what though."

Sharee frowned, "Well, it sounds random to me. Like someone's got a whole bunch of pots and pans and is banging 'em together."

Werim shrugged, "Let's see what Mom says."

"Hold on, let me put on some pants," Sharee said.

Werim tapped his foot impatiently as his sister shimmied out of bed. She pulled down on the T-shirt she was wearing as she walked over to her dresser and opened the drawers. She grabbed what was on top–the green dress given to her by Bud's mom–and quickly pulled it on over her head. A glare at her brother kept his inevitable comment stuck in his throat where it belonged. Shrugging, brother followed sister as she stalked out of the room.

A few seconds later Werim stood, wide-eyed and dumbfounded, in their mother's room. She prevailed before them, clad in a strange, waxy green shirt and clingy trousers, with a rather ornate bow in her hands and a full quiver of arrows with red fletching at her shoulder. Her long, red hair was swept up in a ponytail, except for two stray strands in front that framed her face. Belted to her waist was a large knife, and the leather strip caused the bottom of the long shirt to flare outwards like a skirt. Her right hand was partially covered with a strange, black glove, and her pants were tucked into leather boots that turned over at mid-calf.

She favored them each with a loving look that contrasted starkly with her warlike attire. The cacophony of gongs continued in the background, twisting Werim's stomach with its eerie vibration.

"What are you wearing?" Werim blurted out.

"You don't like it?" his mother asked, twisting around to get a better view of herself. The fabric moved with her, not exactly stretching, but not rustling or bunching either. "I'd like to think it still fits pretty well after all these years," she chuckled.

Werim frowned, "No, Mom, I mean where did you get it?"

The gongs continued their crashing. They sounded like they should be entering the village, they were so close.

"Don't worry about that," his mom retorted. "Right now we have bigger trees to climb."

"Huh?" Werim grunted.

Sharee had wandered over behind her mother during the exchange, eyeing her weapons critically. "Your bow is prettier," she observed. "But the knife is the same."

"Yes, dear," her mother nodded, "I did the best I could with the available materials." She put her hands on her hips, "Now are you two goin' t' listen or not?"

"Yes, mother," they echoed.

"There is a very bad man coming with an army," she explained. "I need to go rouse the villagers. You two need t' stay here and protect the house."

"An army? How do you know?" Werim asked.

At the same time, his sister complained, "But we could help!"

Their mother simply smiled back, "You both will obey me in this. And if I do not return, you both will run t' the woods and hide. Your father will need t' know o' this." She shook a stern finger at the two of them, "Do you hear me?"

"Yes, mother, but–"

"Na!" their mother interrupted. "I'm afraid there isn't time for me to explain more. You're just gonna have t' trust me for now."

Hefting her weapons, she glided out of the room. Werim and Sharee followed at her heels. The gongs continued. If Werim had to guess, he would say they were somewhere among the houses now.

"Both of you keep your weapons on you," their mother ordered. "Mark my words: If I don't return by midday, into the woods with you!"

With that she turned toward the front door and placed one hand on it. Werim could have sworn he heard the soft bleat of pipes underneath the brassy resonance of the gongs and was about to speak up when his mother flung the door open. The sight on the other side caused both Werim and Sharee to gasp. A solid wall of black smoke waited on the threshold of the house. Strangely, though it roiled malevolently, it did not penetrate at all. Their mother took a deep breath before plunging headfirst into the darkness. After a few steps, she was out of sight.

Werim ran a hand through his hair. *What in the world is going on?* Were the houses all on fire? What could create that much smoke? He stood there, staring at the dark wall, watching it pulse. Oddly, it shivered with each blast of the gongs. The windows did not rattle, nor the floor shake, the darkness definitely vibrated with the rhythm of the gongs. It seemed almost *alive*.

"Close the door!" his sister ordered.

Werim shook himself out of his stupor, striding quickly over to the door and slamming it shut. His eyes found his sister's, and they were a mirror of the turmoil that bubbled within his belly. A shiver danced along his spine.

As the two siblings sat there staring at each other, Sharee suddenly broke eye contact and cocked her head. Her eyes narrowed after a moment, and then returned to her brother. Apparently she had heard something that he hadn't, and it had snapped her out of the morose trance that Werim was still stuck in.

"Werim," she said far too calmly, "we have to get our weapons. You heard what Mom said."

Werim nodded reflexively and followed his sister back up the stairs. How could she hear anything with the constant banging?

Even the usual creak at the top of the stairs seemed subdued. Werim stopped to look at the board. How had he even heard it with the racket going on outside? It was like the strange sound of the gongs was in his head rather than around him, but even that didn't fully explain the sensory difference. It was like he was listening to each sound with a different set of ears.

Werim remained rooted in his musings. He tried to come up with a way to rationalize the different sensations. The best he could explain was that it was similar how smell and taste worked. He could do each independently, but they could also affect one another.

"Come on, Werim!" Sharee pleaded from the doorway to their room. "Ignore the stupid gongs; they're not even that loud."

Werim again found himself shaking his head and following his sister. How could she say they weren't that loud? They were tumultuous in his head. It was hard to think with the rhythm pounding on him. *Crash, crash. Crash, crash.* Like huge, brassy footfalls.

He wandered into the room and watched his sister as she dug for something beneath her bed. She was right, of course, he needed to snap out of his pensive mood. Who knew what state the village might be in? His mother was out there, in that strange smoke, probably fighting for her life. He didn't have time to waste sitting around and pondering. He was probably just shaken up anyway, what with a sudden attack and all. The sounds were likely just sounds. He needed to shift his focus to the task at hand.

As Werim forcefully shoved his attention away from the gongs, the pounding beat diminished to far more tolerable levels. It was like he'd stuck his head under a pillow. He blinked a few times, surprised that it had been that easy, and sighed in relief before turning toward his dresser.

Reaching behind the piece of wooden furniture, his hand came back clutching the hilt of his sword. He quickly grabbed a leather strap from his drawers and belted the weapon to his waist. His boots sat at the foot of his bed, and he shoved a foot into each.

When he turned around, he paused for a moment as his brain struggled to make sense of what he saw over on his sister's side of the room.

She wore the same green dress from earlier, but white-fletched arrows stuck out above her right shoulder. Cord in hand, she was hurriedly stringing an impressive bow. *When had she gotten that?* The entire weapon was almost as tall as she was. Once the string was attached, she deftly grabbed a white arrow, notched it, and drew the weapon. She let it relax slowly before fingering the fletching of the arrow and then returning it to the quiver. The familiarity with which she handled it surprised Werim. He felt like he'd missed something.

"'Ree? What is that?" Werim asked.

She shot him an annoyed glance, "Uh, what does it look like?"

"A bow, right, but where... when did you get it?"

"It was my nameday gift, among other things," she said, glancing down at a wooden box that was sitting on her bed, unopened.

"And that is?" Werim pressed, following her glance.

Sharee ran her hand across the lid. Nothing happened. "Doesn't matter," she sighed. "I can't seem to open it right now."

Leaving the strange object on the bed, she ran over to the window and threw it open. Werim joined her, looking out the front of their house and into the village. The thick, black smoke didn't extend very high off the ground–it was perhaps tall enough to hide a man–and it appeared to permeate into what they could see of the village.

From their vantage point, they could barely discern distant signs of commotion within the haze and couldn't really make anything out. Little tufts popped up here and there, punctuated by screams, shouts, and short clashes of steel on steel. Every now and then, the sound of a splintering wooden door added its crack to the din. Some houses were apparently being broken into, but it was difficult with the low cloud to understand why and by whom. Above it all, they could see smoke, real smoke, rising from some of the more distant houses. Whatever was happening had started on the other side of the village from their house, but was quickly spreading their way.

The nearest houses were still standing, however, and there was a wide swath of open land that any would-be attackers would have to cross. A solid mass of black stretched the distance between, making it seem as if their house bobbed just out of port on a dark sea. The sound of footsteps nearby made Sharee jump, and her head turned to the corner of the house below them. Werim saw a single lump in the smoke near where the sound had originated. It moved slowly around the corner of the house, warily approaching the front door. Perhaps it was friendly, but that didn't seem likely.

"Did you lock the door?" Sharee whispered.

Werim shot a panicked look at his sister before turning and running out of the room. He barreled down the stairway, barely avoided tripping, and stumbled out onto the first floor facing the front door. To his horror, he could see the door knob turning as if in slow motion.

Without thinking, he ran straight for the door, lowering his shoulder at the last second even as it swung inward. He thought he caught a glimpse of menacing steel as he rammed into the back of the door. It slammed shut with a loud knock, and he heard a grunt and a muffled curse from the other side. Quickly, Werim turned and engaged the lock, sliding it home with a metallic click. Panting heavily, he turned around and leaned against the door.

Sharee was standing at the bottom of the stairway, bow in hand. Their eyes locked for a moment, and Werim wondered if his were as wide as hers. He didn't know which was louder: the sound of his heart knocking against his chest, or the gongs clashing in the background. He had almost forgotten about them in the excitement, but they were still there.

The sharp sound of someone banging on the door with a piece of metal sent Werim stumbling to the floor and elicited a scream from Sharee. Werim flipped over, drawing his sword and pointing it at the offending door. It stayed silent.

Werim quietly got to his feet, listening for signs of the potential intruder. Sword in hand, he backed up, looking at the door as if it might swing open of its own accord and admit their enemy. Sharee stepped up beside him and tapped him on the shoulder. If he hadn't known she was there, he might have turned and stabbed her. As it was, he jumped, took a deep breath, and then turned slightly to look at her.

Sharee pointed to the kitchen meaningfully. Werim raised an eyebrow. His sister pointed again, more urgently this time and reached back to grab an arrow. Nocking it, she drew the bow and pointed it at the doorway that led to the kitchen. She took a few steps toward the door before Werim shrugged and decided to follow her.

Hefting his sword, he walked alongside his sister as she slowly brought the kitchen into view. Soon enough, he saw what had her concerned. There was a window above the wash basin on the wooden counter. It was unlocked.

Sharee made a move to enter the kitchen, but Werim stopped her with a gesture. He pointed his sword to the window, and they both watched in horror as it slowly slid upward. Someone, or something, was about to let itself in.

◊ Chapter Five

Sharee's breath sounded unnaturally loud in her ears as she watched the window rise. Her muscles strained from holding the bow taut, an arrow nocked and ready to launch at the first thing that came through the opening. Werim stood in front of her and to the right, creeping slowly toward the kitchen doorway. Sharee kept her aim steady and her angle such that she wouldn't accidentally shoot her brother.

She had been relieved to find that Werim had gotten the front door shut in time, but after the initial rush faded, she'd immediately thought of the kitchen window. Her mother usually threw it open when cooking and almost always left it unlocked. In fact, she had caught Werim sneaking a pie from the sill on more than one occasion. It was, perhaps, the only other way into the house besides the front door, and now it was going to admit an intruder.

Sharee focused in on her aim. Werim stood ready to pounce the moment she let fly with an arrow. The window continued its slow ascent.

Finally, the movement stopped, and Sharee held her breath. The first thing she saw was a pair of hands, one gripping the hilt of a sword. Whoever was outside was trying to leverage their body up and through the window. Sharee didn't wait to see more, she fired.

Her arrow went a bit high, glancing off the window and clattering to the floor. The hand and leg disappeared from the opening with a muffled thud. Werim rushed in and made to slam the window shut. He leaned forward and shoved his sword through first, reaching a hand up to grasp the window. Suddenly, he froze.

"Bud?" Werim asked.

Setting his sword aside on the counter, Werim reached an arm out and it was clasped by a hand on the other side of the window. He pulled backward and, indeed, the torso of his friend soon followed. Bud struggled to shimmy through the window, pulling his long sword behind him. Eventually, he flopped onto the floor, chest heaving. Werim stood above and looked down at him worriedly.

Sharee moved into the room to get a better view and gasped when she got a good look at Bud's face. He had a rather nasty cut high on his forehead that stained his blond hairline. Dried blood made a path down the side of a face blackened by soot. Bud's blue eyes were haunted, and they darted back and forth as if searching for something. Sharee set her bow on the nearby table and hurried over to grab a rag from the water basin.

"What were you doing out there?" Werim asked.

Bud didn't respond. He just stared at his friend. Werim frowned and went over to the open window. Eerily, the wall of black smoke again remained just beyond the threshold, roiling menacingly. He looked at it for a moment before slamming the pane shut and locking it in place.

Sharee wet the rag, and then knelt down next to Bud. She helped him into a sitting position and began to gently wipe the dried blood off his face. His eyes settled down a bit, but they were still tinged by despair. Sharee noted that Bud didn't look at her as he stared forlornly into the room.

Window secured, Werim set his and Bud's swords on the table next to where Sharee had left her bow. He also went and picked up her errant arrow. Thumbing the tip, he recoiled when he found it still sharp, then set it next to the other weapons.

Werim turned his attention back to his friend. "Hello?" he asked. "Bud? Are you with us?"

"They killed..." Bud trailed off, meeting Sharee's eyes for the first time.

Something Sharee saw in them caused her to pause in her ministrations. His gaze was laced with pain, and she couldn't help but feel trapped by the stare. She didn't know what else to do, so she put a consoling hand on his shoulder. Something awful had clearly traumatized her brother's friend.

Werim simply pressed onward, "Who's killing people?"

Bud tore his eyes away from Sharee to respond, "The dark men. The Baraban."

"Baraban?" Werim asked, regarding his friend with a look of confusion.

An anxious feeling welled up in the pit of Sharee's stomach. Something was awfully wrong here. They weren't near any borders. They weren't near *anything*, really. People didn't kill up here. It just didn't happen, and looking at Bud's face, she had a sinking suspicion of why he was so shaken up.

"Bud, who did they kill?" Sharee said softly, with as much compassion as she could.

His eyes met hers again, and she was startled to see a well of moisture barely held in check beneath them. Sharee did not deal well with crying. She swallowed the lump forming in her own throat, but couldn't break the stare.

"My mum," Bud finally choked out in a whisper. A held breath hissed out of his lips, and his eyes dropped to the floor. His shoulders shook slightly, but no tears fell to stain the wood floor.

Sharee stood and turned away from Bud, hiding her own struggle with composure. Her thoughts strayed to her mother. When she listened, she could hear little trills of pipe notes in the distance. Somewhere, her mother was still alive and making music. The knowledge gave her a small bit of comfort. Beneath the clear notes, however, was the constant clanging of the gongs. To her, they sounded like a steady, incoherent deluge of noise that buzzed in the background. It was easy enough to ignore, but the sheer size of the undercurrent scared her when compared with the solo notes from her mother. What did it mean? Was there another muse out there?

"Bud, we'll do... something," Werim said, running a hand through his curly hair.

Bud inhaled deeply and then stood. He dragged a dirty hand across an equally dirty face, smearing the soot and obscuring the small trail that Sharee had been able to clean. With a quick glance toward his friend, he grabbed his sword off the table and threw the leather loop over his shoulder so the weapon hung down his back. Composure regained, he looked more angry than anything else.

Werim seemed not to notice and began pacing the kitchen. Sharee cast her brother a dirty look. Could he be any more unsympathetic? His friend's mother had just died. Still, with all the noises going on in her head, she couldn't help but remember that they weren't out of the woods yet. Hopefully, her mother was having success rousing the other villagers.

"Why did you come here?" Werim spit out, stopping for a moment and looking at his friend.

Bud narrowed his eyes, "They burned my house, Werim. Where else would I go? Besides, before she... before they... Mum said to find your mom. I don't know why, but it was important to her." He stopped for a moment as if reviewing the scene in his head. "Killed two of 'em before they got her," he finished, fists clenched.

They were silent for a moment. Foreigners were here, killing. Sharee grabbed her bow and arrow off the table, placing the latter back in her quiver. Werim belted his sword again and left the kitchen, heading upstairs. The other two shared a look of puzzlement and then followed, leaving the bloodstained cloth forgotten on the floor.

As a group, they trudged up the stairs and went back to the window overlooking the front of the house. The scene remained unchanged. The black fog still roiled below. Tendrils of smoke from burning houses rose in the distance, perhaps a few more than before they'd left, but not many. The sounds of forced entry and screams sounded, if anything, more distant. The sun had climbed more than halfway up the sky now.

Finally, Bud looked around, "Where *is* your mom?"

"Out there," Werim answered, pointing vaguely at the village beyond the window. "Probably dead, too."

Sharee bit her lower lip and listened for the telltale trills. She could still hear them, faint but insistent. "No, she's still fighting."

Werim looked at her and raised an eyebrow, but didn't ask the obvious. Perhaps he could hear pipes, too. He heard the gongs, so he must also be a muse, but Sharee wasn't sure otherwise how it worked. He had picked up on the brassy cacophony before both Sharee and her mother, but was that just because he had been awake?

"Either way, we need to be out there, helping or something," Werim said, hand on the hilt of his sword.

Sharee shook her head, "No, Werim, Mom said to stay here."

"She said stay here until midday, 'Ree," Werim countered. "It looks close enough to me."

"It's not even halfway up yet!" Sharee argued.

"Bud?"

The blond-haired boy just shrugged, staring forlornly out the window.

"Two to one, I win," Werim said, turning from the window.

He walked over to his dresser and withdrew two cloth satchels. They had often used the bags to collect odds and ends when out adventuring in the woods. Today, Werim filled his with a few items from his drawers and tossed the other at Sharee. She caught hers and looked down at it.

"What's this for?" She asked.

Werim shrugged, "Who knows what they'll do to the house while we're gone. I'd put anything you don't want burned in there."

Sharee frowned, but turned to her things. The first thing she put in was the box her mother had given her. Even though she couldn't seem to open it right now, there was no way she was leaving that behind. After that, she stared blankly at her drawers. What did she want to lug around? She certainly didn't want her things to burn, but one thing didn't stand out from another. Finally, she settled on a simple change of clothes and the hairbrush that Scrontle had made her. She didn't want to have to face the big man if she let the gift melt. Attaching the satchel to her waist, she turned to find her brother doing the same.

"Someone's coming," Bud said, making them both look up.

Sharee scampered over to Bud's side. Her brother stood behind her, peering over her shoulder. Sure enough, there were several lumps making their way to the front of the house. They reminded Sharee of mice crawling under a smoky rug. She counted three.

"Think they're friendly?" Werim asked of no one in particular.

A small black object puffed out of the fog from near one of the houses. It zipped toward them, sending them all to the ground. The object struck the wall and lodged in with a loud twang. Werim got up and yanked it out, examining it quickly and then passing it to Sharee. It was a smooth rod with one sharpened end, almost like an arrow without fletching. It also seemed to be made out of a lightweight, solid material that was definitely not wood.

Bud was back at the window. Sharee turned just as another dark rod puffed from the fog and streaked toward the house. She pulled Bud down as it bit into the wood just above the window.

"What do you think you're doing?!" Sharee said, alarmed.

Bud ignored her, "I counted four."

"Four of them against three of us?" Werim observed.

"Boys, we are *not* going out there," Sharee said.

Bud stood confidently and headed for the stairs, "Seems fair to me."

Sharee cast a desperate look at her brother, who rolled his eyes and followed his friend out of the room. There was nothing for Sharee to do but heft her bow and join them. A heavy thump with an accompanying cracking noise nearly elicited a scream from her jittery lungs, but she ground her teeth and found herself nocking an arrow as she rounded the corner at the top of the stairs.

Bud and Werim were about halfway down. Bud had taken his long sword off his back and held it in both hands before him. Werim was fumbling with his at his waist. The loud noise had caused them both to hesitate. Whatever was on the other side must be big to have been able to crack the solid wooden door. Weapons in hand, they continued creeping, more warily now, toward the entryway. Sharee stayed at the top of the steps, arrow drawn and trained on whatever was about to burst through the door.

When the boys were two steps from the bottom, the door exploded, sending shards of wood skittering through the room. They raised their hands to shield themselves, freezing in place and struggling to make sense of what they saw. A giant figure stood in the doorway, having apparently just completed a second swing of a very large, heavy weapon. It looked like a giant hammer, with a shaped metal top lashed to a long, white handle.

The hulking behemoth looked to be a man, with huge, rippling muscular arms sprouting out of a thick, black leather vest. Strange, dark markings covered his tan skin, as if someone had drawn on him with ink, and he had short, dark hair. His eyes were covered by what appeared to be dark, tinted spectacles that wrapped around behind his ears with a short shaft sticking straight up on one side. Eerily, the darkness in the lenses swirled like the mysterious fog that provided a backdrop behind him.

With a sneer, he raised one large, booted foot to take a step into the house. Sharee didn't wait to see more. She fired. Amazingly, her arrow flew true and took him right in the neck. The man's eyebrows went up in surprise, and a liquid gurgle escaped his lips as he pitched forward to land facedown across the threshold.

Before the corpse even had time to settle, two more assailants leapt into the room. These two, while smaller, were no less menacing. They wore spectacles as well, with inked arms exposed to the shoulder. Each of them had a curved shortsword, very similar, in fact, to Werim's in size and shape. One was held high, the other low, both at the ready.

With a snarl, Bud launched himself at the newcomers. The one on the left easily blocked Bud's wide, sweeping strikes, engaging him fluidly. The other stalked just on the edge of the brawl, keeping both Werim and Sharee in his sights. He cast a furtive glance toward the open doorway and the darkness beyond. Sharee followed in time to see a little black blur appear out of the darkness and head straight for her. Without time to think, she threw herself back into the hallway and landed with a grunt against the wall. The black rod chunked into the wood behind where she had just been standing.

Sharee pulled herself up to a sitting position with her back against the wall, breathing heavily. She heard a second set of clashing begin and guessed that Werim had decided to join the fray. With shaking hands, she nocked another arrow and rose to her feet. *Be brave now, Sharee,* she told herself. Taking a deep breath, she jumped out from the cover of the wall, sweeping the room with her drawn bow and searching for a target.

Bud and Werim had been drawn apart by the two inked assailants. The men appeared almost bored by the sword fight as it progressed, deftly turning aside every blow thrown at them by the two boys. What was more, they had positioned themselves so that Sharee couldn't get a clear shot at either. No additional black rods flew at her from the darkness beyond the doorway. She stood, paralyzed by indecision, watching the scene play out in front her. What could she do?

As she waited for an opening, she edged to the far side of the stairwell, keeping the doorway in view but not giving anything out in the fog a good shot at her. Whatever had been hurling the black rods, she didn't want to wind up with one stuck in her throat.

Sharee pondered over the goal of the two inked men fighting her brother and Bud as she crept to the side. With how easily they handled the attack of the boys, they should have ended the fight quickly. It seemed as if they were playing with them.

Somehow, Bud managed to slip the guard of one of the men, raking a cut across his chest. It hardly made it through the thick leather, but he cried out anyway, startling them all. Up until that point, the only sound had been the clanking of steel and grunts from the fight's participants. The man with the cut swiftly spun away from Bud, shooting out a leg and tripping the blond boy to the ground. The move left him exposed to an arrow from Sharee. Just as she was about to release her taut string, movement from the doorway caught her eye.

A third spectacled man appeared from the smoke. He held a strange device up at eye level. It looked almost like a miniature bow turned on its side and fitted with a handle. Settled in a groove atop the device was another of the sharpened black rods. It was aimed at Sharee's head.

"I wouldn't be doin' dat, 'twas me," he growled in a strange accent.

As the words were spoken, everyone froze. Bud was still on the floor, his attacker standing over him, sword pointed at the fallen boy's face. Werim stood on the other side of the doorway with his sword weaving in front of him like a live snake while his adversary danced just out of reach. Sharee slowly lowered her bow and turned toward the newcomer.

"There's ta be no killin' o' da chilluns," The man continued, as much to his companions as to the three of them. "We do be needin' ta take 'em to da Warlord, alive, or it be our heads."

"Argh, you think I do no' remember that?" the man over Bud fired back. "Dis here runt done cut up me good vest."

His partner near Werim began laughing. "A chile! T'were marked by a chile!"

"Shut yer trap, or I'll be markin' ya up next," the first snarled back.

"Har, har! 'Twould love to see ya try," the second answered.

The deep twang of a cord caused Sharee to jump. She looked around for the source, but was surprised to see that no one else had apparently heard it. Her brother had turned during the strange conversation, and was looking at the newcomer with determined eyes. While the two inked swordsmen continued to spar verbally, Werim's sword had begun to glow. It was dim, almost unnoticeable, but it was there. Werim looked at it, and then his eyes traveled to the device held by the man, then back to his sword. He changed his grip slightly, flexing his hand.

In that instant, Sharee realized what her brother was planning. He was going to throw his only weapon, hoping to disrupt the man's aim enough to give them an opening. It was a desperate gamble that would leave him defenseless, but, looking at her brother's face, she was positive he was going to do it. *More guts than wits, that boy*, her father had always said fondly. Sharee sighed inwardly as she subtly shifted her balance toward the man standing by Werim. He and his partner were arguing freely now, gesturing with their swords and hardly paying attention to what was about to happen.

Sharee heard that twang in her head again, and her brother's sword began to glow brighter, almost as if it were white hot. Finally, the two men noticed the weapon, and abruptly stopped their conversation. The third man turned his head slightly toward Werim, eyes widening.

"No," he gasped.

Werim chucked the sword. It sailed straight through the air, shearing through the rod launching device as if it were made of butter, and lodging itself between the eyes of the man leaning over Bud. Sharee wasted no time bringing her bow to bear and training an arrow on the man behind her brother. He was apparently too shocked to move, even as Sharee's arrow took him neatly in the chest. He collapsed in a heap, leaving only the single man with the ruined, bow-like weapon.

The man turned toward Werim. "Please, don't ki–" he started to plead, but was cut off when the tip of a sword broke through the front of his chest.

Bud pulled his long sword back through and the man collapsed, gurgling. The three of them stared at each other breathing heavily. After a moment, Werim went over and pulled his sword out of the dead man's head. The broken lenses slid off the corpse, no longer swirling, and revealing brown eyes that stared unseeing at the ceiling.

"Well, that went well," Werim said.

Bud merely grunted in response. The blond boy stood and wiped his blade on the vest of a dead man. Sharee stood motionless, halfway down the staircase where she had fired. Her eyes were wide, and she held her bow limply at her side. They had come so close to dying.

I killed a man, the thought sprang into her mind unbidden. *Two men!* She looked down at shaking hands. Without remembering sitting down, she found herself seated on the stairs, shuddering uncontrollably. Werim and Bud were staring at her worriedly. Why couldn't she stop shaking? *I'm a killer*, her brain reminded her.

"The bodies," Bud said simply, looking at Werim.

Werim nodded, "Right."

Bud came over and knelt in front of Sharee, putting a hand on her shoulder. In the background, Werim began dragging the bodies out of the ruined front door and into the darkness beyond. Sharee focused on Bud's dirty face, trying to block out the carnage and stop her shaking. *I killed two men.*

"Sharee, they were not going to let us go," Bud explained. "It was us or them."

Sharee found herself nodding as tears welled up in her eyes. Bud was right, of course. He'd seen what they were capable of first hand. As she stared into his blue eyes, her breathing began to slow. *I will not cry in front of a boy*, she told herself sternly. She took a deep breath to regain control of her emotions. The shaking calmed.

"Werim's sword..." she said, trailing off.

Bud nodded, not taking his eyes off hers, "Yeah, good throw."

Sharee shook her head, "No. It was *glowing*."

Bud regarded her with a quizzical look, "How do you mean?"

"The steel, it glowed, as if it had been heated up," she tried to explain.

Bud looked down at his own sword as if it, too, would show evidence of her claim. Then, he shook his head. "The mind plays strange tricks in battle," he said simply, like he had heard it somewhere before.

"My mind is fine, Bud," she said, a bit more petulantly than she'd have liked.

Bud just shrugged.

In a huff, Sharee stood and put her bow on her shoulder. She knew what she had seen, and Werim's sword had glowed. Besides, as long as she stayed focused on something other than death, she could keep control of herself.

The glowing sword was probably part of Werim being a muse, but she didn't know how to explain that to either of them yet. She wasn't exactly sure of it herself. Was that even how it worked? She was hardly an expert. Her mother had mentioned muses for the first time the day before. Sure there were tales, little more than whispered rumors she'd heard around the village, but she hadn't committed any of those to memory. The reasonable adults she knew always dismissed stories like that.

Sharee thought about bringing up the stories now. Maybe one of the boys would remember what she had dismissed. Still, she didn't need to give them any more reason to think she was losing her mind. She decided she'd let it go for now. Perhaps she would talk to Werim alone later. Surely he had known what he was doing, somehow. He would have gotten a similar talking to when he'd had his nameday.

Bud stood slowly in front of Sharee as Werim came back in out of the darkness wearing one of the dead men's spectacles. He was grinning ear to ear. Sharee suppressed a shudder as she thought about where they'd come from. *Focus on something else,* she told herself.

"Stylish," Bud said.

"Take 'em off, Werim," Sharee pleaded. "They're not yours."

Werim looked back toward the door, "Oh, I don't think they'll need these anymore." He reached a hand up and adjusted his eyewear. "Besides, I have a feeling they'll come in handy."

"And why is that?" Sharee asked.

"Apparently they let you see through *that*," he answered, pointing at the wall of smoke outside.

◆ Chapter Six

Werim held out a hand containing the other two pairs of unbroken spectacles. Bud snatched one up right away, slipping them over his head and adjusting them. Werim went to give the second pair to his sister, but she shied away.

"Come on, 'Ree. They're not going to bite," he said.

Bud added, "You're not going to be able to see without them."

Sharee frowned, but grabbed the remaining pair out of Werim's hand. He hid his smile at her obvious discomfort. It reminded him of the time he put worms in her hair. That was hilarious. *Girls*, he mused silently, shaking his head. She twisted them in her hands before finally slipping them over her head.

"Whoa," she said, looking out the door, "the fog is gone."

"You think?" Werim responded.

"But... how?"

"Does it matter?"

Bud was flipping his spectacles up and down, alternating his view. He took them off, studied them from all angles, and then jammed them back on his head. A grunt was his only response as he trudged off into the smoke.

To Werim's eyes, the blond boy's form dimmed a bit when it entered the darkness, but was otherwise easily seen. Werim could certainly tell where the smoke started, but instead of being a wall of swirling, pulsing murkiness, it looked like his front yard on a cloudy day. Colors were muted, but visibility was not a problem. Bud paused for a moment as if expecting something to happen. When nothing did, he continued off toward the center of the village.

"Wait!" Werim hollered after his friend. "Where are you going?"

Sharee brushed by, hurrying after the blond boy. "To find Mom, of course," she responded.

Werim cast an annoyed look at her back as she bounced away, satchel at her waist. His pack waited for him at the foot of the stairs. It was far from heavy, but he still grunted as he tossed it over his shoulder. Of course he'd taken the larger bag; it was expected of him. He wasn't sure if he'd even need any of the items he'd thrown in there, but it was better to be prepared than not. Besides, he didn't want to hear Sharee complain if forced to carry useless items.

"Wait up, you two," he called as he left the house.

He turned to shut the door, but there was no door to shut. It had been destroyed by the big man. The same heavy corpse that he'd had to lug around the corner of the house to get it out of Sharee's sight. That had not been easy work, either. Why did he always have to do the heavy lifting?

Catching up to his sister and friend, Werim crouched and took the lead. He *was* the best at sneaking, after all. He'd proven that over and over again when they'd played Hide and Find in the woods growing up. Those two were always finding each other, but never him. They always stayed in one spot, hoping not to be found. The trick, as Werim had figured out, was to sneak back to places they'd already checked. He'd found that people rarely checked the same place twice. Though they hadn't played the game in years, he was still relatively confident that he was the best of the three.

Shortly, they came to the first house of the village. It was the Bourge homestead, one of the harvesters in town. Many families tended the vineyards that provided the main source of income to the village, and the Bourges were typical of the bunch. Old man Bourge lived with his two sons and their wives. There were half a dozen grandchildren, much younger than Werim, that usually ran around in the yard while their fathers worked. Obviously, none of them were out now.

Werim crept around the corner, spectacled eyes sweeping for any more of the inked men, and quickly found a window. Standing up on his toes, he peeked inside. The dwelling appeared to have been deserted. Chairs normally tucked neatly beneath the kitchen table had been overturned, presumably in haste, but otherwise the interior was motionless. If anyone was inside, they were most certainly hiding and unlikely to come out.

Werim settled back into a crouch and turned away from the house, gazing absently toward the center of the village. The crash of the cymbals sounded louder in his head since entering the smoke, but he forced the sound down and did his best to ignore it. He was afraid to pay it any mind lest it overwhelm him, and his sense of hearing needed to be sharp unless he wanted to get caught in another fight. Something told him that they were very lucky to have escaped the last one.

There were several structures near them and on the other side of those bubbled the stream that bisected the settlement. Werim watched for signs of movement in the dim light. Not seeing any, he hurried toward the next house, intending to peek around its side and evaluate the situation. He expected there to be more invaders lurking about. Surely they numbered more than four.

"*Psst*, Werim," his sister hissed from behind. When he didn't respond right away, she repeated a little more loudly, "Werim."

Stopping halfway to the next house, he turned around irritably. "What?" he hissed back.

Sharee frowned, but didn't comment. Instead she pointed to the south insistently.

Werim backtracked to her and whispered, "What do you want to go that way for?"

"Mom," she explained quietly. "She's that way."

"How do you know?" Werim asked.

Sharee hesitated for a moment before replying, "Just trust me."

Werim looked at Bud. His blond friend just shrugged, and started heading south. *Why not,* he seemed to say.

They passed several more deserted yards with equally deserted houses before the familiar rock walls of the smithy came into view. There was no peal of hammer on anvil this time, only eerie silence on top of clanging gongs.

Creeping around to the front of the large building, they found the heavy doors wide open. Werim motioned for them to slip inside. Perhaps Scrontle would be able to help them. It certainly wouldn't hurt to have the big man around. Quickly, they pulled the well-oiled doors shut. They didn't want anyone following them in out of smoke.

Looking around, they failed to find the steel rod that could be laid across the double doors to lock them. Scrontle must have hidden it somewhere, though Werim couldn't think of a reason why. After several minutes of fruitless looking, Sharee strode up to the door and slid one of her white arrows through the two handles. She looked rather pleased with herself.

"There's no way that's going to hold anyone out," Werim observed.

Sharee frowned, "I didn't see you coming up with any ideas."

"Let's just find Scrontle and ask him what he did with the rod," Werim suggested.

"Oh, like he's here," Sharee said. "He wouldn't have left the doors wide open if he were home."

"Both of you, quiet," Bud said sharply enough that they both stopped and looked at him. He pointed once to his eye, and then again at the soot-covered floor. They saw what he had seen: footprints. Lots of footprints.

Werim watched Sharee try to count the sets. There were too many, crisscrossing one another in the black powder. It appeared as if a whole army had stomped through, and they all had gone straight back toward the forge. Bud's eyes narrowed as he followed the path, and he motioned silently for them to follow before he started down the hallway. Werim fell in behind and they both drew their swords as quietly as they could.

Down the hallway they crept, eyes on the closed doors in front of them. Scrontle usually kept the doors to the forge area open, hence the layer of powder on everything. Bud approached along the right side of the hallway with Werim on the left. Sharee stood slightly off center and back from the two boys, arrow nocked on her bow, pointing toward the floor. She was ready to raise and fire at the first sign of movement. Cautiously, Werim used his free hand to push against the door. He kept his body against the wall, peeking through the crack as it widened, looking for any sort of threat. When it was wide enough that a body could fit, Bud slipped through, still hugging the right wall. Werim followed quickly, throwing the door the rest of the way open, hoping to surprise anyone inside. The door swung wide and bounced off the stone wall with a bang.

The room was empty. Emptier than they'd ever seen it. There were certainly no people inside, though footprints scuffed the residue on nearly every open space of floor. All of the metal racks, normally filled with Scrontle's different projects, were vacant. They had been stripped of anything useful.

For the first time ever in their memories, the boys found the forge unlit. The bellows were unmanned. The quenching buckets sat devoid of their usually hissing contents. There was no clang of hammer on anvil. There was no hammer to clang, only the heavy anvil left behind amongst the barren benches and racks in the room. And everywhere, footprints.

"This place looks stripped," Werim pointed out the obvious.

"Yeah, but why?" Bud asked.

Sharee frowned, running a finger across a dirty surface and then looking at it distastefully, "Mom must have gotten here in time."

"What do you mean?" Werim asked his sister.

"Well, she went to warn the village, right?" Sharee explained. "What better place to start than here at the forge?"

"She's right," Bud said.

He was about to explain further when a thump at the barred doors interrupted him. The three friends turned to stare back down the hallway. The door to the forge was still half open from their entry, and they could just barely make out the arrow threaded between the two handles on the inside of the double front doors. It thumped again, harder this time.

Werim sprinted down the hallway, sword at the ready. Surely whoever was outside would soon burst through, and they would be met with charging steel. He was surprised to find Bud alongside him as the hallway raced by. A third thump rattled the doors. The wooden shaft bent, but did not break.

Both boys skidded to a halt as a fourth shudder shook the doorway. It was the strongest yet. The heavy doors bulged inward, straining the arrow, but it held. This close, they heard muffled voices outside, grumbling about apparently being unable to get the door to budge. Sharee crept up behind the two boys, staring incredulously at her improvised doorstopper.

Eventually, the mumbling subsided and the voices trailed off. Apparently, they had given up on getting in. Werim waited a few extra minutes, straining his ears just to be sure. Finally, he slid the arrow out from between the handles, handing it to Bud and cracking the door. With his spectacles on, he peeked out into the smoke. A short ways away, crossing the nearby stream, were perhaps two dozen of the inked men. Only a few of them wore headgear, and those led the pack. They all appeared heavily armed. Werim eased the door closed.

"Where do you suppose they're going?" he asked.

Bud was running his hands along the smooth, white shaft of the arrow he'd been handed, a look of wonder on his face. "I could swear this is made of whitewood, but that stuff is so brittle," he mumbled. He flexed the arrow between his hands. "It's so strong."

"Give me *that*," Sharee said, snatching it out of Bud's hands and putting it back in her quiver.

Bud looked at her, "Where did you get these?"

"My mother," Sharee stated.

"Yeah, but where did *she* get it?" he asked.

"Um, guys," Werim interrupted, "about those invaders..."

Sharee looked up. "Mom," she said simply.

"What now?" Werim asked, exasperated.

Sharee pushed through the two of them and out the front door. She appeared suddenly more agitated. Werim shot Bud a look, and the two of them trailed behind as she ran toward the stream. She was heading in the same direction as the group of invaders. Without hesitation, she bounded over the stream and sprinted past the bakery. Werim hurried to keep up, trying in vain to look everywhere at once in expectation of an ambush. *Fool girl's lost all her sense*, he thought.

She kept going, weaving between houses and heading steadily toward the front of the village. The closer they got, the fewer homes still stood while charred remains became more prevalent. The raid had apparently come from the main road that ran by the village down to the valley, spreading rapidly all the way across to Werim's house.

Sharee only slowed when voices could be heard coming out of the smoke in front of them. They stopped to catch their breath behind the burned out husk of what had once been a storage barn for harvest surplus. The voices sounded like they were just around the other side. Motioning for silence, Werim peeked around the wreckage. Sure enough, the same group of men they'd seen at the smithy stood milling about. They were a motley crew, ink running up their exposed arms. Most carried curved swords, though some had heavier cudgels and battle axes. Only four of them wore headgear.

"Go an' tell the Warlord that the village be empty," one of the men with spectacles ordered.

A second man struck fist to breast and replied, "Aye, aye, sir."

"The rest of ya's, stuff it!" the first man continued after the messenger had run off. "The Warlord'll be plenty pissed if we give away our position. He's got plans for these folk, he do."

"What be important 'bout dis village, huh?" A man without the aid of the lenses grunted. "They didn't even offer up a good brawl."

"Yar," another replied. "Dat blasted woman done rallied 'em before we even got a chance fer some sport."

"Enough out of you's," The first man said. "Dere be silence from now on as we get in position and wait fer da Warlord's signal. Don't make me run you through."

There were several grunts, but none of the men spoke. They moved on silent feet as they loped off southward through the smoke, one spectacled guide up front and one in the rear. Werim locked eyes with Bud and Sharee, asking the question with a look: *Do we follow?* Bud cocked his head once in the direction of men, signaling that he thought they should. Sharee nodded enthusiastically. Werim shrugged and began to follow, sticking to the sides of structures and creeping quickly between them.

Shortly, they reached the last black, skeletal house before the cliff that marked the southern end of the village. Peeking through the charred boards, they saw the group of twenty some-odd men waiting expectantly in the roiling black smoke. They all had their weapons at the ready and appeared to be waiting on some sort of signal. How most of them were supposed to see the signal through the fog without lenses was beyond Werim.

Sharee gasped beside him.

"What is it now?" Werim whispered.

Sharee pointed, "Mom."

Sure enough, a short distance from the house, in what appeared to be a clearing in the smoke, stood a ruffled group of villagers. Werim recognized the odd green dress of his mother out in front of them. She looked majestic, holding her bow at the ready, pointing steadily toward the wall of fog in front of her. The rest of the people huddled close to each other, surrounding what appeared to be all of the children in the village. Werim could see the large bulk of Scrontle in the back, wielding his large blacksmith's hammer and a round shield. A few of the other villagers held varied weapons–swords, spears, wood axes–but the majority were women and children. They wouldn't stand long against two dozen warriors, though they had them almost doubled in number.

Beyond the clearing was another group of inked invaders. They stood before a gigantic beast that Werim had never seen before. It had six legs as thick as tree trunks with giant knees bent that suspended a large, furred body between them. Two short tusks sprouted from its long, hairy snout. A long, reptilian tail with a single spike at the end whipped the air behind it. The creature stood nearly as large as a house, though low to the ground, and on the back of the giant beast, a structure had been lashed on with some sort of rope. It appeared to hold another dozen or so men wielding the same strange bows that spat rods at them earlier. Werim wasn't sure what the structure was made from, but it certainly didn't seem to be wood. He wasn't quite sure what to make of the sight.

Directly in front of the creature stood a man. The darkness of the smoke flowed from his shoulders like a long cape. The man's inked arms were exposed like the rest of the men around him, though he wore what appeared to be a heavy metal bracer on his left wrist. He was the first of the invaders that Werim had seen with any kind of armor on, and though several of the men around him wore headgear, this man's eyes were exposed. What Werim saw of them sent chills up his spine. They were filled with a darkness that appeared deeper than the smoke that enveloped him, pulsing in time to the gongs in Werim's head. Surely, this was the source of the strange fog, though Werim didn't understand how, or why. This man was clearly the leader of the invasion. Not only that, but it was clear his eyes could pierce through the smoke unaided. He stared straight at Werim's mother.

It was at this point that Werim noticed his mother–who appeared to be standing in the direct center of the clearing on a slight hill with the rest of the village huddled behind her–didn't seem to be hindered by the haze either. Her bow was nocked, drawn, and pointing unwaveringly at the strange man with the black eyes. Though she faced away from Werim, her figure radiated a confidence that seemed out of place with the tense situation. For some reason, he pictured her face with a wry smile on it. The eyes of the rest of the villagers were frantic, sweeping back and forth along the wall of smoke as if expecting attackers to come from all directions at once, but his mother was calm.

"A'renee," the dark man called from where he stood. "So it be you that requested parlay. I'd wondered who in this worthless village might know so much of our ways. A clever hiding place if you ask me."

"I invoke the Code," Werim's mother replied in a strong voice. "Present yourself."

The spectacled messenger that Werim had seen a few moments ago ran up beside the dark man. He struck fist to breast and began to report to his leader in a low voice that did not carry. The dark man turned to listen.

Werim was surprised when a bright bolt of light streaked from his mother's bow, spiraling toward the fog. It was an arrow, but somehow it glowed with a radiant, white light, shooting off trails of luminescence as it flew through the air. Where it passed through the smoke, it drilled a clean tunnel away, burrowing until it lodged itself in the messenger's throat. The inked man gurgled and fell backward, his report only half delivered. The villagers all turned to peer down the suddenly clear tunnel, some gasping at the dead man it revealed.

The dark man didn't even flinch. He calmly watched his messenger collapse to the ground. Then, as if nothing had happened, he turned back to face Werim's mother.

"That wasn't very sporting," the dark man observed, seeming amused more than annoyed.

Werim's mother responded, "Neither was your continuation o' hostilities after we called for a parlay."

The dark man spread his arms wide, "What can I say? Sometimes words travel slowly in battle." He regarded her curiously from his position in front of the great beast. "Where is your focus, A'renee? Why have you not fought back?" the dark man asked. "Surely a Warlord of your renown be cravin' to meet me in battle. Yet I sense no resonance. You have not come here for a challenge it seems. Do you doubt your abilities after so many years unused?" He smiled wickedly.

"Tis no longer my burden," she admitted. "Goading me will get you no glory."

"Ah, I see. Then, how is your son?" Werim's heart jumped into his throat at being mentioned, but his mother didn't respond. After an awkward silence, the dark man continued, "Not admitting to that one, eh? How about your husband? Where did he run off to? Loyalty was never one of his traits. I suppose he took the shard too."

"Who would be loyal to a betrayer? A murderer?" Werim's mother countered.

The dark man ignored the barb and continued on, "He would not have taken the child with him, and since my messenger dutifully informed me–before you dispatched him, of course–that the village is clear, the boy must be there in your midst. I *will* meet him eventually."

"Enough banter. Come out from behind your parlor trick an' present yourself, Aarik," Werim's mother ordered.

The dark man did not like that. His face twisted up in a grimace, and he strode angrily forward out of the smoke. Darkness still trailed down his back like a flowing cape, but upon entering the clearing, it swept backward as if by an invisible wind, whipping menacingly and quickly dissipating. For some reason, it appeared that the smoke would not subsist in that area. The man's eyes still pulsed with a dark light, and he quickly suppressed the emotion that had shown on his face, smoothing it to calmness once again.

"Let us talk more formally, then," he growled. "You will address me as Lord Vraika, as I do be Warlord of the Baraban Legion by Blood Rite. And what should I call you?"

"Renee Swift," she announced. "Wife of Rynel Swift. That is all I am now."

"Doesn't seem very Folian," the dark man, Lord Vraika, observed, scrunching up his face in evident distaste. "So eager to hide your roots, then?" he chuckled at his own joke.

"What is it you have come for, Aarik?" Werim's mother demanded.

Vraika reached out and slapped her hard across the face. Her bow went skittering to one side and her head turned so that she was looking directly at the burned out building. Werim nearly dashed out from cover with his sword at the ready. If not for the restraining arm of Bud, he would have. His mother saw him, and her eyes widened. She frowned but turned calmly back to face the dark man.

"You *will* show respect to your betters, Fole," Vraika announced.

Werim's mother spat blood, looking confident despite having been hit. She still had a sheathed knife at her waist. "What have you come for?" she repeated.

Vraika examined her for a moment, and then stepped between her and the villagers, effectively turning his back on her. Projecting his voice, he addressed the crowd. "The price for treason against the Grand Warlord is death. We come to administer justice in his name. However, I will spare your children, as they should not be punished for their parent's sins. Will you accept this fate willingly?"

There was no response from the villagers. Many of them stood, stone faced. A few of the younger children started to cry openly. Werim noticed Andree Peau standing beside his mother. Roland Boulang, the baker was there, arm around his wife protectively. Several of the Bourge children huddled near their grandfather, tears streaking down young cheeks. Scrontle Marteau hefted his hammer at the rear of the group, his dark eyes sweeping over the children with concern. They would all die. And for what? Who was this Grand Warlord to them? Who was Vraika to administer this so-called justice? Werim wondered why his mother didn't simply draw her knife and stab the dark man in the back.

He was doubly surprised, then, when she spoke up, "I can propose an alternate arrangement."

Vraika turned back toward her, curiosity on his face. "What could you possibly have to offer me, Renee Swift?" he sneered. There was an uncalled for amount of disdain in the way he said her name, as if it were a personal affront to him.

Werim's mother gazed past Vraika at the group gathered before her on the hill, a good half of which were children. She turned and looked behind her at all the inked soldiers in front of the large, intimidating beast. The villagers had no way of seeing through the smoke, but apparently Werim's mother could. Her eyes lit on the group that had crept around behind them as she turned in a circle, stepping forward so that her back was to the dark man. Vraika turned to his troops in front, slowly raising a hand as if to give some sort of signal. Werim saw that if they were to come to blows, the group on the hill would be assaulted from both sides, and quickly overwhelmed. They were exposed. What choice did they have? Fight, and they would die. Submit, and they would die. Either way, it appeared that all the children in the village were to become orphans this day. Finally, green eyes found Werim and Sharee, standing in the shadow of the burned out building. Both children stared with wide eyes at their mother as she mouthed four words.

I love you, and then, *run.*

She turned back to Vraika and said in a quiet voice, "My life for theirs. The children *and* adults."

The dark man smiled. "Done," he said simply.

There was an exceptionally loud crash on the gongs in Werim's head, and a dark metal knife sprouted suddenly out of the black bracer that Vraika wore on his wrist. Darkness wreathed the shadowy blade. In one quick, smooth motion, he brought his fist up and stabbed Werim's mother in the chest.

Werim's scream was lost amongst the cries of the villagers as his mother slumped to the ground. Whatever had been holding the darkness back vanished, and the smoke rolled over the hill like a black tsunami. Inked soldiers charged in to disarm the blinded villagers, but Werim didn't see them. His eyes were fixed on the crumpled form fallen at the dark man's feet, blood running in deep burgundy rivulets down the side of her green shirt to spill down the grassy hill. Red hair settled like sputtering fire around a face with lifeless eyes that came to a rest staring directly at her only son.

His mother was dead.

◊ Chapter Seven

The pipes were silent. Sharee hadn't realized how comforting they'd been until they were suddenly and irrevocably muted. Her entire body was numb. She ripped her lenses off, throwing them on the ground in disgust. There was a soft plink as the glass struck a rock, breaking. Sharee didn't care. She didn't want to be associated in any way with the people that had murdered her mother. She'd rather be blind.

Blind she was. Smoke curled around her, almost taunting her as it smoothed out the sharp lines of reality, presuming to soften the jagged edge of loss. She could still hear her brother's anguished scream echoing in her head. There were muffled grunts beside her as he struggled against Bud's strong arms. Did he think he could rush out and take on the entire legion of inked men after her mother had just been silenced so easily? Her invincible mother, the once strong notes of her life cut off so short.

Sharee felt lost. She quietly took out the wooden box from the pouch at her waist, sinking to the ground and cradling the gift in her hands. It still would not open. She doubted it would ever open again.

There was so much she wanted to ask her mother, and yesterday it had seemed like she would have time. If only she had known that their time was limited, what would she have said?

Obviously, she wished she could have talked to her mother about being a muse, about other songs, about where she learned them. Yet, she found it wasn't those lost moments that ached the worst. Deep down, it was the questions that only a daughter could ask of a mother that Sharee felt most robbed of. After all, surely there were other sources to learn about Songs. She'd only been given one mother to accompany her as she began her journey into womanhood. There were things she suspected she would want to ask, about life and love, that could never be answered by another. At least, not as a mother might answer. And when she experienced her first kiss or her first heartbreak, there would be no mother with which to share these moments. Being special was one thing, Sharee wasn't sure if she could manage *normal*. What did being special get her except loss?

Sharee found herself pulled from her dire musings by a strong arm, standing her up again and stepping in. Bud's face swam out of the smoke close by. His breath was cool on her face where it caressed the tears she hadn't realized she'd been shedding. Sharee tried to find his comforting blue eyes, but those blasted spectacles were in the way. Darkness swirled in the lenses, and she saw her own pathetic reflection. There was no sympathy in the murky darkness, only death. Sharee pulled away and wiped the tears off her face.

"Let's go," Bud whispered morosely. "There's nothing more for us here."

"Werim..." she started, looking around her at nothingness.

"I'm here, 'Ree," he muttered gruffly from behind her.

Sharee sniffed once, but nodded, letting Bud lead her through the smoke. She sensed they were going deeper into the village, but she wasn't really sure. To be honest, she had a hard time caring.

Eventually, the bubbling sound of running water alerted her that she was approaching the stream that ran through the center of Kokamongo. The grass and dirt sloped slightly downward as they approached, and Sharee had to slow up a bit to keep her footing.

She heard a thump as her brother leaped the small depression ahead of her, and then Bud stopped to guide her forward with a gentle but firm arm. She put one foot down into the cool water, her boot finding the solid river rock bottom. An arm shot out of the smoke ahead of her–her brother's–and hauled her quickly up on the other bank. The stream didn't cut too deeply into the stone, but footing could be treacherous, especially if you couldn't see. She wouldn't be the first villager to slip and break something.

"Wait a second, Bud," Werim whispered fiercely.

"I know, I see them," Bud responded.

"See who?" Sharee asked.

"You'd know if you hadn't broken your lenses," Werim responded.

Sharee frowned in the smoke where she thought his face might be, "Well, that's helpful."

"Shhhh," Bud hissed.

Werim dragged Sharee southward along the stream. She could still hear its peaceful bubbling next to her, but otherwise had no idea where they might be. The smoke swirled around her, pressing in on her, making her almost nauseous with its constant shifting and moving. Bud's footfalls on the other side of the stream barely reached her ears, and the breathing of both boys was subdued. Every few steps, they would stop for a moment, presumably to look around, and then creep off in the same direction.

"Shoot," Werim whispered. "They're heading for the woods. We won't be able to get by them unseen. Most of them have spectacles."

Bud's voice floated back out of the smoke, "Yes, but they haven't seen us yet. Come back this way. Perhaps they've left the front path unguarded."

"You think we're going to be able to sneak out the front? That they're not watching it?" Werim asked, incredulous.

"Well, they're certainly cutting off our route to the woods," Bud shrugged.

"True, but how many of them can there be?" Werim asked.

"I don't know," Bud admitted. "Here, give me Sharee back and come over here."

"I'm not a trading stone," Sharee replied.

She swore she heard her brother chuckle. He guided her back to the stream, holding her arm as she stepped into the cold water once more. Bud's arm snaked out of the smoke in front of her, and she grabbed his warm hand. He pulled her up a bit more gently than Werim had. A soft double thump announced Werim's arrival on this side.

They began to work their way back through the village, weaving around structures that Sharee couldn't see. She allowed herself to be led by Bud, clinging to his hand and hoping she wouldn't knock into anything solid. It was a disorienting experience, being completely without sight. She soon found herself with her eyes closed, trying to concentrate on hearing sounds. She was saddened by the marked lack of pipes. The whole time they'd been sneaking through the village before, she'd been able to hear snippets of her mother playing. While Werim complained about the gongs, she found that if she didn't pay attention to them, their sound slipped away from her. If she focused on them, she could bring them back, but why would she want to do that? It was just a bunch of racket. Still, she might as well try. Maybe there would be clues in them, melodies or notes she could use. She cocked her head to the side as she tried to tune in to the gongs. They swelled up in her mind, bashing her with their brassy cacophony. Then, suddenly, they stopped. Sharee froze in shock. Had she done something?

She opened her eyes. The smoke had stopped writhing and pulsing as well. In fact, even as she watched, it began to thin out, disappearing swiftly until she could see Bud coming to a stop a few steps in front of her. He turned to look at her. Within the span of a few seconds, the air around her was back to normal. Real smoke from burning houses still hung in the air, but it didn't hover along the ground unnaturally, obscuring vision. Bud noted her expression, and lifted his spectacles, looking around in amazement.

"It's gone," he said.

"But why?" Werim asked from behind her. Sharee spun and found him looking around suspiciously, spectacles in hand. "Don't relax just yet."

The three of them crept over to the corner of a nearby house. Bud handed Werim his spectacles, and her brother shoved both pairs into his pack. Sharee poked her head around the side of the house while the boys were rearranging their gear. What she saw nearly called her to yell out in alarm. A solid line of inked men, walking shoulder to shoulder, was spread out between the houses. None of them wore any strange headgear now, but they were still armed with curved swords and strange bows. Some had axes and hammers as well. They appeared casual but alert, flowing around structures, and steadily progressing through the village from the front path. They were advancing toward Sharee and the boys. The line of men was endless. Each man was scanning the ground before him, occasionally bending down to snatch an item for observation. At each house, a few of the men entered, apparently scouting out the interior. They were scavenging.

"Uh, boys," Sharee began quietly. "You're going to want to see this."

Bud and her brother crept up to the corner and peered around, each a head above the other. Sharee pulled back and looked toward the stream. She could see a good portion of the village between the houses, but didn't see the group of men the boys had mentioned earlier. She leaned up against the house and slid down into a sitting position.

"Bloody knuckles!" Bud hissed. "We're pinned."

Both boys turned away and plopped down next to her. They were stuck. They could hide in a house, but would be found eventually. These inked invaders were unlikely to skip a closet or wood shed.

Sharee looked at Bud, and then her brother. Their eyes echoed the hopeless feeling within her. *We can't get caught, we just can't!* She wasn't going to let these barbarians win. Not after what they did to... she wasn't going to think about it now. If she did, she might fall apart. *Focus*, she told herself, chasing the image of red on green from her mind. *Listen... learn.*

She cleared her mind of everything, letting the sounds wash over her ears. She could hear the heavy footfalls of the men approaching their position from the east, the crackle of a burning house in the distance to the north, the whisper of the wind through the trees at the west, and the sound of the stream accelerating over river stones to plunge off the cliff at the southern edge of the village.

It's the only way. Her eyes snapped open. She found her brother staring at her, an expectant look on his face. She knew in an instant that he had had the same thought.

"I've got it," Werim said excitedly.

"No," Sharee moaned. "No way."

Bud looked between the two of them, confused, "What? What is it?"

"We have to, 'Ree. It's the only way out," Werim explained.

Sharee shook her head, "It's too far."

"No, it isn't," Werim argued. "Scrontle told us that dad did it once."

"Boy stories," Sharee countered. "Mom said he was just teasing us. She was angry with him."

"Yeah, but dad wasn't angry," Werim recalled. "In fact, he laughed about it. You know he did. That's as much as an admission from him."

"No, Werim. We are *not* doing *that*," Sharee pled.

"What in the Composer's name are you two talking about?" Bud blurted.

Sharee and her brother both looked at Bud. "Who's the Composer?" they asked.

"Didn't your mum ever read you stories when you were little?" Bud shook his head.

"What does that have to do with anything?" Sharee asked.

"I'm going," Werim said. "You two can stay here and get captured for all I care."

He took off in a low crouch, heading for the stream. Sharee gave Bud a winning smile, hoping he'd take her side and stop Werim. He raised an eyebrow and followed his friend. Sharee stuck her tongue out at his back, and then trotted after the pair.

They sprinted between the shadows of the houses, heading southward and back toward the stream in the middle of the village. Soon, they had put enough houses between themselves and the line of men that they lost sight of the invaders. They continued until they saw the giant smoke stacks of the smithy. The stream moved quickly in this part of the village, cutting a bit deeper into the river rock. Werim walked up to the edge. He looked back at them.

"Wait," Sharee called, hurrying to his side and looking down.

The view made her a bit dizzy. The water rushed right over, spilling straight down the cliff to a small pool below. It wasn't nauseatingly high, but it was taller than any of the trees that Sharee had climbed in the woods behind their house. Rocks were at the base of the falls, and the virgin forest spread out before them. There shouldn't be any invaders to contend with below. It was wilderness for quite a distance before the path met up with the waterway again.

"You can't be serious," Sharee told her brother, looking at him.

He nodded at her, smiling. Then, he jumped. Sharee's heart leapt with him. She watched him plummet downward. Keeping his legs together, he knifed into the water below with a small splash. Sharee swallowed loudly. She realized Bud was at her side, lips pressed together.

"You're as crazy as he is," Sharee accused him.

Bud glanced back at the village. Small portions of the line of men could be glimpsed between the houses now, steadily heading toward the center of the village and the stream. Sharee followed his eyes, sweeping across the only home she'd ever known, smoke rising from burned houses in the distance. She saw the pain start to creep into his face, his strong jaw clenching, his eyes tightening, as he thought about the loss of his mother. Despite her own pain, Sharee wanted to hug him. Everything had changed for them in the span of a mere half day.

"There's nothing left, Sharee," Bud said morosely. "Only death."

Sharee nodded, trying to suppress her own tears. He was right. Her mother had sacrificed herself. They had to make the most of that. Her eyes traveled back to the pond below. Werim was swimming toward the edge of the water, apparently unharmed. She looked at Bud once more, and he nodded toward the cliff, indicating she should go first. She bit the inside of her lip, but returned the nod. Then, taking a deep breath, she jumped.

The air was a roar in her ears as the ground rushed up toward her frighteningly fast. Her arms flailed beside her in what she was sure was an undignified manner, and her dress threatened to peel itself up off her head. It felt like she was in the air forever, and yet an eye blink later she plunged into the icy water. She'd at least had the presence of mind to straighten her legs and pull her arms in as she entered, slicing through the surface of the water and plunging swiftly below the surface. A belly slap from that height would have surely killed her. Fortunately the pond was a lot deeper than it looked; otherwise she'd have smashed into the bottom. Within seconds, her feet found the rocks at the bottom, jarring her somewhat even having been robbed of most of her speed.

She hadn't managed to get a good breath before she'd jumped, and her lungs soon began to burn from lack of air. A bit of worry bubbled up into her mind, threatening to steal her thoughts and sweep her away into a frenzied panic. She fought the feeling, and pushed strongly off the rocks, propelling her body up. Kicking furiously, she broke the surface of the pond and sputtered for breath. A splash behind her nearly made her scream as Bud entered the water from above. *He should have waited until I was out of the way!*

Sharee quickly swam over to the edge of the pond and hauled herself out of the water next to her brother. She suppressed the urge to shiver in the chill fall air. It was going to be quite cold come nighttime. They would need to get a fire going. Werim was wringing out his clothes and rearranging his pack. He quickly rummaged through the contents, perhaps checking to see if anything had been ruined. Apparently satisfied, he stood and watched Bud swim toward them.

Sharee stood and turned back toward the pond as well. She began to try to wring the water out of her dress, pulling the garment up and twisting the cloth in her hands. Recalling her freefall, she was thankful that she'd thrown on a pair of pants under the dress before leaving. There were a couple small rips at the bottom hem of the dress, and it was a bit shorter than when she'd first put it on. She frowned. It was the first time she'd worn the poor thing.

As Bud arrived at the side, he reached up with one arm and pulled himself from the water. He was favoring the other arm. Sharee noticed that a streak of red ran down it along with the rest of the water as it sluiced off of him. He tried to turn away from them, but she quickly went over and grasped the offending limb. An angry gash ran the length of his left forearm, red oozing up and seeping out. She twisted it a bit, examining the wound.

"I caught it on a rock," Bud explained.

Werim frowned, "You should have jumped further out."

Bud glanced at Sharee before answering, "Yeah. The men above were almost where they would see me. I aimed poorly."

Sharee stared into his blue eyes for a moment. She knew he was lying. He hadn't aimed poorly. He had jumped so that there was no way he'd crash into Sharee and hurt her. Guilt panged her heart as she remembered her initial irritation with him in the pond.

He'd been forced to jump. She should have been grateful that he'd chosen not to land on top of her. Apparently he couldn't admit that in front of Werim, though. *Boys,* Sharee thought.

"*Tsk,*" Sharee said. "This is pretty deep."

She dropped his arm and grabbed a hold of her dress again. Starting at one of the small rips, she tore off a length of cloth. Now she was doubly thankful she wore pants. The dress hardly covered her knees anymore. Taking the cloth, she tied it around the wound on Bud's arm.

Werim laughed.

"What?" Sharee asked testily.

Werim pointed at the pack on his back, "You didn't have to do that. I had bandages."

"*Hmpf,*" Sharee responded, walking away from the boys.

"Nice," she heard Bud say behind her.

"What did I do?" Werim asked.

"Let's get away from the cliff before someone spots us," Bud said, catching up to Sharee.

"Right," Werim shrugged, following. "But which way should we head?"

"Does it matter?" Bud replied.

They were silent for a bit after that. Where *would* they head? They knew their father had gone to Tashaba, the capital, on some sort of business, but how were they ever going to find him? How were they going to tell him about mother? Sharee looked at the trees around them. Oddly, it appeared to her as if they were all drooping, sagging sadly with the early evening light filtering through weary braches. It was as if her pain echoed in their forms. Her mother... *No,* she would not dwell. She would continue forward.

"Knucklesporte," Sharee said. "We should head for Knucklesporte."

It was the biggest town she knew of. She'd never been there, but she'd heard it had walls and soldiers. The road down out of the mountains rejoined the river near there, and the land began its transition from foothills into the plains. Surely a fortified town such as Knucklesporte would be able to hold against a small party of raiders. The inked men wouldn't find it to be easy prey like Kokamongo. She and the boys could get help from the townsfolk there; maybe even get a few horses to make the long trip to the capital easier.

A chill wind blew through the trees and on it, the scent of charred wood wafted. Apparently, the invaders above had finished their searching and were seeing to the final stages of their raid. Hopefully, the dark-eyed man was honoring the promise made to Sharee's mother, but that was doubtful. The man didn't strike Sharee as honorable.

Bud sniffed the air and looked up at the darkening sky. "Savages," he growled.

"What are they doing? Burning everything?" Werim pondered aloud. "Glad we didn't try to hide."

"They're feasting," Bud said. He cast an odd look at his friend. "Your parents really did shelter you, didn't they?"

"What do you mean?" Werim asked.

"Those men," Bud began to explain, gesturing back toward the village as they walked through the woods, "they are Baraban. Fierce savages from the deserts beyond the Pillar of Fire."

"The Pillar of Fire," Sharee interrupted. "What is that?"

Bud shrugged, "A big, lonely mountain, I guess. My da used to tell me all kinds of stories when I was little, before he took off. Tales from the lands beyond the mountains, he said. He talked a lot about the Grand Warlord and his high seat at the foot of the Pillar of Fire. A powerfully evil man. And about the fall of The Nine, stuff like that."

Werim looked toward his friend, "What does that have to do with these inked invaders?"

Bud answered, "Well, there were some stories about the Baraban Legion. They were one of the first nations to renounce The Nine and join the Grand Warlord in his conquest. They're rapists and scavengers. They loot what they please and dine on the flesh of their fallen enemies. Supposedly, it strengthens them. When they conquer a land, they kill you and eat you, or they force you to eat your friends and join them. Either way, they leave nothing behind. It's said that each mark on their skin is for a soul of a person they've devoured. Sort of a sick tribute."

Sharee shivered. Now that Bud mentioned it, she could smell burnt flesh on the fumes from above. It turned her stomach. She thought of one of the boys she'd seen in the group of captured villagers, Andree Peau. He had sometimes hung around with her brother and Bud. Sharee envisioned the savages forcing Andree to eat her mother. The shiver turned into a shudder before Sharee banished the thoughts from her mind. She sought the harp in the back of her head, and gave it a soothing caress. It responded with a pleasant, soft thrumming that filled her. She latched onto that warm feeling and regained herself.

As the noise hummed along quietly inside of her, she cast a look over at her brother. Had he heard? She was sure he had the ability to hear. After all, her mother had said as much, but how did it work? She could easily pick up her mother, but the strange gongs she'd had to focus on in order to hear. Was that how other muses would interact with her, or was she merely untrained?

"Are we going the right direction?" Werim asked, startling Sharee. "I mean, we don't have the stream to guide us anymore."

Sharee looked at her brother and then walked over to a tree. She put her hand on its trunk. The noise was still vibrating quietly in her, and she felt it reverberate off the rough bark. She stood there for a moment, reveling in the strange feeling. She wasn't really sure what she was doing, but like the first time she'd held a bow, it just felt right. She struck another note on the harp and felt it traverse through the woody structure of the tree. It was almost as if she could *feel* what the tree was feeling and how all of its parts fit together.

The wind brushed across her green leaves in a gentle caress. She stretched to the sky, delighting in the last touches of the sun as it turned orange and began to slide off the horizon. There would only be a few hours of sunlight left. The ground below was fertile and moist as her roots snaked through it, giving her a firm anchorage. They stretched deep, weaving around hidden rocks and searching for it. *Yes, there it was.* A source of moisture, deep down. The tips of her deepest roots just barely touched it. The water from the stream continued underground, pointing her steadily southeast.

"Hello, 'Ree? What are you doing? Talking to that tree?" Werim asked, snapping his fingers in her face.

"As a matter of fact, I was," Sharee responded. "And we're going the right way."

Werim snorted, "Well, I guess that's as good as anything. C'mon, Bud. Let's follow the tree." He chortled and continued walking.

Bud turned his head a bit, regarding her with a mild curiosity before heading off after his friend. Sharee frowned. Hadn't she just talked to that tree? Was that even possible as a muse? Maybe she was losing her mind, but it really did feel like she was heading in the right direction.

Sharee turned and followed the boys, music on her mind.

◆ Chapter Eight

Lugar Tyniente, High Admiral of the Baraban Legion, stood before a chair that had been pilfered from the still smoldering village. Warlord Vraika brooded in that chair as if it were a throne. They stood in the middle of what had once been the home of a family. Wooden walls and much of the roof had burned away, leaving only ashes and a shoddy dirt foundation. Emissary Larse lurked just behind the chair to the right, rubbing his sticklike hands together as if trying to start a fire.

That boy be no better than a pit lizard, Lugar mused with irritation. Larse had shown up as soon as the fighting had ended, of course. Up until that point, he'd been ensconced comfortably up in one of the Landshas. *A bit of a chill would serve him right.*

In Lugar's seasoned opinion, the boy needed to get some meat on his bones. The cold winds of the mountain pass didn't reach them in the village. It was balmy by comparison. There was no excuse for catching a shiver. In fact, with fall not yet yielding to winter, it was still warmer than most of the frigid desert nights Lugar remembered from his youth. That was a different time, and though the Admiral might reminisce fondly on certain memories, he did not miss the harsh weather.

"The Grand Warlord will not be pleased that lives were spared," Bir Larse contemplated aloud.

Lugar watched Vraika, waiting for the furious response he was sure would come. The dark Warlord didn't even look up. He was contemplating the new symbol on his forearm. Oddly, after killing the green clad woman, he'd insisted on performing her Last Rites himself. As a result, a fresh, ash-darkened carving of an intricate tree had been added to the designs on his arms. It still bled a bit from the repeated needle piercings needed to bury the dark ash permanently beneath the skin. Lugar had been a part of many Rites himself, though he didn't feel the urge to commemorate each and every one of his numerous kills. *What do that woman be to him?* Lugar thought curiously. It was odd that the Warlord should take personal interest in a simple village woman's ceremony, though her blood had been shed by his hands.

Larse continued, a bit louder this time, "Of course, the mistake can still be rectified."

Vraika ran a hand through dark, curly hair. He sighed and finally raised his head to fix Lugar with tired, hazel eyes. They were calm now, not swirling with darkness like they had been all day. Not for the first time, Lugar admitted to himself how much he found muses unsettling. He preferred the consistency of steel over inexplicable trickery.

"Admiral, what do you think?" Vraika inquired.

Lugar had to focus to keep his eyebrows from popping up. The Warlord had been acting strange all day. He didn't normally ask for Lugar's input on decisions. In fact, making any suggestion recently had been like walking into the den of a desert rattler. One misstep and he would find himself marked for death. *Be this a test?*

"A deal do be made," Lugar said, shrugging. "By the Code, the villagers be protected now."

Lugar kept his face calm. It was the truth and if nothing else, the Admiral prided himself on adhering to the Code. He led with honor.

"Codes matter not the Grand Warlord," Larse hissed. "He *is* the law."

Vraika stood and began pacing. He kept looking down at both the bracer he wore and the fresh, bloody mark on his skin. Uncertainty radiated from him. Lugar found himself equally vexed. Normally, the Warlord had the only barest of regard for the Code. Though the correct decision was clear in Lugar's mind, he didn't expect Vraika to pay heed to the simplicity dictated by honor. The dark man had chosen a different path long ago, one that followed the wishes of the Grand Warlord more than the traditions of the Legion. Lugar supposed that was just one of the hardships of being branded a muse: being forced apart from your people.

"Bring the dark haired boy to me," Vraika growled. "I've seen him among the villagers. He be the only child of sufficient age. If he can listen, then the villagers do be spared."

"The Grand Warlord will not be–" Emissary Larse began.

Vraika interrupted, "Leave Vral to me, Larse." He turned toward the skeletal youth, eyes flashing. "If that boy can listen, then he is Renee Swift's son, a true child of Two Keys. Surely the Grand Warlord will be pleased to have him, whatever the cost."

The Emissary bowed his head obsequiously, "Then, let us put him to the test."

Lugar waited for a nod from his Warlord, then struck his breast with a fist and left the room. *Best be off 'fore the good grub spoilt.* He stepped through the blackened frame of a doorway, one hand going up to steady the triangular hat resting on close-cropped, gray hair, and walked toward the front of the village. It felt good to be able to don his hat again. The high winds of the pass had caused it to blow off so often that he'd put it away for safe keeping. Only this morning had he gotten the covering out prior to the raid. After all, one had to look the part when going to battle.

The Admiral surveyed the Landshas that were resting in the village as he strolled by, settled onto their enormous bellies with eyes closed. Ladders had been unfurled. They hung down the furry sides of the animals, allowing the men atop access to the ground, where they bustled about. Lugar nodded to a few as they went about the business of setting up camp. Many of the Landshas had been sent ahead to prepare for assaults on other, larger mountain towns. What remained in the village was only a small sliver of the force they'd brought with them, though it consisted of many of their elite troops.

Lugar's chest swelled with pride as he strolled among his men. Such an armada of Legion warbeasts hadn't been amassed in the Admiral's lifetime, which was why it was his honor to lead the crew personally. Somehow the Grand Warlord had discovered a way to open the mountain pass, and he wanted to send in a large fleet of his finest troops before the Resistance became aware. If they could capture the Tashers without much of a fight, then the remaining kingdoms would face battle on two fronts. With the odds stacked against them, they would fall in no time, and the Grand Warlord's grip on the land would be complete.

Not that it be any business of mine, Lugar reminded himself. He was a simple soldier, concerned with keeping his people from being eliminated under the rule of the Triumverate. So long as they served faithfully, they retained some of their autonomy. It was up to Lugar to make sure his Legion performed admirably in battle. He needn't–and shouldn't–concern himself with the motivations of muses. The spoils of war found their way home, back to his people– to his children–and that was enough.

The sun threatened to dip completely into the valley, creating long shadows with its slanting rays. Nightfall was almost upon them. Heat from a large fire sent wavy lines rising into the air on the tail of black smoke. The ceremonial fire had been built in what had once apparently been a sparring field.

'Tis a poor excuse for a sparring field, Lugar reflected. In fact, the whole village appeared rudimentary to the Admiral. The air was more of a temporary refugee camp than any sort of permanent habitation. The wooden houses were just one step up from tents, and the storage and production facilities were barely enough to provide adequate supplies for the residents. *Why would anyone be choosin' ta live here, what with the valley below?*

A large structure stood between him and the fire. It was the only structure left uncharred in the village. Inside, the men had found casks of wine. If there was one thing Legionaires would spare from fire, it was drink. Lugar's eyes crinkled around the edges as he smiled at the thought. Surely a few of those barrels were being cracked open even now. If all went well, the Admiral might even get to relax with a cup of wine tonight himself. *It do be too long since I been havin' the pleasure of a good wine*, he admitted. Mostly, what they had from home was grog, and a man of his seasoning could only drink so much of the sour rum before acquiring a Lasha-sized bellyache.

Lugar rounded the shoddy, wooden warehouse to find a large tent pitched near the fire. Men covered by ash symbols surrounded the tent solemnly, Legionnaires. The revelry would not begin until the sun had hidden its face, and the villagers were being held inside, awaiting their induction into the Legion. Lugar recalled his own indoctrination with a shudder. *The poor bastards be in for a long night.*

Long torches had been stuck into the ground at the corners of the tent, adding their smoke to the haze above the camp. The smell of flesh was heavy in the air, though Lugar found it not altogether unpleasant. He had long ago grown used to the smell. Bodies were still being brought and piled up next to the pyre as the dead were counted. The Admiral found it surprising that there had even been a few casualties among his seasoned troops. The green clad woman had done a good job of uniting the villagers before they'd managed to surround her. Red fletched arrows protruded from several of the bodies lined up next to the fire, evidencing the woman's success. *It do be a shame a saucy wench like that had ta die. 'Twould have made some lucky bastard a fine tentwarmer.*

Two large men framed the entrance to the tent, and they struck fist to breast as Lugar approached. He nodded, and then pushed the leather flap aside, bending his head slightly as he entered. His dark eyes swept the room as he let the flap drop behind him. There were two more guards, sitting at a pilfered table near the front of the chamber, throwing bones. Before them was a bundle of green clothing, several more of the red arrows, an ornate bow, and a ceremonial dagger. The colored cubes rattled on the wood once more before the men noticed him, snatching them up and standing at attention. The remaining villagers sat together in the back half of the tent on the dirt floor. Surprisingly, they appeared calm, though tear streaks stained the sides of many faces. Lugar approached the table and nonchalantly lifted the bundle, slipping it beneath an arm.

"T'were good that you be dicin' for first watch tonight," Lugar said with a straight face. "Course, we be needin' you both, so t'were for naught."

Both men grimaced, but bowed their heads in acquiescence. First watch was not likely to trade off until after the wine was gone. They knew better than to be caught dicing on duty. Especially for loot that wasn't theirs by Rites. It was fortunate for them that on the eve of victory, the Admiral was feeling lenient. *There be a time when t'were me in their shoes, dicing for the spoils and lustin' after wenches.* Lugar suppressed a smile as he turned from the men to face the villagers.

A large, bear of a man rose to his feet in front of the group, jaw set as if prepared for a confrontation. Several of the other men and women were at his back, with all of the children gathered behind them, mostly young girls. From the wariness in their eyes, apparently they had about as much faith in the Warlord's adherence to the code as Lugar did.

He was not here for the villagers, however; he was here for the boy. The lad stood proudly with the men, jaw set in a fair imitation of his elders. He appeared to be shielding a brown haired woman, who stood just over his right shoulder, frowning. Young men did tend to be rather protective of the women in their lives. *If only they knew.*

Chocolate brown eyes stared back at the Admiral defiantly, yet Lugar could see the fear in there as well. *Good.* The boy was brave, but not stupid. He would need both courage and wits to survive where he would be going. His straight brown hair was cut precisely a finger's width above each ear, and Lugar scanned the grown men, trying to figure out which was the father. None bore an obvious resemblance. *He be dead then*, Lugar decided.

"Boy," the Admiral said, pointing, "you be summoned by the Warlord."

The boy's eyes widened in shock, and the woman behind him placed a restraining hand on his shoulder. Motioning the others to remain calm, the bearish man stepped forward. Black hair covered every exposed part of the man's bulky arms.

"What do you want with him?" the man asked.

Lugar resisted the urge to chastise the man's lack of respect. They were not in the Legion yet. They could not be expected to abide by the Code. *That be changin' soon enough.*

"That be the Warlord's business," Lugar said sharply, then waved a hand at the boy. "C'mere now. We no be wantin' that pretty thing to be hurt, do we?"

Lugar didn't make a habit of threatening women—he didn't like to make threats he was unwilling to fulfill—but in this case it was true. The fate of the entire group of people was on the boy's shoulders, not just the woman. Lugar hoped, for the Code's sake, of course, that the boy would prove to be who they thought he was. Besides, several of the men looked as if they would be useful in a scrum. Lugar was not fond of needless killing, especially when numbers could be bolstered.

No one moved, and Lugar's frustration began to rise. *They do not know their place,* he thought irritably. They would need to be broken, but not tonight. He wasn't even sure they were going to live. Chances were that the boy would hear nothing. Slowly, deliberately, Lugar reached a hand up to remove the triangular hat he wore on his head. *Yet, if they be yearnin' for a fight...* He was halfway through a turn to hand the hat to one of the two guards when a messenger burst into the room.

"Sir!" he said, striking fist to breast, and then proceeded to take in his surroundings with wide eyes.

Lugar waited for the message, however, the man continued to stare pointedly around the room. When it became apparent that the man was hesitant to relay his message in front of unknown ears, the Admiral calmly placed his hat back on his head, turning back around to face the villagers. They were still bristling before him, though they were unarmed, having been searched thoroughly, and the Admiral carried his customary sword. Lugar wished he had more time to deal with the situation appropriately. The duties of an Admiral of the Legion were many, however, and time fleeting. *Duty be what duty be*, he intoned in his head.

"The boy will no be harmed tonight," Lugar promised, which was true enough. The Code forbade executions the night after a battle. Their revelry was meant to celebrate winning another game of bones with the Fates, not provide further feeding for Death's fiery furnaces. Lugar met the big man's eyes unyieldingly, letting him see the sincerity in them. *There no be hidin' of the eyes when the truth be spoke.* Then, he stepped up to the group and grabbed the boy's arm, pulling him from the grip of the woman. She made a little yelping sound, but the villagers made no move to stop him, which was fortunate. *Poor bastards*, Lugar thought as he fingered the ornate sword hilt at his waist.

The Admiral pulled the boy out of the room, casting a meaningful glare at the two guards left behind. They would *not* be late for their watch. The messenger followed him out. Lugar shoved the boy toward one of the guards standing outside of the tent.

"Take the boy to the Warlord. He be expectin' 'im," Lugar ordered. He handed the bundle he'd snatched from the table to a second guard. "This be goin' to my tent and nowhere else, savvy?" he dictated to the other guard. Both men nodded their heads and then trotted off, boy and bundle in tow. Lugar pulled the messenger aside and then asked, "Now, just what is it you no be wantin' the others to hear?"

"Sir," the man began haltingly, "we did run afoul s'more bodies. 'Cept... well, you be wantin' to see 'em, Admiral. Dey be a bit oddly marked up."

"Aye, fine," Lugar responded. "Lead the way, then."

The younger man started off with a nod, the Admiral striding swiftly behind him. They took the main path, making use of the small stone bridge that still spanned the stream in the middle of the village. Not for the first time, Lugar reflected on the temporary nature of the wooden structures in the village. *Rickety things, these be,* he thought while passing the remnants of one particularly shoddy structure. It was as if they had all been constructed by folk that hadn't meant to stay. Still, the vineyards were well established, and paths had been worn into the ground. The village hadn't sprung up yesterday. It was as if the people had all expected to leave, but had never quite gotten around to it.

It puzzled Lugar. The view from the cliff down into the valley was breathtaking, and the land was far more hospitable, even this high up, than what he was used to on the other side of the mountains. In the desert, such an oasis would most certainly have had high walls and a constant watch. The people here had been relatively surprised by the raid, though they hadn't simply surrendered. *They certainly had reason for fightin'. One don't be givin' up one's home easily.*

Lugar wondered where the young Legionnaire was taking him. They continued all the way through the village to where the houses stopped, and kept going. There was a large field and then a tree line bathed in shadow. They continued across the field and soon the Admiral was able to make out a house nestled on the very edge of the wood. In fact, it almost appeared to be strung between some of the trees, its roof drooping from trunk to trunk. It was an unusual structure, and Lugar wasn't quite sure what to make of it. It certainly blended well.

The messenger led him around the side of the house where Lugar found the three other men of the scouting party standing around a pile of bodies. They'd been hastily thrown behind a wood pile, mostly hidden from view. It was a testament to the sharp eyes of his scouts that they'd even been found. When the messenger simply nodded to the corpses, Lugar approached and, with a grunt, bent over to examine them.

The body on top had a nasty cut in the center of his forehead. Lugar had seen its like before on a man whose skull was split with a thrown axe. This one was a bit neater than that had been–*normally there be more gore*–but otherwise not unusual. Surely many of the villagers kept wood axes around. It was easy to throw a wood axe. The second body evidenced a simple stab wound; the man had been impaled by a sword. Likely from behind, judging by how his leather vest bent outward slightly. Such wounds were common on any battlefield. *Dere be nothin' to these two,* Lugar puzzled.

Apparently, it was the final two bodies that had brought him out here. Each had a single arrow sticking out of them, one in the neck and the other in the chest. Each arrow displayed white fletching and deep penetration. The one in the neck had nearly come out the other side, telling Lugar that they were not fired from a long distance, but up close.

"There be blood in da house," the messenger pointed out. "They be drug out here."

Lugar nodded. Reaching down, he yanked the two arrows from the bodies. At first, they got hung up on bone, but with a lurch they came out accompanied by a wet, sucking sound. Drawing this thumb across each tip, fresh blood sprang up from two shallow cuts; the tips were still razor sharp. The Admiral's brows knitted together in puzzlement. It wasn't that arrow wounds were uncommon. It was just his experience that, in the heat of battle, arrows were rarely placed so expertly. In fact, many of his soldiers carried a multitude of puckered wounds from arrows in battle. He could recall battles himself where he'd broken shafts off and continued fighting. The wounds hurt something awful to heal, but they were rarely fatal, so long as you cleaned them properly and cauterized them. *And these arrows do still be in pristine shape. Curious that.*

The bowman that had done this was obviously skilled, especially to have done such damage in close quarters. The weapons themselves were apparently made of the finest of materials, and he was only recently familiar with them. He'd pulled one from the neck of a messenger earlier, and seen them peppering his other dead. The simple answer was that the green-clad woman had done this; however, he wasn't so sure. All of the arrows in her quiver had been fletched red. Of course, it didn't preclude her from having a second set of arrows.

"Be there more arrows like this in the house?" Lugar asked.

One of the scouts shook his head, "Da house be searched 'troo. Dere be no more arrows. Of any kind."

Lugar nodded. He tucked the arrows into his belt and stood from the bodies. It occurred to him that perhaps the Warlord was wrong in looking for a son. *What if the child do be a daughter?* While there was only one boy of proper age in the group, there were several girls that would fit. Lugar hadn't even bothered to look at the girls. He needed to get back and inform the Warlord before he made a mistake with the boy. He would hate to see the Code broken for such a simple oversight.

"What should we do wit da bodies?" a scout wanted to know.

Lugar realized he'd been staring at the strange house and brought his attention back to his men. "Take 'em to be honored."

"Aye, sir. And da house? Should we burn it?" another asked.

Something about the house tugged at him. *Where be the like been seen 'fore this?* The structure looked so out of place compared to the shabby nature of the rest of the houses. It was such a solid, graceful construction.

"Leave it be. Wouldn't want to be settin' the woods on fire," Lugar answered.

"Aye, aye," his scouts replied.

Lugar turned to let them go about their work. He started back toward the front of the village, picking up his pace as he went.

He didn't want to be too late. *How long be a test for a muse anyway?*

Soon enough, Lugar found himself crossing the stream in the middle of a village at near a trot, old wounds causing him to limp a bit. Of course, near a trot wasn't quite a trot. There were appearances to maintain, and the High Admiral of the Baraban Legion was always in control. *The house be just up the way a bit now, no' far at all.* Surely, he'd not been gone long enough for the test to have been completed. Lugar was just beginning to slow his pace when the scream of a young boy broke the peace of the camp. He lurched into a full trot.

~ + ~

Werim sat bolt upright, ripped suddenly and painfully from a dead sleep. His hands flew to his ears. A sharp, painful noise had wakened him, knifing into his brain and grating along his spine. The sound itself had been quick and pointed, leaving only a hollow echo in its wake. Werim poked a finger into each ear and focused on blocking out the pulsating echo. To his surprise, it abated almost immediately.

He glanced over at the sleeping forms of Bud and his sister. A gentle snore sawed out of Bud's lumpy shadow, and Sharee's chest rose and fell peacefully under her blanket. The hoot of an owl sounded in the distance, but otherwise the night was at ease. Apparently nothing else had been disturbed by the sound.

As Werim reflected on it, it reminded him of the time he'd dragged a knife down the side of Scrontle's anvil in an attempt to startle Bud. The terrible screech had set all their teeth on edge, and the blacksmith had kicked them both out of the forge for the day. He'd been furious that Werim had dulled one of his good knives. This noise was similar to that, only instead of being drawn out, it was as if the entire prickliness was concentrated in one pointed burst. The fresh memory of it was enough to turn Werim's stomach.

Surely something else, an animal even, should have been jittered by the sound. Yet, silence reigned around him and the night passed by unperturbed.

Werim moved his fingers to his head where he tried to rub out the ache that the sound had caused. He'd been hearing strange things lately. First those gongs, and now this weird metallic screech. It was like he couldn't trust his own ears anymore.

A soft wind blew through the trees, hardly reaching the hollow where they slept. Werim shivered. He'd packed only one blanket which he had given to his sister. It was cold at night, especially with clothes that were still a bit damp, so he'd figured it was the right thing to do. She was younger, after all.

The faintest hint of smoke poked at Werim's nostril. They had made it quite a ways from the base of the cliff, jogging in the direction Sharee had indicated, until they'd felt safe enough to stop for the night. The ruined remains of the village were far behind and, with them, the mysterious spectacled raiders.

Mom too, Werim thought, but he quickly suppressed it. They needed to find his father. No amount of dwelling on the past would help them achieve that. He was the oldest; he needed to be strong. It was his duty to see that they got safely through.

Werim shrugged off the strange sound and other thoughts that assaulted his brain. He had only just drifted off to sleep and was staring down a long day of travel on the morrow. He couldn't afford to fret away the night. The sound had probably just been part of a nightmare anyways, since apparently no one else had heard it. Surely, he'd been through enough today to warrant a few nightmares.

Sword and pack were still where he'd left them at his side, comforting Werim for some reason. As long as he had his sword, he could fight. He *would* fight. Thoughts began to thicken in Werim's brain as he laid back down, punching at the shirt wadded beneath his head.

As long as I have my sword, he thought before drifting back to sleep.

◇ Chapter Nine

Sunlight streamed down through the canopy of trees, dappling the forest floor in a kaleidoscope of light. Sharee perched on a rock next to Bud, enjoying the cool morning breeze in silence. Every now and then, she picked up the stick that was lying on the ground near her, reaching out to poke her still sleeping brother. He was such a heavy sleeper.

Bud finished stuffing most of their things in the pack and slung it over his right shoulder. He was still favoring his left arm where he'd been cut after jumping into the pond. He didn't complain, but Sharee could tell it was hurting him. She wished there was something she could do, but they didn't exactly have poultices and tonics around for healing. The bandage she'd ripped off her dress would just have to do.

Another poke in the side elicited a grunt and some mumblings from Werim, and she suppressed a giggle as her brother went right back to drooling on his shirt. She looked over to Bud and found him grinning, too. Her brother's blond friend was holding Werim's sword on his lap, studying it curiously every now and then, but otherwise enjoying watching Sharee torment her brother. They should have just shaken him to wake him, but prodding him with a stick was far more fun. He would swat the air belatedly, missing the stick, and snuggle back into his wadded makeshift pillow.

Sharee poked him again, and this time he rolled onto his stomach, his hands pawing around him as if searching for something. He appeared to be grasping where his sword and pack had been before Bud snatched them up to prepare to leave. When his hand closed around nothing, Werim's form went rigid. For a second, Sharee thought he might have gone back to sleep, but then he surprised them by quickly flipping over and presenting the two of them with balled up fists.

Sharee yelped at the suddenness of the movement, falling backward off the rock she'd been sitting on, and Bud chuckled. She shot him a glare, and he stopped. Nodding approvingly, she stood and looked at her brother.

Werim's eyes slowly cleared of sleep, and his hands dropped as he realized what had been going on. He fixed his sister with annoyed eyes, taking in the stick that lay near her feet. She knew he would try to get her back for the prodding later, but she would be ready. Her brother wasn't very good at tricking her. She knew him too well. That's how she'd always been able to fool him into angering Mom and.... Sharee locked those thoughts away. She wasn't going to dwell. She was just going to move on.

"Give me my sword, Bud," Werim said.

Bud handed it over. "No notches," he observed.

Sharee watched as Werim took the blade and ran his hand along the side, confirming Bud's observation. A quick look at the larger sword strapped to Bud's back revealed dents in numerous places from their fight the day before. Sharee suspected that her father had likely taken the same care in making Werim's weapon as... as was fitting for such an important gift. Her brother's face grew troubled as he stared it, and eventually he simply shoved it into his belt and went back to glaring at the two of them. Sharee made a mental note to talk to him about muses later. She wasn't sure she wanted to bring it up in front of Bud, lest she be accused of losing her mind again. If she talked to Werim alone later, perhaps then he would listen.

Noticing that Bud had shouldered the pack, her brother smiled slightly, and then turned to continue in the direction they'd been hiking yesterday. Sharee shook her head and shared a giggle with Bud. She'd already communed with a nearby tree this morning, letting her music flow into it, and discovered that they were slightly off course. Some rather hard rock had diverted the underground flow to the east.

Werim stopped and turned around, "Are you two coming or just going to stand there telling jokes all day?"

"We need to go this way, Werim," Sharee explained, pointing in the new direction.

Her brother frowned, grunted, and then trudged in the new direction. Sharing another laugh with Bud, they started after him. Sharee walked between the two boys, only occasionally having to dodge a stray branch that her brother *accidentally* lost hold of.

They stopped only briefly for lunch and a quick course correction, and then continued walking. Werim had thrown a few loaves of bread and some dried meat in his pack before they'd left. It wasn't a feast, but it was better than nothing. He'd also brought a wooden water canister along, but hadn't thought to fill it. Sharee wanted to wring his neck about that, but she'd kept her mouth shut and munched on the dry bread. It wasn't like they were in a desert or anything. They would fill the canister easily enough.

The afternoon passed quickly, and when they finally decided to stop for the night, the sky was already a robust orange. The boys began to slowly remove some sticks and stones from the open area, and Sharee spread out her blankets. There was little talk as they were all bone-weary. She watched the boys for a bit, moving as if they were wading through molasses. *Poor guys*, she thought. *A cool drink will perk them up.*

Standing, Sharee retrieved the canister and walked over to a nearby tree. Little, muddied streams were common enough in these mountains, but Sharee wanted a cleaner source of water. Perhaps it was only extra work, but it gave her an excuse to experiment with her newfound abilities. Closing her eyes, she struck several chords in the back of her mind. The music swelled inside of her and she pressed her hand to the tree. Now that she had done this a few times, it came more easily. In fact, she was beginning to notice that specific notes reverberated better along the bark, and others echoed more fully in the leaves and roots. It was subtle, but by weaving each different note together, she felt like she got a better feeling for the tree. In fact, she thought she could almost feel healthier growth in response to her ministrations.

This tree had exciting news for her. Its roots weren't struggling nearly as deep as some of the previous ones she'd studied. Water was closer to the surface here. Quite clearly, it indicated that the underground stream had made its way back to the surface. In fact, she suspected from the pattern that it might issue forth out of a spring or cavern nearby. Keeping her notes steady, Sharee left the first tree and walked to a second that was several paces in the direction of the water.

It was odd the things trees had written in them. Sharee reflected on what she heard even as she sorted out the melodies. Echoed in every fiber of the tree was a pattern that seemed to tell about how tall to grow to see the sun and where the nearest source of water was. The notes of the trees reflected which direction the wind normally blew and what season it was. They also possessed a sense of other things growing nearby and how the land rolled around them. It was even stranger to Sharee that, if she played the right notes on her end, she could hear these things more clearly. It wasn't exactly like the tree was talking to her or playing with her, more of an echo if anything, yet still she felt as if knowledge was made clear to her. It wasn't a specific knowledge, like a number or a word, but a vague understanding of the way of things. To Sharee, it was like hearing a familiar melody, but not being able to place it exactly, so she hummed along with her notes, trying to get a better feel for what the song of the tree was telling her.

Listening to her effect on the trees, she moved from trunk to trunk, letting each lead her a bit closer to water. She began to notice that the echo of an oak was a bit different from that of a whitewood, or pine. Each new tree she came across filled her anew with a sense of wonder at the elegance of the songs they reflected. There was a depth to the notes that belied their simplicity. Sharee wasn't exactly sure she could even describe what she was doing, her fingers flying from string to string in the back of her mind, notes flowing into notes, a symphony playing in her head, echoing off the trees, and returning with new layers of sound. It was beautiful, and as she drifted through the trees she lost herself in the melodies. At one point, she thought she might simply find a stump to sit on and be one with the forest, never moving, ceasing even to breathe until she became a tree.

Her thirst brought her back to reality. She was still humming, and humming with a dry throat had become uncomfortable. Slightly chapped lips reminded her of what she'd set out to do. She refocused, cutting out the extraneous notes and returning to simpler melodies. In a way, she was not surprised when she rounded the particularly large trunk of a fir to find a wide stream burbling out of a cave nestled in the side of a cliff. It had been here longer than the trees, and their songs reflected that fact clearly. Many of the trees would not have grown nearly so tall had the water not been near, nor would they encroach upon land claimed by water or rock.

She put a hand on the tree to steady shaky legs, and then immediately recoiled as her fingers sank into something sticky. Her eyes went first to her hand, and then to the side of the tree. It was sap, leaking down from an angry wound in the bark. Someone had hacked into the side of the tree with a wide blade. Sharee was astonished. Who would do such a thing to a defenseless tree?

In anger, she struck some notes in the back of her mind and put her hand to the bark. She was a bit surprised when the tree didn't reflect anything all that different from any other tree. Perhaps she expected it to be in pain or something, but that was silly; trees didn't have feelings. To the tree, healing a rip in its bark was just another part of the natural growing process. It couldn't comprehend that this wasn't supposed to be happening to it, that if some human hadn't taken a blade to its side, it wouldn't be bleeding sticky blood. Disregarding the tree's apathy, Sharee decided she had to do something to make it right.

Without really thinking about it, she began to play the notes her mother taught her for Knitting. If it worked on the vine necklace, why wouldn't it work on bark? After she finished the song, she stared at the gash in the tree. Nothing happened. She replayed the notes in her head. Surely, she'd gotten them right. Again, nothing happened.

Frustrated, she stuck to the simple notes that allowed her to commune with a tree. The echo remained unchanged. As expected, she could feel leaves, roots, and branches, all growing as usual. Her eyes widened as she pondered the echo. *Leaves, roots, branches... of course!* They were all related, yet unique, just like a vine would be similar to, yet different from, bark. She realized that she needed to modify the original song slightly in order to match the subtly different tonality. Leaves and vines were similar, and bark was a bit lower and more rigid than leaves, so perhaps if she tried....

She played the modified song in her head. The tree responded immediately, its bark knitting back together before her eyes. When the song had completed, Sharee held her hand up to touch the new surface. It was indistinguishable from the rest of the tree. Yet, as she pulled her hand away, she noticed that the fresh sap still remained. Wiping it back on the tree, the realization struck her: *fresh sap. Fresh! As in, recently shed. Was someone nearby?*

Sharee surveyed the woods around her warily, wishing she'd have thought to bring her bow. She fought down the eerie feeling that she was being watched and uncorked the top of the canister, kneeling down to refill it with cool, clear liquid. It was the same water from her village, guided down the mountain by porous rock, yet there was so much more of it here. The stream was wider and its flow swifter than Sharee was used to in the village. As a result, it cut more deeply into the surrounding earth, forming higher banks. She had to lie on her stomach and extend her arm all the way out in order to dip the canister in the water.

After the container was full, Sharee shoved the cork back in the top and then set it beside her. She was about to use her arms to leverage herself up off the ground when she noticed something shiny in the water. She reached back down, fished it up, and then held it for a look. Her hand began to quiver as she examined what she'd found. Her mind went blank with terror, refusing to process the object. Scooping up the canister, she stood and looked around her warily. It suddenly felt as if an entire legion of eyes were on her back.

Skin crawling, she crept back into the safety of the trees. She cowered beneath the boughs of the large fir and held her breath, peering out into the darkness of the surrounding forest. Nothing moved. She tried to convince herself that there was no one there; that the item in her hand wasn't real.

She failed. Turning, the fresh amber sap dripping down the side of the tree suddenly took on a crimson hue to her. Instead of being simply part of the natural healing process, the tree blood now struck Sharee as something more sinister. Spinning, she sprinted back to the camp, never daring to look over her shoulder.

She burst into the clearing, startling the boys who were nibbling on their last bits of food. Bud was on his feet in an instant. The blond boy tried to reach back and grab his sword with his wounded arm, winced, and snatched it with his other hand, holding it a bit awkwardly and scanning the woods around them. Werim rose more slowly, hand on sword at his waist, and fixed Sharee with a stare.

"Find a spider?" he asked with a smirk. Sharee hated spiders.

"No, bark-for-brains," Sharee whispered fiercely. "I found something worse."

"Worse than a spider, is there such a thing?" Werim whispered back.

Sharee huffed at him.

"Why are we whispering?" Bud added, joining them.

"Look," Sharee said simply, holding out her hand. She had the entire run back to dwell on what they were: a pair of spectacles; the same kind that the raiders had been wearing when they'd broken into the house. Werim's demeanor turned instantly serious.

"Did you take those from my bag?" he demanded.

Sharee shook her head. "I found a stream nearby. These were in it," she explained. Bud swore.

"What were you doing looking for a stream?" Werim pressed.

Sharee rolled her eyes and handed him the canister, "We needed water."

Bud grabbed it, removed the cork, and took a long pull. "Ahh," he sighed, and then stood and stalked to the edge of the clearing without saying a word.

"Stay here," Werim ordered, standing up and following his friend.

Sharee glared at her brother's back as he disappeared into the surrounding trees. She didn't need to be left behind like some defenseless waif. Her unstrung bow and quiver waited for her next to her blankets. Nimble fingers looped the sinew around wooden knobs, and plucked the string once. The familiar hum comforted Sharee, and she pulled out an arrow, nocking it. She walked to the tree line and sat beneath a bough with her back to the trunk of a maple. Bow resting across her lap, she slowed her breathing and watched for any sign of movement. There was enough brush nearby that she was well hidden yet retained a good view of the clearing, so she waited. And waited. The only marking of the time was the gathering darkness.

After shadow had all but claimed the clearing, Sharee heard a rustling near her. She tensed up and readied her bow. If whatever showed itself had ink on its arms, she was going to shoot first and ask questions later. Footsteps neared, and Sharee slowly began to pull back on her bowstring.

Directly to her right, Werim and Bud came traipsing out of the woods. Sharee relaxed and stood to follow them. Upon entering the clearing, the boys paused, searching around for a moment with puzzled looks, obviously wondering where Sharee had gone. They'd not even noticed they'd walked right by her! *Clumsy boys, stomping around everywhere. Making noise enough to wake the trees.*

"Think you two could make any more noise?" she accused from behind. To her satisfaction, they both whirled around, blades at the ready.

"Bloody knuckles, Sharee!" Werim exclaimed. "We almost killed you, right there. You don't even want to know how close it was."

Sharee smiled, "Sure you did. Did you find the raiders?"

Bud shook his head, "They must have just been passing through. We can scout further in the morning."

"Yeah, let's get some sleep. I'm bushed," Werim added, flopping down on the ground.

"I'll take first watch," Bud sighed.

"What?" both Sharee and Werim asked.

"Watch," Bud explained wearily. "You know, where someone stays up to make sure we don't all get our throats slit in the middle of the night?"

Sharee gulped and lay down, pulling her blankets tightly around her.

"Yeah, good idea," Werim said. Sharee could tell he was a bit shaken as well. The thought of someone sneaking up while they slept hadn't occurred to them. "Wake me up for the next turn."

"Don't worry," Bud replied, settling down on a nearby rock. "I will."

◊ Chapter Ten

Werim was surprised to wake up naturally to the light. He'd expected to be woken in the dark for his turn at the watch. Apparently Bud had forgotten, or fallen asleep. Remembering what his blond friend had said about slit throats, Werim rolled over as slowly and quietly as possible, his hand reaching out and finding his sword next to him where he'd left it this time. *Thank the stars for that*, he thought.

"Hey, 'Ree," he whispered, trying to surreptitiously scan the woods for any raiders.

"I'm already up, Werim," came the annoyed reply.

Sitting up, Werim surveyed the scene. His sister sat on a nearby stone, munching on some bread with the water canister in front of her. She was looking at him with her head cocked. Werim realized he was lying on his stomach, sword in hand, tensed to spring. It was only the two of them in the clearing. With a blush, he stood and brushed the dirt of his clothes.

"Where's Bud?" he asked.

Sharee shook her head, "I don't know."

"He didn't wake you, either?"

His sister's eyes widened, "You let *him* take watch the *whole* night?"

Werim held up his hands, "Hey now, what about you?"

That shut her up. Werim walked over to look at his meager choices for breakfast. Bread, or bread.

"He apparently came back for breakfast," Sharee noted. "This stuff was out when I woke up. I just figured you two had swapped at some point. We should go look for him."

Werim nodded, picking up a piece of bread and shoving it into his mouth. It was their last piece. He hoped they'd come across another village soon so they could get more supplies. A horse would be nice, too. He'd had enough walking, though he doubted anyone would be so generous as to let them have a horse. He washed down the dry bread with some water and then went to grab their stuff. Sharee was bouncing on her toes, ready to go and obviously anxious. Werim rolled his eyes. Bud wouldn't have gone far. Likely, he had just fallen asleep against a tree nearby.

"Let's get this search party started, then," Werim announced, picking a direction at random and heading toward the woods.

"This way," Sharee called from behind him with some exasperation.

Werim spun, "What makes your direction any better?"

"Um," Sharee said, "because this is the way Bud went?"

"How do you know?" Werim countered. "The trees again?"

She pointed, "There's a path through the brush."

"Oh." Joining his sister, he looked at where she was pointing and saw the slightest indication of passage. He hated when his sister was right, and she seemed to be more often than not lately. It was like she had developed a sixth sense in the woods. "Lead the way," Werim said, gesturing grandly with a hand.

Sharee wound around several trees before they found Bud, not very far from the camp. He was wide awake and crouched behind a bush, peeking through it. He glanced back as they approached and motioned for them to be quiet. They took the cue and crept to his side.

"Why didn't you wake us?" Sharee demanded in a whisper.

Bud shrugged without looking up, "Wasn't tired."

Sharee saw the lie in the bags beneath his eyes but didn't call him on it. Something told her that he had his reasons.

"What are you looking at?" Werim asked.

"Enemies," Bud answered, moving aside to let Werim take a look.

Just beyond the bush, the land sloped sharply down into a large clearing. Nestled in the meadow was a cluster of tents. Around the edges, it even appeared as if some trees had been cut down to increase the space. There was enough for perhaps a hundred men, with a much larger tent at the center, the rest lined in neat rows. Shirtless men lumbered through the camp, dark symbols evident on their tan arms and chests. They appeared unperturbed by the nighttime chill that still clung to the air and appeared to just be milling about–a man cleaning his sword here, a couple men walking off a patrol there–nothing menacing.

"What are they doing here?" Werim whispered.

Bud answered, "It appears to be a supply camp. See the tents on the far side?" he pointed. Werim looked and saw a couple men exit one of the larger tents with loaves of bread and a wooden barrel in their hands. As he watched, Werim thought he heard a buzzing sound, and he swatted at the air though there didn't seem to be any insects.

"Knucklesporte isn't too far from here," Sharee said, leaning against a tree and favoring Werim with an odd look. "They're probably reserves."

Bud nodded, casting an appreciative eye toward Werim's sister. "That'd be my guess. They'll be used to surround the town once the gates fall."

Werim was still watching the supply tent. A steady stream of men were going in and leaving with their arms full. "You think they'll miss some of that food if we borrow a little bit?"

Bud grinned, "No, I'd imagine not."

"Oh, and I'm sure you can just go down there and ask nicely and they'll just give it to you," Sharee snorted.

"The tents are at the edge of the camp," Werim pointed out. "If we sneak over to the far side, we could be in and out before anyone's the wiser."

"We should wait for dark too," Bud suggested. "Fewer guards at night."

Sharee crossed her arms, "Great so now we're thieves *and* refugees."

~ + ~

Werim tapped Bud's shoulder. The blond boy was sitting with his back against a tree and his eyes shut. After the tap, his blue eyes opened smoothly, and he was instantly alert. Werim couldn't decide if his friend had been sleeping or not.

In any case, the sun had finally gone down and many of the men below were retiring into their tents. The day had been rather uneventful, with various groups of the invaders coming in and out of the camp, always leaving with armfuls of supplies. Werim was bored out of his mind. Bud had been sitting in the same position for most of the day, and his sister had gathered several fallen tree limbs and pieces of bark and had been studying them intently. When he asked what she was doing, she simply shook her head and told him to ask later. Now that the sky had darkened, Werim was getting excited about the prospect of some action.

"Bud, it's time," he whispered.

Bud yawned and nodded, "Leave your sword and pack here. We wouldn't want any clanking to give us away."

Werim directed a forlorn look down at the sword belted to his waist, but nodded and complied, stacking the items neatly beside him. "'Ree, you stay here and watch the stuff," he said.

Sharee pouted but didn't argue. The boys were faster and stronger–though it surely pained her to admit that–plus if things went sour, she could cover them with arrows from the hill long enough for them to escape. At least that was the plan.

They waited for a bit longer until the only men left outside were the watch patrols that ringed the camp and the handful of men stationed outside of the larger supply tents. Raucous laughter could be heard from inside the central tent, and Werim had seen several of the wooden barrels rolled in there earlier. He suspected they didn't contain water.

"Let's go," Bud said, eyes following a pair of men as they patrolled past. "Now's our chance."

Werim nodded and turned to his sister, flashing what he hoped was a winning smile. "Be back in two shakes," he said.

The two boys dashed down the hill and toward the supply tent. They made relatively little noise, and were confident that any errant sounds were being drowned out by the loud guffaws coming from the middle of the camp. Once on the flat ground, they crept into the darkness that gathered along the tent's sides. They tried pulling at the bottom edge of material, but it was too taut to slip underneath. Foiled, they looked toward the front corner. Lit torches burned on a post just beyond, and they could see the shadows cast by two guards.

"How are we going to get by them?" Werim asked.

Bud shrugged, "Throw a rock? Hope they chase after it?"

Werim rolled his eyes, "They're not dogs, Bud."

"You got a better idea?" his friend asked. "I guess we wait for an opening."

Werim frowned and studied the situation. Motioning for Bud to stay put, he slowly crept up to the front corner to get a better look at the two men. They both wore a simple leather vest with no shirt underneath and had curved swords belted to their waists. Dark symbols covered their arms, mingling with what looked like a plethora of scars. Sadly, they did not appear to be sleepy or pushovers.

Heavy footsteps from the left appropriated Werim's attention. Another man was approaching. From the way he stumbled into the light, Werim guessed that he was after another one of those wooden barrels. The man passed close, and Werim ducked into the shadows that pooled around the tent and held his breath. It wouldn't do to get caught without even having stolen a thing, so he watched silhouettes of the guards from the safety of the darkness.

"Anuzzer cask o' rum, 'ere!" the drunken man blurted out, his shadow pointing at the two men who stood guard and then at the ground in front of him.

One of the guards stepped forward. "By da Admiral's orders, we be handin' out no more barrels tonight," he said firmly.

"Aye, an' which one o' you be stoppin' me from takin' one, huh?" the drunkard asked.

The first guard that spoke laughed. "You do be stone drunk, Borach. You'd not be lastin' tree slashes 'gainst us. Best be gettin' back to yer tent, me thinks," he said smugly.

Werim flinched as the post in front of him vibrated loudly. The drunken man, Borach apparently, had thrown a large, double bladed axe and embedded it deep into the wood. Werim had hardly seen the large shadow move, yet the weapon was there, rattling loudly. He was amazed it hadn't passed completely through the thin post.

"By da Gran' Lord!" one of the guards exclaimed.

Borach's shadow stepped forward menacingly, "I belee dat be a challenge." He appeared more sober all of a sudden.

The first guard began to stammer, "I be no... I mean... where be you-?"

"Dere be no reason t-" the second guard said, talking over the first.

"What?" Borach roared, interrupting both. "Be ya's both yella?"

Both guards straightened up at that. "No," they denied vehemently in unison.

"Den tree slashes it be," Borach said. "Challenge accepted."

There was an audible gulp from each of the guards, but they nodded and unsheathed their swords anyways. Werim watched as the big shadow that was Borach stepped back and cracked his knuckles loudly. The two guards approached the bigger man warily. One shadow circled left, the other right. Borach seemed unconcerned at being surrounded, simply flexing his arms calmly between them and waiting.

It was over before it began. Both guards danced in, swords slashing at the same time. Borach's shadow jumped backward with a litheness that was at odds with his immense size and apparent drunkenness. Their target gone, the two guards sliced through air which offered much less resistance than flesh. As they stumbled, Borach reached out and grabbed them each behind the head with long, strong arms. Off balance, the guards' momentums carried them forward and Borach helped with a push, smashing the two silhouettes together with a sickening crunch. The smaller outlines slumped to the ground, and Borach's larger shadow walked unimpeded into the supply tent. A short moment later he reemerged and walked over to the post, wrenching his axe free with a massive hand. Werim huddled in the darkness, terrified at the thought of being seen. Borach didn't even spare a glance around the side of the tent as he walked back over to the two lumpy forms on the ground.

"Shoulda made it two," he muttered, and then began loudly humming a tune to himself as he stumbled away, drunk once again.

He left the way he came, passing by Werim, still frozen with terror in the shadows. He caught a glimpse of the big man as he sauntered back into camp with a barrel under his arm and an axe propped on his shoulder. Two fresh, shallow cuts ran unheeded across his back and chest, the blood already drying.

Werim wetted his throat before turning back to Bud, "I think we've got our opening."

Taking deep breaths, the two boys stepped around the corner of the tent and into the light. The two heaps in front of the tent were the guards, breathing shallowly but otherwise dead to the world. Werim followed Bud into the tent.

Inside, they found crates, barrels, and sacks, all arranged neatly along the canvas walls. They poked into each, finding various salted meats, liquids, dried beans, and grain. There were even several satchels with hard loaves of bread that they discovered sitting atop some crates in the back. Bud snatched up one of the bags of bread and tossed a few loaves out, replacing them with some meat and beans. Werim went over and hefted one of the smaller casks of liquid. He wasn't sure what was in it, but with how the wooden containers appeared to be coveted by the men, stealing a small portion would surely be worth it.

A muffled groan from outside the tent caused them both to freeze. The boys stared across the room at each other, eyes wide. They waited breathlessly for a few moments, but didn't hear anything else. Shoving a few last things into the bag, Bud slung it over his shoulder and ducked out of the tent. Werim followed, holding the cask in front of him with both arms underneath.

Back outside, they realized that the groan came from one of the stirring guards. They were both rolling on the ground with their hands on their heads. Bud and Werim crept as silently as possible toward the corner of the tent. They were almost back in the safety of the shadows when a more coherent grunt made them flinch.

"Hey!" one of the guards called out behind them groggily.

Werim turned to see that the guard had gotten to his feet and was pointing toward the two of them. His partner was still on the ground. Arm raised, he took one unsteady step toward the boys.

That was all they needed to see. Werim and Bud ran. When they'd taken several strides without being stabbed in the back, Werim dared to hope that they would escape. As they were stumbling up the incline and into the woods, he spared a glance back over his shoulder. To his surprise, the guard hadn't gotten very far. He'd apparently only taken two steps after them before falling again. As it was, he was back on the ground a short way from his partner, staring blankly toward the woods. He certainly wasn't giving chase, or even raising the alarm.

Werim allowed himself a deep breath of relief once they reached the top of the hill and were back in the cover of the forest. Sharee appeared almost immediately to his right, startling him with her drawn bow. *How did she always seem to blend in?*

"You two got lucky," Sharee said, slinging her bow back over her shoulder and folding her arms across her chest. She handed him his things.

Werim grinned at her as he set down the heavy cask and sat on top of it, belting his sword back to his waist. He ran his hand along its hilt, glad to have it back. Bud had dropped the satchel and was back at the bushes, watching the camp with his sword strapped to his back. He was probably making sure that no one was following them. Sharee just stood there, looming above him with a disapproving frown.

"What's in the cask?" Sharee asked.

Werim patted the side of his seat, "We'll find out." He cocked a finger back toward the camp, "*They* obviously love it. Probably some expensive wine."

Sharee rolled her eyes, "You stole wine. Ugh. Like we're going to be celebrating any time soon."

"Beats the pulp out of water," Werim shrugged.

Sharee pointed a finger at him, "There's nothing wrong with plain old water."

Bud grunted.

"What? You too?" Werim asked.

Bud turned and frowned. Instead of answering, he motioned for the two of them to join him. They complied and stared through the bush at the camp below. From their vantage point they could just make out the two guards standing alongside the supply tent where they'd just left. One of the patrols had come around and was talking to a still-unsteady guard that leaned against a post with a hand on his head. As they watched, he pulled his hand down long enough to point at the woods in their general direction. The patrol nodded, and disappeared into the camp.

"What do you suppose he said?" Werim inquired.

Bud frowned, "I don't imagine he's gone to accuse Borach, if that's what you're getting at."

"Who's Borach?" Sharee wanted to know.

Werim stood and swatted her question away, "Don't worry about it."

Sharee slapped at his hand, "Well, maybe I am worried about it. Why do you expect me to just–"

"He's back," Bud interrupted.

"Who, Borach?" Werim hoped.

"No, the patrol. And he brought friends," Bud explained, standing up and grabbing the satchel.

"What do we do?" Sharee asked.

Werim hefted his cask with a grunt, "Run."

~ + ~

Vraika is pleased. His march progresses. There have been no more surprises, pleasant though the first may have turned out. From his vantage point in the lookout nest that rests upon a standing Landsha, he looks out over the wooden walls of the fallen enemy stronghold. Behind him, the rising sun spills over the peaks of the mountains. He can see foothills flattening to plains in the distance. His Legion is nearly out of the mountains, yet the Tashers still do not know of his presence. He will be halfway to Tashaba before their squabbling council even begins to discuss his invasion. That is as it should be.

The sound of stretching rope alerts him that someone is climbing up. Sure enough, smooth hands appear over the side, gripping the bone that serves as a platform. They pull up the head of a Legionnaire. As the rest of him comes into view, Vraika notes that his tan arms bear only a few markings, evidencing his inexperience and unimportance.

Vraika turns back to the picturesque scene before him, leaving his second to address the messenger. Such chores are beneath a Warlord. The Legionnaire takes the cue and addresses Lugar instead.

"Admiral, sir," says the man, pulling himself up and striking fist to breast, "dere be an urgent report from one of da supply camps."

"Aye, what is it?" Lugar responds.

"Last night, sir..." the messenger begins, but then halts and seems uncertain.

Vraika turns around to observe the Legionnaire once more, interested now. It pleases him that the young man squirms under the Warlord's scrutiny. That is proper.

"Out with it, son," Lugar assures.

"Well, a couple of da men dat were on watch, they got knocked on da head and when they came to, dere be raiders about," the man explains. Then he hurries to add, "Dere be some things missing, though not a lot they say. They rallied the men and chased dem off."

"Be there a count of the raiders?" the Admiral asks.

The messenger fidgets some more, "Not exactly, sir. Must be near to a dozen, they think, to get da drop on 'em."

Lugar nods thoughtfully. "Then there do be some that are aware of us. Relay the order for increased patrols. They no be gettin' at us again."

The young man salutes the Admiral. Then, he turns to shimmy back down the rope. Vraika is just a small bit perturbed that he didn't get a salute as well. It is only fitting that a Legionnaire should also pay respect to his Warlord.

"My Lord, the men do need a night of rest, I believe," Lugar Tyniente suggests after a moment. "I be suspectin' that they may have been fighting, and thus left opening for raiders. They tend to do that when they be drunk and weary."

"No, Lugar, we press on," Vraika responds. "There are no captives here. There is no cause for celebration, initiation, or rest. We will flood the plains 'ere Tashaba marshals any resistance. By then, 'twill be too late. This land *will* belong to the Triumvirate."

"And the girls from the village?" Lugar presses, switching tracks. "Be they tested?"

"The child of Renee Swift is a boy, as I have already told you," Vraika says through clenched teeth. "See to your men, Admiral. Fate is not to be slowed by frivolous questions and traditions."

Lugar's face remains impassive as he strikes fist to breast, "Be it as you command, Warlord," he says.

Vraika frowns as his second walks away. It is quite obvious that the grizzled man does not share his pleasure. Why not? Admittedly, they have been pressed hard, but they are the chosen of the Grand Warlord. Outdated superstitions and pageantry have no place in the new world being forged by Vral's hand. The old must perish to make way for the new.

The Legion is performing admirably, slaughtering all in its path. Apart from the surprising appearance of a muse in the first village, resistance has been as weak as expected. The Tashers are a soft people.

Renee Swift was dealt with. The very thought of the name nearly brings Vraika's blood to a simmering boil. What are farce! But that is past, and past is not now.

Now, a child of Two Keys is on his way to the Grand Warlord. From there, he will go to the Academy for training. Perhaps one day he will return to fight under Vraika's command. Vraika reflects that he would very much like that. It has the feel of... *destiny*.

The Warlord smiles, a feral, mirthless thing. Emissary Larse took the boy. It is nice to be rid of them both. Without the sniveling watchdog looking over his shoulder, Vraika can lose himself in the simplicity of spilled blood. Finding the child means that he will not have to waste any more time. Larse would have sided with Tyniente and taken the others for testing had he not been so focused on the boy. And for what? The chance for a few untrained muses with little talent? *Pah!*

The discovery of A'renee also means that her husband will be along shortly. It is puzzling that he has not turned up yet, but he can't be far. Vraika's mouth waters at the thought. He looks down at the fresh symbol etched into the skin of his forearm. It is a tree, inscribed in ash. She is now a part of him. And next to it, space for another. The husband will be found and dealt with. It is Vraika's destiny as told to him by the Grand Warlord. By the Fates. It *will* come to pass.

His gaze returns to the land before him. The Tashers will fall. The land will make a fine gift to the Grand Warlord. There is nothing that Rynel can do to stop it.

◊ Chapter Eleven

The sun was only just beginning to wane orange when they decided to stop for the night and make camp. After staying on the move throughout the night and most of the day to make sure their pursuers were far behind them, the three companions found themselves quite exhausted. Werim was pretty sure they'd traveled in circles for a bit, but Sharee assured them that they were very near Knucklesporte. With a sigh, he set his large, wooden cask down and stood looking at it in irritation. Bud began clearing away debris wearily while Sharee pulled some of the food out of the stolen sack. After a moment, Werim wound up with his leg and kicked the cask out of disgust. It wobbled a bit before settling, and Werim resisted the urge to reach down and rub his toe.

"Why did I even bother with that thing?" he asked no one in particular. "I lug it around all night and all day, and we don't even know what's in it or how to open it."

"They probably use some sort of wood screw," Bud suggested, rolling out Sharee's blankets in the first area he'd cleared.

"Well, I haven't got a screw," Werim whined. "I didn't know I'd be trying to break into a blasted heavy wooden barrel. Burn this thing!" He kicked it again, a bit softer this time.

"You could have dropped it at any time today," Sharee pointed out from where she was examining the foodstuffs.

"Buzz off, 'Ree," Werim answered.

Sharee put her hands on her hips, "Do you want dinner or not?"

Werim frowned but nodded and trudged over to see what his sister had dug out of the bag. She handed him some salted meat, a hunk of bread, and a wedge of cheese. It was hardly a feast, but after a full day of fleeing and only previously having eaten the bread he'd nicked from the cupboard at home, it was more than enough. He found himself shoving large bites into his mouth and licking every last crumb off of his fingers.

So focused was Werim on his food, that he didn't notice when his sister served Bud and pulled an apple out of her pouch to supplement her own meal. The three of them ate in silence, the sound of smacking lips competing only with the simple song of soughing branches. When he finished, Werim eased onto his back, content, and stared up through swaying limbs at the early evening sky as it began its ritualistic passage from warm orange to bloody red in preparation for night. He was sure that he could hear the crickets buzzing, warming up for their starlit performance.

"I found an opening!" Sharee exclaimed excitedly, startling her brother.

Hopping to his feet, Werim ran over to where his sister was crouched by the cask.

"Where?" he asked dubiously.

"There," she pointed.

Sure enough, there was a small separation high on the cask in the middle of one of the wooden slats that made up the sides of the container. Below it, the wood was stained a bit where some of the liquid had just leaked out. Werim stared in disbelief.

"Where did that...? How did you...?" Werim stuttered. "That wasn't there before!" he finally spit out.

Sharee just shrugged and smiled sweetly at him. "I'll go figure out some sort of cup," she said cheerily.

Werim bent over and examined the hole, running his fingers along the edges as if it might be a mirage. He was surprised at how smooth it felt. It felt as if the split was simply a natural growth in the wood. Sharee had not made it with an arrow. It would have been far more jagged and he would have noticed her shooting at the cask in any case. Perhaps his kicking had knocked a previously unseen knot out of the wood. His toe did still hurt. The buzzing of the crickets grew louder in his ear for a moment as he contemplated the possibility.

"Here," his sister said, disturbing Werim's line of thinking.

She had three green cones in her hand, and handed one to each of the boys before crouching down to pour some of the liquid into her makeshift cup. Werim stood, dumbfounded, looking at the drinking implement in his hand. He twirled it around, trying to figure out where it came from. It had the same texture as a leaf, but there didn't seem to be any seams or creases on the thing. What tree had leaves shaped like this?

"How did you–?" he began, but cut off when Bud slapped him on the back jovially.

"Let's find out what's in this cask, eh?" he said with a smile.

Werim realized it was the first time he had seen his blond friend smile since they'd left the village behind. For that matter, something had finally worked out in their favor. The last few days had been decidedly unpleasant, and though his sister's peculiarities were bugging him–tugging at hidden strings in the back of his mind that he felt he wanted to pluck out–Werim decided that it'd be better to just let things lie and enjoy this turn of luck.

He handed his cone to Bud, who tipped the cask forward and poured them each a bit of the amber liquid. Standing up, the three companions faced each other and raised their glasses to the darkening sky, just as if they were at a village celebration. Touching the edges, they shared a smile and took a sip of the contents. For a brief moment, the night was still. Then, they all spit the liquid out.

"This is wretched," Sharee exclaimed, looking at her cup in disgust. "What in blazes did you steal, Werim?"

"It's not that bad," Werim returned.

"Well, it's no wine," Bud pointed out and went over to examine the cask more closely.

"I'd rather drink goat's piss than this stuff," Sharee continued, waving her arms around.

Werim cast his sister an odd look, surprised and a touch amused by her language. "I'm sure I can work out a trade in Knucklesporte if you want a goat, 'Ree," he suggested.

Sharee threw her cup at him. "I'll stick with water, thanks," she said.

Werim chuckled as he watched his sister stalk over to their bags and pull out the water canister. She then trudged off into the woods, probably to find another of the strange green leaves. Bud had lifted the cask up off the ground and was peering intently at the bottom.

"Rum," he declared. "It says rum."

Werim went over to look at what his friend had seen. Sure enough, there was writing on the bottom of the cask. It looked to have been burned into the wood.

"What's rum?" he asked.

Bud shrugged, "A kind of drink. My da used to mention it in stories he told about dicey taverns. Mum hated those stories."

"Well," Werim said, raising his glass, "we may as well enjoy it."

He then knocked back another swallow, trying, but failing, to suppress a grimace at the taste. Still, it wasn't as bad as that first swig, and there was something... *manly* about it. His sister could drink all the water she wanted. He and Bud would make a roaring fire to sit around, tell tales of battle, and drink rum. Except they had no tales and it wasn't exactly smart to make a roaring fire in the middle of the highly combustible woods. At least they could drink the rum.

Bud appeared to share the sentiment, because he set about topping off both of their small cups. Raising his own glass with a look of trepidation, he took a sip. Werim laughed at the face his friend made, and then did a salute of his own. After a small swig, as the liquid raced down his throat by way of his spine–or so it felt–Werim gritted his teeth and wiggled his arms, hopping around as if he were doing a jig. Bud burst out with a chuckle of his own.

They traded tentative sips and laughter, settling eventually into seated positions on the ground around the cask. The sips became drinks, the drinks became chugs, and soon they found themselves having to refill their little cups anew after each imbibing. The bitter drink grew on them, and they found that they didn't have to fight a grimace as much. The night seemed to mellow out with the setting of the sun, growing blurry at the edges, and the two boys leaned back, contentment smoldering in their warm bellies and the full moon couching them in its soft, blue light.

"Tell me one of those stories about dicey taverns," Werim suggested.

Bud eyed his friend for a moment, and then took a long pull from his cup. "All right," he said. He leaned forward, setting his cup on top of the cask. "My da used to spend a lot of time in taverns. And as he tells it, he was sitting next to an old man once when the man surprised him by ordering three pints of ale." Here Bud held up three fingers and waggled them. "My da, trying to be helpful, says, 'Perhaps they do things differently where you come from, friend, but 'round here it's best to drink them one at a time. Otherwise, they'll go stale.'

"In reply, the old man shook his head and explained, 'I gots two brothers, an' when we parted ways many years ago, we promised each other that we'd drink like this, three pints, to remember the good times we shared.' " Bud tipped back his own cup for emphasis.

"So, naturally, my da bought the next three pints for the fella to apologize for having doubted his wits. He was a good man like that, mind you, no matter what mum... well he just was." Bud pointed at Werim with narrowed eyes and an unsteady finger, as if challenging him to say otherwise.

When Werim nodded sober agreement, his friend continued. "Anyway, was about a month later when my da runs into the man again. This time, though, the man's only ordering two drinks." He held up two fingers this time. "So my da, thinking quickly, leans over and says, 'Sorry for your loss, friend.' He was figuring one of his brothers had died, y'see?" Werim nodded that he saw.

"Well, the old man screwed up his eyes at my da like he was a mad man. Then he says, 'Ain't no one died, friend, I just quit drinkin' ale!' " Bud let out a huge guffaw at the end, refilling his cup, while Werim just sat staring.

"I don't get it," Werim admitted.

"He said he'd quit drinking ale when he was obviously still drinking ale," Sharee said from behind him, startling her brother upright. She'd apparently snuck up at some point during the story and was favoring them both with an annoyed look. Werim tried to turn and fix her with a dirty stare, but fell over in the process. She giggled at his expense.

"Shut up, 'Ree," Werim slurred.

Sharee ignored him and sat down near the cask, joining the boys.

"Tell us another," Sharee ventured. "How about one of those stories you were mentioning earlier. Not about taverns."

"What's wrong with taverns?" Werim mumbled.

"Please, Bud," Sharee said.

Bud put his hand to his chin, stroking stubble that was hardly more than the down on a fledgling, and looked up to gaze at the sky. Stars had begun to poke through the dark blue canopy as night strengthened its hold on the valley. In the distance, an owl cried out and the nearby buzzing of the crickets faded.

"Okay, how about this one," Bud said finally. "My mum used to call it the Birth of the Nine." He raised his glass and took a swig.

Sharee cast him a thankful grin, getting a sheepish smile in return. Werim sipped disconsolately on his drink. He leaned back and tried to resist the urge to pull up clods of dirt and fling them at his sister.

"Supposedly," Bud began, "all of this was created by a being known as the Composer." Bud spread his arms grandly, leaning back and almost falling over. Werim started to snicker, but was cut short by a sharp look from his sister. He glared back at her.

Bud steadied himself and continued, "The Composer came with his children from across the heavens. It was he that sang the first song, and, as a result, the sun grew bright. Next, in the same fashion, he brought forth the moon and then finished his song with the sky.

"The song of the heavens moved his spirit, but it was incomplete. So he set about the land. Over countless days, he sung the rivers, mountains, and forests into existence, blanketing the once barren landscape with the vibrant new melody of life. This song was more orderly than the first, the song of nature, and he found in it a different sort of pleasure. Yet, there was still something missing." Bud held up his empty glass with a look of dismay. Sharee grabbed it swiftly and refilled it, obviously wanting the tale to continue.

Bud nodded his thanks and carried on, "So, the Composer sat down to think. Silence fell over both land and heavens, and he listened. To nothing but silence. It was in that silence–the silence of the Composer's own being–he discovered a third song. It was far too chaotic to be of nature, yet not spiritual enough to be of the heavens. Still, the Composer found in it the missing muse he'd been searching for. It was the song of man, and as he listened, he envisioned people down among his creations below.

"The Composer closed his eyes and lost himself in that song. It is said that he was so moved by its beauty that he shed a tear." Bud had been swaying with his eyes closed, but now he opened them and took a small drink. "Just a single tear, and it fell to the silent world below. When it struck, it solidified to pure crystal, and all three songs began anew, intertwined forevermore. The Composer gazed on the symphony he had created, and felt it finished.

"Before he left to rejoin the heavens, he gifted his creation to his children, of which there were nine. He charged the Nine with safeguarding all that he had created. In order to do this, he instructed them to shatter his Tear into nine pieces—one for each of them—and divide up the land. They each assumed dominion over equal portions of the people, and departed to form their own nations. Ours was founded by Tash, of course," Bud explained, holding up his cup reverently and taking a drink.

"The Nine were happy for a time, and the world flourished under their watchful eye. Others arrived, sent by the Composer, but the Composer himself never returned. They remained vigilant, each taking charge of some of the people, and longed for the day when their father would return. The years stretched on and eventually, they grew heartsick and homesick. Together, they reassembled the Tear, in the hope that they could find their father."

Here Bud lowered his voice, and his speech slowed, "However, their plan backfired, and the power of the Tear nearly tore the world apart. They were forced to shatter it once more. In doing so, it is said that they lost a part of themselves inside of each piece and thus became mortal. As such, they all eventually died and the shards of the Tear were lost." Bud drained whatever was left in his cup and threw it over his shoulder dramatically. "Some say that the Nine had children of their own, and passed the shards along to them, keeping them separate and secret in order to prevent the Tear from ever being reassembled again. Thus, the souls of the Nine still wander... and... sleep," Bud finished, leaning forward on the cask.

"Well that was a dumb story," Werim complained.

Sharee glared at her brother, "You wouldn't know a good story if it dug roots and sprouted right up under your butt."

Werim pointed a finger, "Yeah well, you're... you're..." He trailed off, sputtering incoherently. They stared daggers at each other.

A loud snort startled them both. They turned to find Bud with his head flat against the cask's top, eyes closed. He was snoring. Loudly. Sharee stifled a giggle and despite feeling like it was still his duty to come up with a witty retort, Werim found himself smiling as well. Crawling over to his friend, he put a hand on the blond boy's shoulder and shook him gently. Bud mumbled something and waved halfheartedly as if to swat a fly, but did not wake.

"He sounds like a mill," Werim remarked, splashing a bit more into his cup.

Sharee walked over and grabbed one of Bud's arms, pulling him away from the cask. She grunted as she tried to drag the much larger boy toward her blankets, but didn't get very far before her grip slipped. Bud toppled over like a sack of straw as Sharee stumbled backward. Werim laughed.

"Oh, put a cork in it and help me get him to bed," Sharee scowled at her brother.

Werim stood and wavered for a moment. Hands out to his sides, he found his balance swiftly and drained the drink he'd just poured. Apparently pleased with himself, he sauntered over to grab Bud's other arm. Together, brother and sister navigated their friend to the blankets. Once Bud had been deposited, Werim plopped on the ground nearby, panting. Sharee laid the sleeping boy's things next to him and covered him up. Another incoherent sound issued forth from Bud's drooling mouth as he turned onto his side and snuggled into his makeshift bed.

Her job finished, Sharee smiled with satisfaction and walked a short way to the edge of the camp where she'd gathered another pile of leaves and sticks. Werim watched from his drunken perch at Bud's side as she started to sort through them. He wondered idly what was so interesting about simple forest droppings. Unless whatever tree had produced the cups also produced cots, Werim wasn't all that interested in the forest at the moment. Indeed, he felt his gaze drawn skyward.

In an effort to make himself comfortable, Werim unbelted his sword from his waist and laid it beside him. He then eased onto his back and put one arm under his head in an attempt to stop the stars from moving. Had they always danced so?

As the world spun around him, his mind was forcibly drawn back from sky to earth despite his better intentions. The crickets had started up again in earnest, and a chill breeze stirred the tops of the trees that brushed the edges of his view. Cold, rough ground prodded an already aching back. Winter would be along before too long, and Werim figured they needed to be well onto the plains before that happened. It would be slow enough trying to trudge through the snow all the way to Tashaba. They didn't want to risk getting stuck in the mountains, too. That would be miserable. And what choice did they have? They no longer had a mother, and the only place they knew to look for their father was the capital city. It wasn't like they could just hole up somewhere until spring. Besides, surely there would be soldiers or someone that would want to know about the raiders. The mountain villages needed more support.

Werim's head really was awhirl. Heavy thoughts slipped away as easily as sand through a sieve. The harder he tried to grasp at an idea, the quicker it spun away. He was so tired, too. Perhaps he'd had enough thinking for one day. There was always tomorrow. He switched off the light in his brain and encouraged sleep to ease the lids down over his eyes.

Surprisingly, the forest spun all the faster in the resultant darkness. *I'm going to vomit,* the thought popped in. *And those blasted crickets sound like they've crawled into my ears.* Between the noise and the nausea, Werim forced his eyes back open and fought the rising bile. Green eyes stared back at him. His mother!

No... Sharee.

The revolving earth slowed somewhat as he stared into his sister's concerned eyes. The forest had suddenly gone silent. For a moment, Werim had the oddest sensation that time itself had stopped. Leaves did not stir. Branches didn't creak. The wind was no longer tugging at his hair. She looked *so* much like his mother.

With a deep breath, Werim heaved himself to his feet. Trees pirouetted around him once, but then settled. It definitely felt better being on his feet. He decided he wouldn't let sleep claim him just yet.

As he gazed at his sister, a fierce sense of responsibility tugged at the strings of his heart. She'd never gotten on with the girls back home and, as such, had always tagged along with him and Bud. In his tired state, Werim admitted that there were definitely times when he'd thought of her mostly as an annoyance–a pest that needed to be swatted away before the real adventures could begin–but he'd tried to be a good older sibling. He really had! And now they'd both lost their mother.

Werim stood, battered by a sandstorm of thoughts and emotions. He felt a coolness on his face and swiped a hand at some moisture that had somehow crept out of the corner of his eye. Viewing the offending dampness on his finger, he scowled. What had that rum done to him? He was being a weepy girl.

He took another deep breath to compose himself before walking over to join his sister. She had returned her attentions to the sticks and leaves–missing his little bout of tears–and was completely engrossed with the array in front of her. The crickets picked up again as he stood there watching. Sharee was touching each of the pieces quickly, letting her fingers linger for a moment, and then swiftly moving to the next one. Every now and then she'd return to a previous piece of foliage as if comparing the texture between the two, but she never seemed to do more than just touch them.

"What are you doing?" Werim asked finally.

His sister looked up, noticing him for the first time. "Oh, um, just getting a feel for the different trees around here," she explained.

Werim raised an eyebrow, "By poking them?"

Sharee pursed her lips in thought for a moment, apparently considering how to respond. "Werim, there's something you should know about... about us."

"That we could be orphans?" Werim replied blunty. The sad look that briefly tugged at his sister's features caused him to regret the comment immediately.

Sharee didn't respond. Instead she reached down and plucked one of the leaves from the ground. She held it up between them, and gazed intently at it.

"Can you hear that?" she asked.

"Hear what?" Werim responded. He heard nothing but the incredibly loud buzzing of insects.

She dropped the leaf, and then reached out and laid a hand on Werim's shoulder. Even through his shirt, her fingers were warm in the cool night. Closing her eyes, she concentrated again. A chill climbed up his back, popping gooseflesh out on his arms, but the only thing his swirling mind could focus on was the crickets. They were *so* loud.

"*That*," she emphasized.

Werim twisted a finger in his ear. "The crickets?" he offered.

"What crickets?" Sharee asked in puzzlement.

"A whole army of crickets," he said, gesturing widely around him.

"You don't hear a harp?" Sharee wanted to know.

"Who has a harp?" Werim shot back, shaking his muddled head in confusion. The turns of the conversation were making him dizzy. Or perhaps it was the rum. He stumbled backward a step and eyed his sister, "Were you sneaking some of the rum?"

"Rum? You mean that nasty stuff?" She pointed at the cask. "No way." She paused for a moment. "You really don't hear anything?" she pressed.

Werim smiled and stuck out a finger, "You're just messing with me because you think I'm drunk, aren't you?"

In reply, Sharee tossed a stick at him. It had been a soft toss and the twig traveled in a lazy arc toward his face. Werim's hand shot out confidently to swat it away but, magically, it missed. The projectile hit him in the eye.

"Ouch!" he cried. "What the blazes did you do that for?"

Sharee half stood and stuck out an arm, "Sorry, I didn't mean to hit you."

"It didn't hurt anyways," Werim waved her off, rubbing his eye. No way was she getting the satisfaction of tears. "I'm going to bed," he announced. The world had mostly stopped spinning now anyway. He turned and walked away from his sister, ignoring the poorly suppressed snicker. Halfway to the area he'd planned to lie down in, another need made itself known. "Well, perhaps I'll visit the woods first," he amended over his shoulder.

"Don't touch any of the bushes with three shiny leaves," Sharee cautioned. "Trust me on this one."

Werim frowned in confusion, but nodded as he plodded away from their camp. Even when he was relatively sure he'd put several trees between himself and his sister, he continued walking. The movement cleared his head, and the awful buzzing of the crickets quieted down. He reflected that it was actually rather nice out. The night sky was clear, and a full moon shone brightly through the branches. Camp had been made uphill from another stream that Sharee had found, and Werim embraced the slope of the land to stumble down toward the running water. The soft burbling reminded him once more of the need that had led him out here in the first place, so he veered off toward a nice big tree. He was in the middle of creating his own stream, peering idly around the side of the trunk when he thought he detected the haze of a torch up above him on the opposite side of the ravine. He craned his head as far to the side as he could without falling over but couldn't get a good view.

He finished as quickly as he could and pulled his pants back up, however when he walked around the side of the tree and looked up, the light was gone. Rubbing his eyes did not affect its absence. *Stupid stick,* he thought. *Probably injured my eye.*

A few more steps took him down to the stream, and he bent slowly to one knee, still staring at where he thought he'd seen a glow. He scooped up some of the cool water and brought cupped hands to his mouth to drink. A soft footfall behind him caused him to freeze.

"Ye be a long way from da village, boy," a voice growled from beside him.

Werim turned to find a slim man, his bare, heavily inked arms marking him clearly as one of the raiders. The clean steel of a sword glinted in the moonlight. Werim calmly swallowed his drink.

"I don't know what you're talking about," he replied evenly.

"Be ye alone?" the man queried.

"Do I look like I need to bring my mother with me?" Werim knew he should feel afraid, but the only emotion he could summon up was annoyance.

The man just grunted. "Ye'll be comin' wit me," he ordered. "Quietly, if ye know what be good fer ya," he added.

"Sure," Werim replied, wiping his hands casually on his pants. "Where are we going?"

The man didn't answer. Instead, he crossed the stream and began walking up the far slope. Feeling that it was fortunate the group was headed away from their camp, Werim didn't argue and hurried to keep up. *At least I can keep the other two from getting caught. Then, they'll spring me in no time.*

"Back on yer feet, ya louts," the man called once he reached the top. "It do be one o' da ones we be lookin' fer."

At first, Werim couldn't see who he was talking to, but then several other men appeared out of the bushes behind him. They each wore a sleeveless leather vest that left their inked arms exposed. They all had blades belted to their waists and one had a shielded lantern, which he held up and shone in Werim's face. The light temporarily blinded Werim, and he stumbled backward on an exposed root. The first man caught him roughly in an iron grip and turned back to the group.

"One of ye's best be goin' back ta check da far side as well," the leader called back over his shoulder. "Dere supposin' ta be two of dem."

Werim felt his nausea return with a vengeance, only this time he suspected it wasn't simply the rum.

◊ Chapter Twelve

From the tall, wooden gate of the conquered village, Lugar Tyniente observed as yet another fleet of Landshas plodded away down the mountain road. The men were executing his battle plan flawlessly. Surprises had been few and far between, but that only served to worry the Admiral. War never went according to plan, and it was still very early in this campaign. As the giant beasts lumbered off into the distance, he wondered idly what unexpected things awaited his men.

The plan was simple. His Legion poured down out of the mountain pass into the stronghold at Knucklesporte. In truth, Lugar had expected more than the wood walled village he found–it was hardly more than two score buildings–but it would serve just fine as a temporary command post. From here, his fleets would launch down into the foothills and onto the plains beyond. They were to press forward, and the command post would move up in their wake, leaving the rear guard to cover their flanks and keep supply lines open.

Not that there would be much of a threat from behind. Their directive made sure that no combatants were left alive. Young boys were to be immediately conscripted and indoctrinated. Women and girls were to be rounded up and shipped back through the pass under light guard. Men were to be killed. None were to be granted quarter.

Lugar was shaken from his mental musings by a small, white flake that drifted down past his face. *You don't be seein' them out in the sea of sand,* he thought. His eyes followed the frozen moisture to the ground, where it touched lightly and immediately melted, soaking into the dry dirt. His gaze swept upward. Gray clouds drooped low, blocking most of the sun and spitting out the occasional icy flake. *Winter do be on the doorstep.*

This reluctant admission pulled Lugar back to the here and now. Turning, he strode quickly among the wooden houses toward the town hall at the center of the village. It was by far the largest building, and the only one made of stone. For now, it would serve as his command center. Large double doors perched atop a half-dozen stone stairs. Lugar's eyes strayed for a brief moment to the squat, grated windows at ground level, and then he was up the steps and pushing through the doors.

A bustling scene greeted him as Legionnaires scurried this way and that, carrying messages, reports, and other papers between the long wooden tables they'd commandeered from the hall. Lugar wove through the room while the men sifted around him like grains of sand about a slithering snake. At the rear of the room there was a doorway to a small kitchen where Warlord Vraika sat brooding. Once more the dark man was staring at the new marking on his wrist and did not look up when Lugar entered. *He sure do be pensive of late.*

"The weather be about to turn," Lugar noted.

Vraika appeared not to have heard him.

Lugar shifted his weight to his other foot. "It be only a matter of time 'fore the Tashers respond. We be stirrin' the pot too much ta stay hidden."

Vraika waved an arm. "Let them come. The Song left these lands years ago."

Lugar bit his lip and said nothing. The Warlord's overconfidence worried him. True, the Tashers were unlikely to have any muses of their own. It was well known that their kind had been outlawed for years in the Tasher Nation. Still, men did not give up their homeland easily. There most certainly would be a battle, and men would die. It was up to Lugar to see that the other side lost more than his. He doubted they'd just graciously accept Triumvirate rule.

"The fleets be on their way. I suspect that we be to Kinnsley 'fore Tashaba reacts," Lugar tried again. "However, snows do be threatenin', Warlord. 'Twill be slowin' us down."

Vraika finally lifted his head and met the eyes of the Admiral. Lugar suppressed a shiver. There was nothing comforting about gazing into those chaotic pools of darkness.

"I will take my troops west around the top of the lake, Lugar," Vraika said.

Lugar cocked his head. "But it do be swamp land to that side. All of the maps agree."

"Aye," Vraika nodded. "A perfect place for a prison, don't you think?"

Lugar frowned. He did not understand what a prison had to do with their campaign but was afraid to question the Warlord further. Though Vraika's temper had been more subdued as of late, the Admiral knew better than to assume it would stay that way.

Vraika's eyes cleared and glazed over as if he were seeing a distant scene, "Yes, I believe all kinds of secrets may be hidden there. Dismal Renard, they called it years ago. It still stands; I'm sure of it. Just because something is hidden from common eye does not mean that it has been done away with. In any case, it is there that Destiny leads me." He seemed to be talking to himself.

An awkward silence seeped into the room. Lugar reviewed what he knew of the Tasher Nation in his mind–he had committed all of the maps and history books to memory, of course–and couldn't recall having come across any habitations located in the swamp. *What madness be this?*

All he lent voice to was, "Such a place do no be on the maps."

"You doubt me, Lugar?" Vraika said, eyes flashing dangerously.

Lugar averted his gaze, "If you say there be a prison there. Well, there it be."

The Admiral's eyes unconsciously veered to a rather unique corner of the kitchen floor. Someone had crafted a hole there, perhaps to allow food to be lowered to the basement below. He wondered just how far their voices might carry down such a hole. Then, it dawned on him just where he was staring. *Can't be playin' my hand too open now,* he cautioned himself. *The Warlord would not be lookin' favorably on the latest... development. Best to be decidin' what I be doin' 'bout it first.*

"Be you expectin' to rejoin the fleet then?" Lugar asked, raising his head and lowering his voice.

Vraika's demeanor settled back into pensiveness. "Aye. Eventually," he said, pausing for a moment. Then, he continued with, "Hole up in Kinnsley once it has fallen, Lugar. Wait on my coming there. Offer parlay to stall the Tashers if you must. Lure them into believing that you lust after *peace.*" He spat the last word out as if it tasted foul in his mouth. "I will sweep in with my elite troops–bolstered by some... allies–and we will crush them between us." He smacked his palm for emphasis.

Once more, Lugar found his head cocked. *Be this madness, or genius? What be he expectin' to find in this prison?* Yet he knew better than to push his luck. *Best to be stayin' out of the schemes of muses,* he reminded himself.

"It be as you command, Warlord," Lugar saluted formally. "When do you be takin' your leave?"

"I've not... decided yet," Vraika admitted, stuttering a bit as if something had interrupted his train of thought. His eyes had gone black again.

A nervous trill raced up the Admiral's back as Vraika's head turned toward the hole in the floor. Lugar's pulse quickened as dark eyes stared daggers into the opening. *Seein' troo solid stone be beyond even a muse, don't it?* Sand suddenly caked the Admiral's mouth and throat, or so it felt like.

"Do you hear that?" Vraika asked the room at large, still focused on the hopefully unseen.

Lugar's face remained impassive, "Hear what, Warlord?"

Vraika shook his head as if casting off a disquieting thought, and eyes cleared to hazel. He stood and walked over to a window on the opposite wall. Lugar let out a pent up breath. As simple as that, the tension boiled away like water in the desert. As he watched, Vraika began to rub his forearm once more. His eyes were unfocused as they gazed out into the dim day.

"Soon, Lugar. Very soon. Destiny will no be waitin' on me, I think."

~ + ~

Had a small woodland animal been climbing up the side of the stout oak, Sharee was certain it would have run away terrified upon seeing the face of a girl poking out from *inside* of the tree. Her head was just small enough that it fit through the hollow that opened on the side of the old trunk. A human might have been baffled at how an almost fully grown girl like Sharee had gotten into such a hollow, but there were no humans around. Sharee made sure of it, poking her head out and looking right, then left before disappearing back into the darkness.

If Sharee were on the ground, she judged that the maw of the tree would open just slightly above her head. Far enough that, had the tree possessed a tongue, it might have been able to lick her dirty auburn hair. Fortunately, Sharee was not outside of the tree, nor was the tricky tree hiding any human appendages. To a casual observer, it was just another tree, perhaps providing a nice wooden home for an owl or some squirrels by way of the hollow. In reality, though, it housed a young woman who was even now reflecting that her new home was a little too dark and just a bit cramped. And though the tree's trustworthy embrace stirred up raw memories of her mother, Sharee knew she had to get out and face the world again. Alone.

Sharee sniffled a bit and dragged a hand across her face, smearing the moisture that had been running in rivulets down her cheeks on and off throughout the night and well into the morning. She took a deep, shuddering breath and tried again to find the harp in the back of her mind. It was there, as expected, but it felt as if someone had pushed it just out of her arm's reach. She couldn't pluck a cord no matter how hard she strained.

Waves of fatigue smashed up against the thoughts in her mind, scattering them in a mist and causing the deeper flow of her emotions to froth up angrily. She couldn't decide whether she wanted to cry or thrash about in a rage. Why couldn't she make it work? It had all come to her so easily before. *Why now?*

Sharee curled up into a ball, pulling her knees to her chest and rocking a bit in the darkness. Her nerves were raw and frayed. Her eyes felt like someone had shoved handfuls of splinters into them. She hadn't slept well since... well, since her nameday really. *Heck of a way to start another year*, she ruminated.

For whatever reason, she'd only slept for short spans of time since she'd embarked on this adventure. She just wasn't tired at night. Then, it would all hit her full force around dawn and she'd drop off for a couple winks before waking to face another day. She supposed a lot could be blamed on the harrowing events of the past several days, as well as on missing her bed back home. The forest floor was hardly the most accommodating lodging. Still, Sharee didn't feel like it was simply discomfort or emotional trauma keeping her awake at night. She just... couldn't sleep. Her mind hopped around like a frenzied jackrabbit, bouncing from one idea to next.

At first, she'd been able to sleep more than she'd been awake, but those precious portions were shifting the wrong way. Last night had been the worst yet. When Werim had wandered off and not returned, she fought down her worry for what felt like the span of days. She guessed he was probably just teasing her, watching from the edge of the woods, waiting for her to grow impatient enough to come after him. Then he would jump out and scare her. Such a prank was typical.

Instead, she'd spotted a splash of light in the night and heard gruff voices that certainly didn't belong to her brother. She'd been leaning against the big oak on the edge of the clearing when two men, arms covered with the markings of the invaders, burst out of the underbrush. Sharee panicked upon seeing them again. She'd reached instinctively for the harp in her head and plucked her little heart out. The first melody that had risen to her mind, of course, had been the one she'd used to open the hole in the cask. It played just fine on the oak, widening the existing hollow into a dark crevice. It was a simple thing to knit the wood back together, and then she'd found the perfect hiding place.

The song for separating wood was simple, but Sharee was still proud that she'd figured it out. It had seemed pretty obvious to her that one might take the Song of Knitting and reverse some of the notes in an effort to do the opposite. Working out the actual melody had taken a bit of experimentation on sticks and other bits of wood, but she'd been confident that if a muse could coax bark to grow together, than a muse could most certainly inspire it to separate. When her experiment on the cask validated her guess, she'd been excited, though she could hardly have explained to the boys the enormity of her accomplishment. Bud wouldn't understand and probably think her strange, and Werim would seize upon any opportunity to tease her.

Poor Bud, the thought hopped in. Sharee had watched helplessly from the hollow as the marked men had found her sleeping friend. They ruthlessly kicked his bandaged arm in an effort to wake him, nearly causing Sharee to cry out and reveal herself. Fortunately, the men had taken one look at the nearby cask and apparently figured out what had happened. They had a good laugh before performing some sort of ritual with fists and hands that appeared to discern which one of them was to hoist Bud like a sack of grain and throw him over their shoulder. At that point, Sharee surmised that these same men had probably stumbled upon her drunken brother, and the heavens only knew how he'd handled it. If Sharee had to hazard a guess, her brother had probably offered them a drink. Mother always said that he had more guts than wits.

Sharee had been profoundly disappointed when Werim had failed her little test. She had thought for sure he'd be able to hear her play. She'd even been able to probe into him in the same way she'd done with the trees. Not that what she'd found had made any sense to her. Her mother had told her Werim was special too, but maybe it worked differently for him than it did for her. What did Sharee know? One thing was for sure, though: there was no way her brother would believe her unless he could experience it for himself. The problem was, if what her mother had done for Sharee didn't work on her brother, what under tree and sky would? Surely their father would have an answer, if they ever found him.

Her eyes roamed the darkness around her. *Settle down,* Sharee commanded herself. The meandering path of her musings kept her from focusing on what was important. Instead, her mind jumped from one errant thought to the next without any regard for the struggles of the present. Sharee forced her concentration onto deep breaths and a slow count. *One Folish kitten, two Folish kittens, three Folish kittens...* she numbered off.

She didn't get very far. The counting reawakened pleasant memories of warm hiding places and childish games. Vaguely, her mother's voice swam into her languid thoughts, cooing to her like she had when Sharee was little. Exhaustion began to get the best of her, and her eyes sank shut. She tried to fight them, but they... just... wouldn't... listen.

What felt a scant moment later, Sharee blinked herself awake, reflex shooting her arms out to both sides and smacking painfully into the trunk of the tree. A vast majority of her fatigue had retreated, and her thoughts settled to a manageable level. Immediately, she reached back and plucked the string of her harp.

Its wonderful resonance filled her, almost bringing tears along with relief. With sure, careful intent, she plucked out the melody for separation. She reached a hand out, pointing with a finger and drawing a line where she intended the split to form. She wasn't sure if the motion was strictly necessary–after all, she hadn't touched the cask–but she found it helped to have direction for the notes. It was easier to feel how the tones mingled with the song of the wood.

She finished with a flourish and was rewarded as the tree yawned wide and spat her out. Her smile of satisfaction was quickly replaced by a frown when she discovered that the sun had all but given way to the wiles of the moon. A retreating red stained the bottom of gray clouds, and a deep chill had taken hostage of the late evening air. Sharee rubbed her bare arms and cursed herself silently for not thinking to grab any of their belongings–or Bud– when fleeing into the arms of the oak. She desperately hoped the invaders hadn't ruined any of her things. *Mom told me not to let the bow out of my sight. Fine job I did of that*, she chided herself.

Striding out of the tree, she shook off the last lingering vestiges of sleep and surveyed the surroundings. The marked men had left nothing. Not even the cask.

Sharee turned back to the tree and played Knitting on the wood. The bark slid back together, intertwining without any evidence of her intrusion. She nodded and ran one hand over the rough trunk. The oak may have been an unpleasant place to spend the night, but it had saved her from being captured.

She quickly probed the tree, both checking that she hadn't ruined anything with her manipulations and getting her bearings. Knucklesporte was nearby, she was sure of it. Perhaps she would be able to get some clues about the whereabouts of the raiders from the townsfolk there. Surely they had been able to hold out against the small force.

A moderate-sized branch on the ground caught her eye, and Sharee walked over to pick it up. It was nearly as long as she was tall and would make a good walking stick. Plucking in her head, she combined the two songs she knew in order to remove knobs and knots, smoothing out the branch into a nice, straight staff. She even carved a little design into the bulbous top with small, focused melodies of separation. The artwork took the form of three leaves from an oak tree, revolved about a point at the top of the solid rod. She was rather pleased with the work. Perhaps this was how her mom had crafted the wooden items she sold among the villagers.

With memories and thoughts firmly in hand, Sharee started down a slope toward the stream that ran nearby. She followed it, comforted by the burble of water over stone, and gazed up at the colorful foliage. Fall was preparing yet another brilliant entrance for the cool gray of winter. Sharee reflected that, having lived on the verge of wilderness for much of her life, she had never fully appreciated the transition of the trees. Reds, yellows, and oranges jumped out at her in droves. The poor leaves always tried to hang on until the last possible moment, as if they were reluctant to allow winter to have its way with the world once more. Then, as if orchestrated by some benevolent spirit, they all became convinced that since winter's coming was inevitable, they might as well relinquish their hold of the branches in favor of carpeting the ground. Perhaps in doing so, they hoped to keep the barren earth warm like a blanket, buffering it against the snows and ice.

As Sharee strolled, darkness began to ooze forth from the shadows beneath the trees, reaching out with formless fingers to snuff out the last traces of light. The sun fled once and for all, and any chance of an appearance by the heavens was disrupted by the low-hanging clouds. Sharee fought back a shiver as she walked and was thankful she didn't have far to go.

Leaving the stream behind, she soon topped a rise and found herself looking down at Kuncklesporte. Fires burned brightly in torches where the mountain path entered the village. Several also lit the streets, illuminating the shapes of people there. For a moment, Sharee simply leaned against a tree and looked on. What she saw was not at all like a city as she'd imagined from childhood stories, but it was certainly the largest collection of houses she'd ever witnessed.

Sharee took two steps out of from the cover of the trees and froze. Something about the scene below unnerved her. The townsfolk patrolled around the outside and raucous laughter wafted out from somewhere on the other side of the pointed wood wall. Though she had never been to Knucklesporte before, the overriding pattern of the people below resonated with her somehow. Her sense of caution mysteriously inflamed, Sharee ducked back into the shadows.

No sooner had she concealed herself beneath the boughs of a tree than a group of men crept out of the woods a short way from her location. One of them was carrying a lantern that cast light out before them. In that dim luminance, Sharee could make out a detail that made her blood run cold; their bare arms bore the markings of the invaders.

As Sharee watched from her hiding place, the group approached the gate to the town and was allowed through without even so much as a nod. She half expected a shout from inside the city, but when none came it confirmed her fears. Kuncklesporte had been captured by the invaders. How was she going to get help now?

Fighting unsuccessfully with despair, Sharee sank into a seated position in front of the tree. She laid her staff across her legs and reflected. In all likelihood, the marked men had taken Bud and her brother here. It was the closest settlement, especially secure with the knowledge that they had taken control of it. There was no black smoke above the village, which Sharee expected she would have seen had they been cooking any prisoners. It also meant they hadn't simply burned the town to the ground. Perhaps some of the townsfolk were still alive inside. If she could get in undetected, they could still help her, and they might also know where the boys were being held.

I can't give up, she said to herself, *Bud and Werim are counting on me.*

Picking up her staff, she used it to leverage her body into a standing position. The captured town still rested peacefully below. It all felt odd to Sharee. Shouldn't they be fighting or something? How strong and quick could these invaders be? How many of them were there?

The gate was well guarded. Patrols strolled around the outside at regular intervals, groups of four men all heavily armed, their steel glinting in the torchlight. The wood walls were more than twice her height and pointed at the top. *But they're made of wood,* Sharee realized. Hadn't she just played her way out of a previously solid tree? A wooden wall wouldn't be enough to keep her out.

Another group of four men rounded the far side of the town, passing by the gate to her left and continuing around the corner that pointed almost directly to where Sharee stood. As they passed, Sharee began to count in her head; *One Folish kitten, Two Folish kittens....* She got to thirty before the group passed out of her sight. Another ten later, and a second group of men appeared again to her left, following the same route as the previous batch.

It took them approximately the same amount of time to arrive at the corner facing her, and the same again to disappear. Another ten cats later and the first group reappeared. That meant if she ran straight to the corner facing her, she had somewhere around sixty cats to find a way through the wall and knit it back up before the guards would be upon her. She desperately hoped that the thick posts that made up the wall were of a wood she knew.

As the current group of guards passed by the gate, approaching her corner, Sharee crept down the rise toward the city. She danced from shadow to shadow, staying low, and cast an appreciative glance toward the low clouds that obscured the moon and stars. It was a perfect night for sneaking around, the kind her brother used to relish when they were allowed to play games after dark.

She paused in a depression before the wall, dropping to lie flat, and waited for the guards to pass around the far side. As soon as they had, she popped up and went straight to the corner nearest her. Putting a hand to the wall, she probed the wood. Immediately, a sigh of relief escaped her lips. It was oak.

With sixty cats to go, Sharee began playing separation. As she released the song, she expected the post she was touching to begin to split. It did, but not quite as anticipated. A hairline fissure bisected the post from top to bottom. It was not nearly large enough for her to fit through. She stepped back and poked at it with her staff. Why hadn't it worked?

Sharee leaned in close to see if perhaps there was something inside of the wood that she had missed. Fingers wedged into the rift, she tried in vain to pry the wood apart. It didn't budge. The posts on either side prevented it. *Of course! There's not enough room for the wood to split.*

Fifty cats left.

The problem with playing on cut posts was that her ministrations only worked on one post at a time. If she could play on several, perhaps it could create enough space for her to slip through. Sharee played separation again, though this time she tried to direct it outward at three of the posts in front of her. Once again, they cracked, but the result was smaller, sloppier cracks in the middle of each post. By dividing her focus, she seemed to be decreasing her effectiveness. Plus, the splits weren't together, so that while she had more of them, they didn't add up to a wider gap in the wood.

Forty cats left.

Sharee poked her head around the corner. One of the patrols had just rounded the opposite end was headed her way. If she ran back to the woods now, it was likely that she could make it without being seen. If she waited, her chances of remaining undiscovered decreased with each subsequent kitten counted. Standing at the corner, staring at four inked and armed men pacing toward her, Sharee tried to decide what she should do. Bud and her brother needed her, but she couldn't help anyone if she got caught.

Thirty cats left.

Sharee turned back to the wood and laid her hand on the corner post. Indecision held her frozen. They could be starting a cook fire right now to roast her brother and Bud. *How can I retreat when every second could be the difference between life and... dinner?* As if to underscore her concerns, a thin tongue of smoke wafted over the wall, following the breeze in a sinuous curl up toward the clouds. It was not the heavy smoke of carnage, but it could certainly be a cookfire. *I won't leave the boys to that fate,* she decided.

Think, Sharee, think. She knew she could create a big enough split if the wall were one, giant post, but a collection of unique entities was too much for her. She couldn't divide her focus with any discernable effectiveness. If only they had used contiguous pieces of wood.

Twenty cats left.

Knitting! The idea sparked her mind to life. *Of course!* If she knitted the posts together, she could treat them as one big piece of wood. She would still need space for the split on at least one side, though. She looked toward the nearby corner, expecting to see the glow of an approaching torch. Then, it dawned on her: corners weren't hemmed in by definition. Connecting several posts up to the corner should work. Striking the harp, she quickly knit together the four posts closest to the corner, one at a time.

Gruff voices from the approaching patrol set her heart aflutter. They were almost upon her. There was no turning back now.

She surveyed her work. It was not pretty. Instead, it looked like the posts had been cut from some strange, four-headed, freak of a tree. Probing the wood, she verified her success. It would work, no matter what it might look like. The posts were joined.

Ten cats left.

Taking a deep breath, she played the most precise song of splitting that she could manage in her frenzied state. A small hole opened near the bottom, bowing the corner out slightly. It was just enough for her to get down on her hands and knees and crawl through. She desperately hoped that the approaching men wouldn't notice the bulge. As she wiggled through her little doorway, she listened for the shouts of alarm that would indicate discovery.

Even as she was pulling her feet through behind her, she began to knit. There was no elegance to the tune this time as she banged the notes out furiously. The wood glowed faintly and flowed together behind her like a strange, brown liquid, before settling in a swirl of grains. There was nothing natural looking about it.

Her breath coming in deep gulps, Sharee stopped playing and leaned her back against the wall. She counted with her heart in her throat. *One Folish kitten, two Folish kittens....* When she got to twenty cats and no alarm was raised, Sharee allowed herself a small smile of satisfaction. She was inside.

Now, to find those boys.

◊ Chapter Thirteen

"How did you two get caught?"

The voice came from the brown-haired young man sitting in the dingy corner of the cell, directly under a makeshift hole in the ceiling, and startled Werim. He looked up to regard the man with bleary eyes. Why was he breaking his silence now? He hadn't responded to any whispered overtures all day.

With a wince, Werim recalled waking up on the uncomfortable dirt floor to find the midday light lancing down through the squat, grated openings that served as windows to the dungeon. Thankfully, the day had been cloudy, and darkness had swiftly claimed its rightful place, giving Werim's overly sensitive eyes a much needed respite. Upon sitting–which turned out to be no simple task–he had tried to ask where they were, but repeated questions had only been met with silence from the unknown occupant.

Sitting in the darkness, not feeling much better despite the agonizingly slow passage of time, Werim tracked a lethargic hand across his grimy face and took a deep breath. The simple movement threatened to elicit another wave of nausea. In an effort to steer focus from his complaining body, Werim tried to bring up what he could remember of the night before. There was not much to distract him. After following the group of marked men a few paces into the night, they'd hit him over the head with something solid.

How long he'd been unconscious, Werim did not know. To be roused with a bucket of water inside of a cage was not a very pleasant surprise either. Neither was finding Bud in a similar state nearby. He had been spared a knock on the head, but blood had soaked through the bandage wrapping his forearm, turning the previously green fabric a dark shade of brown. Apparently his captors had reopened the wound that Sharee had tried to cinch up. And unfortunately–or fortunately, Werim hadn't decided yet–in place of his sister was the other occupant, who repeated his question.

"I said: how did you get caught?"

Werim examined the man for the dozenth time. Oily hair hung limply down to his chin, framing a face that was both dirt-stained, and rough with stubble. He wore the simple clothes of a farmer, tan breeches and a coarse, off-white shirt. When he moved, though, there was a litheness that was more than one might expect to find in a simple worker of the land. Werim wondered, not for the first time, if this man was a soldier.

"So, now you want to talk?" Werim replied.

The simple vocalization pounded at Werim's temples. He wished his head would either explode or quit throbbing altogether. It certainly wasn't helping him in trying to figure a way out of their current predicament. In fact, it wasn't conducive to much of anything.

"We'd been drinking," Bud spoke up from the other side of the room, attempting a shrug. He, too, cradled his head in his hands and appeared beleaguered by the previous night's events. The third man snickered from his perch in the corner.

Werim cast him an annoyed glance. "Do you have a better tale?" he challenged their companion.

"Why yes, as a matter of fact I do," he stated grandly. His voice had a melodious quality to it, deep and sonorous, and he spoke with an odd tempo. "And, as to your first... observation, I now choose to talk for the simple reason that the guards at the door have gone, leaving us quite alone."

"How do you know that?" Werim groaned back.

The brown haired man favored them with a mischievous smile and pointed at the hole above his head. "You can hear just about everything through the food passage in the ceiling."

"And your tale?" Werim pressed, frowning.

"Right, right," the man waved a hand. He stood and glided to the middle of the room. "First, though, introductions *must* be made. I am properly named Sornwa Voleur," the man made a grand bow. "But you can call me Sorn," he added, straightening. "And with whom might I have the pleasure of sharing this delightful cellular abode?"

"I am Lua Costeau and this is my friend Wil Aboitte," Werim invented.

Bud and Sorn both favored him with a quizzical look, but fortunately neither saw the other.

"Very well, Lua," Sorn nodded. "Pleased to make your acquaintance, both of you. And now, you shall hear my tale of woe." He cleared his throat. "It began a scant two nights ago when the captain of the guard here in fair Knucklesporte favored me with a missive. This Legion of savages had besieged our gates for nigh on a week, yet we valiantly persisted. Still, it was a losing cause, and we knew it for what it was.

"The Captain, sensing the inevitability of defeat, charged me and two others with a mission. He told us we had been selected as the swiftest on horse, and were to carry warning of this barbarous invasion to the very domes of Tashaba. Thus, it was in the face of great personal peril that I fled into the night, even as the city fell beneath the dark cloud of this terrible invasion.

"The hounds of the Legion were on me from the start. But, being of stellar horsemanship, I led them off into the wood on a wild chase. Dodging branches and arrows, I expertly wove my steed around like a shuttle through the loom. Right up until I dismounted and turned myself in, of course."

Werim gaped, "Why would you do that?"

Sorn flashed another cheesy smile and answered with confidence, "Why, my aim was to merely create a diversion so that the other lads might get loose. Obvious, I should think. And valorous, to sacrifice one's self for the greater good."

"You were under siege for a week?" Bud questioned.

Sorn nodded slowly, "That's what I said, is it not?"

"The invaders weren't even through Kokamongo less than a week ago," Bud pointed out.

Sorn looked troubled for a moment, but quickly recovered. "Have you seen the grandiose size of this Legion?" he asked. "They ride upon gigantic beasts that must carry nigh on a hundred men. Who can say the speed of such a host? It may simply be that such a small village was only recently discovered by a scouting party whilst the siege was being pressed, having been overlooked because of its inherent triviality."

"Why would they scout back up territory they just crossed?" Bud wanted to know.

"And who are you to know the movements of such an armada? Are you an Admiral? Have you commanded troops in the field? You look far too young for the part, if so." Sorn countered. "Tell me then, what dire mission were you forsaking when you took to drink?"

Bud scowled, but said nothing.

"We are simple... merchants," Werim answered for his friend. "We were hoping to sell our wares in Knucklesporte, before we ran into these invaders, of course. Came up from the south, we did, and weren't expecting so much trouble. Last night, we sat down to have a bite to eat and something to drink, and were knocked over the head. Very uncivilized, I might add." Werim wasn't quite sure if that last was appropriate, but it seemed like something this man might appreciate, with his flowery speech and all.

"Yes! A difficult lot these marked men are. And who can speak to the minds of such savages? Can one even trust their words?" Sorn expounded. He paused, casting an annoyed look up at the ceiling, and then continued in a lower voice. "They burn all in their path and dine on the flesh of their victims. They are horrible to behold with their markings and wicked swords. And they are led by one of the outlawed. I have seen him with mine own eyes. He wears darkness like a cloak! The armies of our peaceful nation will be hard pressed to hold this Legion at bay. We must stick together, or we will most assuredly be torn apart and fed to their fires." He stopped and cocked his head as if listening for something.

After a moment, he continued in a louder voice, "But why do they come, these new overlords? What spurs them onward at such a pace? What could they possibly want with Tasher lands? I say, show me the man that can guess their motivations, for that man is certainly not I." He spread his arms wide in emphasis, his chest heaving with emotion.

"Aye," a gruff voice wafted in from the shadowy stairwell. "Certainly it no be you."

Sorn dropped his arms and calmly approached the metal bars. The fire that had fueled his previous ranting was suddenly snuffed out. From the darkness across the room strode a sharply dressed older man. Slate gray facial hair underscored a strong jaw line, leaving his chin bare. Unlike most of the other invaders, this man wore a long, black coat that covered his arms fully. The brass buttons gleamed dully in the sputtering torchlight that trickled in through the squat windows. Atop the man's head was a black, triangular hat.

As he walked over to them, Werim noticed he evidenced a bit of a limp, though his gaze was strong. Indeed, it felt as if the man sized up each of them in the half dozen steps it took for him to cross the musty dungeon. Werim found it odd that instead of feeling scared as he thought he ought to, he felt the desire to rise and present this man with a more dignified front.

"Lugar Tyniente be my name," the man growled, "and I do be one of these... savages."

He favored them with a grin that sent a shiver skittering up Werim's spine. Though he laid no such claim, here was a man who was much more than just a common soldier. Authority radiated from every facet of his demeanor, and his firm stare required solid returns. Werim would need to be cautious of his words and actions.

"That hole," he pointed, "do indeed be workin' both ways it seems."

Werim's stomach flipped, and he thanked the stars that they hadn't confided their real names to their cellmate.

A square table that was cluttered with junk stood in the opposite corner of the room, surrounded by several discolored wooden stools. Lugar retrieved one of them, dragging it across the floor roughly, and sat directly in front of the bars of their prison. Brown eyes bored into them hungrily. *Is he going to kill us and eat us right here?* Werim pushed the thought away before his nausea got the best of him.

Sorn smiled with confidence. "I take it that I held up my end of the bargain."

"None too quick," Lugar mumbled.

"It's all about timing, my friend," Sorn replied smoothly. "Besides, it would have looked suspicious had I been too free in front of your guards. You might have left us alone earlier if you were concerned about timeliness. Now, about my freedom." Sorn stuck an arm through the bars and held it up as if to receive an item.

Werim gaped at the traitor revealed in their midst. Bud stood and reached behind him as if for his sword. When he recalled its absence, he sank back with a defeated look.

Lugar pulled a twisted, charred piece of metal from a pocket inside of his coat and placed it in the man's hand without fanfare. Sorn's previously confident façade fell off his face. His eyes narrowed, and he brought them back up to meet his captor's.

"What's the meaning of this?" Sorn asked.

"This be your first time barterin' with Barabans, don't it?" Lugar replied.

Sorn cocked his head to one side in unspoken question.

"The deal be made as: their names and intentions for the key from the jailor, and I be holdin' to my end," Lugar explained. He shrugged, "It do be seemin' that the jailor be an unfortunate casualty of our... *meal* when we be takin' this town."

Sorn threw the useless, charred remains of the key down in disgust. "You savages have no honor," he accused, and then retreated back to the rear of the room to sulk.

Werim and Bud glared at the snake as he passed, but otherwise remained where they were. They turned back to find the old man watching them with renewed interest. He appeared to be examining their reactions.

Just then, something occurred to Werim. He approached the bars. "You must have another key," Werim stated with confidence. "Why not honor the bargain with that?"

"Why be you thinkin' there be another key?" Lugar inquired.

"We're in here, aren't we?" Werim replied.

Lugar chuckled, "Clever boy. What be your name again?"

Without hesitation, Werim answered, "Lua."

"Well, Lua, he be specifyin' the *jailor's* key. The Code be requirin' me to be exact, y'see?" He spread his arms wide as if to absolve himself of responsibility. "Now that you be knowin' the way of things, what be you goin' to do with the knowledge?"

Werim thought for a moment before replying, "It seems to me that you're willing to trade freedom for information."

"Aye," Lugar replied, his eyes sparkling.

"Perhaps there is something we can tell you that would earn our way out of this cell," Werim offered. "And free passage out of your camp," he added quickly. He thought it better to be safe than sorry.

Lugar nodded, "So it be. And fortunate for you, I be knowin' already exactly what I be wantin' from you."

To Werim's surprise, the man reached into his jacket and pulled out a white fletched arrow. He watched with a growing sense of dread as the man twirled the arrow in his hands, apparently examining it. With a sudden motion, he brought it down swiftly over one knee, as if to snap the thin wooden shaft. It simply bent and returned to its original shape.

"It be a curious thing, no?" Lugar mused aloud. "It do be obvious that these be finely made, perhaps even with a Song at that. And it be told to me that there be more of these amongst your things," he jerked his head toward the table across the room. "A full quiver and a bow t'boot." He paused before coming to the request, "What I be wantin' to know is-"

"They're mine," Bud blurted out.

Lugar stared at the blond boy.

Werim thought fast, "What he means is that he stole them. We're not merchants, we're thieves, as you no doubt already know."

He decided that this man probably knew more about them than he was letting on. Perhaps he had heard of their little visit to the supply camp. Such an admission might earn a bit of credit to their favor.

"If these do be the work of a muse, then how be you expectin' me to believe that two young boys could be sneakin' off with 'em?" Lugar asked.

"We got your rum didn't we?" Werim pointed out.

"A muse?" Bud asked. "Their kind are not allowed on Tasher lands."

"And you think that be stoppin' a muse?" Lugar arched a gray eyebrow.

"They would stick out," Bud argued.

Werim glared at his friend. Who cared about some stupid muse? Werim was trying to barter their way out. Couldn't Bud see that?

Lugar chuckled, "Boy, your neighbor could be a muse and you would no be knowin' of it 'lest they be wantin' you to."

That apparently shut Bud up.

"We took these from a carpenter's tool shed," Werim explained. "He had all kinds of the things, in all types of wood.

These looked to be the most expensive. You can have 'em as part of the deal if you'd like."

He looked to Bud to back him up. No one paid him any attention. Lugar was staring intently at Bud, who was in turn studying his hands.

Werim shook his head. First his friend jumps in and now, at the mention of some muse, he clams up again. It didn't make any sense to Werim. The arrows weren't anything special. They were his sister's nameday gift. It was just fine wood, and that was all. What was going through Bud's head?

Realizing he wasn't going to get any help, Werim switched tracks, "Fine. Let's say we managed to get these off of a... muse. What, then, did you want to know?" It was apparently what the man wanted to hear.

Lugar frowned but answered, "It be simple, I just be wantin' the name of the owner of these arrows. I want the name of the muse."

"We don't know her," Bud blurted again.

"Who said it be a *her*?" Lugar asked.

Bud's jaws clapped shut and he stared at the floor. *Blast him*, Werim thought. *What is he doing?* Of course they didn't know any muses. Why was he acting all nervous instead of helping to lie their way out of this place.

If it was a name this man wanted... "Magie Chanson," Werim offered.

It was a name he pulled straight out of his britches. He could vaguely remember hearing it mentioned by one of the teamsters that came up to the village in early spring to haul casks of ice wine back down the mountain. Werim fondly remembered their coming as soon as the passes thawed. They were always after the freshest samples of the winter harvest. In a way, they seemed to bring spring with them. He doubted this foreigner was familiar with any of their stories.

Lugar chuckled and cast Bud one last look before standing up. "It be unfortunate for you that I only be lookin' for confirmation of what I already suspect. Chanson no be the name I be expectin' to hear." He turned to Werim, "I do believe your friend be knowin' of whom I be askin' after, though. You'd best be getting' him to talk if you want out of that cell."

Silence dominated for a while as Lugar studied them, and Bud surveyed his knuckles. It appeared that the old man was content to wait them out. The creak of the door leading down to the dungeon caused both of the boys to jump. Lugar swiveled around to see a sleeveless, marked man clomp into the room.

The man approached and saluted, "Admiral, one o' the patrols do be requestin' your presence."

"For what reason?" the old man wanted to know.

Admiral, Werim thought. *Certainly not a common soldier.*

The messenger shifted his weight on his feet, but still stood at attention, "Well, sir, that do be the thing. They say there be somethin'... odd about a part of the outer wall. They do be waitin' on you now."

Admiral Tyniente raised an eyebrow, but stood and waved the man ahead of him.

He took a few steps toward the door before turning and adding, "If this be what I think it be, then you may soon be findin' yourselves short of anything to be bargainin' with. In that case, you be makin' a fine dish to be served with your muse." He chuckled as he left.

"We have to get out of here," Bud said.

Werim nodded and tried to swallow, but for some reason he only tasted blood.

~ + ~

The glow of torchlight bobbed away from Sharee, sliding down the wall of the building across from her and finally disappearing around a corner. Gingerly, she crawled out of the bush she'd been forced to dive into when the patrol had turned the corner at the end of the alley. After picking a few twigs out of her hair and returning them to the shrubbery, she approached the wooden wall across from her and probed it, picking up where she'd left off.

Upon entering the village, she'd darted from shadowy corner to shadowy corner, hoping to chance upon something that might point her in the direction of the boys. The only thing she'd noticed was a small section of town that was far more heavily patrolled than the others. It was a simple square with the doors of the four buildings on each corner all opening onto a small plaza. The paths leading to the plaza were partially barricaded with carts, and marked men with torches stood guard in whatever openings remained. One of the buildings appeared to have been a tavern and inn, while the others were simply larger houses, perhaps with storefronts on the bottom floor. Sharee had no way of seeing what was in the buildings as all of the windows were boarded up.

The city hall nearby lorded over the wooden structures, but otherwise they appeared to be among the largest that Knucklesporte had to offer. Sharee had made her way into one of the alleys that ran behind the buildings, and guessed that she was directly across from the stone hall. Dusty walkways leading to hidden hovels branched periodically off of the alley, a bush marking each entryway. These much smaller houses huddled in the shadows of the buildings on the square. Sharee had endeavored to avoid detection and approach the rear of what she thought was the tavern. Each of the floors above the tavern were dedicated to the inn. She suspected that if anyone had been taken prisoner, they might be festooned here. It wasn't like the invaders would be expecting to fill the rooms with travelers.

Probing revealed that the walls were pine. Sharee was relatively familiar with pine trees, since they all but took over the forest at higher altitudes. The wood itself was somewhat smoother and softer than oak. In fact, Sharee discovered that pine trees grow much faster than oak trees, so it only made sense to her that pine was a bit easier to manipulate. Applying the trick she'd learned with the city's exterior wall, she knit a handful of boards together and then split a small sliver down the middle that was approximately her height.

Hiding in the bush afforded Sharee the opportunity to reflect on what she'd learned with the posts. At the time, she'd been hurried and scared to death of being caught. With a calmer mind, she had quickly devised a new method for creating an opening and was anxious to see if it would work. It helped that the safety of the bush was only a short leap away, so in the event that her plan failed, she could easily retreat to rethink her strategy while waiting for the patrol to pass.

She had another twenty cats until the next patrol rounded the corner. They were much more closely spaced here in the city, but they also had to make sharp turns down the gridded streets. They couldn't see nearly as far, and the shadows from the buildings further aided Sharee's cause. She could wait up until the very last kitten before plunging back into the bush.

The harp was ready in her mind's eye, shimmering, almost eager for her touch. Sharee began to play the notes for splitting slowly and confidently. At the same time, instead of simply directing the notes into the wood and letting the song flow as it wished, she tried to impose a more rigid sense of form. With one hand on the smooth wall, she could sense the song dancing along the wood, coercing the previously inert grains into action. As they begin to split at the urging of the song, she subtly pulled the tune back toward her.

The result was immediate. Along the crack she'd created, the conjoined wooden boards warped outward, bending at her command like petals peeling back from a flower and glowing faintly around the edges. Heat and light washed over her from the room beyond, spilling out into the dark night. With the once solid wood pulled back like heavy curtains, Sharee stepped confidently across the threshold. Switching to knitting, she pulled the wooden drapes closed behind her.

She still had a full ten cats to spare.

◊ Chapter Fourteen

As the wooden curtains joined back together, Sharee began to wrap up her song. With a last flourish, she knit up the original crack and disconnected the boards. The wall looked just as it had before Sharee had imposed her will on it. She nodded with satisfaction, running a hand over the smooth wood.

Several gasps from behind froze her. She hadn't considered that there might be people on the other side of the conjured doorway. With a hollow sense of dread, she turned around slowly.

Sharee was surprised to find that she was in a kitchen. The roaring fire in an overly large oven explained the heat, and lit sconces on the walls provided light. Pots and pans hung from racks, and cabinets ringed the long, rectangular room above the counters. There was a small square cutout about chest high on one interior wall with a platform inside and a rope running down its center. Far to the left and right, closed doorways led off to other areas of the building. The room was quite spacious despite the clutter, and had probably served guests of both the tavern and the inn. Sharee cringed as she imagined the amount of dishes to be washed in such a workshop.

The gasps had originated collectively from the three other women in the room, all of whom were now staring at Sharee in open astonishment. It looked like she had caught them in the act of baking, since they were holding large mixing bowls and wore aprons dusted with flour. Several trays filled with finished loaves of bread cooled on a table in the center of the room. Even as Sharee was paralyzed with surprise, so too were these women, though from the looks on their faces, Sharee thought it might be more appropriate to say horror. *They're afraid of me?* The idea was not a familiar one for the young girl.

The standoff stretched on. Sharee stared at the women. The women cowered before her. No one moved. Sharee suspected that if she were to take another step–or even to twitch–that all three would run screaming from the room.

To her right, a door flew open and banged against the wall. One of the previously paralyzed women threw her bowl up in the air and dove to the floor. A second screamed. The third began babbling incoherently and pointing. *Not exactly the entrance I was hoping for,* Sharee thought.

The stern-faced newcomer stopped and surveyed the scene with a frown. When her chocolate eyes finally came to a rest on the travel-stained intruder, Sharee realized that she recognized the woman. It was Andree Peau's mother, Marie. If the woman were surprised at Sharee's presence, she certainly didn't show it.

"Oh knock it off," Marie snapped at the panicking women. "Haven't you all seen a girl before?"

"S-she came through the wall!" the Screamer screamed.

"M-m-muse," babbled the Babbler. "Muse, she's a muse. Musey muse muse."

The Diver poked her head above her hiding place behind the table and vigorously nodded agreement.

"What's going on in there?" another voice called from the doorway to the left.

"Nothing, nothing," Marie announced, going over quickly to block the view from the half opened door. "Just had a little spill is all. Here," she snagged a loaf of bread from a nearby counter and handed it through the crack. "Take this upstairs and make sure the girls are still in bed. You know how they like to get up and go adventuring in the middle of the night."

Marie slammed the door and marched back to the table at the center of the room. Along the way, she picked up the thrown bowl and wooden spoon. Glaring at the other three women, she corralled them into a huddle. Wielding the spoon like a scepter, she pointed at each of the women in turn.

"You three will tell no one about what you saw, and I mean *no one*," she commanded.

Babbler, Screamer, and Diver nodded in unison, eyes on the spoon.

"If you have any doubts, rest assured that I've known this girl her whole life. I know who and what she is. I know where she comes from," Marie continued. "She is most certainly *not* the enemy. Keep that firmly in your minds."

The three women turned large doe eyes on Sharee. They did not look convinced. Marie shook the spoon at them. They all flinched, but she had regained their attention. They stared again at the simple utensil.

"Now, each of you take a loaf of bread and get back to your rooms. That's enough for one night. I'll finish up here," Marie ordered, somewhat soothingly. "Go. Get on with you."

Without so much as a peep, the three women burdened themselves with loaves and exited through the door to the right, casting scared looks over their shoulders. Marie patiently waited for them to leave before turning toward Sharee. Spoon still in hand, she came around the table. The stern look had not left her face.

"I-I'm sorry I scared them," Sharee stammered.

Marie didn't acknowledge the apology. As she stood directly before Sharee, she let her eyes sweep up and down, taking in the dirty, torn dress and overall state of uncleanliness. Sharee resisted the urge to cringe and fiddle with her hair. It felt like she was about to be sent upstairs for a bath with firm instructions to scrub behind her ears. Not that she couldn't benefit from some scrubbing, she just had more important things to be about. *The boys*, she recalled. *They need me.*

"You might have used the back door, you know," Marie said, pointing toward one of the doors far down to Sharee's left. "They've locked it for us, but I'm sure that's not a problem for someone like you."

"I didn't know there was one," Sharee admitted. She hadn't thought to look around the corner of the building. "Wait, someone like me?"

"Here," Marie handed her the spoon. "Show me."

"Show you what?" Sharee asked, taking the spoon and turning it over in her hands.

"The women obviously saw something, and I don't think you just waltzed in through the front door," Marie explained. "I have a hunch... but I'd like to see for myself."

Sharee blushed. Being a muse was her secret, something she shared with her mother. She was proud of it, sure, but she still felt like it was something to keep hidden. For now, anyway. If other people knew about her abilities, how long before they expected her to do something important with them. Sharee wasn't sure she was ready for that kind of responsibility. A very large part of her wanted to just go back into the woods and seal herself up in a tree.

But she couldn't. Werim and Bud needed her. The three of them needed to find her father. After that, well... he would know what to do about everything. *Surely father had known of mom's abilities.* For now, she would do whatever it took to get to him, brother and Bud in tow with vines if need be.

So she probed the spoon, discerning immediately that it was neither pine nor oak. On the spectrum of hardness, this wood fell squarely in between those two extremes. If she had to guess, she would say it was wood from a cherry tree, though there weren't many of those up high in the mountains. She'd not encountered cherry wood since learning of her abilities, and thus had nothing with which to compare the spoon's song.

As she felt along the grain, an idea began to form in her mind. Wanting to bring it to life, she reached back and plucked her harp. Knitting and splitting flowed out, twined together as one, and the familiar feeling of working with wood played its own soothing melody on her nerves. She soon found herself humming as the spoon began to respond to her overtures.

Marie's eyes widened as the previously inert utensil came alive in the hands of the younger girl. Sharee smiled a bit at the look of wonder, relieved that it was not fear. Her hands revolved around the spoon, cupping it both above and below, as the wood rearranged itself at her direction. There was a faint glow to the wood and bits of light leaked out through her fingers, colored reddish by her skin. The ambient glow gave the proceedings a perception of warmth, though the only real heat came from the ovens. When the work was finished and the songs wrapped up, Sharee pulled her top hand away to reveal a perfectly formed–if somewhat larger–representation of a cherry in her palm. She plucked the faux fruit from her hand by its wooden stem and held it out to Marie in offering.

"Amazing," the older woman breathed, taking the cherry and examining it. "I had always suspected it of your mother but could never drum up the courage to ask."

"Is confronting a muse that scary?" Sharee wanted to know.

"Oh yes, dear one. Muses have been outlawed within the borders of the Tasher Nation for nearly a century, for good reason too. Plus, they're coveted by the Triumvirate, which makes them doubly dangerous," Marie explained with a touch of sadness in her voice. "Still, though most serve the Grand Warlord, not all are simply... evil."

"Well, I am not a bad muse, nor was my mother," Sharee stated.

"Of course not, dear." Marie smiled. "In fact, your being here can only mean hope."

"Hope for what?"

"Hope for a fight. Hope for freedom," Marie said.

That quickly, Sharee recalled her original purpose. "Madam Peau, have you seen my brother or Bud?"

Marie's face hardened again, "Have they been taken, too, then? Like they took my Andree."

"They took Andree?" Sharee asked. She remembered the brown haired boy as being quiet and perhaps a bit shy whenever he had joined with Werim and Bud for some fun. "What would they want with him?"

"They seemed to think he was *your* brother," Marie shook her head ruefully. "They wouldn't believe me when I called him son!" She took a deep, shuddering breath. "If Werim is also a muse... well then, I suppose that might make sense. Though if they expect to find it in my Andree, I fear they will be disappointed." Marie's voice had gained an edge that made Sharee's skin crawl.

"I'm sorry about Andree," Sharee offered.

"I *will* find out where they took him, Sharee. I will," Marie resolved, staring daggers at Sharee.

"I believe you, and if there is some way I can help you..." Sharee trailed off.

Marie smiled, "You already have helped me, dear. Hope costs little, but is worth much." She put her hands on her hips. "I'm supposing they just caught your brother recently, then?" When Sharee nodded, Marie continued, "Well, we will have to get a message to Scrontle. Unfortunately, only the girls are sent here. *Stored*, they say. For what, I could not tell you. In any case, Scrontle'll know where they might be keeping the boys. With any luck, they haven't been sent off yet. You'll have to brave the tavern, though," she cautioned.

"Thank you, Madam Peau," Sharee replied, not fully understanding the warning.

Marie favored her with a curious look. "Think nothing of it dear. I owe your mother far more than this simple favor. And call me Marie, Sharee-imba." At Sharee's puzzled looked, Marie explained, "That is what you call a muse, dear. An honorific, if you will."

Sharee nodded thoughtfully, filing the information away. Marie picked up two baskets and filled them with bread and other foodstuffs. When she returned, she examined Sharee with a critical eye.

"Give me the stick," Marie ordered, holding out her hand.

Sharee intended to argue–she wanted to keep the staff close to her–but the look on Marie's face made the futility of such an argument clear. Sharee blushed and offered the staff. Marie set it aside. Then, she leaned in, licked her thumb, and used it to wipe some of the dirt off Sharee's cheeks.

Marie stepped back. "That'll have to do."

She handed a basket to Sharee and then led her through the door to the left, which apparently opened out into the tavern. Several Baraban men were seated at the various wooden tables. They looked up as the women entered with dark, hungry eyes. One even whistled. Suddenly, Sharee felt even more grimy and underdressed. She couldn't help but blush as a few of the men leered openly at her. The warning was starting to make more sense.

Marie was unfazed by the brutes. Casting a confident smile toward Sharee, she cocked her head toward the men. Apparently, they were to serve food.

"Yo ho! Dere be a new wench tonight," one of the more heavily inked men hollered. "Pretty little ting she be."

He's talking about me, she realized with a start. But why? She looked dreadful. Sharee couldn't help herself and turned a bright shade of red.

"Har! Ye be makin' 'er blush," another voice yelled.

"I do be likin' 'em rosy," a third voice grunted.

Torrents of laughter flooded the tavern.

Sharee followed behind Marie sheepishly. The older woman was unaffected by the stares and jests of the men as she made her way across the room. A few even reached out to try and pinch her bottom! Sharee kept her chin up and tried not to think of the marked hands reaching for her. Her effort to ignore the men only to spurred them on.

When Marie stopped abruptly in the midst of the tables, Sharee nearly skidded into her. The older woman turned and slapped a dark hand as it reached out for Sharee, earning raucous laughs from all around. Sharee found herself blushing again. *I have never been so embarrassed in all my life*, she thought. *The boys must never hear of this.*

"My dear, go and serve the men that just walked in," Marie ordered with a significant look.

Sharee glanced over and saw a group of marked men settling in. She swallowed hard and nodded at Marie. *Why is she making me do this?* Basket held high, she wove lithely between the tables, dodging hands as she approached her assigned table.

"Aha! Dis one be havin' some wiggle ta 'er," one of the men leered as she stepped up. "I tink I may be needin' more dan da usual..."

A knife appeared in the middle of the table, driven downward in the wood with a crack. Sharee shamed herself with a little jump and squeal. *What would the boys say?*

The beefy hand clutching the hilt of the blade displayed white knuckles, punctuated by darker burns here and there. Sharee's eyes traveled from hand to hairy arm, slowly moving upward past muscular shoulders and bulging neck until she came to the rough-looking face. She blinked in surprise; it was Scrontle Marteau.

Her dirty face must have been clean enough, for the man's dark eyes widened in recognition as well. After what felt like a long moment, he ripped his eyes away and turned an angry glare on the other man. Up until the moment the knife assaulted the table, the first man had been reaching out for Sharee as if to pull her into his lap. He had frozen in the act with one eye on the blade.

"She's mine," Scrontle growled. "Unless you're gonna challenge me fer her."

The first man looked from the burly blacksmith to Sharee and back. He appeared to be struggling with a particularly difficult decision. Scrontle was much larger than the wiry Baraban. If a challenge entailed what it seemed it might, he would be hard pressed to fend off the bigger man. His eyes returned to Sharee, and then back to Scrontle again. Finally, he turned back to Sharee with a look of regret.

"Ye can have 'er, smith," the man grumbled, his eyes roving. "Best be goin' b'fore I be changin' my mind."

"Same as you changed yer mind earlier this evening 'bout my throw," Scrontle rumbled.

The man stiffened while the others around the table hid smirks. After an uncomfortable moment, Scrontle yanked his knife from the table and stood. He walked around and grabbed Sharee roughly by the arm.

"Leave the basket, wench," her friend ordered.

Sharee hesitated. Something about the blacksmith's demeanor felt off. She put the basket down slowly and examined Scrontle more closely. He wore garb similar to the rest of the men at the table. Wide pants and a leather vest without sleeves. His arms were covered with curly black hair, obscuring most of the skin, but this close Sharee noticed something she had missed the first time: a skull atop a pile of bones etched into his skin. *He's one of them!*

She tried to jerk her arm away, but his grip was like iron. With wild eyes, she searched over her shoulder for Marie, but the woman was engaged with another table, dodging idle hands and earning laughs. Scrontle was pulling her inexorably back toward the kitchen. She dragged her feet, trying to slow him down, but he was far too strong. She tried her arm again, but the struggle was only causing those few still paying attention to laugh. The knowing look in their eyes only fanned her panic.

She had no hope. Scrontle was going to take her away and... and what? She didn't know, but if Scrontle had eaten another person, who knew what he was capable of? That was what the marks meant, wasn't it?

"Let go of me!" she screamed as she was pulled through the swinging door.

Surprisingly, Scrontle obeyed. The vise of his grip loosened and Sharee stumbled free. She took three staggered steps away from the bigger man, regaining some of her composure. Then, she whirled, plucking the harp in the back of her mind furiously. She wasn't sure what exactly she was going to play on this brute of a man. Though his arms might mimick the size of tree trunks, they were certainly not made of wood.

He took one menacing step toward her, and she held out her hand helplessly. What good was being able to sing to wood when faced with a human threat? For all that the thought of a muse had stricken fear into the three women earlier, Sharee felt powerless.

She searched around desperately for a weapon. Her eyes found her staff, still sitting wher Marie had left it. She dashed over to it and picked it up, holding it sideways before her. If he came any closer, she would whack him with it.

Sensing her determination, Scrontle scowled and glanced back at the door to the tavern. Perhaps he was regretting his choice of target. He only hestitated for a moment, though, before coming at her. Sharee swung with all of her might.

He was expecting the blow. One big hand shot up and caught the wood. It didn't even seem to make him strain. He put his other beefy hand on her shoulder and steered her toward the back door. She thought about reaching up to claw at his eyes, but his arms were too long for her. Instead, she let herself be led out into the dark alley.

Sharee shivered and probed the blacksmith for lack of anything useful to do. The song of a human was obviously much different than the song of a tree, but Sharee noticed some similarities as well. Both had a strong undertone that Sharee associated with water. Without thinking, she started playing the song of splitting. What would happen if she directed it at a human? Perhaps if she twisted the notes just right....

She waited until Scrontle dragged away from the door and across the deserted street. If she timed her attack right, maybe she could twist out of his grip and slip away into the gloom. The hand on her neck seemed like a good focus, so Sharee let the song loose. When nothing happened right away, she frantically began shuffling in notes. She tried to focus on the commonality of water and used that to construct the melody. The alley grew even darker as panic threatened to overwhelm her.

"Ouch!" Scrontle pulled his hand back. "Burn it all!"

When the big man backed away, Sharee just stood. Scrontle stared at his knuckle, where a bead of blood was welling up on top of a previously solid scar. *Run*, part of her yelled. Yet another part was celebrating. *It worked!*

"Something bit me," Scrontle said, turning back to regard Sharee with softer, kinder eyes. He shook his head, and like that, all of the threat washed out of his features. "Lady Swift, my apologies," he rumbled. "I hope I didn't go and hurt your arm. Had to be convincing fer those men, I did."

Sharee blinked, "What?" She shifted her grip on the staff.

"Well, that's sorta how they do things, y'see? It's not women, it's wenches, and they's supposed to play all coy and shy, just like you were doing. Are ya saying Marie didn't warn you before sending ya out there?" He scrunched his bushy eyebrows together.

"N-no," Sharee forced out. "Not really."

Scrontle frowned. "Well then, apologies on top of apologies." He bowed low and appeared genuinely abashed. He then straightened and looked her in the eye. "This the way we gotta play it, though. The Legion ain't used to taking on adults, and unless we fit in... well, we's fearing that they might yet kill us."

Sharee relaxed a bit at his explanation, but then remembered something. "Your arms! They forced you to...." Sharee couldn't bring herself to say it.

Scrontle looked down sadly at his markings. "It's not what you think. Ah, well, we did what we had to, to be sure they honored their end of the bargain. Y'know, the bargain that your m–"

"They caught my brother and Bud," Sharee interrupted, perhaps a little loudly.

"They did, did they?" Scrontle looked around worriedly and lowered his voice a bit more before continuing. "Those boys always did go getting themselves in trouble."

Sharee took the cue and moderated her own volume. "Marie seemed to think you would know where they're being held, if they're still here."

"Aye," Scrontle smiled. "They'll be holdin' them in the cellar of the town hall." He coughed. "Forgive the accent, I been practicing it, I have. Fer ta fit in, o'course."

Sharee waved the apology off. "How do you know they're in the hall?"

"Well, a while back I constructed a jail cell in there. They called me down from Kokamongo to do it," he explained.

"Why did they need a cell?"

"Well, they had a problem with a thief, I guess. Needed to hold him fer a bit 'til they could send him down to one of them bigger cities. Knucklesporte don't have a proper jail y'see." Scrontle turned and looked toward the end of the alley. "C'mon, let's go an' fetch 'em a'fore the Admiral gets back."

The big man turned and began walking down the alley. Sharee took a deep breath to settle her nerves—she was still a bit jumpy—and followed. She cast one look over her shoulder toward the inn, thinking of Marie in there alone with the rambunctious men. *I will help you, Marie,* she promised in her head. *Just let me find my father first.*

The dirt path took them directly to a wider road that ringed the town hall. One of the large stone walls loomed before them, a shadowy behemoth in the night hinting at the cavernous space it hid. In better times, the people of Knucklesporte might have been in the midst of decorating the area in anticipation of the festival that marked the start of winter. Frostingfest, they called it in Kokamongo, celebrating with food and dance the coming of the first frosts. It was viewed as a last night of fall fun before the grueling winter harvest. Sharee lamented the fact that no harvest would happen this winter. Frostingfest would go uncelebrated.

Scrontle walked all the way to the wall and then began creeping along it in the darkness. Sharee followed, trailing one hand along the cool stone. She found herself wishing it were wood. How else were they going to get in? She doubted that even a makeshift jail looked favorably upon visitors.

At the front corner, there was some green space between the road and the long stone stairway that led to the entrance of the hall. A large tree grew out of the small patch, its heavy limbs stretching over the lower part of the stair. Bright torches burned at even intervals on the sloping wall, casting plenty of warm light on the area before the building. Two marked guards lounged out front, leaning on the large blocks of stone that bracketed the end of the entryway.

She followed Scrontle as he slunk up to the trunk of the tree. They huddled there, keeping their heads down so that natural rise of the wall shielded them from a chance glance by one of the two guards. Scrontle approached and poked his head over quickly, and then returned back to Sharee.

"I'm not sure how we're gonna get by the two of them," he admitted. "These Legionnaires are no strangers to a scuffle. I could whack one over the head, but the other'll see me, he will." His shoulders slumped. "If it were just me, I'd do it, but surely they'll blame the rest of the folk what came with me. Probably say I broke the deal."

Sharee patted the big man on the arm. "It's okay, I have an idea."

While Scrontle had been surveying the scene, Sharee probed the tree next to her. It was a majestic oak, of course, and it had been planted to provide some shade on the stairs during the day. She was pretty sure she could split off one of the lower limbs and have it drop on the nearest guard. Unfortunately, there was nothing above the other guard's head but the stars. Looking at the ground around her, she found a heavy stone. She picked it up and handed it to the blacksmith.

"Scrontle," she whispered. "See that limb there? It's going to fall on the nearest guard. Think you can chuck the stone at the other one?"

Scrontle looked confused, "Sure, but how do you know the li–"

"You leave that to me." She turned to the tree. "Just be ready."

He frowned, but dutifully crept forward so that he could see over the wall, casting the occasional dubious stare back toward Sharee. She ignored the glances and plucked her harp. The resonance filled her, and she resisted the urge to hum along with it. Her hand found the rough bark, and she deftly began to play a split into one of the low branches that hung over the wall. It was quite a ways for the song to travel up the trunk and out to the limb. Sharee found that she really had to focus on the notes to keep them from slipping out of tune or wandering off on their own. What sounded strong in her head was deadened a bit by each length of wood, forcing her to play more loudly than she was used to.

Eventually, she saw a neat line begin to glow up on the tree where she was focused. It widened to traverse most of the heavy limb before a sharp crack startled her. She paused in the middle of her song as the guard looked up. The wood that remained connected could no longer support the weight. Time slowed as Sharee watched the guard's eyes sweep up to the tree. The limb broke loose and began to hinge down toward him, still partially attached. She quickly finished her song, splitting the wood cleanly, and it crashed down, striking the man on the head. He went down in a heap of limbs and leaves.

The second guard had been staring in surprise as the events unfolded. So baffled was he by the fallen branch, that he didn't notice when Scrontle rose and hurled the stone. It struck the man in the temple, and he dropped like a grain-filled sack. Sharee finished her song by knitting the end of the stump. There was no reason to leave the tree with an open wound.

Scrontle moved quickly around to the bottom stair. There, he cast a look up at the tree, and then back to Sharee. He surveyed the motionless forms of the guards, and then back to Sharee. He pointed and opened his mouth, but finally just grinned.

"Just like we planned, eh?" he said.

Sharee smiled sweetly and came around the end to join him. She prodded the man beneath the branch with her staff, pleased to find him still breathing. Killing an armed and ready man was one thing, but she hadn't wanted the blood of a defenseless guard on her hands. Even if he was Baraban.

"Shouldn't be anyone else inside at this hour," Scrontle noted. "Like I was saying, I happen to know that the Admiral is off looking at an oddity in the wall."

Sharee cast him a panicked look.

"What?" he asked.

Before she could answer, a blast from a horn shattered the stillness of the night.

◊ Chapter Fifteen

Water shimmers in the distance. Tasha Lake. Due to its sheer size, it is impossible to view one bank from the other. For most of the Baraban men, this is the largest body of water they have ever seen.

The great lake of the sun in Solestar is larger, Vraika recalls. Beside him, the West Tasher River rushes onward to where it will plunge into Tasha Lake, warring with the waters of its eastern twin. On the south side of the lake, the flow emerges as the Great Tasher River, roaring by the capital and out to sea.

Vraika does not intend to follow it any further. That the lake is on the horizon tells him that they must depart from the road. Before they reach the north bank of the lake, he and his elite guard will need to cross the river and strike out across the grassy plain. Then comes the swampland. There, on the western landing of the Tasha Lake, in the midst of the swamp, is where he will find Dismal Renard. Where he will find his destiny.

The rest of the Legion will turn in the other direction, aiming for where the lake swallows the East Tasher River. From there, they will take Kinnsley and hold it, awaiting his arrival. And what a glorious arrival it will be. His Legion will become unstoppable in these lands, and his victory here will go even further toward assuring compliance in other lands. He will march unimpeded to the capital and raze it to the ground. He will capture the Oracle. With the wayward shard in hand and the denizens of the prison in tow, he will return triumphant to his surrogate father. He will returned having secured his place as Warlord.

And yet... Vraika is plagued by a deep sense of unease. A confrontation is looming. A confrontation orchestrated by the Fates.

He looks down at the tree on his forearm. A testament to one victory already. *But it was too easy, she did not fight me.* Doubt gnaws. *Could I have beaten her?*

It does not matter. Vraika brushes the thoughts away with a wave of his hand. The black shard on his wrist glitters mischievously in the dull light from the full moon overhead. The only sounds around him are the huffing of his men. They have been marching hard since setting out from the captured Tasher city at midday, leaving it far behind. Their Warlord urges speed from them, yet now....

"Commander Borach," Vraika shouts.

"Yes... Warlord..." the man pants next to him.

Vraika hides his surprise. Of course the man is next to him. "Order a halt. We will camp for the night."

"As... you... wish... Warlord."

The big man turns, pulling a smooth, white horn from one of his packs. Stopping and taking a deep breath, he blows two quick bursts. They thrum lowly in the cool night air, and the men stumble to a halt. Each man takes out the goggles they carry as a member of the elite troop. They breathe heavily as they cover their eyes. All except for Vraika. He watches with a sense of detachment.

Resonance hums in him. Cymbals crash. The Warlord reaches out to grasp the shard. His sound echoes and amplifies, churning among his troops like a vicious sandstorm.

The rightful one will have his vengeance, the voice skitters across his mind.

Be silent, Vraika answers. *Your time has passed.*

Tragedy is recorded in flesh to remember its Song.

Vraika ignores the voice, drowning it out with even louder cymbals and shrouding his camp in a thick, dark fog. *Destiny or demise?* The question that bubbles up is his own. In the gathering gloom, he finds himself once more staring at the empty space next to the tree on his skin.

~ + ~

A loud crack yanked Werim back from the edge of slumber. He peered through the darkness toward the grated windows. It sounded like wood splitting. Perhaps all the crickets out there had congregated on a tree limb and broken it. There seemed to be enough of them. Did everywhere further down the mountain have so many of the insects?

Werim sat up and looked around the room wearily. Across from him, Bud was leaning up against the bars. The blond boy had been even more sullen since the Admiral's departure. Werim tried to pry out the reason behind his friend's unusual behavior, but Bud only shook his head and repeated that they needed to find a way out. *Not that he had any ideas for how to accomplish that feat,* Werim thought. *There has to be some way we can lie convincingly to that old man.*

A blast on a horn somewhere outside ripped Werim from his plotting. He stood and approached the door to the cage. No way was he going to be able to get back to sleep with so much spinning around inside his head and such a racket on the outside.

"What was that?" Bud asked.

"They've raised the alarm," Sorn responded from his corner in the darkness of the cell.

Both of the boys turned to regard the traitor. It was the first thing he'd said since the Admiral left. In fact, Werim had thought him asleep. Sorn stood and walked into the light and over to the side of the cell closest to the windows. He had a curious look on his face.

"Who would be attacking at this hour?" Sorn wondered.

"Perhaps Tashaba has finally sent an army," Werim offered.

Sorn waved the idea away. "That is not possible. That loathsome city likely hasn't even caught the faintest whiff of these dogs, embroiled as they usually are in their own philandering and pomp. Nay, there is no force close enough to pose even a remote threat to the Legion that has fallen upon us."

"Maybe it's Sharee," Bud spoke up.

Werim laughed. "How would she get passed the guards?" *Much less cause enough trouble to raise the alarm.* "No way. She's probably wandering around in the woods, waiting for us to figure out a way out of here."

The door to the dungeon creaked open. Three heads turned toward the gloomy stairwell. Airy footsteps pattered down the wooden risers. Light spilled across the floor from the high set windows, and into it stepped Sharee, a triumphant smile on her face and a strange staff in her hands.

"They're down here, Scrontle," she hollered behind her.

"Lost, huh?" Bud mumbled.

Much heavier footfalls thumped down the stairs. Werim gaped as the big blacksmith followed his sister toward the cell. He was dressed like a Baraban–and were those *markings* on his arms?–but there was no mistaking the warm face of their friend.

"Well, she obviously had help," Werim defended under his breath.

"Master Swift!" Scrontle rumbled. "Master Suppe!"

"Scrontle," Bud replied with a nod.

"How did you find us, 'Ree?" Werim asked.

"Simple," she smiled, "I followed the smell." She wrinkled her nose.

"Har har," Werim responded.

The light on the floor flickered a few times, drawing all five pairs of eyes upward. Shadows moved around the exterior of the building, and muffled voices echoed down. Scrontle frowned and walked over to the cluttered table in the far corner.

"We have to hurry," Bud noted.

Sharee nodded and walked up to the bars, examining the metal lock on the door. "Scrontle, can you get them out?"

The big man grunted from where he was rummaging around on the table, "Yes, yes... just need to find... ha!" He came back over with a thin, crooked piece of metal.

"Hey! That's my lockpick," Sorn whined.

"Lucky they left it, thief," Scrontle shot back. "Don't worry, I won't break it."

Thumps from overhead warned of imminent discovery. There were men in the hall. At least if they could get out of the cell, they could fight. Or so Werim told himself.

"Hurry, Scrontle," Sharee urged. "I'll buy you a few minutes and seal off the door." She disappeared back up into the stairwell.

The three cellmates clustered together, watching intently as the big blacksmith fiddled with the door to their prison. Werim felt a buzzing in his ear, and swiped at it blindly, unwilling to tear his eyes away from the lock. Bud was staring where Sharee had gone, frowning in thought. Sorn bounced on his toes next to them both.

"If you'll just allow me," Sorn said, stepping forward.

"It's my lock, thief," Scrontle argued. "I know how the tumblers are set."

"Yes, but your big, oafish hands obviously lack the necessary dexterity to–"

A loud thumping at the door startled them all. Sharee stumbled back down the stairs with a wild look in her eye. She hooked an arm back toward the doorway.

"That'll hold them, but not for long," she said. "Is there anything else that might help around here?"

Nobody answered. They were all staring intently at the clicking of the pick inside the lock. Sharee paced around the room for a moment, casting nervous looks toward Scrontle, but apparently not wanting to break his concentration. Not knowing what else to do, she went over to the table in back to rifle through the things.

Sorn's hands were twitching. "Honestly, blacksmith, if you would please just–"

There was a loud click as the lock disengaged. Scrontle tossed it to the floor and swung the big door outward on squeaky hinges. He flashed a satisfied smile at an angry Sorn, who snatched the offered pick out of the bigger man's hand.

"Lack the dexterity my arse," Scrontle commented.

The thumping continued at the door, punctuated now by the occasional crack of the wood beginning to give way. It was only a matter of time before they got through. Werim rushed out of the cell and into the center of the room, spinning to look at all of the corners as if they might have magically changed since his release.

"Is there another way out of here, because I seriously doubt they're going to just let us walk out," he asked no one in particular.

"Look, Werim, our things," Sharee said, walking up with her pack, quiver, and bow on a shoulder. She rubbed a hand across them fondly.

Werim frowned. "That's great, but how do we get out, 'Ree?"

His sister shrugged. A sharper thump followed by a more drawn out crack caused them both to jump. It sounded as if their captors had found some axes.

"Here," Bud stated.

He alone was still in the cell, staring up at the ceiling. Everyone turned toward him, and then crowded into the cell to see what the blond boy had in mind. Werim jostled between Sorn and Scrontle, craning his neck upward. He found himself staring at the hole in the ceiling used to lower food to the prisoners. The same hole the Admiral had eavesdropped through earlier.

It was roughly square, having been cut out of the wooden floorboards sometime after the original construction. It was not very large. In fact, Werim was doubtful if he could even get his head up into such a space, much less his shoulders. Even the willowy Sharee would find squeezing through such a small hole impossible. It was meant for a plate of food, not to convey prisoners. Likely by design.

Werim slapped his friend on the shoulder. "I think you've been in here too long, friend."

Scrontle was scratching his chin. "We might be able to work at it with the swords, but we ain't got no axes, and they's beating down the door, Bud."

Sorn snorted and stalked out of the cell without comment.

"No, no," Bud said. "Have *her* do it." He pointed to Sharee.

"Ha," Werim laughed, "you really have lost it, haven't you? Tell him he's crazy, Scrontle."

But Scrontle was nodding at Bud. "Yes. I saw what she did to that tree. Just need to get her up there." He turned and headed back for the table.

There was another bone-jarring crack at the door. Werim looked over at his sister. She was frozen, her bottom lip caught between her teeth, eyes wide.

Sorn returned wearing a long, brown jacket that he'd liberated from the table. He was brushing it off, though it didn't look to be making it any less dusty. He fished a floppy hat out of an inside pocket and shoved it on his head.

"Well, if I'm going to die, a few of them will join me." He pulled a strange knife as if from air and flourished it. "And I'll look a damned sight better on the way."

Scrontle was dragging the table back toward the cell. "Grab them stools," he grunted.

Bud obliged, taking his sword off the table in the process and strapping it to his back. He came over and handed Werim his things. Together, Bud and the blacksmith positioned the table beneath the hole and stacked two stools atop it. Werim stood with his things in his hands, eying his dumbstruck sister.

"Will you please tell them this is crazy, 'Ree?" he insisted.

Something in his tone snapped her out of it. Her brows turned downward and she fixed her brother with a frosty green stare. She laid her things down on top of her staff, and walked briskly over to the table.

"I'll do it," she announced.

"Do what?" Werim cried as more cracking filled the room. "There's no way you can fit through that hole."

Sharee ignored her brother and laid her hands flat on the table. Her chest inflated with a deep breath and she closed her eyes. Werim swatted once again at a buzzing near his ear, turning to try and catch the culprit in the act. There was nothing there. Swearing under his breath, he turned back to see his sister climbing, unaided, up the precariously stacked furniture. He rushed over and grabbed the feet of the stool to steady it.

"You convince her to climb up there, and now you're just going to stand while she falls and breaks her neck," he accused. "What in the blazes is wrong with all of you?"

Sharee paused and stared down at her brother. "Werim, the stool isn't going anywhere, relax. Look around your hands."

Werim frowned but did as he was told, examining the two feet of the stool that he gripped. It took a moment for what he saw to register. Then he jumped back from the table as if he'd been holding hot iron, shaking his hands. Where before the stool had been separate from the table, it now appeared that they had grown *together*.

Even as he was staring, wide-eyed, the buzzing in his ear grew louder. It was far more than mere crickets could account for. *What is that?*

He looked up at his sister and gawked. She had her feet on one of the rungs in the middle of the stool, hands held above her and pressed to the floor above. The edges of the boards that ringed the hole in the ceiling began to glow faintly. Even as he watched, they appeared to grow together into one solid, square board. Then, it appeared as if the floor warped toward him around the hole, widening and splitting into four separate flaps.

When the opening had grown wide enough to admit his sister–and then some–the boards dimmed back to a normal luminescence. As if an afterthought, Sharee touched the bottom edge of one of the flaps and it descended even more, splitting away from the board above it and rotating to form a hanging step. With a final nod, she climbed atop the stool, stepped on the rung, and easily pulled herself up to the floor above.

She turned around and waved at her awestruck brother. "Well, hurry up."

"What did... how did you..." Werim sputtered.

"She's a muse," Bud explained, passing his friend and handing Sharee her things before climbing up to join her.

"There you go with that crazy word again." Werim flailed. "Will someone please tell me something that makes sense?"

"Disparage not, young hero. This fortunate turn means that not all is what it seems. Which is very good for us, I should think," Sorn said, climbing up next. "Hmm, fancy that! Looks like I live to die another day, and thanks to a creature straight from the tales no less."

"My sister is *not* a... a... fairy tale!"

"No, she's much more than that," Scrontle noted soberly. "Now, up with you."

The blacksmith handed the remaining items they'd cleared from the table to Werim. It was his sword and his pack. Still somewhat in a state of shock, he accepted them and hoisted himself up. Bud's strong arms reached down to pull him the rest of the way, and Scrontle followed quick on his heels. The big man could just barely squeeze through the widened hole and grunted with the effort.

Werim stood and was surprised to find himself in a kitchen. Instead of cooking implements, however, maps and other papers were strewn about the surfaces, some with markers on them. Drawn to them, Werim wandered over and stared, trying to decipher their meaning. He may not have understood all the markings, but one thing was clear, the recipe followed by this chef apparently called for war. Sorn had been right in describing the size of the Legion as grandiose. There were dark markers everywhere.

Suddenly, the buzzing started up in Werim's ears again. He whirled and found Sharee bent over the hole with her hands against the floor. She appeared to be humming in time with the crickets.

"It's *you*," he accused.

She favored him with a quizzical look and looked about to say something, but Scrontle interrupted.

"Not now," the big man said. "We have to get out of here before they figure out you're gone."

As if to punctuate his concern, there was yet another loud crash at the door below, this time accompanied by the clatter of larger wooden chunks.

"They're through the door," Bud noted.

"Quick, help me block the hole."

Werim watched the maps in front of him get swept from the table as Bud and Scrontle flipped it over. Something inside of him came back to life, and he helped them maneuver the heavy wood to cover their escape route. When it was in place, Sharee bent down and with two quick buzzes, joined the table to the floor.

"We'll talk about this later." Werim cast a stern look at his sister.

Adding to his consternation, she giggled and shrugged.

Werim ignored it for now, and let his eyes sweep the room. They still needed to escape. The room had only one door, and it led back out into the hall. He doubted they would like what they found behind it, but he approached it anyways.

Opening it a crack, he flinched back when a black bolt nearly took out his eye. Instead, it lodged just to his left in the frame, vibrating a warning. The men were flooding back out of the stairwell to his right and running for the kitchen. Werim slammed the door and stood with his back against it. Sorn was rummaging around in the cabinets, probably looking for something to steal. *What are we going to do with that blasted traitor?*

Several more thumps told him that they hadn't stopped shooting. Werim stepped away, afraid that one of the bolts might somehow make it through the door. When Sharee came over and did her cricket imitation again, he didn't even have the heart to complain. They were trapped.

"Blast!" Werim swore. "There's got to be at least a dozen of them, and that's the only way out."

"What are we going to do?" Sharee wanted to know.

"We fight," Bud answered.

He had taken his sword off his back. With a crack, Scrontle broke a chair against one of the counters. He hefted the jagged remains of the feet in his hands and wielded them like clubs. Sharee was busy stringing up her bow, though it wouldn't do much good in close quarters. Sorn was apparently trying to look for loot *behind* one of the cabinets. There was a sharper thump at the door. The marked men had arrived.

"Seriously, traitor?" Werim asked, drawing his own sword. "We're about to make a last stand here, and all you can think about is stealing? Why don't you try and help us? Who knows, you might just live."

Sorn didn't answer, but put his shoulder against the heavy cabinet and shoved it, grunting.

"Aw leave 'im be, Master Swift." Scrontle waved a big arm. "He was a no-good thief a'fore these men showed up. He'll die a no-good thief all the same."

"Wouldn't be much help in a fight anyways," Bud mumbled.

Sorn had wedged his way in behind the container and was using the wall to push it out further.

"They're still going to find you back there," Werim pointed out.

A loud crack at the door spun them all around in time to see the shiny metal blade of an axe protruding through the door. Even as they looked, it was wrenched out. A few seconds later, it made another noisy appearance.

Sharee sidled up next to the door, reaching out a hand to touch it. Werim heard the telltale buzzing again, but this time wondered how he'd ever confused it with crickets. There was something different about it that he couldn't quite put his finger on.

When the next swing of the axe came, the sound rose in a crescendo. The door glowed faintly and the wood wrapped itself around the blade, trapping it. *She's a freak! Just ignore it,* he told himself. Grunting and cursing could be heard through the door as the invaders attempted to free the blade.

"Good work, Sharee," Bud complimented.

She favored him with a smile and stepped back. "It won't hold for long I'm afraid. It's still just wood."

The four of them positioned themselves in front of the door, steeling themselves to face the inevitable. Werim twirled his blade and felt a thrill race through him. *What is wrong with me?* Here he was about to face death, yet instead of the fear he expected, there was only... *excitement.* If anything, his senses were sharpened. The grains in the door jumped out at him. Footsteps from beyond the door pounded in his ears along with his racing heart. Behind him, Sorn still labored away, and the occasional scrape of the cabinet on the floor was easy to discern.

"Stupid thief," Werim muttered. "He's going to miss all the fun."

Scrontle cast him a strange look.

"Ha!" Sorn exclaimed. "Found it!"

They all spun around to see that Sorn had uncovered a door.

"Of course!" Sharee said.

"How in blazes did you know that was there?" Werim asked.

Sorn smiled. "Every kitchen has a back door. In addition, there were already marks along the floor that would lead any truly observant man to the conclusion that the cabinet in question had not always existed in a single location."

"He's still a traitor," Bud grumbled.

"Ah yes, but a clever traitor!" Sorn amended. "Shall we?"

He opened the door and gestured grandly. The darkness of night pressed in from beyond. More importantly, there was no telltale glow from a torch.

A sharp crack alerted them that the men had freed the axe from the wood; they were back to chopping again. Sorn jumped and darted out. Bud and Sharee were quick on his heels. With a sigh, Werim shoved his sword back in his belt. *Am I... disappointed?* He shook off the feeling and let Scrontle lead him out into the night.

◊ Chapter Sixteen

Sharee followed the lanky thief as he loped down the alley. His strides were silent and smooth, like just another shadow sliding along through the night. In stark contrast, she could hear Bud huffing along behind her, the slight click of the sword strapped to his back punctuating his heavy footfalls. She didn't even need to glance back to know that Werim and Scrontle were following as well. *At least they haven't run away scared of me*, she thought. *Yet.*

The twig-like man froze, and Sharee nearly climbed up his back. She took a few steps away and leaned against the wall as Sorn peered around the corner. The heavy thwack of axe on door reverberated far behind, and the stone wall shuddered in sympathy. The remainder of the crew clattered to a rest beside Sharee, eyes searching the night.

Sharee passed her staff to her left hand and hefted the items slung over her right shoulder. The additional weight of her burdens was reassuring. It was a comfort to have her bow and arrows with her, as well as the pack that she'd strapped about her waist with the wooden box inside. She still felt a touch guilty about losing them in the first place.

After a brief hesitation, the man called Sorn cocked his head and then darted across the wide street and into another dark alleyway. The rest of them followed in a clump. To Sharee, this new alley was eerily similar to the one Scrontle had dragged her down, though they were on the opposite side of the central square. He seemed to share her sense of recognition, for he slowed to a stop once they'd left the street safely behind, head swiveling from left to right.

"Scrontle, what's wrong?" Werim hissed.

The big man's eyes found Sharee, and his brows scrunched together.

Sorn had doubled back to join them. "Come on, blacksmith. We don't have time to dawdle."

"I hafta stay here," he replied.

"What? Why?" Werim asked.

Sad, dark eyes found Sharee. "The other men, they know I left with Sharee, y'see? If'n I don't show up somehow..." he trailed off.

"They'll blame the villagers," Sharee finished.

Scrontle nodded.

"We can't just leave you," Bud objected.

"Ah, sure you can," Scrontle said smiling. "Someone's gotta watch over the rest of the villagers. Besides, a big man like me'll just slow ya down."

Sorn turned to go. "So it's settled then. Now, may we continue on?"

"Wait, wait," Sharee grabbed the thief's sleeve. "We can't just leave him standing here. How will he explain missing the warning horn?"

Shouts wafted through the air. Everyone turned back toward the hall. Their pursuers had discovered that they had escaped from the kitchen. While the rest of them were staring worriedly, Sorn snatched the staff out of Sharee's hand. Before she could even cry out, he took two steps and smacked the piece of wood into the back of Scrontle's head. The reformed branch splintered and the big man toppled over like a felled tree.

Werim's blade was in his hand in a heartbeat. "Big mistake, traitor," he growled, stepping forward.

"What did you that for?" Sharee cried out.

Bud put a restraining hand on her brother. "Explain yourself," he ordered calmly.

Sorn rolled his eyes. "Bloody bones! The man needed a way to explain his absence from yonder fray. A nasty lump on the head'll do just nice. Besides, the way I see it, I owed him one for concocting that blasted enclosure we were locked up in. Served a pair of purposes with one stroke of a staff did I."

"You could have warned him," Bud pointed out.

"I suppose I didn't figure he'd be too keen on the plan, but I assure you it's for the best. Now, he can honestly say he got cracked upside the head without achieving so much as a glimpse as to the perpetrator." He folded his arms. "Now, if I've assuaged your tender sensibilities, may we depart this wretched locale? Surely they will stumble along this way eventually, if the sound of that catchpenny staff shattering hasn't brought them already."

"Hey, I made that staff," Sharee whined.

Sorn cocked an eyebrow. "Sing a stronger wood next time then, eh?"

He turned and glided down the alley. Werim put his sword away and scowled. Sharee thought she heard him mumble something about "itching for a fight" as he begrudgingly followed. Bud favored her with sympathetic eyes before motioning her along. The blond boy brought up the rear.

They made their way steadily outward from the centrally located hall. Every now and then, they were forced to double back when the glow of a torch warmed the corner ahead of their route, but more often than not they found the streets deserted. Sorn appeared to have the town memorized, as he never hesitated before ducking down yet another darkened pathway.

In short order, they arrived at the thick wall of posts that ringed the town, emerging from an overgrown pathway into a small yard tucked between the houses of the outer row. The dwellings stopped several armspans from the wall, and a short fence enclosed a well-tended garden in the middle of the area. Neat rows of herbs were demarcated with spikes driven into the soft earth, their different names whittled into the wood. Where the fence met the outer wall, a raspberry bush grew on either side, its vibrant fruit simply a light shade of gray in the colorless night.

Sorn hopped into the garden–ignoring the nearby gate–and picked his way toward the center, avoiding the growth as much as possible. Most of the greenery was turning a shade of brown this late in the season, but Sharee figured they appreciated not being squashed underfoot all the same. Whoever tended the garden obviously took good care of the plants. Near the center, Sorn bent down to examine one of the stakes.

"You were in a hurry earlier, now you want to pick weeds?" Werim huffed.

Sharee shook her head. "They're not weeds, they're herbs, Werim. And over there are some vegetables too." She pointed.

"Whatever," Werim said. "They're going to die come winter anyway."

"Hibernate," Sharee corrected. "They don't die, they hibernate."

Werim threw up his hands, turning away from her. "Sorn. Hello?"

Bud had approached the wall and was studying it. "They probably have guards posted at the gates, so we'll have to figure out a way through," he mused.

Werim kicked at a stone, eyeing the sharpened tops of the posts. "Well, we're not going to climb it."

Bud turned and walked back to Sharee, "It *is* made of wood."

"Yeah," Werim spoke up. "Do your freakish, buzzing thing."

Sharee frowned at her brother. With a cheery nod to Bud, she approached the wall. She was just about to start joining the posts together when she was interrupted.

"Not necessary!" Sorn had one of the stakes in his hand.

As they watched, he tapped it twice on the top with the palm of his hand and a glinting metallic object popped out of the bottom. Before it could hit the ground, Sorn snatched it out of the air and examined it in the dim light. He then trudged over to one of the bushes and began rummaging around between it and the wall. Sharee and the boys came over and clustered behind him.

"You never know who might be listening, and you've already made enough noise," he mumbled. "Besides, this will be just as adequate."

"A stone?" Sharee queried, catching sight of something gray hidden beneath the bush.

"There's always a back door," Sorn smiled, brushing aside more of the branches to reveal a large, flat stone set flush with the ground.

At first glance, it appeared to be just another block, nearly swallowed by the ground. Closer inspection revealed a small, circular depression in its center. It was into the depression that Sorn inserted the object he'd retrieved from the stake. Sharee would have called it a key, but it was not really key-like at all. It was more like a large coin. Instead of being long with teeth at the end, it was squat and circular with no apparent ridges or patterns.

The smooth device fit perfectly into the depression, and Sorn pushed it home with a soft click. No sooner had he done that than a small square above the coin began to glow a dull red, pulsating slowly. Sorn laid one finger atop the light and waited for a moment. There was a soft chime, and the glow turned green. Sorn removed his finger, and a deep grinding noise shook the ground at their feet, causing them all to look around nervously.

When the noise stopped, Sorn pried the strange key out and pocketed it. "Unpickable lock," he explained, and then gave the stone a gentle shove.

To Sharee's surprise, it swung downward to reveal a pitch black hole in the earth. Sorn lowered himself in and quickly disappeared. Sharee, Bud, and Werim all looked at each other and then back to the hole. Muffled shouts in the distance urged them on.

"Beats staying here," Werim said and dove into the hole.

Bud motioned for Sharee to follow. She gulped and obliged, placing her hands on the ground to either side. Her feet led and kicked blindly about, hoping she wouldn't connect with her brother's head. She was surprised when her leather boot encountered a step carved into the wall. One after another, she climbed down into the darkness.

She didn't have far to go. Bud's worried face hovered in the opening above her only an armspan away when she encountered solid ground. There was a rustling before her, followed by a tap, and then a faint blue light blossomed in the underground tunnel. Sharee was surprised to see that she was surrounded by smooth stone, no hints of how the passage had been made evident on the walls. It might have been naturally formed, but why here?

Sorn and Werim stood together a short distance away huddled beneath what appeared to be the stone covering for the exit. Sorn shook the glowing stick in his hand, brightening it, and then held it up to examine the surface. Werim was staring in amazement at the device. It appeared to be made of glass with a strange cork stopper in one end, a heatless luminescence within. Two footfalls behind her let her know that Bud had joined them.

Sorn glanced their way and nodded, apparently satisfied that everyone had made it down, and then pressed the coin key into the stone. Once again, he laid his finger on the stone and the sound of boulders scraping against one another resounded in the hallway. Sharee found herself resisting the urge to cover her ears. Instead, she simply turned back and grimaced at Bud. To her surprise, the weak shaft of light that speared down from the opening behind them was slowly being sluiced off. Apparently the opening of one door closed the other. Hopefully they wouldn't find themselves trapped on the other side. There was no retreat.

When the unpleasant noise abated, Sorn turned to Werim, who was still standing slack-jawed. "It's a Dagaran glowstick," he explained. "Very difficult to acquire unless you are acquainted with the proper people."

"How does it work?" Werim wanted to know.

Sorn shrugged. "Not my area of expertise. All I know is that it does, indeed, work." He held the small glowstick up so that he could see each of their faces. "Now, there may be malevolent men beyond this door, I know not. There could be a patrol standing atop us even now. The woods are not far from our position. In the event we are surprised, I suggest you run for them. We will fare much better amongst the foliage."

With that, he reached up and grasped a small length of rope. The stone door above them swung downward with the tug, and the ashen light spilled once more upon them. Sorn hid the glowstick somewhere in his long coat and started up the wall using the carved out notches. Werim was quick on his heels. The hole was only deep enough to fit the two of them, so Sharee and Bud waited at the bottom. Sorn paused for a moment at the top, head poking out warily, before pulling himself the rest of the way up. Once there was enough space, Sharee followed her brother.

The night was a lot brighter outside of the city walls, though the moon remained veiled behind clouds. A wan light filtered through to bathe the wavy grass in gray light. Sharee was surprised to find they were only a few paces from one of the town's four corners. A gentle breeze blew her hair into her face, and a small bit caught in her open mouth. She sputtered and pulled it out, examining the greasy strand. *Gross.*

At first, she thought the reddish tinge at the corner of the wall was simply due to her sight being filtered through wisps of auburn hair. Then, as the glow grew, she recognized it for what it was. A patrol was coming. She glanced back toward the edge of the woods, but the dark wall of trees may as well have been a league away for all it was worth to her. They would never make it beneath the comforting boughs before being seen. She turned back to the group just as Bud emerged from the hole and Sorn was bending down to close it.

"Patrol," she announced, pointing.

"Make for th–" Sorn began. "Oh, bloody boulders," he finished instead.

Werim had sprinted away as soon as she'd uttered the word, his sword in hand. Unfortunately, he was sprinting *toward* the corner. Bud, recognized his friend's intentions and followed, struggling to get his own weapon off of his back.

Sharee turned back to Sorn. "We have to help them."

"Yes, yes," he waved a hand. "Bloody fools if you ask me, but I must close up this passage first. Wouldn't do to have them finding out about it, eh?"

"Who cares about that?" Sharee hissed. "They're going to get killed!"

She turned and took her bow off of her shoulder, thankful that she had left it strung. An arrow was notched in an eye blink, and she was moving away from the wall in order to give herself a better angle for firing. The men would appear any moment now, and she didn't want to be trying to shoot between the running boys.

When Werim was only a few strides from the corner, the patrol appeared at the edge. Sharee let loose an arrow, aiming at the first thing she saw, and it caught the torch bearer in the chest. The flame fell to the ground, and then Werim was upon them. His blade was glowing again as he whirled amongst the marked men. There were six of them, and they were caught off guard by the ambush. Two more had fallen before the remaining three drew their swords to fight back.

Werim danced back once they had armed themselves and appraised the situation. Suddenly, he found himself struggling to defend against three trained blades. They smiled and darted in. Elongated shadows flickered and melded on the wall behind them, illuminated by the torch that guttered on the ground. Fortunately, before the larger men were really able to press their attack, Bud stomped up with his long blade in hand. He fielded two solid blows aimed at his friend before both groups stepped back out of striking range. The glow had left Werim's blade, and he realized for the first time that he was at a disadvantage. He held his sword in front of him, shimmying backward each time one of his attackers so much as flinched. *Who does he think he is?* Sharee wondered.

The patrolmen, aware that an archer was waiting somewhere out in the darkness, kept their backs to the wall and moved around enough that even had it not been dark, Sharee couldn't be sure of her target. They waited with the patience of an overwhelming force, and it looked to Sharee like her brother was favoring a leg. How long before the experienced men took advantage of the relative youth of the boys? Or, even worse, another patrol stumbled upon the fray, further skewing the numbers.

Sharee reached reflexively for her harp. She had to do something. Directing a song outward, she tried to coax one of the posts in the wall to split, hoping to distract the men. However, when she released the song, she felt it travel out from her and then swiftly dissipate in the cool night air. There was no way her quiet noise could make it across a length of field to the wall. Once again, having her special power did her no good. She watched helplessly as Bud fielded another blow with his sword, followed by a vicious kick to the middle that sent him sprawling backward. Werim stepped in before the attacker could close the distance on his friend, parrying a few quick blows. Two of the men forced her brother backward with flashing blades while Bud scrambled to get out of the way. *Where had the third man gone?*

A gasp left Sharee when her brother tripped and fell on top of Bud. The two boys frantically tried to untangle themselves as their attackers pressed in. Sharee fired another arrow without aiming. It sailed over the men and lodged into the wall harmlessly, yet it caused the two men to flinch and duck, their dark eyes scanning the night. She ran toward them, hoping to distract them further. It was difficult to notch an arrow on the run. Sharee's fingers fumbled and failed her. One man kept his eyes on her while the other turned back to the boys, his foot snaking out to kick a sword away from a searching hand.

Then, suddenly, the two men pitched forward into the grass. Sharee slowed to a halt, bewildered, while Werim and Bud regained their feet. A shapeless lump uncoiled itself behind where the men had just been standing. It took her a few seconds to recognize the shadowed form of Sorn. The thief bent over the two bodies and then stood back up. Dim moonlight glinted off of something in his hands before he dipped them back in his long coat.

Sharee approached warily as the boys picked up their swords. Sorn went around kicking each of the bodies, apparently making sure that they were as dead as they seemed. He took the sword from one body, walked a few steps, and then shoved it in another. It made a sickening wet sound. Sharee decided to switch her focus to the boys.

Blood ran down Werim's leg from a shallow gash in his thigh. When he noticed his sister's eyes, he picked up some dirt and rubbed it on the wound as if by obscuring it she would think him unscathed. She frowned and turned to Bud. He had blood on him as well, though it didn't appear to be from a blade. It seeped from the bandage on his arm and trickled down to his fingers. The old cut would need tending again. Sorn returned to the group with a scowl on his face. He returned two arrows to Sharee, one bloodstained, and then rounded on Werim.

"Just what did you think you were about, hero?" he said.

Werim looked at the ground, "I-I just felt like... I was so... I mean, I guess I thought that if we ran then... I don't know."

"Why did you stab the men with their own swords?" Bud broke in.

Sorn turned to regard the blond boy. "Why, to buy us a step or two, of course. Perhaps they'll surmise that the guards quarreled amongst themselves. They are, after all, savages. Not at all unlike your friend here."

Werim shoved his blade back into his belt angrily and trudged off toward the woods. Sorn shook his head, mumbled something about a "bloody irrational whelp," and followed. Sharee looked to Bud, who motioned back at her. She hid a smile as he brought up the rear.

~ + ~

"They be dis way, Admiral."

Lugar nodded at the young lieutenant and picked up his pace. It wasn't time that concerned him—he was sure his escapees were long gone by now—it was more that his irritation was getting the better of him. *You'd think the men be knowin' what to do 'bout a muse.* But he supposed it had been a long time since they'd faced one as an adversary.

"Here dey be," the young man said, pointing.

Sure enough, there were crumpled forms strewn about the ground. In the soft light of early dawn, Lugar examined the surroundings. It was obvious that a fight had taken place. There were scuff marks from boots all over the ground and patches of dark mud clustered around the corpses.

He removed one of the swords and examined it. It was definitely one of theirs. *My men do be better than runnin' themselves troo with their own swords.* He glanced quickly at each of the other bodies. They all had Legionnaires' blades buried deep in their torsos. His eyes glazed over as he attempted to play the scuffle back in his head.

From the pattern of the boot marks, he could discern that there were two distinct groups of men. One had turned on the other just as they were rounding the corner, or perhaps had been hidden there. They had taken out the strongest men first, the squad leader and his torch bearer. Then, the remaining men had been backed up against the wall.

Why? If there were reason enough to fight, if this were truly what it seemed–a quarrel between his own men–then the men should have faced each other evenly. Such duels happened all the time in the Legion, though usually not ending in death. *Wagers, wenches, or wars... all be proper reasons fer Baraban blades be bared.* His father had been fond of the saying.

In a daze, Lugar allowed the flow of the battle to take him near the wood posts. The memory of the swirled grains from the night before rose unbidden to his mind. *Blasted muse,* he thought. He didn't have time to pursue this properly now. His presence was needed near the front as they prepared to assault Kinnsley.

A notch in the otherwise smooth wall caught his eye. He reached up and ran a finger along the groove. It was placed up too high to be made by a sword and too wide to be from a sidebow bolt. He knew immediately what it was. If he were to retrieve the white arrow from among his things in the town, he was sure the arrowhead would fit both the width and depth.

"These men no be duelin', Lieutenant," he announced. "If you be searchin' close, you be findin' some wounds apart from swords I believe. It be an ambush."

"A-ambush, Admiral?" he stammered.

"Aye, an' you should be knowin' better too," he accused. "On patrol be no time for duelin', especially when we be on alert!"

"'Course, sir. S-sorry."

Lugar felt his irritation rising. *It no be his fault,* he reminded himself. This young Lieutenant had drawn the short straw–honestly, he'd probably been swindled by his seniors–and had not even been leading the squad that had first found the bodies. None of them had wanted to admit it. The more seasoned Legionnaires had likely realized this was no simple brawl and hadn't wanted to be held responsible for the escape of the prisoners.

Unfortunately, upon finding the evidence of a less-than-natural infiltration, Lugar had gone straight to the section of town they'd been using as a warehouse. He'd originally been afraid that the muse would go for the remaining villagers in the inn.

Otherwise, he might have been closer to the real mayhem. *Why be she choosin' the few over the many? And two gangly boys at that.*

"Sir?" the young Lieutenant prodded.

Lugar realized he'd been staring at the wall. "The fallen do be earnin' the full Rites. See to it, Lieutenant." After receiving a salute, he added, "And be sendin' me the Lead Engineer. I do be havin' a problem fer him to solve."

The Admiral strode away quickly, content that the man would carry out his orders. As he walked, he went over in his head what he was going to say to the man that led his corps of Engineers. They were a strange bunch, and it was wise to be clear in speaking with their kind, lest you get a lot more than you bargained for.

A muse may be handlin' a tracking party, Lugar ruminated, *but we'll see how she be dealin' with a lone Engineer.*

◊ Chapter Seventeen

The leaves on the tops of the trees were just warming to the first caresses of the dawning light when Werim blinked himself awake. He noted that they were no longer green, but shades of red and yellow, and many had already fallen. A shiver chased after the cool morning breeze that ran him through. Winter was Werim's least favorite season. Usually, it simply meant staying indoors and hauling endless buckets of hot water up the stairs. This year, however, promised to be different, and as much as he hated playing mule, he wasn't sure that change was worth the cost.

An annoying buzz stole his attention from the weather. He turned to find Sharee seated against a tree nearby. She had several leaves in front of her and was pouring a bit of water from the canteen onto them. To what end, Werim did not know. He watched as she focused on the moisture and buzzed. As far as he could tell, nothing happened.

"Can you cut it out, 'Ree?" he whined. "Some of us were trying to sleep."

She looked up. "Sorry. I forgot you can hear it, too."

Werim scowled. "If you do it any louder, Bud will be complaining."

They both looked to the blond boy sleeping not a stone's throw away. With a snort, he rolled onto his back. A loud snore rumbled out.

"Yeah, he seems really bothered," Sharee noted.

Werim pushed himself into a seated position. His leg screamed at him, wrenching his eyes down to the hastily concocted bandage. Sorn had provided a few long strips of cloth when they had finally stopped. Werim insisted that it was merely a flesh wound and that he could continue on just fine. After all, it hadn't really hurt until this morning.

A groan escaped as he stood.

Sharee regarded him with sympathy. "Let me have a look at it."

"What? Are you going to buzz me?" He frowned.

She nodded. "If I can."

"No thanks," Werim said, shaking his head. "I don't need my freakish sister doing... whatever it is you do, to me. You'll probably buzz my leg right off."

"Hey, that's not fair," Sharee said, pouting. "Besides, if you can hear me, you're a fr– a muse, too."

Werim frowned. "People seem to love to use that word. I don't even know what it means."

"That's what I am, Werim," Sharee explained. "And Dad is a muse too, I think, and so are you. There's no use denying it. You can hear me."

"You leave Dad and me out of your little freak show, okay?" Werim retorted.

Sharee narrowed her eyes. "I wish he were here. Maybe then you would listen."

"What are you doing up, anyway?" Werim countered. "We can't have slept more than a couple hours."

Sharee shrugged. "Couldn't sleep. I kept remembering the fight yesterday. I can't help but think I should have been able to do more to help."

"What, like buzz at them and scare them away?" Werim snickered.

"Funny, Werim, but it doesn't work like that," Sharee replied. "At least, I don't think so."

Werim frowned. He wanted to tease her some more. *What did she know anyway? Nothing!* But something held him back.

Instead he asked, "Where's Sorn?"

Sharee pointed. Werim followed her finger to find the thief propped up against a tree opposite of them all. His hands were folded neatly on his lap and, disturbingly, his eyes were open. He was staring straight at them.

"What are you looking at, traitor?" Werim prodded.

Sharee came over to stand next to her brother. "Werim, I think he's sleeping. He sat down like that and hasn't moved in hours," she whispered.

"Who sleeps with their eyes open?" Werim wondered.

He limped closer to the man, and Sharee followed. The thief's eyes were light brown, almost golden, and stared unblinkingly outward. During their approach, Werim noted that the pupils didn't seem to track or follow them; Sorn was staring at the same point they had just vacated.

When they were close enough, Werim stuck out a palm and waved it in front of the man's face. There was no response. If it weren't for the steady rise and fall of his chest, Werim might have thought Sorn dead.

As he and his sister stood looking down at the gangly thief, Werim remembered the shiny weapons that Sorn had used to kill the last two savages. The man had struck so quickly that with all of the excitement of the battle–*Excitement! When I almost got us all killed. What am I becoming?*–clouding Werim's recollection, he hadn't gotten a good look at the blades. He cast off the disturbing thoughts and bent in slowly with the intent of slipping a hand inside of the thief's long jacket. Just one look wouldn't hurt....

Sorn's hands leaped off of his lap and moved in a blur. Suddenly, Werim felt cold, sharp metal across his wrist and behind his neck. Sharee let out a small yelp and jumped back. Werim froze and glanced down, The thief's eyes still stared straight ahead.

"And just what discoveries do you expect to unearth within my truncheon coat, hero?" Sorn said.

"I don't know what you mean. I was just going to give you hug," Werim replied dryly. He didn't know why he felt like goading the man, but on the other hand, *why not?* He *was* rather pompous. "After all, you did save me from myself."

Sorn blinked. His eyes darted up to lock with his would-be pickpocket. To Werim's surprise, they appeared to twinkle with amusement.

"I do not believe that fantastical farce for an instant," Sorn admitted.

He slowly pulled the knives away.

"Well then, perhaps I just wondered if you were armed," Werim tried.

Sorn slid out from the tree and stood, leaving Werim still bent over. He flourished a pair of unusual knives before him. The blades were curved and instead of protruding vertically from the longer metal hilt, they stuck straight out, almost like hooks, but thicker. The hilt on each was black, wrapped with leather on the lower half, and appeared to have a small leather thong attached to the bottom that wrapped around Sorn's wrist.

The thief twirled the blades, making a show of them. When he stopped, Werim noticed that sharp metal had disappeared, folding down into a slot. The hilt was more than long enough, so they nested easily, though due to the curvature a shiny bit still protruded. Sorn crossed his arms beneath his jacket and, not a moment later, they reemerged without the weapons.

"Yes, I *am* armed," he stated, and then spread his arms wide. "One exists on the right there, and the other prefers to reside on the left. Not at all unlike you, you see."

Sharee giggled. Sorn favored her with a toothy grin, and folded into a bow. Werim frowned.

"What were those?" he asked.

Sorn rose. "Where I hail from, they are called Kama. Though, you might have just asked in the first place instead of intruding upon my being." When Werim snorted in reply, the thief swept a hand toward the only remaining member of the party still asleep. "You might deign to go and wake–What was his name again?–ah, yes, Wil. Wake Sir Wil and let us be about this sojourn."

With a nod, Sharee went over and began to gently shake the blond boy. Her efforts only served to increase Bud's voluminous snoring. With a grunt, the much smaller girl flipped the boy onto his side, and the snores abruptly abated. There was, however, no waking.

Werim turned back to the thief. "You don't even know where we're headed," he accused.

Sorn raised an eyebrow. "Well, I had assumed simple merchants such as yourselves might not mind accompaniment. The road can be a lonely place."

"And if we do mind?" Werim narrowed his eyes.

Sorn chuckled. "Well then, I suppose I shall have to insist." He crossed his arms again, this time bringing one hand up under his chin. "It may be, mind you, that I have something to offer that you would not otherwise be knowledgeable of."

It was Werim's turn to cast a quizzical glance, but he said nothing.

Sorn smiled. "I see I have your ear. Well, when one considers that if, say, they were to desire to go to Tashaba by way of Kinnsley, there might also be a rather large army sharing the path. One might be interested, then, in a faster and more direct route. The kind of route known by another who is more accustomed to traveling... unseen, as it were."

"You know of a back way?" Werim simplified.

"My dear boy," Sorn spread his arms wide, "if there is one thing I might have imparted on you by now, it is that there is *always* a back door." He grinned.

"Get. Up!" Sharee screamed.

Both thief and young rebel turned toward the lady of the group. They watched as she wound up and kicked Bud squarely in the side. The blond boy bolted awake.

"Ow!" he cried.

"Well if you'd wake with a more gentle prodding, I wouldn't have to resort to the boot," Sharee defended.

Bud rubbed his side but said nothing.

"Let me see your arm," his sister ordered.

Bud complied.

Gingerly, she unwrapped the bandage and examined the wound. It was an angry red color at the edges, and still appeared to be weeping. Werim had to give his friend credit, though; he did not flinch as Sharee investigated. A small pang in his leg reminded Werim of his own injury.

Sharee's brows knitted. "Don't jerk away now, I'm not exactly sure how this is going to feel."

A buzzing started up in Werim's head.

"Sharee!" Werim shouted. "Don't! You don't know what you're doing."

The buzzing subsided as Sharee let go of his arm and bit her lip nervously. "You're probably right..." she began.

"No," Bud said. "Go ahead."

Sharee searched his clear blue eyes, but the boy did not appear afraid. He grabbed one of her hands and placed it on his arm. The buzzing began again.

"You're crazy." Werim threw up his arms.

Bud ignored his friend and nodded to Sharee.

Werim turned away and shut his eyes as the noise reached a crescendo. Visions of his friend's arm exploding flashed in his mind. After a moment, when he heard no screams and the buzzing had stopped, he dared to crack an eyelid.

Sharee grinned ear to ear. Bud was looking at his arm in wonder, flexing it a bit. Where before an angry wound wept, there now existed a long scab. Its edges were still red, but the cut was no longer exposed to dirt and grime.

Bud and Sharee locked eyes and something passed between them. Her hand was still on his muscular arm. She was grinning gratefully and a small smile tugged at the corners of Bud's mouth.

Werim couldn't stand it. "You two are both crazy! She could have blown your arm off."

Sharee shook her head. "That's not how it works, if you'd just let me explain...."

"I don't want to know." Werim held up his hands. "You probably buzzed some of your freak into him now, too."

"It did tingle a bit," Bud noted.

"Blech!" Werim gagged.

"Oh, seriously now." Sharee crossed her arms. "You're making a show of yourself."

Sorn had been watching the proceedings with a distracted air. Werim had almost forgotten the thief was still there. Business at hand abruptly returned to the front of his mind.

"Come on, *Wil*." Werim shot his friend a significant glance. "Let's be off before those savages have a chance to catch up with us."

"Yes, that would be dreadful, indeed," Sorn noted. "We shall endeavor to head in this direction." He cast one last look at the party and started walking.

"We're trusting him now?" Bud asked under his breath.

"I don't see as we have much of a choice," Werim admitted. "Do you know how to get to Tashaba without running into that Legion?"

"I thought you were rather keen on fighting them," Sharee broke in.

Werim scowled at this sister, and then turned to follow Sorn. As he took his first step, pain shot up his leg, and he hissed. He narrowed his eyes at his sister, daring her to say something, and then started off. The next step was easier than the first. Same with the step after that. *This isn't so bad*, he thought.

Sharee rolled her eyes at Bud, as her brother limped away. The blond boy calmly motioned for her to follow, but not before cracking a smile of his own.

~ + ~

"My Lord, what orders be ya havin' fer da men?"

Vraika lifts his head. Blinking twice, a fog lifts from his mind. He regards Borach, Commander of his elite forces, with a questioning glance.

Borach shifts nervously. "It just be, Warlord, dat da day do be gettin' on fer ta evenin'."

Is it that late already? Vraika feels as if barely a moment has passed. The cymbals continue to crash in his head, and he silences them with a thought. Abruptly, the fog enshrouding the camp disperses, and he can see the tents that his men have pitched. Goggled men walk between them, backs bent to various tasks. He sits on the ground in the center. Next to him, his tent has been put together by some of the guard, but he has not used it. Thought has consumed him all through the night and most of the day.

True to the Commander's words, the sun is past its apex in the sky. The light bathing the long grass that surrounds them is beginning to tarnish a bit. Still the shimmer off of the lake looms on the horizon, no closer than when they had stopped. Time has been wasted.

Or has it? What had his father always said? *Time be more precious to the man it be runnin' out on.* Was his time running out?

Destiny or demise?

"Allow the men to sup, Borach. They have earned some rest," he orders. "I will not be holding up the fog tonight, so post an extra watch or two. If I am needed, I will be in my tent. I have much to plan for. Do not disturb me unless the news is dire."

"Aye Warlord." Borach salutes, and then stomps away.

A part of Vraika wishes he could join the big man. Surely, his guard will make raucous use of the night off, and he knows his Commander to lead by example. It reminds him of his father.

Memories begin to surface. Unpleasant, uninvited. Vraika hurries into his tent, lest his men see his struggle. Inside, he begins pacing. He grinds his teeth together. *Why did you make me do it father? Why couldn't you see? Why?*

The Warlord realizes that tears are streaming down his face. He swipes at them, but they return in force. They are a foe that he has yet to eradicate.

He finds a chair and table set up for him. With a smooth motion, he pulls out his sword. Approaching the table, he swings. Metal bites hungrily into wood. A shudder travels up his arm.

Again and again, he lets the blade feast. Splinters fly, and his arm begins to ache. When he regains control of himself, there is nothing left but crumbs, kindling.

He rights the chair and sits down. The sword drops to the ground beside him. He rests his hands on his knees and turns them, palms upward. Their shaking betrays him. His eyes focus on the tree.

You could have stayed. You could have saved me this fate. You could have chosen us *over* her.

The dark branches on his arm seem to stir in the breeze. To Vraika, they are alive. They know what he is thinking. They mock him.

You will pay, brother.

~ + ~

By the time that they stopped the next day, Werim was feeling pretty good about himself. Not only had he avoided a buzzing, but his leg was surprisingly pain free. As he stood from gathering loose wood for the fire, there was not even a twinge. He'd had deep cuts before–from sparring with Bud or simply the result of general mischief–but even with proper bandaging they seemed to linger. Perhaps it hadn't been as bad as it looked.

Returning to their makeshift camp with his arms full of kindling, Werim found Bud and Sharee off to one side, sitting amicably next to one another. She had her usual pile of foliage, and Bud looked on with interest as she examined them each in turn. Even as Werim watched, a telltale buzz tugged at his ear. The small stick she was holding looped over into a circle, seemingly of its own accord. He shuddered and turned away.

Sorn was watching the encounter with a mild interest as well, but the thief quickly returned his attention to the fire pit he had dug. With careful movements, he arranged the tinder just so. Werim had been skeptical when the man had promised a "mostly concealed" flame and was interested to see it in action.

He dropped the sticks near the pit, nodding back when the thief mumbled thanks. A strange clicking noise caused Werim to peer more deeply into the wooden construction. Sorn had something shiny in his hand and was flicking it with his thumb. Small sparks briefly illuminated the interior, falling on a small, wrapped bundle of dried grass that Sorn had produced, but not immediately lighting.

"Should have refilled the liquid reservoir... damned firestarter," he grumbled. "Ah, there we go."

One of the sparks caught and a flame sprang to life. Sorn withdrew his hand, flicking the firestarter closed, and it disappeared into his jacket. He turned to the pile that Werim deposited and began to sift through the loot. Some sticks he tossed into the makeshift furnace, others he threw back into the surrounding woods.

"What's wrong with those?" Werim wanted to know.

"A trifle damp," Sorn explained. "You see, the moisture within the wood will produce an unwanted amount of vaporization. We desire a mostly smokeless fire."

Werim nodded. By the time Sorn had finished sorting through the bundle of brushwood, the fire was crackling with life. It was a small blaze, but it fit their purposes. Sorn had dug the pit deep enough and kept the fuel low enough that, apart from the faint glow cast up out of the pit, the actual flames were mostly unseen unless you stood nearby. True to his intentions, there was also very little smoke.

"Now, how about we have a look at that wounding of yours?" Sorn suggested.

Werim's hand went protectively down to his bandage. "Why?"

"Though I have not poultices and powders, I assure you that it is in your interest to renew the dressing, and I possess clean cloth. In addition, I consider myself moderately schooled in such traumas." He shrugged. "After all, one shouldn't wield sharp weapons without expecting to suffer the occasional cut. Indeed, stitching may be required. Especially, if you are not keen on *her* methods."

"Stitching?" Werim swallowed.

He looked back at Bud and his sister. They were still playing with sticks and leaves. Another buzz nipped at his ear. Another piece of nature performed an unnatural back bend. He swallowed again.

"Fine," Werim said. "Let's have a look, then."

Sitting near Sorn and sticking his leg out, he began to unwind the wrapping. It didn't take long. In the interest of expediency, Werim had simply bandaged over top of his pants. A dark bloodstain greeted him, radiating out and down from the slice in the material. Some rivulets had run down his leg to stain his socks too, but there wasn't much he could do about that now.

With care, Werim rolled up his pant leg with the intent of examining the still-healing wound. When he'd gotten past the rip and then some, his eyes widened in alarm. There was a distinct lack of marring amidst the hair struggling to make itself known on his thigh. Mistrusting his eyes, Werim ran his hand across the skin and around back all the way up to his buttocks. He could feel no wound either. Sorn stared at him with narrowed eyes.

"I swear it was there," Werim defended. "I was not faking it, I promise. I did not simply tear my own pants. Who would do that? I mean, how can this be? There are blood stains. See?"

He frantically rolled up his other pant leg. Perhaps his legs had exchanged places without his consent at some point the night. Unlikely, sure, but what else could it be? Unfortunately, unblemished skin greeted him on that side as well.

Sorn's puzzled look persisted. The thief raised his eyes from the examination of legs, and fixed them a short ways away on Sharee. His gaze returned to Werim, and a sort of understanding passed behind his amber orbs. Slowly, the man raised a hand to rub ponderously at his chin.

Werim's eyebrows climbed skyward as his brain made the connections. His sister hadn't buzzed him *that he was aware of*. However, she *had* been awake each morning before him. Could she have done it without waking him? *She must have!* She was, after all, a freak. Who knew what she could do?

He met Sorn's eyes, and his breath escaped him. "She did this to me," he whispered.

To his astonishment, the man's eyes rolled as if Werim had completely missed some obvious truth. It only served to further stoke the fires of fury. Brother rounded on sister, stomping across the small clearing.

"You! You buzzed me!" he accused. "Even after I asked you not to, you still went ahead and did it anyway."

"I did no such thing," Sharee replied, her back straightening.

"Unwind your arm," Werim ordered Bud.

The blond boy looked from brother to sister, and then down at the contorted leaves and twigs, completely forgotten now. A frown crept onto his face, and he shot Sharee a questioning look. She shrugged in reply as if to say: *go ahead.*

Bud slowly began to unravel his binding. Sure enough, when the cloth had been removed, virgin skin–though a bit hairier than Werim's–was displayed for all the world to see. All eyes turned to Sharee.

The young girl's brows knitted together. "I swear that I had nothing to do with this. Perhaps you did it without knowing."

"No," Werim spat. "Don't even think about blaming this on me. For the last time, I am not like *you.*"

As the two sat staring daggers at each other, Werim noticed small pools of water threatening to burst forth from the bottom of his sister's eyes. *She's about to cry,* he noted, and it felt like someone had punched him in the gut. He wasn't sure why he should care so much–it wasn't like he hadn't ever made his sister cry before–but something was different. Perhaps it was losing a mother–or perhaps he was just tired–but Werim suddenly felt awful about what he'd said. It was not a notion he was used to.

Unable to think of how to take back words that had already been said, Werim decided instead to flee. He turned and went back to sit by the thief and the fire. Strangely, he was almost thankful that Bud stayed behind and comforted Sharee in rumbling tones.

"You know, I believe there is more to this than you are willing to admit," Sorn pointed out upon his arrival.

"What do you know, traitor?" Werim retorted.

"Traitor. Freak. You seem quite keen on labeling everyone. Except for yourself, that is. And I must wonder: what special knowledge do you possess that allows you such freedoms?" Sorn asked.

Werim didn't answer. The thief was right. What did he know?

He stared deeply into the small fire and was surprised to find himself envious of the flames. Their existence was simple. They crackled and burned. There was no question about their purpose.

Soundlessly, he rose and went over to settle where he'd set his pack earlier. Alone. He lay awake for a long time, listening to nothing in particular. Bud and Sharee went back to the leaves, the occasional buzz prickling Werim's ear. Eventually, they joined Sorn around the fire for a small bite to eat. The little food they still had among their things was enough for a decent meal, but Werim worried about the hungry nights ahead.

The thief kept the fire low, eventually snuffing it out when it began to burn too brightly. A while later, when Bud began snoring, he could hear Sharee shift him to his side to quiet him, and still sleep eluded Werim. He didn't think he would drop off until he worried out an answer to the question bouncing around in his head.

What was his purpose?

◇ Chapter Eighteen

Eclectic Marcko was several days out of Kinnsley when the
clouds gathered ominously above him and began to spit icy
rain all over the narrow path he was following through the
woods. His hand reflexively went to his head as a cold breeze
stirred the nearby trees, but his red hat was not there. It was
packed away along with many of his other belongings in the bags
strapped to the sides of the horse beneath him. Advertising his
station along this road would not be wise. Instead, he pulled up the
hood of his heavy traveling cloak and cinched it tighter around his
shoulders. Here and there in the shade were bits of morning frost
that the noon-high sun had failed to burn off before the storm
rolled in. Fall always passed in the blink of an eye. Winter chased it
off without remorse.

Perhaps part of his perception of the brevity of autumn was
due to his habit of meandering north so late in the year; he wasted
much of it on the road. Marcko didn't always spend his winters up
in the mountains, but he did try to return to the grounds of his
youth as much as possible. Though he enjoyed the comforts of
Tashaba immensely, Knucklesporte had its own charm. Besides, he
felt it important to spend time among those he represented. If he

stayed in the city like many of his peers, how would he hear the real issues of his people? Mountain folk danced to a different drum than city folk. It would be a disservice to them to remain aloof.

Beneath boughs that hurried to shed the last of their leaves, Marcko rode slowly despite the weather. *Too often we hurry through life without enjoying the journey*, he reflected. It was a common thought for him whenever making this trip. Time itself seemed to stretch out the further he got from the capital, and the stress that characterized his time among the other Eclectics bled out of him. The effect caused him to revel in each moment even as it slid slowly by.

This most recent session had been a particularly grueling one, too. He had tried so very hard to convince his peers to heed the dire warning that his close friend had brought. Unfortunately, none of them had been keen on listening to a murderer. That Rynel claimed to have acted in defense against an agent of the Grand Warlord failed to stir their compassion as well. After all, what would interest such a distant leader? Only Marcko's finely spoken words–and a few favors, of course–had kept Rynel's head off the chopping block. A small mercy, that. He cringed at the thought of bringing the news north.

The man was lucky to be alive. Marcko had advised him to remain cooperative until spring. His actions would be all but forgotten by the time the Summit reconvened, and then Marcko would be able to get him released from the swamp quietly and quickly. He might have to leave the country, but at least would be free. In the meantime, it was best that he lay low, even if it meant his family would be without him for another few months. From what he remembered of Rynel's wife–Renee if memory served–he was sure that the woman would manage. She didn't strike Marcko as one to fall apart in times of struggle.

Rynel had agreed contingent upon two conditions. First, Marcko had to get the Summit to mobilize the Tasher army. He had already accomplished that one, though it had taken him the rest of the session and many concessions which he might never get back.

The second was that he bring word to Rynel's wife as soon as possible. She needed to know he'd been locked up after an encounter with an agent.

As Marcko reminded himself of the second part, he kicked his heels into the sides of his horse. It wouldn't do to dawdle *too* much. As much as he'd like to enjoy the colors of the falling leaves around him, the trek was already going to be tough up into the mountains, and he would hate to get stuck somewhere until the thaws.

No, what he needed was to hasten up to Kokamongo to check on Renee and the kids, and then head back down to Knucklesporte for some much deserved rest and relaxation. Hopefully the neighbor he paid to take care of his home had done his job, and the house stood ready. Then, he could bribe away one of the young men that worked the stables at the inn to help around the house during the cold season. There were never many travelers in the winter, so a few silver should be enough. He certainly didn't want to lug his own hot water up the stairs.

Marcko was daydreaming about hot baths and soft towels, slouching contentedly in his saddle when voices ahead of him straightened his back. Reaching beneath his cloak, he loosened the knife that was strapped to his waist. Bandits and thieves often used this path to move unmolested–and more swiftly–between Knucklesporte and Kinnsley. Also, it allowed them to avoid the army patrols on the North Tasher Road, though surely those had been pulled away by now to man the borders like Marcko suggested to the Summit.

As for bandits, a sufficient bribe and hint of a knife was enough to placate most of the nefarious characters found along this narrow road. Thieves and ruffians were loathe to risk a wounding when a decent amount of coin could be had without a fight. Had they a vote, it would perpetually be cast for the smoothest path.

With that in mind, Marcko readied his knife while at the same time freeing his coin purse. It jingled pleasantly as he rounded a bend and saw the source of the noise. Two young men leaned up against a large boulder on the side of the path, the cold drizzle making their hair cling to their heads. They fell silent when they saw him. While both had swords–the blond one with a large two-handed blade strapped to his back and the dark-haired one with a shorter saber at his waist–neither had the look of a ruffian. He frowned, letting his steel slide back into its sheath, his cloak dropping to cover it. They lacked the characteristic predatory gleam in their eyes. Though, taking in the rough state of their dress, they certainly looked capable of mischief. Just not the sort of mischief that might involve the law. Rather, the kind that their mothers might switch them for later. Marcko absently wondered if he might be able to hire these two in lieu of the young men at the inn. It would be nice to hear some new tales for once, and these two certainly looked like they had a few to tell.

"Ho there!" Marcko called out, raising a hand in greeting.

The boys failed to return the gesture and simply shifted their feet.

Marcko jingled his coin purse. "I don't suppose you two are looking for work?"

The boy with black hair met his eyes and fingered the hilt of his blade, while the blond one studied his feet. Neither so much as glanced at the purse. Marcko pulled up short and studied the boys more closely from his steed.

Blood stains marred the pants of the dark-haired one, though the leg in question appeared strong. *Stolen then? Why steal ruined pants?* Otherwise, their clothing was unremarkable. Their shirts were made of the same type of plain, brownish cloth that could be found everywhere in the mountains. The blond boy had the beginnings of a beard and blue eyes that peered up every now and then to regard the eclectic with suspicion. Marcko's gaze returned to the hazel eyes of the other youth. There was a challenge in them, as if the boy were itching for a fight. As Marcko studied them, the back of his mind was prickling. There was something familiar about the boy.

He tried to piece together their story. Perhaps they were no more than they seemed: a couple of village youths run off to seek adventure. Marcko could understand that. He was once their age. Perhaps they were running from something, or someone. Or maybe they actually were thieves, just new to the game. Either way, they surely wouldn't turn down a friendly offer of food and perhaps some coin. Then, he could be on his way.

Just for a second, the hazel eyes flicked off to one side. Marcko nearly missed it, but the damage was done. A new theory formed in his mind: *they're not alone.*

He had time only to draw his knife and spin, slashing wildly upward. There was a low grunt as his knife grazed flesh, but all Marcko saw was a swiftly moving shadow, and then pain exploded in his head. His vision flashed crimson, and he felt himself sliding forward and falling, falling into an endless blackness that swallowed him whole.

~ + ~

If it weren't for the throbbing pain at the base of his skull, Marcko might have thought he was still unconscious. The blackness that surrounded him was deep, at first, but then it slowly resolved as blurred shapes slid into focus. He counted four forms, outlined by a very slight glow from a banked fire. Two of them were likely the young men he'd seen on the road, but the other two had been hidden.

The rain had stopped, but a damp chill remained in the air. Marcko took care to remain motionless, suppressing a shiver. So long as they didn't know he was awake, it was possible that they might reveal something useful. At the very least, it might buy time for his headache to subside.

"For the last time, 'Ree, we'll ask him when he wakes," one of the dark forms was saying.

"I know, I know," a second replied. A young woman's voice. "Aren't you the least bit eager, though? News from the capital! He could have seen Father."

"Don't get excited. We don't even know that all of those things are his," the first cautioned. "For all we know he could have stolen them. Or killed someone for them."

"Oh, come on," the second said. "Look at him. He looks more like a... what did you call him?"

"An eclectic," a third voice jumped in smoothly. "A paunchy agent of democracy, the overly nourished voice of his people in Tashaba."

So they'd found the hat. And if he had to guess, the third man was the experienced one amongst them. It was likely he who had knocked Marcko on the head.

"Right," the girl continued, "he looks more like an Eclectic than a thief or a murderer."

"I was not aware there existed much to differentiate the two," the smooth one elaborated.

There was a snort of laughter from the fourth shape in the darkness.

The girl rounded on that one. "And what do you know, *Wil*?" She stressed the name as if it were a dirty word.

"Only what my mother told me," Wil answered solemnly, all trace of laughter gone. "That our representative lives in Knucklesporte, and we are fortunate that our taxation is kept low."

Marcko smiled to himself. At least someone appreciated his work.

"Fortunate?" the smooth one scoffed. "Taxation is a crime, perpetrated by the few on the many. After all, are any of you at all cognizant as to where the money goes? Whom does it benefit? Transparency should permeate the rule of the land, not obfuscation, and politicians are all masters of the obtuse. It is theft under the guise of societal beneficence. Extortion in the basest sense! Mistake it not, for if you do not forfeit your tribute willingly, it will most assuredly be taken from you by force."

The diatribe was met with silence.

"Bah, you are all yet young. You have not experienced their dirty hands in your coin purse," he finished.

"In case you haven't noticed, none of us have coin purses," the first voice pointed out. "Besides, it doesn't matter any more. I doubt the Legion will be keen on paying taxes for the land they've invaded."

Invaded? The Legion, up here? Marcko struggled to push aside his concern for the bigger picture for a moment. He needed to focus on the here and now, so he instead turned to the quality of the voice he'd just heard. In the dark, it struck him as even more familiar than the hazel eyes had earlier. He immediately paired it with the dark-haired boy. If only he could dredge up the memory behind the familiarity. He could not afford to remain waylaid for long.

"What are we going to do with him?" a deeper voice asked. Marcko paired it with the blond boy, Wil.

"Well," the smooth one began, "once he regains consciousness, we shall question him to ascertain the purpose of his trip. Likely, he was simply attempting to return to his abode for the winter. Politicians, much like vermin, spend the months between fall and spring barricaded in their lairs, plotting reemergence once the weather turns favorable."

"Then, we're just going to let him go?" the dark-haired boy asked. "Waltz right into *their* hands?"

"Of course not. We can't allow them so easy an eyewitness to our departing vector. We'll tie him to a tree and leave him for the vultures."

The young woman gasped. "You can't do that. It's... not right."

"Hardly," the smooth one scoffed. "More than likely he'll win over the carrion gobbling horde with a rousing speech and false promises of feasts and fortune. In a fit of passion, they will loose his bonds and then deliver him home slung between them. It will only be later that they discover the missing feathers."

"No," the woman said resolutely. "We take him with us. What harm can it do to leave him in Kinnsley when we get there?"

"He'll have us arrested, or worse," the smooth one pointed out.

"He is another mouth to feed, and we don't have a whole lot of food," Wil added.

"And he cut Sorn with that knife of his," the dark-haired one threw in.

"Which I tried to heal," the woman defended, "and I only made a scab like I did with you two. Just like I said."

"Probably because you didn't buzz him during his sleep like you did to us."

"Werim Swift, I have had just about enough of you," the woman threatened.

Swift? The name jolted his mind like a lightning bolt. It took a conscious effort not to cry out. *Could I really have stumbled across Rynel Swift's children? What are they doing all the way out here?* He recalled the talk of the Legion, and immediately imagined the worst. Smoke and flames smoldered in his mind.

"Great job, Sharee. Now you've done it. It's bad enough you go around buzzing everything, but then you go giving away my name," the boy, named Werim, accused.

"What difference does it make if Sorn knows your damn name, Werim?" The woman stood and began shaking her finger at the shadow next to her. "The man has been nothing but helpful to us since leaving Knucklesporte, and yet you insist on treating him like dirt. Why don't you grow up already?" the young woman, Sharee, yelled.

The smooth one–Sorn apparently–chuckled, but said nothing.

"Oh, buzz off. Don't you have some leaves to collect or something?" Werim retorted.

"Werim," the blond one spoke up, "what your sister can do is special, and she must practice at it. Like us with swords."

"Not you too, Bud," Werim lamented. He turned to the girl. "You've gone and buzzed his wits out, haven't you?"

"Werim, you are *so* dense sometimes," she replied.

"It's outlawed for a reason, Sharee," Werim yelled back. "You ought not be messing with things you don't understand."

"Since when have you cared about following the rules?"

Werim turned to Sorn for support. The man shrugged. "I cannot speak in your defense. After all, you did just reveal Sir Wil's true name after berating your sister for doing the same. Not that I blame you for lying about it. To be fair, I never believed you anyway. If it would please you, I can continue to call him Sir Wil."

The shadow that was Werim stomped away, cursing angrily. When he got far enough away that they could no longer hear him, the remaining forms all shared a laugh. Marcko had to suppress a chuckle of his own.

The more he listened, the less frightened he was. These appeared to be reasonable folk. If things in the north were as bad as he feared, then they were simply taking care along the road. The Fates know, he might have done the same. Besides, it was especially important if these were truly the children of Rynel Swift. Though why they would be so far from home without their mother had Marcko concerned.

When the laughter had died down, the one called Sorn stood. "It is time we roused *your* prisoner, then." He gestured toward the girl. "As we delve the mind of this esteemed Eclectic, however, be sure to hold fast to your coin. You may find it does strange things around a politician. Lady Sharee, Sir Wil... if you will accompany me please."

They both giggled and stood with the man. Marcko relaxed his eyes and lolled his head forward. It wouldn't do to give away his advantage. In the darkness of his mind, he could hear the three sets of feet pad over to him. He steeled himself for a rough slap, but it never came. Instead, a small satchel of aromatic salts was shoved under his noise, causing him to recoil. The reflex was so strong that he smacked his head up against the tree and nearly knocked himself back into unconsciousness.

A groan escaped his lips as he blinked his eyes. "I have... more coin than what you've undoubtedly already found in my purse."

"It's the people's coin in the first place," Sorn grumbled.

Sharee cast him a look, and the older man bowed his head in acquiescence. *Interesting that he should let her take the lead*, Marcko noted. It appeared that he might not want to reveal his experience. *Or perhaps he's just used to playing the accompanying lyre.*

"We apologize for cracking you over the head Master...?" she trailed off. She gestured to Sorn and the theif loosed the Eclectic's hands. Narrowed eyes communicated more than enough warning to mind his manners.

"Marcko. Eclectic Marcko of Knucklesporte," he filled in. "And yes, that was quite unexpected. I'm surprised that I'm not bleeding from the scalp." *Best not have them think me adversarial.* "Though, I can't say that I blame you along these roads. One can never be too careful."

Sharee's face reddened. "Your head *was* bleeding. I... uh... tended to the wound."

Marcko's eyes widened. He reached back and felt along the sorest part. There was no wetness, though no dressing either. *Must not have been very bad.* "Then, I am indebted to you."

Sorn snorted, but said nothing at a quick glance from Sharee.

"So, what are you doing along this road, Master Eclectic?" the girl asked.

"Please dear, Marcko," he amended. "As to my purpose, well I was simply on my way to visit a friend in Kokamongo before retiring to my home in Knucklesporte for the duration of the winter, as is my habit. This road tends to get me there a bit faster, provided I don't run into any ne'er-do-wells, of course."

"You have friends in Kokamongo?" the blond boy blurted.

"A few, yes." Marcko smiled easily. "I do, after all, represent this area."

"And who are they?" Sharee pressed.

Marcko waved a hand with feigned disinterest. "No one you would know, unless... well, unless of course you happen to hail from there." He paused, scratching his chin for effect. "Seems unlikely to me though, as everyone in that village is most assuredly preparing for their winter harvest."

A look of deep sadness welled up in the girl's eyes, but she said nothing. Silence settled between them. Disowned leaves tumbled across the clearing, pushed by the unseen hand of the wind as the moment stretched on. Marcko thought briefly of pressing his luck, trying to draw some information out of her, but something held him back.

Instead, he merely surveyed his inquisitor as she stared down at her scuffed leather boots. Her dirty auburn hair fluttered loosely, along with the tatters of what once would have been a very nice green dress. She looked the part of a pauper, though without the typical stoop to her frame.

Abruptly, having finished the waging of some internal battle, Sharee raised her chin and speared Marcko where he sat, her eyes ablaze with emerald intensity. The taller companions to her right and left faded into the background in the face of her stare. It seemed almost as if a shaft of moonlight had somehow been directed to light just the spot between them. Marcko's heart fluttered. The blond boy turned to regard Sharee quizzically while the older man flashed a knowing smile.

Appearances can be deceiving, Marcko reminded himself. Despite the ill repair of the girl's clothing, despite her thin frame and delicate features, despite being wedged between two men–one quite thick, the other more spindly–the young woman commanded attention. Here, in the middle of nowhere in the woods, Sharee was a queen.

"If I told you my name is Sharee Swift, would that mean anything to you?" she inquired.

Even as the name left her lips, Marcko's memory suddenly snapped into focus. Like it had only happened yesterday, he recalled when Rynel and his young wife had first come to him. They had been on the run as well. She'd been pregnant, and they'd arrived in the dead of night to ask the local Eclectic's help in finding a quiet place to have the child. *Oh, how she ordered Rynel around*, Marcko recalled. That young woman, too, had donned a regal air like others might a favorite cloak. It was a fond memory of his, and not only because he had been able to help. They'd also reimbursed him beyond his wildest dreams. Not with coin, mind you, but with knowledge. And hope. Both of which Marcko held in higher esteem than any number of metal discs.

Now that he knew what to look for, Marcko saw traces of the father as well. It wasn't as plain in her demeanor, but there was a spark of wildness that danced about her, same as he'd seen in Rynel on occasion. *Surely this is a Swift child.*

"My lady," Marcko said, bowing his head without realizing it, "it would only confirm what I already see before my eyes, and would also mean I have found that which I seek."

She squinted her eyes at the remark and the strange formality of the reply. "Why would you be looking for me? Don't play any games now."

He raised his head to meet her gaze. "It was your father that set me on this fool path, my lady. Him and his recklessness, that is for sure."

"You know my father?" she asked.

The odd trance of her intensity wore off, and Marcko found himself once again simply talking to a young woman. "Rynel Swift, yes, if I am not mistaken, my dear. You bear a striking resemblance, you see." Marcko gestured with his hands as he spoke, continuing when she didn't stop him. "Your father came to me in Tashaba. He said he had a warning to deliver and wanted me to provide him access to the Summit. It was all very strange, but then again, your father was no ordinary man."

"Where is he now?"

"I'm afraid his brashness got the best of him. There was an... ah... incident, and he's been sentenced to a rather lengthy prison term," Marcko explained. "Not before delivering his message, though, I might add."

"Prison?" Sharee echoed.

Marcko bobbed his bald head. "I'm afraid so. Do not worry, though, I've already set plans in motion to see him released come spring. This is the very thing I was on my way to advise your family about. Speaking of, where is your mother? There is more to the message, but it is meant solely for her ears, I do believe."

The girl turned away, one hand going to her face. Both of her male companions stepped in as if Marcko had committed some grievous offense. From their demeanor, he quickly assessed the verity of what he'd overheard earlier.

"It's true then, isn't it?" he said. "The Legion really has invaded from the north."

The man called Sorn smiled. "So you *were* listening. It had seemed as if your reaction to the salts was a bit superfluous, even for a politico."

Marcko waved a hand. There was no reason for pretense anymore, no time. It appeared they had been tricked into playing right into the Grand Warlord's hand. "Of course I was. I thought you were simple bandits and that I was going to have to bribe my way free. All of that is irrelevant now, anyway."

"If we were bandits, we wouldn't have taken on a prisoner," Sorn pointed out.

"Well, it seemed odd to me, too," Marcko admitted. "But I must protest, we have more important..."

"They burned Kokamongo," Bud broke in, his voice deep and haunted. "They killed my mother.

The two men turned to regard the blond boy. He was staring off into the distance, his eyes glazed over. Marcko's mind was racing as he began to put it all together.

"They must have opened the pass," he muttered, "and that also means that the Archon is... Sharee, what happened to your mother?" Marcko knew what she was. Surely she couldn't be....

"Dead," the girl turned around, tears brimming. "The dark man... she made a deal... to save the villagers."

"Vraika," Marcko growled. "So the Grand Warlord truly has sent his Right Hand. The Summit must hear of this invasion, and quickly. Perhaps it is not too late to salvage something of this."

"I'm not certain we can outpace them, and I would advise you not to continue north, should you have means of communication from there. You will discover Knucklesporte quite occupied," Sorn noted.

"No, no." Marcko waved distractedly. "Of course not, I'm...."

"You're what?" Bud asked.

Marcko met his blue eyes. "I'm coming with you." He nodded as his mind caught up to the decision. "Yes, I was sent to find the Swifts, and so I have. What remains, anyway. Now, I must return to serve my country. Untie me, please. We have no time to waste."

◆ Chapter Nineteen

The sun was long gone by the time they decided to stop. In addition to sore feet, their aggressive pace gifted everyone with sharp hunger pangs. Fortunately, Marcko turned out to have plenty of food in his packs and offered to share for as long as it lasted. And fine food it was. The best the capital had to offer, they'd been assured.

Werim glared at Sharee and Bud sitting off to one side as he took a hunk of cheese and some spiced jerky that had been set out. His sister was playing with foliage again, making cups out of leaves and then filling them with water. Turning away, Werim scratched at his ear and sat down on a fallen tree next to the portly Eclectic. He was surprised to find the man appraising him with thinly veiled amusement. Werim struggled to shrug off his rising anger. They were, after all, eating the man's food.

"So, you know our father?" Werim ripped off a piece of jerky with his teeth.

Marcko smiled and nodded. "Yes, he and I go way back."

"And he's still alive?" Werim asked with his mouth full.

Marcko replied, "I should hope so, though Dismal Renard is no pleasant lakeside village. Still, if I were a betting man, Rynel Swift would have my money." He raised a sausage-like finger and scratched his chin. "Come to think of it, I believe he does have a good bit of my money."

Werim swallowed and raised an eyebrow.

The man laughed heartily and slapped the boy on the back. "Lighten up, lad. We'll get you to your father, I promise. Just give it time. First things first; we must get to Tashaba. There will be paperwork to complete, and I'm in no hurry to return to that, trust me. But once all that's taken care of, we'll hire a swift river runner to take us up the Grand Tasher River and straight across Tasha Lake. Besides, it's not like we could approach the place on foot anyway." He frowned. "Can you imagine how much it'd cost to keep a road passable in a swamp? A dock is much more practical."

"If you say so," Werim groused.

"I do!" Marcko said. "I do say so. And if you can't trust your own Eclectic, who can you trust?"

Werim glanced over at Sorn. After constructing another fire, the thief had settled near Sharee and was watching her with thinly veiled interest. Every time she did something strange with a lost bit of the forest, Werim could swear he saw the man's lips twitch in the slightest hint of a wistful grin.

"I certainly don't trust that traitor," Werim admitted.

Marcko studied Sorn for a moment. Finally, he said, "Don't you worry about him, he's harmless. He may not like me, but I can assure you, he is no traitor. At least, not in the way you think."

"What does that mean?" Werim asked.

The bald man just smiled. "Wine?" he asked, producing a full skin seemingly from thin air.

Werim accepted with a nod. It was a far cry better than rum. A particularly loud buzz caused him to swat at his ear.

"She's coming along nicely, isn't she?" the Eclectic asked, inclining his head toward Sharee. "You both can't be much older than sixteen now, right? She's not had much time to practice, then."

"Doesn't it bother you?" Werim asked. "I mean, she's breaking the law, and isn't it sort of your job to see that it's followed?"

Marcko rumbled out a chuckle. "Son, I just help write the laws. I don't need to make sure people abide by them. That's up to the Polemarch. Or the army. Either way, it's out of my hands." The Eclectic shrugged. "Besides, it isn't like I supported every law that's ever passed through the Summit."

"Are you saying you're okay with freaks like her?"

Marcko laughed again. "Freak, huh? That's what you call her? I suppose it is a brother's love..." he trailed off, some thought seeming to snag his attention. Eventually, his eyes refocused. "There are worse things than being a muse."

"Yeah, like what?" Werim asked.

"Well, being a Warlord for one," Marcko said. "Having the weight of an entire people on you. Better men than I have buckled under that sort of pressure. At least I get to share my burden with the rest of the Summit."

"It just seems so... *unnatural*," Werim said.

Marcko shot him an odd look. "Don't be so quick to judge. Perhaps it might be something you would enjoy, given the chance."

Werim shook his head. "No way. I'm not like her."

Marcko laughed. "If you say so, son. She *is* your sister, you know."

Werim ignored that and ripped another piece of jerky off. In between bites he asked, "How far away are we?"

"Oh, perhaps another few days if we keep up the pace. I wasn't too far down this path when I ran afoul of you ruffians." He rubbed his head for effect and grinned. "And I was taking my time."

"Why wouldn't you hurry if you had a message for us?" Werim asked.

"Would you be in a hurry to tell someone's family that their father had been sent to prison?" He took a swig of the wine. "Besides, a slow trip north is one of the few luxuries I allow myself."

Werim looked at the fine cheese he was about to bite.

"Have some more wine, boy," the Eclectic urged, shoving the skin in his face.

Werim recalled quite keenly his run-in with the rum. He had promised himself that he wouldn't drink so much again. Then, he thought of the walk ahead of them and the rough road they'd left behind. With a shrug, he took a small drink to wash down the cheese. It really was delicious wine. Not that Werim had a whole lot of experience to compare it to.

"So, what did my father do to end up in prison?" Werim asked.

"It is mostly just a misunderstanding, nothing that won't be cleared up with time," Marcko answered evasively.

"I should think a city as grand as Tashaba would have jails of its own," Werim pointed out.

Marcko coughed several times before responding. "Ah, I'll let him explain that when you see him. It's not really my place."

Werim frowned and took another bite of cheese. After he swallowed he asked, "Do you think Kinnsley will be able to hold back the savages?"

It was the Eclectic's turn to frown. "Honestly, I'm not sure. If the bulk of the Legion truly is here, then they will be hard pressed. Also, unfortunately, your father and I may have done more harm than good."

"What do you mean?" Werim asked.

The man shifted his bulk. "Well, your father came to me with warning of an imminent invasion. Of course, we assumed it would come, by necessity, through one of our open borders. The mountains have protected us to the northwest for many years. Why did they fail in this case? Has Vral grown strong enough that he can now move them? If so, then I fear our battle is already lost."

"Vral?"

"The Grand Warlord, of course. Leader of the Triumvirate. They rule all land to the north and west of the Knuckle Mountains. Hardly a benevolent outfit either," Marcko explained. "Anyway, your father had me rouse the army, which we promptly sent off to bolster the border strongholds. Kinnsley will be even more depleted than usual. They will not last very long, I'm afraid."

Werim swallowed another bite of food as the thought hung between them. It didn't seem like they could do much to stop the Legion. *So,* Werim thought, *assume they do succeed in taking Kinnsley. What next?*

"Who leads the Legion? We met an Admiral, but there was also the dark man. Which one is of higher rank?"

"Vraika is Warlord of the Baraban people, leader by right of blood, though his High Admiral does most of the actual leading," Marcko explained. "Why?"

"I'm not sure it matters, I just wondered," Werim admitted. After another bite, he decided it wouldn't hurt to share his thoughts with the Eclectic. "While we were in Knucklesporte, in the jail in the basement of the hall, we heard the Admiral and the Warlord talking. Taking Kinnsley was only part of their plans. It seemed almost like a distraction for the Warlord."

"How do you mean?"

Werim shrugged. "Well, the Warlord mentioned that Renard place, the prison. Said something like destiny was bringing him there. He told the Admiral to wait for him after taking Kinnsley. Even if it meant pretending to talk about peace. Why would it be more important to go to a prison than attack a city?"

Marcko was silent, staring off into the night, lost in thought.

"Doesn't that seem backward?" Werim pressed. "Shouldn't the leader be at the most important battles?"

Marcko didn't answer, instead he mumbled, "Vraika knows of Dismal Renard, then." His eyes found Werim. "Well, you're correct in deducing that Kinnsley pales in importance. If Vraika succeeds at the prison, I fear our army would not be enough to turn the tide at any city, much less Kinnsley. The Legion would overwhelm us."

"What is so important about this prison?" Werim asked.

Marcko brought his eyes back to the boy's. "It is where we send people like your sister. That has to be what is drawing Vraika.

He can't have found out that... no." He shook his head. "Anyway, many of the prisoners once served the Grand Warlord, and the rest? Well, for their freedom they may very well join him."

"A prison for freaks?"

Marcko nodded. "I believe you've seen what your sister can do in a pinch. Imagine what a trained muse could do. A normal jail would not hold them. And they are worth many men in any army."

"Then why are they outlawed in the first place, if they are so useful?" Werim asked.

"Yes, why not endeavor to repeal the law, Eclectic? Explain that to the boy." Sorn had sidled up, surprising them both. He stood on the other side of Marcko, his long hair acting like a hood in the gathering gloom, casting malevolent shadows across his face. "And while you're at it, why don't you explain to him the legal basis for the denial of foreign asylum."

Werim squinted. "What are you talking about, Sorn?"

The thief held up a finger. "Shhh. Don't allow him time to formulate a lie."

Marcko frowned. "Why would I lie? Those laws were passed before my time. I believe them to be outdated, if you must know. If it were up to me they would be changed, but such are the frustrations of a democratic government. I have tried to bring them to table at the Summit, but the Traditionalists hold a majority. The Archon Basileus would love nothing better than to toss me out, too." He held out his arms. "Besides, there are no muses left that are native to the Nation. The bloodlines died out many years ago. Any people evidencing abilities in our midst are agents of a foreign power at worst, illegal aliens at best."

"Bah," Sorn waved a hand in disgust, "the Tashers are so scared of the *Grand* Warlord that they willingly turn their backs on those in need."

Marcko cocked his head. "Are you suggesting that the Folians and Illunites can't take care of their own?"

"No, but what of the Dagarans?" Sorn said.

Marcko's eyes widened, but he said nothing.

Sorn spat on the ground. "Anything to save your own skins. Nothing's changed."

Werim wouldn't have been surprised if the thief pulled out one of his Kama and took a hack at the Eclectic. The air boiled with the man's frustration, though Werim didn't really understand why. He replayed the exchange in his mind, hoping to catch a whiff of a clue.

"Wait a minute," Werim spoke up, "so you're saying my sister is a foreigner?"

Thief and politician stared at the boy, their quarrel momentarily forgotten.

"But we were born here, in Kokamongo," he added.

"Which begs the question about the integrity of some among us," Sorn said. "Didn't you say you were sixteen? Sixteen years is a long time, even in a remote village."

"*Especially* in a remote village," Marcko amended with a sly smile. "It would seem we are not all as lawful as our station suggests, if one were but to refrain from holding the sins of the father against another, one might discover as much."

Sorn raised an eyebrow and Marcko stared back levelly. The tension deflated, replaced by some sort of tenuous truce. Werim's head spun. All of a sudden, life was a whole lot more complicated. Up until this point, he had simply been trying to find his father. Along the way, his sister had turned into a freak, and he had somehow gotten embroiled in a war, accompanied by a thief and a politician. Not to mention the strange bloodlust that had been plaguing him lately. Now, he found himself in the midst of some sort of philosophical argument where it was being suggested that he and his sister were foreigners. On top of it all he still hadn't answered the question of his purpose. *What's my part in all of this?*

"In any case, what is the plan upon arrival in Kinnsley, assuming we make a timely entrance?" Sorn asked.

Marcko shrugged. "I'm not sure we will. The gates may fall quickly. Even if we do warn them, there will not be sufficient help nearby. We would likely only be prolonging the inevitable."

"Then let them in," Werim said suddenly.

Both of the older men turned to regard Werim with puzzled expressions.

"To what end?" Sorn asked.

"You heard Warlord Vraika, Sorn. He instructed his Admiral to play at peace," Werim said.

"Yes, *after* taking the city."

Werim's eyes darted between his two companion's faces. It seemed so obvious. "So, let them have it. Even if we're late, there's bound to be a back door, right? We'll have no problem getting in." He inclined his head toward Sorn. "We tell them to open the gates and ask for"–he searched for the word–"parlay. Without a fight, there will be no bloodshed, plus under talks of peace they'd surely not cut off supplies or messengers. It will buy us time *and* serve to alert the capital."

Marcko was nodding. "Yes, yes. I know the Archon there. He'll listen to me. And peace talks would have to go through Tashaba and the Summit. They can begin pulling the army back, correcting my blunder."

"Surely you'll lose standing, Eclectic," Sorn pointed out.

The big man shrugged.

Werim shook his head. "The army doesn't matter. If the muses fight on the side of the Legion, we won't stand a chance. You said so yourself." When Marcko nodded, Werim continued. "So what if we free them first? Surely, they'll fight for us just as easily."

Sorn's eyes widened. "You're talking about raising a foreign muse army on Tasher soil. I thought you were supportive of the laws, what with all your talk of freaks and traitors. This goes quite a bit beyond petty theft."

"I know. But if Sharee is an illegal foreigner, then that means I am, too. I've already broken the law by existing. Might as well save the army the trouble and go straight to prison." Werim grinned.

Marcko was nodding again. "I like it. It has panache. Though we will probably all be tossed back into prison if we succeed, worse if we fail."

Sorn still wasn't sold on the idea. "What if we are too late, though? To the prison I mean. Surely, they've gained a significant lead on us by now. Won't we just be delivering ourselves into the hands of their Warlord?"

Werim shrugged. It was the best idea he could think of. Risky, sure, but a darned sight better than doing nothing and leaving his father to rot until spring. Who knew what the savages would do to the prisoners who didn't fight for them. *Or what if father does?*

"I don't think you should worry too much about that," Marcko announced confidently. "We have the advantage of coming by water. It will take them far longer to sludge through the swamp. Remember what I was saying about a proper road, son?" A jolly twinkle danced in his eyes. "The Summit specifically chose the location of the prison for its inconvenience. A boat is the only practical way of entry, and they haven't got any."

Sorn frowned. "How do you know that? Or what if they commandeer one along the way?"

Marcko's smile widened. "Barabans can't swim. They won't go anywhere near a boat." He chuckled, his massive belly shaking. "More wine?"

~ + ~

"Bud, wake up."

Sharee shook the snoring boy gently. Only the very first blushes of dawn were staining the undersides of the clouds, but Sharee was wide awake. Come to think of it, she'd not slept the night through at all recently. She glanced worriedly at the deep shadows that congregated beneath the trees.

"Wake up," she tried again.

Bud snorted, rolled over, but did not wake. He really did sleep like a lumberjack. Complete with the sounds of sawing logs.

Sharee sighed and went over to try her brother. "Wake up," she whispered with a gentle shake.

His eyes fluttered, but then he rolled away from her.

"Wake up," she tried again, a harder shake this time.

Werim groaned and swung at her sleepily before returning to stillness.

Sharee glanced over at the sleeping forms of Sorn and the Eclectic. She didn't really want to try the men. They probably wouldn't take her seriously. It was also likely that her sleep starved mind was simply playing tricks on her. She looked back at the trees. *But what if it's not?*

With a deep sigh, she closed her eyes and reached for her harp. There was no way she could wake Bud short of causing an explosion, but with her brother she had a different option. Striking a single note, she let it ring out and waited. Surely, his ears would "buzz" him awake.

True to her expectations, his eyes fluttered again, and he brought one hand up to lazily scratch at his ear. Sharee dropped the note, hoping not to scare her brother. Unfortunately, he simply settled back to sleep. Sharee started again, just a little louder this time. His hand shot back up. Sharee cocked her head and dropped the note. Werim's hand eased back to the grounds. *It's like playing with a puppet*, she thought, her curiosity distracting her.

After a moment, she started up again, only this time she tried to focus on his other ear. When the other hand came up, she couldn't help herself and a giggle slipped out. Slowly, she pulled the note back to the first ear. The hand followed. Choking on her laughter, she reached out to pull his hand back down. As fun as this was, she needed him to wake up.

The moment her hand touched his, the note shot up of its own accord. The suddenness of the crescendo scared Sharee, disrupting her focus. Instead of simply dropping off, the note bounced out of her control. It took a life of its own, rising in pitch and volume until it was almost a screech. Sharee's hands flew up to her ears, and her eyes squeezed shut as she struggled to sever the awful shriek in her mind. Abruptly, the sound dipped in volume, and then silence crashed back in as she drew back from both the harp and her brother. The morning was still again, except for an odd and unpleasant echo reverberating in her skull.

She opened her eyes to find Werim wide awake, both hands massaging his temples. "What the blazes was that, Sharee?" he hissed.

"I–I'm sorry," she stammered.

"Baker's bloody bread-basket. I told you not to buzz me while I'm sleeping. You just couldn't resist, could you?"

Sharee shook her head, still trying to clear it. "I swear I didn't. I mean, before. I did just now, but that was different. I didn't do it before though, and I wasn't trying to do anything bad. I was just trying to wake you up. Promise." She spread her arms.

Werim opened his mouth wide and stuck a finger into his ear. "What did you do anyway? I don't think I have any more cuts for you to mess with. And I'm not a leaf."

"I–I don't know what happened," Sharee admitted. "I was just trying to wake you up with a simple note, not any sort of song or anything like that. But it backfired."

"Backfired?" Werim fixed her with an angry gaze.

Here it comes, Sharee thought. It never did. Even as she prepared her defense, her brother's gaze softened.

"Well, whatever you did, can you please not do it again?" Werim asked with a sigh.

Sharee nodded, thankful.

"What are you two whispering about over here?"

The voice was Sorn's, and it was abnormally loud. She realized that she and Werim had been talking in hushed tones without realizing it. Even so, they'd apparently wakened the thief. Instead of annoyance, though, the look on his face was concern.

Werim rubbed his eyes. "Yeah, 'Ree, what did you wake me up for?"

Sharee looked around. She'd nearly forgotten. "The woods. I heard something moving around out there."

"Where?" Sorn asked.

Sharee pointed in the direction of the road nearby. "I thought maybe it was someone following us but wasn't sure. I didn't want to wake everyone for nothing."

"Probably just an animal," Werim said through a yawn.

She looked to the thief. Sorn didn't appear convinced by the simple explanation, but neither did he argue. Sharee frowned. "Sorry, I guess I'm just a little frazzled."

"It's all right," Sorn said. "While I harbor a healthy dubiety that a Legionnaire could have followed us, or even found this path, it doesn't hurt to be careful. Likely, we should depart anyway. I'll rouse the Eclectic."

Sorn drifted away. Sharee marveled at how silent he was, sliding around their small camp like a dark leaf riding a breeze. A snort nearby reminded her of Bud.

"I'll go and get the horse ready," Werim said quickly before slinking away.

Sharee looked over at the lumberjack, sawing away, and sighed.

◇ Chapter Twenty

"**D**a "Da men do be standin' ready."

Up high in a Landsha, Lugar Tyniente nodded toward the Captain and let his eyes sweep the field of battle. His fleet spread out before him. Giant, hulking beasts sprouted here and there. The great, bone-wrought riggings strapped to their backs looked not unlike the skeletons of the burned buildings they left in their wake. Large, thick masts of flame-darkened bone stuck straight up and were joined together by rope, suspending giant sheets of thin animal hide at angles to shade the men below. Boiled leather stretched across smaller areas, providing cover for the sidebowmen that would ascend the rigging to rain bolts on the enemy from strategic perches. Atop the highest point of the structures, just above the vulture's nest, the emblem of the Legion flew proudly, a white Landsha skull atop a pile of white bones on black background. Around each of the plodding beasts' six stout legs scurried a sea of men. Together, they rolled over the hills toward Kinnsley, a black cloud as numerous as the blades of grass they trampled beneath them.

A single spire pierced the sky above the great city, the giant bell at its apex strangely silent in the face of their approach. High stone walls greeted them, and even at this distance Lugar could tell they were poorly manned. What was worse, the city gates stood open. *At least the surrounding fields be properly drained of civilians.*

The Admiral frowned, and not for the first time. *There be no honor in this.* He had hoped to lead his historic fleet into glorious battle against a worthy foe. Instead, he felt like a thief in the night, sneaking in and slitting the throats of the unaware. *Where be their army?* Surely word of the great invading host had swept before them like grains of sand pushed by a mighty wind. Even a poorly patrolled nation should have noticed an uninvited army moving across its open plains. The mountain villages had been caught unaware, as expected, but this was different. There was nowhere to hide in the fields that surrounded the road they followed since leaving the foothills. His men did their best to pick off scouts, but Lugar Tyniente was no fool. Scouts *always* found a way of getting through, especially in their own land.

"Captain, be they launchin' any boats?" Lugar asked.

The man shook his head. "It be mighty strange, Admiral, but da city do be seemin' ta be waitin' fer us like a wench in a brothel."

Lugar nodded at the man and returned his attention to the open gate. *Strange indeed.* He had expected–anticipated even–a bloody battle. Or at least to find a flurry of boats aimed at escaping the soon-to-be-besieged city. Any scout that had seen them cross the bloody river–*Surely, they be postin' scouts at such a key crossing!*–would have witnessed firsthand the reticence of his men to trust even a stout span so long as the smothering blue lurked below it. Lugar had worried of mutiny with all the grumbling that had gone on. Fortunately, a few of his more worldly men had gone first, celebrating with rum on the other side as an example. The Admiral had been at a loss about how to contain any launched ships. Unless they happened to be carrying rum, that is. *Be there one thing to get a Baraban movin', it be the promise of rum.*

From his perch on the captain's deck of his Landsha, Lugar raised a looking glass to his eye. He looked down the tube, and the city gates sprang toward him. It almost appeared as if he stood right before them. The Admiral didn't always understand the things his engineers made, but he certainly appreciated them when they worked.

Disturbingly, there didn't seem to be any armed men in the entryway. Perhaps Lugar had expected to find them scrambling to get the heavy doors shut, but he was disappointed by a lack of activity. Instead, he saw a lone man on a pristine white horse ride forth, unarmed. Lugar felt his frown deepen. *What game be this?*

The Admiral slapped the looking glass against his other palm, collapsing the device, and shoved it back into his jacket. He descended a half dozen stairs to the main deck and approached one of the coils of rope lying on the bone planking. Winding the rope around his arm, he jumped from the side of the Landsha. The ground rushed up at him in a hurry. Before he crashed into it, however, the rope snapped tight. His descent slowed and curved into a smooth arc. At the bottom, when he had swung into the shadow of the great beast, he released the rope. The ground wasn't far, and he hit it running. Within a few steps, he was walking again. He heard thumps behind him as several of his men followed him, no doubt sensing his mood and itching for a fight.

He had walked halfway to the front when a messenger skidded to a stop before him, breathing hard.

"Catch your breath, boy," the Admiral ordered.

The young Legionnaire nodded, hands on his knees. He was bulky with fair hair, Lugar noted, and his sun darkened skin bore only a single mark on his left shoulder. It was the Mark of Conscription, a simple outline of a skull resting on a pile of bones. Among the bones was a darkened sun. *A Solestan conscript, then,* Lugar noted. There was always the occasional skirmish in the occupied lands, and the Baraban Legion was often called upon to deal with it, which resulted in a steady influx of conscripts. Lugar found himself wishing that his mission in these lands were as simple as that. They already had more conscripts than they could safely handle, and wenches in droves to send back to the brothels.

After a couple gulps of air, the messenger straightened and saluted. "Sir, they sent me from the front. A man be askin' for you by name."

Lugar raised an eyebrow. "Be he givin' his?"

"He said to be tellin' you that the Archon Base-uh-ah..." The man's brows knit together.

"Archon Basileus."

The conscript nodded. "Aye, that he do be havin' a message for you."

"And he came alone, unguarded?"

The man screwed up his eyes. "Yes, sir, how did you know?"

"I be havin' good eyes," Lugar replied.

He left the messenger digesting that. His guard followed respectfully behind him, shadowing him as he picked up his pace. Together, they walked between the ordered rows of men waiting for battle. As they passed, every eye was on Lugar. He could almost hear their question: *When do the fightin' begin?* His Legionnaires marched long and hard expecting a battle. Lugar had the sinking feeling that he was about to disappoint them. Ever aware of the effects of morale on his men, the Admiral took a mental inventory of the rum in the supply Landshas that followed them. He hoped the city had sufficient stores.

The man waited for him a good distance from the front ranks of men, well out of sidebow range. He stood next to his horse patiently, while two of Lugar's black-clad men waited beside him with blades drawn. The Admiral turned and instructed his guard to remain behind. It was bad enough that he was to meet a lone man with an entire fleet at his back. If Lugar didn't possess confidence in his own sword to protect him, he was unfit to lead and should retire to the boneyards along with the other beasts of burden that had given in to death's call. Or so he told himself.

So it was that the High Admiral of the Baraban Legion found himself walking alone to meet the Archon Basileus of the Tasher Nation as if they were simply two old men about to play a game of ivory towers in the middle of a field. When Lugar arrived, he returned the salute of his two men before sizing the newcomer up. As expected, the defining characteristic was *soft*. Lugar expected no less from the leader of such a lush land.

The Archon Basileus wore gaudy white robes trimmed in crimson that bulged around his ample waist. On his head was the traditional wide-brimmed hat that matched the trimming on his robes and was a symbol of his involvement with the Summit. A giant sapphire adorned one pudgy finger, nested in filigreed gold. The stone marked him as the political leader of the nation, his only equal being the Polemarch that commanded the armies. While the Polemarch was out among his men, the Archon Basileus normally remained in the capital, presiding over the Summit. Lugar would rather have been confronting the former.

"Salutations and greetings, High Admiral Tyniente," the fat man said, inclining his head as if between equals. "I am Eclectic Alexzandar, Archon Basileus of the Tasher Nation."

"Aye, I know who you be," Lugar replied. "What are you doin' out here all alone? 'Tis no place for a policitian."

Alexzandar chuckled, a response that appeared to set his whole body shaking. He casually reached one hand in his robe, but before he could pull it out, he found Baraban steel inches from his throat. Lugar's men didn't trust the politician, either.

"Oh, dear me," Alexzandar said, removing his hand anyway and evidencing a small fan. He splayed it out and waved at his face where sweat beads had begun to form despite the cool air.

Lugar gestured for his men to stand down. Even had he possessed the sharpest of knives stashed somewhere in that voluminous robe of his, Alexzandar would not have been able to cause the High Admiral any harm. Lugar wasn't even standing within striking distance. What was this man doing out here alone? He was certainly no warrior.

"Very good, High Admiral," Alexzandar nodded at him. "Your men display their loyalty. Color me jealous." His eyes had a hungry look as they swept over the two muscled guards. "Still, they need not worry. A man of my... physique should pose no threat to a renowned warrior such as yourself." He raised his pencil-thin eyebrows suggestively.

Lugar took the hint. "You two be goin' back and lettin' the men know to be ready. In no more than a moment, I be joinin' ya."

Both men struck fist to breast before stalking away.

After they had left, Alexzandar spread his arms wide. "A fine day, no?"

"What be your purpose here?" Lugar growled. He wasn't about to chat about the weather. "Speak quick. My *loyal* men do be itchin' to have a go at that city of yours."

"Unnecessary," the man replied, fanning himself again. "You may have noticed that our gates–as well as our stores and taverns, I might add–are open to you."

Lugar's eyes narrowed. "Where be your Polemarch? If we be havin' an accord, I'd rather be makin' it with him."

Alexzandar looked about him as if he expected the grass to answer. Then, he leaned in conspiratorially. "It seems our Polemarch was convinced of the imminence of an invasion. Silly, no? Taking the news to heart, he is off securing our borders, as befits his position. I tried to stop him, but he never listens to me." The man leaned back. "And will your Warlord be joining us soon? I'd rather hoped to meet the great Vraika, Right Hand of the Grand Warlord." He squinted back toward the fleet.

"Don't be expectin' him any time soon. He be havin' other plans," Lugar admitted. "Muses be muses, after all." He shrugged.

The big man fanned his face. "Well, hmm, well." For the first time, he appeared a bit disconcerted. "I was *supposed* to have met *him* here, and then escorted the Hand through to the capital. You and your men were to remain at Kinnsley, as honored guests, of course."

Lugar scratched his head. It made no sense. "It be seemin' to me that someone be holdin' of a parlay without my knowledge."

Alexzandar nodded. "Apologies Admiral." He closed his fan and tapped it twice. Then, he turned it on its side and dumped something small out of a hidden compartment. "Do you know what this is?"

He held up a small chain that might have fit around a more slender wrist. From the chain, a single ruby dangled, the size of a raven's egg, burning in the sunlight. Lugar had seen its like before. The Emissary, Bir Larse carried one. The Admiral wasn't quite sure how it worked, but apparently it allowed one to communicate directly with the Grand Warlord. Larse had referenced its use on many occasions. Lugar had never desired to learn more.

"Aye, 'tis a charm," he said noncommittally.

The Archon chuckled. "A test, then, is it? Surely you know that if I were to throw this into a fire, it would not melt. Indeed, it may even deign to speak with me, no?"

Lugar's face remained impassive. Perhaps that was how it worked, perhaps it wasn't. He couldn't say. Instead, he pressed, "And what be the charm sayin'?"

Alexzandar's face got serious. "Unfortunately, I believe the details are only meant for the Right Hand." He brought a hand up to scratch at his foremost chin. "I suppose I can tell you this much, however: A deal has been made."

The charm disappeared back inside of the Archon's fan before he continued. "It seems that I am in possession of something that the Grand Warlord desires, even as he," the Archon made a gesture at the fleet behind Lugar, "holds a dagger to my throat. In case you cannot tell by looking at me, my throat is one of several parts that I'm interested in retaining the use of. Thus, I asked him: 'Why take what is offered freely?' And so we find ourselves here today, on this field."

"Why not be havin' your Polemarch come and be layin' down his arms then?" Lugar asked. "I'm sure you'll be forgivin' me if I be findin' this all a bit murky."

Alexzandar laughed heartily. "It's not my *land* he wants, dear man. It is something else entirely. Truly, I was astonished as well. However, did you really think you were going to be able to hold all of this? How long do you suppose the Foles and Ilunati would stay their blades whilst an enemy nests between them? Had they any notion that I was allowing your people to... pass through unhindered, they would have met you here in force themselves. Keeping the free peace is a delicate task, I assure you. One that would require many more of the Grand Warlord's men than he has sent here. Or... a man of my talents."

Lugar had to admit, the sentiment mirrored his own doubt. Even when he was first assembling this command—large though it may seem when viewed through the lens of the Legion's history—it wasn't nearly enough to occupy a whole nation, especially one that sat between two other fierce enemies. They would likely be besieged from both sides, and that was simply a swift way to an early grave. Yet, what choice did he have but to follow the orders of his Warlord? He had hoped that Vraika was not such a puppet of the Grand Warlord that he would coldly throw his own people to the grinders. After the first leg of their march, it would be a lie to claim that his confidence was without cracks in the mortar.

"I may be an overindulged politician," Alexzandar continued, "but even I know enough about the art of war to see the truth: You were sent in as a thief, not a warrior."

Lugar removed the hand that had been resting on the hilt of his sword and straightened his own symbolic hat—black instead of red with three points as opposed to rounded—before letting the hand drop back to rest at his side. "Let's say I do be believin' you. On what dune does that be puttin' us?"

Alexzandar smiled. "Well, perhaps you'd like to amend your previous answer to my inquiry about the expected arrival of your esteemed Warlord?"

Lugar evidenced both hand, palms upturned, to go along with his frown. "Warlord Vraika only told me that he be comin' to Kinnsley in due time. Didn't say when."

The Archon's previous smile turned to match Lugar's expression. "Hopefully it won't be too long. I cannot promise to keep the army away forever, and there are many that wouldn't share my same sense of... diplomacy when it comes to dealings with the

Triumvirate." He turned and waved a flabby arm back toward the open city gate. "As it stands, I own what little guard Kinnsley has left, but I'm afraid there are many cracks in the city that a rat might slip through. I would appreciate it if you would lend me the use of your men to, ah, keep the peace."

Lugar raised an eyebrow. "How be your stores o' rum?"

Alexzandar's jowls were set back to shuddering again as the man chuckled. "Kinnsley is the axle that the trading wheel of my great nation spins 'round. I believe you'll find the stores plentiful."

"I be askin' about rum specifically. I be havin' many men that t'were hankerin' for a fight, savvy?"

"Of course, Admiral," he said soberly, and then smiled. "There's plenty of rum."

~ + ~

Destiny.

It is decided.

Doubt shall not be master. Vraika, Right Hand of the Grand Warlord, Sword of the Triumvirate, Warlord of the Baraban Legion will not be cowed by the mere idea of a man. He pats his sword. Steel will prove effective, as always. *And if not...* he glances at his bracer.

Aarik Velos does not exist. There is only Vraika. Vral is his father. The Grand Warlord has shown him the truth of The Blood.

The Fates are brotherless.

"Commander," Vraika bellows, sweeping the flap of his tent aside.

He steps out into a night peacefully asleep under the comfortable blanket of clouds. A chill wind blows through the camp. There are no lights. Vraika cannot guess the hour as the moon is obscured, but the stain of dawn has yet to bleed onto the bottoms of the dark skirts of the sky. It may yet be far off.

"Commander," Vraika bellows again.

Vraika strikes the gong in his head. Its vibration crashes through him. He swiftly pounds out a known cadence and a green film washes over his eyes. The night around him leaps into sharp relief. Dim shapes move around the outside of the camp, visible only because of his enhanced vision. They are the extra patrols that he'd ordered posted. Though expected, he is nevertheless pleased to find his command faithfully followed. His cloudy eyes track the men for a bit as they move soundlessly through the night, adhering to both vigil and duty.

Long grass undulates rhythmically around the camp. The clouds press lower, a colorless backdrop to the waving horizon. Another cold breeze sets tent walls flapping. Vraika suppresses a shiver as gooseflesh rises on his bare arms. Winter is only a state of mind. In his lands, there is only summer.

"Warlord?" his Commander asks sleepily from behind him.

Vraika whirls to find the man blinking bloodshot eyes, squinting at him in the near lightless night. The man's face is all angles, a block of stone set above a mountain of a man. He, too, is sleeveless, proudly displaying his earned markings. That is as it should be, despite the rebellious temperature of the air. The people, the land, the very weather is theirs to subdue.

"Sound the march, Commander," Vraika orders.

The man rubs at his head. "Now? My Lord, it is–"

Darkness seeps in among the green in Vraika's eyes as he claims the shard on his wrist. His sound amplifies, filling him near to bursting. The experience borders on pain, and in it Vraika exults. The power. The Blood.

The usurper shall fall, the Song has been sung.

The voice is not his own.

Destiny, Vraika answers forcefully.

The Fates' motif, the voice seems to agree.

Vraika nods his acceptance as the voice retreats from him. The Fates still lead him. He turns back to his Commander.

"It is what?" Vraika asks.

"Nothing, Warlord. As you command."

The man strides away. Several moments later, three sharp horn blasts are heard. Activity burns through the camp. Torches are lit, voices are raised. Tents begin to disappear. Vraika watches as his company prepares to move.

Once the commander returns to his side, Vraika hammers out the song for the Fog of War. Dark streaks coalesce in the air and begin to swirl, knitting together to form a wispy fabric that cloaks his men. Vraika aligns the strands in his eyes to threads of the fog, and the brief obscurity drops away, allowing him to see just as he did upon leaving his now-dismantled tent. The Warlord watches as his men pull on their goggles. Only a muse can see through the fog unaided, and none of these men are muses.

With another horn blast, the company is on the move. They trot along at a comfortable jog, the grass pushing around them like the sands of some great, green desert sea. Vraika's mind slides out of focus, lost in the song he plays for their concealment. The elite troop glides along, a dark cloud beneath dark clouds.

Nighttime hours pass as they move. Yet, they could be days for all that Vraika acknowledges. Eventually, the sun begins its initial assault on the sky. The land starts to slope downward beneath their feet. Mists gather at the bottom of the ravine below them. They almost seem to beckon, longing for the Baraban fog to add its own sinister wisps to the mass. Perhaps they hope that, in doing so, they will gain the strength to persist against the coming onslaught of daylight.

Vraika realizes a lost cause when he sees one. He brings his men up short of the malicious mists. A rushing sound fills the air. Together, they watch without mercy as the quickening sun thins the enemy brood. While the thick tendrils of their own black fog persist, these gray cousins are swiftly burned away. Beneath their concealing arms rushes the West Tasher River.

His men shuffle with unease. They part for their Warlord as he strides forward. They are all breathing heavily, though Vraika appears untouched by their long run. A side effect of the song in his blood.

He steps confidently to the very bank of the river and peers down. The smothering blue thunders by below him, pushed ruthlessly onward. Rocks bravely stand in the way, but in the end, only provide a harsh tune for the furious frothing to dance downstream.

Hesitant footsteps bring Vraika's head around. His Commander stands just beyond his shoulder, anxiety plainly written on the man's face. *Brave to stand so close*, the Warlord admits.

"Da smotherin' blue be quite fierce here, Warlord. Perhaps we need be travelin' to da North or South some," he suggests.

Vraika shakes his head. "No. Here will do."

"Lord...?" he trails off, afraid to question further.

That is as it should be.

"I am going to drop the fog," Vraika says. "Have the men keep their goggles on. The reason will become apparent in due time."

Confused, his Commander dutifully salutes. He casts one last tremulous look at the raging water and then steps quickly away to rejoin the men. Word will be spread.

Vraika takes a deep breath and stills his gongs. The fog retreats. It does not dissipate like the mists, chased off by the sun. Rather, it is as if the air itself inhales, sucking the dark threads into nonexistence.

Silence reigns for a moment as the Warlord collects himself. His men still shift from foot to foot, but goggles remain in place. Vraika turns back to the river and embraces the shard. The thunder of water seems louder somehow, but the voice of the shard is thankfully drowned. Focusing on the air before him, the Warlord begins to beat a rhythm, much more complicated than that of the fog, but not wholly dissimilar. His entire focus is held hostage by the task. The world drops away behind him. There is only the Song.

The first threads are inspired in pairs, one crossed with the other. For simplicity sake, Vraika does not play darkness. When finished, the goggles will render his work visible. There is no need for it to be seen outside of his men. As the Song quickens, Vraika carefully lays the threads close together. He infuses the melody with a bit of Knitting, joining the pairs together in a complicated chord. It cannot be seen yet, he must first finish the Movement.

The Warlord labors on the arrangement for an unknown amount of time. His hands wave in front of him, bobbing in time with the notes. The gestures get wilder, larger as he approaches the finale in a rush. Finally, with an ominous clang, he releases the Song, and it snaps into focus. His arms drop back to his side. The world explodes into view around him, and he can hear the men behind him gasp. Vraika breathes heavily. Gently, he plays a film back onto his eyes so he can see if the Song has worked as intended.

Indeed it has. Across the rushing river, seen only to Vraika and his men, spans a bridge. Its material is not wood or stone, but air. Colorless, yet not transparent. More substantial than a mist, it appears as a curved, ethereal surface extending to the far bank, radiant in the sunlight. There are no walls, no supports. Rarely has Vraika needed to plumb the depths of his ability so deeply, yet pride fills him as he gazes upon the beauty of the work. It will not last–only until the Song fades–but it will serve his purpose.

"Cross," he orders, and then turns to lead his men across.

Their Warlord is halfway before they follow. Yet follow they do, footfalls soundless as they traipse across the bridge. Vraika almost allows himself a smile as he sets foot on the other bank. *And they think a swamp will stop me.*

Destiny, it comes.

◊ Chapter Twenty-One

"How are we supposed to get in there?" Werim groaned. "The place is crawling with savages."

"Walls are stone, too," Bud added.

Both boys eased their heads back below the crest of the hill and turned to flop on their backs. Next to Werim, Sorn had some sort of metal contraption held up to his eyes and was swiveling his neck to look back the way they'd come. It wasn't clear what he hoped to see with the strange device, though the glass lenses at least appeared to allow sight through it. Upon closer inspection, they weren't completely unlike the Baraban spectacles that Werim still carried in his pack, quite a bit thicker though, and they had to be held up to one's eyes; there was no strap.

"There's always a back door," the thief mumbled, moving the device away from his face and easing down beside them.

He clapped Werim on the shoulder before working his way back down the hill. The boys followed, Werim wearing a deep scowl. His impatience was getting the better of him, he knew, but he couldn't help it.

Sharee and Marcko were waiting with the horse. The trees had given over to grassy plains a while back, and after leaving the relative concealment of the woods, they'd taken care to stay off the rolling hills, instead taking a winding route among the shallow valleys. Sorn had explained that it was necessary to avoid the eyes of enemy patrols. Werim wondered if there even were any. They'd found the great bridge spanning the East Tasher River deserted, and surely any army–be they friend or foe–would post a sentry there. Surely.

The bridge had been magnificent, the largest he'd ever seen. If Sorn hadn't been herding them across like cattle, Werim should have liked to stay and examine the structure. He and his sister had never been this far from home and, though he wished the reason for the trek were more cheerful, he didn't see a problem with taking advantage of the chance to see some of his birth nation. After all, it wasn't likely to ever be the same again, especially if they couldn't find a way to board a boat in Kinnsley. Who knew what their enemies would do to the land?

"It appears as if the garrison had no need of our warning. They must have capitulated without even so much as a fight," Sorn announced once they had returned to the group.

Marcko raised his eyebrows but said nothing.

"Those beasts of theirs are milling around in the surrounding fields like giant, evil goats," Werim said.

"If the goats had six legs and fortresses strapped to their backs, maybe," Bud amended.

"Whatever." Werim rolled his eyes. "Even if there is a back door, there's no way we'll be able to sneak around and find it. It's open field." He sighed.

"How easily you succumb to despair, young hero," Sorn said. "Ofttimes the tendrils of a city reach much further than its walls might indicate."

"And that means?" Werim asked.

"What of the boats?" Marcko wanted to know instead.

Sorn shrugged. "It appears that the port is yet full, which is the opposite of what I had expected. As for the gate and wall, the transition of power appears to have been peaceful. It is almost as if the Baraban were expected guests."

"I find it hard to believe that the local Archon would give over to an invading force without at least a token fight," Marcko said. "As I mentioned, I know the man, and even if he were facing overwhelming odds, he would not have simply gifted his city to the savages. Think what you will about politicians, but the vast majority of us appreciate our freedom foremost. Besides, Kinnsley boasts stout walls. Even an inept commander could hold off a siege for a month, at least. Certainly long enough to send word to the capital by boat."

"Futhermore, it would decrease one's bargaining power to surrender so easily," Sorn said. "Come to the table after several weeks of siege. Let them think you mean to hold out until you secure the most favorable of terms."

Marcko cast the thief an appreciative nod.

"So, what do we do?" Sharee asked.

Werim turned to regard his sister. For a moment, he was struck by how alien she appeared. Though she still wore the tattered green dress she'd had on when they'd set out from Kokamongo, underneath it, she had added some tight-fitting brown pants from her things. With the nights turning colder, Marcko had given her a dark green cloak fished from the packs of his horse. It was quite big for her; its ends reached all the way down to her scuffed leather boots. The hood was thrown back just now, but had it been up, it would have swallowed her face in shadow. Her auburn hair had bits of the forest still clinging to it. She'd pulled it out of her face by twisting strands in the front and tying them around back with a bit of cloth. It was the first time Werim had ever seen her willingly wear anything in her hair. One hand held her strung bow with confidence, and the quiver peaking over her shoulder bristled with arrows. Her face was dirty, but her green eyes sparkled.

In short, she looked nothing at all like the timid girl he'd grown up with. Before him was an unknown warrior princess of the wood straight out of a child's tale. *Probably comes with being a muse*, Werim reasoned. He wondered absently if he looked any different.

"We steal a boat," Bud said, answering her.

Werim chuckled. Bud was still Bud. He was dirtier than normal with the stubble on his face starting to fill in, but the blond boy remained unchanged.

Werim fingered the sword hilt at his waist. "It wouldn't be stealing so much as liberating."

Sorn chuckled. "You sound like a politician."

"I would have used *repossessing*," Marcko noted.

Werim scowled. "I still haven't heard anyone explain how we're going to get past all those men." He paused for a moment, thinking. "Maybe if we set one of those big beasts on fire, we could cause enough of a distraction that we could run by. A muse can do that, right?" He looked to his sister.

Sharee shook her head, but it was Sorn who responded. "A bit ambitious, don't you think? Why risk a confrontation when I've already devised an alternative route?"

"But they're surrounding the *entire* city" Werim said. "Unless you can fly, there's no way in, doesn't matter what your route."

Sorn looked expectant.

"Can muses fly?" Bud asked.

Sharee sighed loudly. "What is your alternate route, Master Voleur?" She cast each of the boys an exasperated glance. "It's not going to hurt to see it," she said to her brother.

"Thought you'd never ask." Sorn flashed a smile. "Follow me."

The thief crept off on silent feet. Marcko grabbed the reins of the horse before joining him. Bud motioned Sharee forward. She smiled as if the blond boy had just told a particularly funny joke. Werim raised an eyebrow at his friend before trotting after his sister. He decided he didn't want to know.

"You sure you can't set one of those things on fire?" he asked.

"Or fly?" She giggled. "I doubt it."

"But how do you know?"

Sharee shrugged. "I guess I don't. It could be that I can. Somehow. I just don't know the Songs for those things."

Werim's brows pinched together. "How'd you learn the... Songs that you do know?"

"Well, one I learned before we left the village. The rest I guess I just sort of figured out." She cast a sideways look at her brother. "Why all the interest anyway? Am I no longer a freak?"

Werim held up his hands. "Whoa, now. I never said that."

Sharee narrowed her eyes. A smile broke out across her brother's face. She punched him in the arm.

"Ow," he cried, rubbing the spot.

They walked in silence for a while, watching as the sun sped toward the distant horizon. The sky was swiftly reddening, and the grass around them seemed to be waving good night. Fortunately, the wind was light and the clouds relatively sparse. It did not seem ready to snow yet, though Werim imagined winter was in full swing back home.

"Do you think she's watching?" Sharee asked.

Werim knew what she meant, but he wasn't quite sure how to answer. It wasn't the first time that he wished their father were here. He cast a worried look at his sister, but she had become very interested in her boots.

It was in that moment that Werim saw her for what she was again: his sister. Not a warrior princess or a dirty vagabond, but a frightened girl from a small village. *His* village. *His* sister. Sharee could be the only family that he had left. Werim hated to pay any heed to the worry, but he could not deny it was there. There were no promises where they were going. As much as he wanted to believe Marcko that their father was alive, it was still a prison. A prison about to be attacked by a powerful muse. Werim needed to be strong. For his father. For his mother. For Sharee.

"She'd be proud of you, you know," Werim said. "Of the Songs and stuff."

To his surprise, Sharee took a step closer and hugged him. Even more surprising, he let her. Out here, where *anyone* could see.

"Thanks Wer," she mumbled.

He rubbed her shoulder with his hand. "You're the only sister I have," he said. "Even if you are a freak."

She pulled away and smiled. After a moment, she cocked her head toward the front of their party. "Where do you suppose he's taking us?"

Werim shrugged. "I'll go ask."

"Nicely," Sharee cautioned.

Werim rolled his eyes, but nodded. Then, he trotted up to Sorn. He was still phrasing the words in his mind when they were suddenly forgotten.

As they rounded another low hill, Werim saw that they were nearing the shoreline of Tasha Lake. The great lake had been a constant companion since they'd left the trees along the thieves' road. At first, it had just been a shimmering speck on the horizon, but as they'd gotten closer to Kinnsley, it had swelled quickly as if anxious to boast of its size. Besides the mountain streams, Werim had only ever seen ponds. This was the closest they'd been yet to a proper body of water, and Werim found his eyes drawn inexorably off to the horizon.

The dying rays of the sun bathed the tips of small waves in gold, mirroring their fluffier friends in the sky. Werim's eyes followed along the razor's edge of the meeting of sky and water until the boundary grew jagged. The coast cupped the lake, curving back to where they were standing. Relatively nearby, shadowy turrets thrust up into the gathering gloom, torches winking to life along their tops like fireflies in the tops of big, stone trees.

Werim noticed that they had moved from the northeast side of the city to the northwest. The entire western side of the city was dominated by the dock, with the tall walls to the north and south running right out to shore like man-made cliffs. Lookouts were posted in the turrets, seen now and then in silhouette before a torch. Werim wasn't sure what Sorn hoped to gain by leading them toward the water, though he still appreciated the view.

Interestingly, the span of open land between them and the walls was clear of Baraban men; they all were camped on the sides furthest from the water. Perhaps that was the gain, though a beach approach would still likely elicit a shout from the men atop the walls before they were even a stone's throw away. Werim was willing to bet that, should a cry go up, men both on horse and foot would follow quickly. Though they were less likely to stumble on a patrol here, their situation did not seem much improved if their goal remained the penetration of the imposing walls.

Werim noticed that Sorn's attention, rather than on the wall, was focused in the exact opposite direction along the beach.

"There," Sorn said, pointing.

Werim followed the finger to a small inlet a short distance away, just off the coast. A few trees crowded around the cove. Water ran out at a steady rate down a narrow channel to join with the lake, carving deeply into the sand to expose the rock beneath.

"Do you suppose there's a boat hidden in there?" Marcko asked. "Maybe he means us to row in under the cover of darkness?"

Werim pointed back toward the towers. "We'll have to make use of Sharee's bow and take those guards out."

"Would have to be a small boat to fit down that channel," Bud added. "Doubt it could fit all of us."

Werim turned to regard his friend. "There could be more than one boat."

Sorn shook his head. "Come on, hero." He started toward the copse of trees.

"What about the men on the wall?" Sharee whispered. "Won't they see us? There isn't very much to hide us once we're out from behind the hills."

Sorn turned around. "You're right." He held a finger up along his nose, and then replied, "Approach with stealth and haste.

We will be somewhat vulnerable until we arrive at the shelter of the cove."

"That's it?" Werim asked.

Sorn shrugged. "I'm counting on them being lazy... or drunk." He turned to Marcko. "Perhaps it would be best if I ferry the horse. Do you mind?"

The portly politician chuckled and handed the thief the reigns. "You'll have a far easier time of it than I will, I'm sure. While I can handle the stealth, the haste may have me tripping over my own feet."

Sorn inclined his head with a grin and then was off, gliding over the beach toward the cove. Werim had to admit, he admired the delicacy with which the man moved. Even the horse seemed to stir up fewer grains of sand simply by virtue of being near the thief. It was only a few short moments before Sorn's elongated shadow merged with that of the thin trees. No cry of alarm went up.

Werim released a breath he hadn't realized he'd been holding. Echoed sighing around him proved his was in good company. The remaining four passed trepid looks among each other and then back at the trees. None of them wanted to go next. *It's up to me, then.* Werim eyed the trees with determination. In a slow, steady movement, he drew his sword.

"What do you need that for?" Sharee hissed.

Werim turned to regard her. *What* do *I need it for?* His mind groped for an answer.

"Didn't want it to clank," Bud replied for him.

The blond boy nodded at him, pulling his own blade over his shoulder. Werim turned and passed the nod along to his sister. She parried with suspicious eyes. Before she could so much as open her mouth, Werim turned and fled.

The sheltering hill fell away, exposing him to the full glare of the city. Tall dune grass surrendered to beach soon thereafter, and Werim discovered something about sand that wasn't shared by the more familiar dirt or rock. It did not hold well underfoot.

With each step further away from safety and toward the cove, it felt as if the soft earth was plotting against him, pulling at his boots, desperately trying to hold him in place so that he would be noticed. Once, he nearly pitched forward, shooting up a spray of fine particles behind him. Reflex required him to drop his sword, so that he had to stop, turn, retrieve it, and then continue on his frenzied dash.

Was it really this far away? It hadn't appeared so far from the safe arms of the hill. Werim refused to turn and look back. Surely, Bud and Sharee were having quite the laugh at his expense as he stumbled along the beach.

Sorn was waiting for him just inside the trees. With a strong arm, he pulled Werim up the last small slope of sand and onto far more stable ground. *Rock! Blessed rock.* He hardly even noticed the heroic effort Sorn was expending to suppress laughter. Between the fire in his chest and the matching blaze in his legs, he simply didn't care. He had made it.

He was still gasping, hands on his knees, when Sorn pushed him aside. The thief leaned out again and this time came back with Sharee on his arm. Apparently she'd been right on her brother's heels. Werim righted himself and turned to accept the bow she offerred. Thus relieved, Sharee bent over and tried to steady her breathing. Still, there was no cry of alarm.

Both Werim and Sharee had caught their breath by the time the last two members of their party crashed up the slope. Bud was bringing up the rear–literally–pushing Marcko from behind even as Sorn pulled. Once the barrier of the trees had been broken, the three of them collapsed in a heap.

"Sand... tripped me. Reached right... up... strong arms," Marcko said between gulps of air.

"I thought we were going to be seen when you tripped halfway here," Bud admitted to Marcko.

"Pulled... me up. Thank... you."

"Strong boy," Sorn laughed.

When they'd all recovered–or, in Marcko's case, could at least stand–Sorn led them deeper into the cove. The foliage quickly yielded to bare rock, but instead of a pond or spring in the middle, Werim was surprised to discover a cave. Even more baffling, the cave that yawned on the face of the rocky ledge didn't appear natural. It looked more like someone had used the rock purposefully to hold the sands at bay with squared off ridges sheltering the opening. On either side, intricate columns were fashioned as if they'd been shoved in to hold up the cliff. A closer inspection revealed that they were, indeed, made of the very same rock.

A steady stream of water ran down a channel that cut the dark entryway in half. The rivulet was neatly squared as well, further evidence of unnatural origins. It reminded Werim of the irrigation trenches that the villagers fashioned back home in order to water the vines during drier days. Wood was usually employed in that case, however.

"What is this?" Werim asked.

"Our back door." Sorn smiled.

As they neared it, an offensive odor wafted out to assault Werim's nose. He shoved his sword back into his belt and reached up to wave the smell away. Around him, his companions were displaying similar reactions. Except for Sorn, who was smiling even wider.

"Yuck," Sharee moaned. "What is that smell?"

"That would be the sewers," Marcko explained. He turned to Sorn, "However did you find it?"

"Followed my nose, of course." He chuckled.

Bud frowned. "He saw it with those spectacles of his."

"Well, I saw the trees anyway," Sorn admitted. "It was merely a lucky guess as to why they might congregate in this particular locale of the sandy beach."

"But how did this all get here?" Werim asked. "Did people from the city make this?"

Sorn shrugged.

"The Traditionalists would have you believe the wind had carved these pillars and shaped the trench," Marcko said. "Historians might offer another explanation."

"A muse?" Sharee suggested.

"Just so, my dear." Marcko nodded. "There was a time when our nation's relationship with muses was more amicable. Their songs can be used for much more than war."

"An interesting thought, Eclectic," Sorn said. "Muses as civil servants? To whom does the creation then belong?"

Marcko held up a finger. "There was a book I read—restricted, of course—it indicated that muses were limited by what already exists; they cannot create something from nothing. Or, more existentially, they simply inspire something to happen that might have happened anyway. It is not conjuration in the purest sense."

"So the claim of ownership might be pre-existing, or at least not pursuant to any interaction with a muse," Sorn concluded.

"Precisely," Marcko nodded. "It really is a moot point anyway, as the laws following the Silent Summit have dictated for centuries that—"

"Guys," Werim interrupted. "Can you discuss this later?"

Marcko shrugged. "I suppose history is not going anywhere."

"So, um, we have to go in there?" Sharee asked, wrinkling her nose.

"You get used to the smell," Sorn said.

"Perhaps *you* do," Marcko mumbled.

"The horse will not fit," Bud spoke up from behind.

Sorn turned. "Ah, yes. I had almost forgotten. I am sorry, Eclectic, but it seems we must leave behind your loyal steed. Please tether him to a nearby tree."

"But won't he starve?" Sharee asked.

Marcko waved a hand. "He'll bite through the reigns long before that happens. Always was a nippy old nag. Let me just take a few things from the packs."

The big man went over and began rummaging through his saddlebags. He took some things from one and put it into another. Then, he took things from that bag and put them back into the first. To Werim, it didn't seem like the Eclectic was getting anywhere, so he took the opportunity to move away from the smelly cave and back toward the trees. Casting an appraising look back over his shoulder, he decided to chase a clever idea.

Approaching one of the thin trees, he pulled out his sword. He proceeded to hack at a low hanging branch until he'd separated it from the trunk. Picking up the wood, he began to methodically go about removing the smaller offshoots.

"What are you doing?"

Of course it was Sharee.

"I'm not hurting it," he held up his hands. Then, looking back at the mangled trunk he amended, "Much."

His sister giggled. "That's sweet, Wer, but trees don't really have feelings. Not in the way you or I do. At least, not that I can figure out."

"I just thought..." he started awkwardly, and then shrugged. "Torches. I figured we might be able to make a few torches. Perhaps the Eclectic has some cloth he's looking to get rid of that will help. Or maybe Sorn has some stuff in that coat of his."

Sharee held out her hand. "Here. Let me."

Werim handed over the branch and stepped back. Expecting the buzz, he was not as startled when she began to work on the wood. In fact, as he watched the extra growth fall away smoothly, he decided that it was more of a hum and not as unpleasant as he'd first believed. It reminded him a bit of his mother, truth-be-told, and he found himself eerily fixated on the workings. When Sharee had finished and was handing him one of several arm-length, sturdy sticks, Werim was surprised to find himself almost wishing she hadn't stopped.

"Thanks," he said.

His sister smiled, and they turned back to the group. Marcko had hefted a few bags and was tucking the others alongside the cave. The unladen horse was munching away at some scrub grass further down from the cave.

"Marcko, do you have some scraps of cloth we could use to make a torch or two?" Werim asked.

"Torches?" Sorn replied, alarmed.

Werim nodded. "It is rather dark in there."

Suddenly, he had a glowstick in each hand. He shook them, and there was a sharp cracking noise. Orange light bloomed within each device. "Trust me, fire of any kind is a bad idea in a sewer," he said.

The thief handed one of the strange devices to Bud and then turned toward the cave.

"Why'd you give it to him?" Werim asked.

Sorn didn't turn. "Sir Wil always remits himself to rearguard. It is one of his many noble qualities that I admire." And then he was striding away.

Sharee giggled–a nasal sound considering she was pinching her nose–and ducked into the darkness to follow Sorn. Marcko was next as the thief's orange light bobbed away. Werim stood puzzled.

"Wait," he called. "Who's Sir Wil?"

The laughter echoing off the stone walls was his only answer.

"Come on, Lua" Bud said, putting an arm around his friend's shoulder. "We can't all be as clever as the thief."

◇ Chapter Twenty-Two

Sharee couldn't have said how long they'd been walking. It felt like ages since they'd turned a corner and lost sight of the entrance behind them. Likely the sky was still dimming outside of the tunnel, but being underground did strange things to you, Sharee noticed. Time and the outside world felt far away, less real. Deep in the rock, the most pressing matter was the weight of the walls above. If they had much further to go, she thought they might be crushed. Not that the construction was unsound–as far as she could tell–rather that the very air seemed compacted, suffocating. Not to mention stinky.

The orange glow of Sorn's stick ahead of her did little to help. It only provided an eerie ambiance to the smooth, featureless walls. *Has this passage been carved through solid stone?* Sharee wondered idly what folly might cause someone, even a muse, to do such a thing. Surely rock was harder to manipulate than even the hardest wood.

Murky water gurgled slowly down the trench in the middle, harmonizing with the awkward silence. Sharee had tried speaking to the other members of the party, but the echo set her teeth on edge. Every now and then she heard a deeper rumble from behind that led her to believe Bud and Werim were chatting in low voices. Despite her desire to drop back and be nearer to them, she didn't dare try to dance around Marcko's bulk. The ledge was narrow, and she certainly wasn't going to dip her feet in the disgusting water.

Many steps ago, she'd dropped her hand from her nose. It had started with a few tentative sniffs, but Sorn was right: the stench mellowed after prolonged exposure. If nothing else, she needed the added air through her nose in order keep her breathing steady. Sorn was setting an aggressive pace. The sound of Marcko rasping behind her bounced off the walls, layering a steady hiss over the sound of their footfalls. Sharee pushed down a vision of snakes rising out of the trench behind her and flicking their tongues at her ankles.

She walked a little faster.

In her head, she tried to find the harp. Like the time in the tree, however, it was being elusive. The fact that she hadn't slept well in a few nights probably had something to do with that. As did the concerns currently bouncing around in her mind.

She'd heard enough of Werim's plan to know that the invaders weren't supposed to be in the city yet. They were to have remained outside while peace was brokered, or at least the capital warned. The idea was to stall, not invite them in with open arms. *Why were the savages inside, then?* It didn't make sense. Surely, her countrymen wouldn't have simply left the gates open to anyone. Especially *them*.

What if the marked men had laid some sort of trap? It was a silly thought; who could even know they were coming? Why would Baraban and Tasher work together? The doubts rattled round and round in her skull, creating a cacophony that Sharee desperately wished she could silence.

Even as she was contemplating a second, renewed fight against the echoes in the form of a frustrated scream, she was plunged into darkness. Fear leapt up and clutched at her heart. She clawed against a crescendo of panic. Her eyes widened until she felt sure her lids had been pressed to the bones of her face like unwanted sheets against the wall on a hot night. She didn't dare take another step.

When Sorn's face appeared next to her, bathed in orange light that was partially shielded by a fist, she couldn't help it; she yelped. Quickly, she clapped a hand over her mouth, but the damage was done. Everyone had heard the melody of her cowardice.

To the thief's credit, he didn't laugh at her. He almost appeared apologetic. "There's an exit in the ceiling just there." He pointed. "The flicker of a torch illumined it for but the briefest of moments."

By now, the rest of their party was catching up. Bud's untended stick revealed them all clustered uncomfortably on the ledge, looking questioningly at Sorn. He motioned for Bud to cover his light, and the blond boy complied.

"We will be taking our leave of this corridor soon, and I'm afraid a patrol may be in the vicinity," Sorn explained.

"What is our plan of attack?" Werim asked.

In the muted light, Sharee regarded her brother with an odd look. *Why is it always a fight with him?*

"Patience," Sorn replied. "We need not engage them if we are clever."

"We don't?"

Sharee thought Werim could have done a better job of hiding his disappointment.

"They are not expecting visitors from below. Provided we slither out whilst their backs are turned, we should experience nary an encounter."

"And if they're facing us?" Bud asked.

"Patrols patrol, my dear boy," Marcko responded. "Our friendly thief has the right of it. We need only be patient and observe the path they tread."

With that, they crept ahead. It was a bit more treacherous with the sticks hooded, so they all stayed within touching distance of the person in front of them. Sharee could just barely make out her feet in the gloom and, from time to time, felt Marcko tug at her cloak from behind. She hoped that the big man didn't lose his footing. If he did, it was likely she'd join him on a bone-breaking fall into the murky water.

Sharee pushed the worry from her mind and tried to focus on emulating Sorn's stealthy movements. The thief hovered before her, seeming to glide forward as they followed the curve of the wall to their right. Sharee was trailing a hand along the stone for balance as much as direction, when suddenly it fell away. One minute there was cold solidity beneath her fingers, and the next empty air.

Sorn abruptly ducked into the crevasse, completely extinguishing his light. Sharee's hand shot out and clutched fearfully at his jacket. She felt a heavier tug on her own back. Thankfully, the thief didn't jerk away or hack off her arms with those knives of his. *Not that he would do such a thing*, she reminded herself. *He has been nothing but helpful.*

Chained together, they completed the abrupt turn into a small notch, deep enough to just barely hold them all. Bud hid his stick away as soon as he realized Sorn's was out, and then they all stood in the pitch black, breathing heavily. Sharee fought again against a rising panic. This time she was aided by the nearness of the others. At least she could feel where everyone was.

Sandwiched between Marcko and Sorn, Sharee felt like a shrub among trees. She craned her neck back, taking a deep breath of air. It was then that she noticed a slightly lighter patch of color among the black, high above where they stood. She could not have jumped to touch it, but if she climbed up Sorn's back, she might be able to reach it.

It took a long moment of staring for her to realize that she was seeing the night sky. A few stars twinkled in the limited sampling, and a fresh air breathed down on them. The cool draft sent a shiver down her spine. It also threatened to reawaken her deadened sense of smell. Sharee fought the urge to plug her nose again.

As she was staring, the flicker of a torch passed by. From her vantage point, it was not much more than a brief glow that warmed the stone edges of the rectangular opening. She wondered how Sorn had even noticed it.

"All right, give me a bit of space, darling," Sorn whispered.

"Where are you going?" Sharee asked.

"Up. Wait here until I complete my reconnaissance."

"Your what?" she hissed back, but he had already turned and did not answer.

She squashed back into the bulk of Marcko as the thief began to scale the wall. *How is he doing that?* With her eyes adjusting to the thin light, Sharee found that she could now just barely make out his form as it ascended. Soon, his boots were above her head, and she could spread out again. She stepped forward and felt the stone. Deep notches had been carved, perfect for foot- and hand-holds.

At the top, Sorn stopped and poked his head out. After a few seconds, he lifted himself up and over the lip, disappearing into the night. Sharee waited with everyone else, trying to keep her breathing as quiet as possible.

She counted out a dozen Folish kittens. The darkness was cloying, the stench trying to reassert itself. She shifted the weight of her quiver and counted a dozen more kittens. *What is he doing up there?* It was taking an awfully long time. Finally, her impatience got the better of her and she started up the wall. She would just have a quick look. Make sure he was all right.

"What are you doing, 'Ree?" Werim hissed.

Halfway up, she turned to answer. "I'm just going to make sure he doesn't need any help."

"Wait... I'm coming too."

She heard rustling and grunting below. It sounded like Werim was trying to squeeze around Marcko in the narrow notch. Muffled cursing soon followed. Apparently, it wasn't going very well. Sharee shrugged and continued up.

The fresh air tasted *so* good. It had begun to feel like her tongue was coated with decaying moss. She resisted the urge to spit as she peeked over the rim.

A cobblestone courtyard spread out before her, hemmed in by high stone walls. She was surprised to note that she was not at ground level. Instead, the stone shaft poked out of the ground. It reminded Sharee of a well, though it lacked any wooden structure to assist with lowering a bucket. Also, there was no water below. None that anyone would want to retrieve anyway.

A full stone's throw on the other side of the plaza was a large, blockish building. The entrance was lit by a single torch that bled light out into the courtyard. The hulking structure appeared to have several levels, and darkened windows riddled the front face. Sharee thought it might be an inn, but even the occupied inn in Knucklesporte had displayed a colorful sign out front accompanied by the sounds of a tavern within. This building was silent and unadorned.

To her immediate right was a wooden gate set deep in the stone wall. Fortunately, the gate was raised so that only the sharpened bottoms were visible within the wide archway. On the other side of the gate, there appeared to be another torch, as warm light spilled back through, illuminating the short corridor. Two long shadows flickered with the flame; a pair of men stood guard. Sharee could just barely note the rumble of their low voices. Sorn was nowhere to be seen.

A path of worn stones ran directly from the gate to the building, evidencing heavy traffic. *Perhaps he went to see what the building is for.* She pulled herself up, pushing down with her arms and swinging her legs over the side of the stones. Dropping lightly to the ground, she smiled at how little noise she had made. Juggling an unstrung bow, a quiver, and a pack on her hip was no easy task, but she marveled at how she was growing used to the gear.

"Get down."

Suddenly, Sorn was behind her. *Where had he come from?* His hand pressed gently, but firmly on her head and pushed her into a crouch behind the well. A scant moment later, an orange glow licked the inside of the walls and the metallic clink of armor echoed around the courtyard as a group of men entered through the gate. She counted four shadows as they clanked by, talking amongst themselves.

"I don't like it," one was saying. "I don't like it at all."

"They should not have been allowed in," another agreed. "The Polemarch won't stand for it when he hears. I've heard whispers of what those savages have done to the north, and we're sheltering them!"

A third voice broke in. "But did you see the size of their army? They outnumber us five to one, easily. I, for one, am thankful that we're trying diplomacy before swords."

The men stopped just beyond the well. Sharee felt her heart hammering away. *What if we're discovered?*

"Why doesn't our Archon request the army?" It was the first again.

"Alexzandar has him locked up, that's why. He's in league with the savages, I tell you."

"Quiet! What if you are heard? You will be discharged from the guard or worse."

A long silence stretched out, and Sharee could almost see the men looking around nervously. With a huff, they started walking again, heading further away.

"Why the hell would he do that anyway?" they started again.

The reply was lost in echoes. Sharee glanced at Sorn and saw that he was slowly rising to look over the top of the well. He had his kama in hand, but the danger appeared to have passed. Sharee figured it was safe, then, and poked her head up as well, just in time to see the last of the four men enter the squat building on the far side of the courtyard. Sorn pushed her back down. After a few seconds more, he joined her.

"I thought I instructed you to wait," Sorn whispered.

Sharee shrugged. She was saved from explaining by the sounds of commotion that bubbled up out of the well. When Sorn stood, she followed suit. They both peered down into the darkness. Marcko froze halfway up the wall with a guilty look on his face. He kicked and shushed the two boys that were apparently forcing him up from below.

"It seems the patience of the children has worn out," Marcko explained. "Is it safe to come up?"

"It is. But please do so quietly," Sorn replied. "We have entered the den of the lion."

When the rest of the party had exited the shaft, they paused for a few moments to consider their next step. Marcko was seated, leaned heavily against the well with Bud nearby. Werim peaked around the corner, surveying the entryway. At a suggestion from Sorn, Sharee strung her bow.

"Where are we?" Bud asked.

"The barracks," Marcko replied, "where the city guard is housed."

Werim returned, pointing back toward the wall. "They're not patrolling."

Sorn scowled. "The last of the watch returned just before you ascended. We should be safe in the courtyard for a time. There are two guards outside of the entrance, and it seems to be the only break in the wall."

"How will we get by them?" Bud asked.

"With steel, that's how," Werim replied. He had drawn his sword.

"*Werim*," Sharee whispered. "They're not bad men. They're just doing their jobs."

Werim shrugged.

"I believe I can propose an alternative solution," Sorn said.

He fished around in his long jacket and produced a small vial. His other hand darted back into a pocket and returned with a couple bits of cloth. He gave one small square to Sharee and kept the other.

"In a moment, I shall place a few drops of this liquid onto the cloth. Be sure to keep it well away from your nose." He removed the cork from the vial. Sharee was holding the cloth out, looking a bit fearful. "Keep it righted... thus." He turned her palm upward and spread out the square. "Ah, there we are."

"What does it do?" Sharee asked.

"One smell of this concoction, and they will drop like a satchel of stones." He repeated the procedure with his own cloth, dripped liquid onto both, and then stoppered the vial. It disappeared back into the jacket. "Simply follow me in. We shall endeavor to creep up behind the fellows–I'll take the far one–and then–"

"Wait, why does she get to go?" Werim asked.

Sharee scowled at her brother and opened her mouth.

"She's the lightest on her feet, that's why," Sorn answered with a hint of annoyance.

Sharee's tart reply died in her throat. Her hastily prepared remark would definitely have accused Werim of "thinking with his sword" and perhaps elaborated on her sharper mind. Instead, she found herself unprepared for the compliment and felt her face redden.

"Now," Sorn said, "let us proceed before the drops do dry and thus provoke a reapplication. Just press the moisture to the guard's face. Gently, mind you. No reason to break a nose."

Nodding, Sharee followed the thief forward. They crept along the outer wall until they reached the entryway. Torchlight spilled just beyond, and here Sorn paused a moment in the last of the cloaking darkness. He poked his head around the corner and then turned back to Sharee. He pointed once to her and then to the near wall, signaling with his hands that her target was just around the corner. Then, he pantomimed a three count, and dashed off.

Sharee thought she'd been prepared, but the moment the thief left in a blur, her heart leaped into action. It beat frenziedly against her chest like a vast multitude of acorns flung repeatedly against a wooden board. Yet, for all the activity in her breast, her feet remained rooted.

I can't fail in front of Werim and Bud, she thought. She looked back to see their faces huddled around the edge of the well, barely discernable in the gloom. Gritting her teeth, she forced one foot out into the light.

Once around the corner, movement became easier. It was as if the warm glow of the torch had thawed her previously frozen limbs. Sorn was nearly to his man, gliding along like a shadow that had detached itself from the fabric of the night. Sharee's man was just a few steps away. As she watched, he shifted his weight from one foot to the other, facing forward with the stature of a man bored to the verge of sleep.

Sharee stepped up lightly. She cast a quick glance at Sorn. The thief had his own cloth at the ready, and caught her eye with a nod. Sharee turned back around, slowly bringing her hands up.

He was a bit taller than she'd expected. When she'd extended herself all the way up, she realized for the first time that it was going to be no easy task to wrap her arms around from behind and press the cloth against the guard's nose. It wouldn't be a problem for Sorn, but Sharee wasn't as tall as the lanky thief. She bit her lip.

There was no time to consider other options. A muffled sound to Sharee's left snagged her attention. Sorn was cradling the limp form of the guard and laying him slowly to the ground. It was almost noiseless. She looked back at her target.

Almost wasn't enough in this case. The guard had turned as well. Sharee could see the man's face as he processed the scene before him. It was as if he'd woken from a particularly pleasant dream to find himself in the reality of a nightmare. His hand strayed toward his sword.

Sharee did the first thing that came to her mind. She jumped. Her legs wrapped around the man's midsection, and her arms flew up around his neck. It was just like she'd done before to

Werim when they were playing at home, except instead of covering his eyes, she threw her hands across his nose.

For a split second, danger had been averted. The night was silent. The guard's hand dropped uselessly to his side. And then she was falling.

The guard toppled like a tree. He hit the stones with an awful cacophony. The wind whooshed out of Sharee, and stars danced before her eyes. For a moment she worried that she'd killed the man, but beneath her, the armored chest rose with a shudder.

When Sharee was able to disentangle herself from the guard's limbs, she rolled over onto her back. The first thing that popped into view was Bud's worried face. She flashed a crooked smile to let him know she was all right, though she'd likely alerted the entire barracks to their activities.

The second thing she saw was a disapproving frown from her brother.

"Don't you say a word, Werim Swift," she warned.

"We should move the bodies," Bud said.

"He's not dead," Sharee noted.

Bud shrugged. He and Werim hooked their arms around the man, dragging him back into the darkness. She leveraged herself up to catch Sorn and Marcko doing the same with the other guard. While they were gone, Sharee stood and dusted herself off, checking to make sure she had all of her gear.

"Fortunately, I don't believe the garrison has been alerted to our presence," Sorn said when they returned. "The building slumbers still."

"Lucky," Werim grumbled.

Sharee shot him a sour look.

A clink of metal on stone sounded behind them. They whirled, several hands reaching for swords, and stared back into the plaza. Nothing moved. Sorn took a few steps to give him a view behind the well, but returned satisfied.

"One of the guards shifted," he said.

They breathed a sigh of relief.

"We should make for the docks," Marcko suggested. He turned and pointed. "They are straight down this way."

They followed the Eclectic across a paved street and into the alley. Sharee's heart still pounded against her chest, but she started to regain her composure. As she did, she noticed the city around for the first time.

She'd never been to Kinnsley or, to be fair, any of the larger cities. She nearly made herself dizzy trying to look everywhere at once. As far as she could see, there were buildings stacked upon buildings. It was difficult to tell where one began and the other ended. She found it hard to imagine so many people living so close together. What did they all do for food? For water? For green trees?

From what she could see in the gloom, much of the construction was a strange combination of stone and wood topped by slate roofing. Dark beams accented stout walls of dried clay, while here and there rose an occasional tower of solid stone that stretched several stories up into the night. Many of the windows were dark and shuttered, but every now and then a candle bloomed high in the home of some night owl.

The sky cleared, and the moon shone down to illuminate their path. Marcko led them along a narrow backstreet, every now and then darting across wide avenues. Each time, Sharee was sure that a patrol waited just beyond her view down a stone stair or around a corner.

They skirted around what Sharee was sure must be a tavern from the noise that spilled out. Even several buildings away they could hear the laughter and revelry. A high-pitched squeal sent a shiver down Sharee's spine. She wasn't quite sure whether it was a noise of pleasure or pain. Perhaps both. Surely, such a place was crawling with marked men. The memory of hungry eyes roving over her nearly made her shudder. She bit her tongue and followed as close to Marcko's heels as she dared.

When they crossed yet another avenue, Sharee's wonder deepened. Knucklesporte had always seemed large to her, but she felt like they could have already walked from gate to gate and back again in the smaller town. *Just how big is this place? It's like a man-made forest.* She almost wished she could scale one of the towers to get a better view of her surroundings. Almost.

Crouched in the shadows of the alley between two large, multi-storied houses, Marcko waved them to a halt. They had reached their destination. Sharee peeked around the big man and was surprised to note that the stone ended as abruptly as the houses. Wood planking covered the ground before them, extending out into three long piers with several large ships moored to each. The sheer size of the vessels awed Sharee. The biggest ship she had ever seen was a rowboat.

Open space separated them from the piers. Stacks of crates were scattered about, and lamps burned along the outskirts of the dock. Her eyes, however, were drawn to one ship that blazed with light. The vessel appeared to be preparing to leave, which was odd considering the late hour. There was no activity on any of the other boats, though the docks swarmed with soldiers. Sharee noted that the Baraban men—easily denoted by their bare arms covered with markings—clustered as close to the buildings as was practical while still blocking off access to the boats. Other armored men—which she assumed were part of the city guard—patrolled up and down the piers. Several were clustered around a plank that led onto the sole active ship. Dirty men in ragged clothing carried crates between the guards and onto the boat. A gasp beside her pulled her attention away from the scene.

"That's Alexzandar!" Marcko exclaimed. "What is *he* doing here? And who is he talking to?"

Sharee saw a large, robed politician waddle into view. Alongside him was a familiar man wearing a triangular black hat.

"That would be the High Admiral of the Baraban Legion. One Lugar Tyniente," Sorn said.

"What is Alexzandar holding?" Bud asked.

They all squinted. The man appeared to be dangling a red charm in the Admiral's face and speaking animatedly. Sorn let out a growl.

"A resonant charm," he said. "Only men who are in the service of the Grand Warlord possess them."

Marcko made a choking noise. "I would never have suspected... to betray one's own country... the man is a...." He trailed off, sputtering.

"At least it seems like there'll be a boat ready to sail," Werim pointed out.

"Yes, but how to approach it?" Sorn wondered. "I had not been anticipating such a showing of strength here at the waterfront."

Marcko had regained his composure. "Yes, generally the dock is quiet at this time of night. I wonder of the nature of this launch. Where could it be headed do you suppose? Surely, not to Tashaba. I doubt the Baraban would allow that."

"Doesn't matter," Werim said. "We'll be changing its course anyway."

"Just how do you suppose we're going to do that?" Sharee asked. "And if it involves your sword, I swear to the Composer I'll brain you."

Werim frowned. "We're far too outnumbered for a fight. No, I think I can do better than steel, 'Ree."

◇ Chapter Twenty-Three

"**I** don't like this plan."

Werim looked down at his sister and smiled. Then, he slid the lid of the crate over her face.

"You can buzz it now," he said to Sharee-in-a-box.

Small streaks of light illuminated the cracks for a moment, and then the crate was whole again.

"Remind me again why she had to go into a box," Marcko suggested.

Werim hooked a thumb over his shoulder, pointing at the ship through the stack of crates. He hoped they were still loading it. "Did you see any girl dock workers?"

"Ah, good observation."

"Besides, she can always buzz herself out of there. Unlike the rest of us," Werim added. He looked down at his dirty, travel-stained clothing.

The politician ran a hand over his smooth head. "I wish I would have thought to bring my hat. It has a certain air of officiousness about it." He pulled up his gray hood with a frown. The robe bulged around his ample middle.

"Alexzandar will still recognize you, and then he will be ensnared," Sorn explained. "If our young hero is correct about the guards–and I believe he is–Alexzandar will not dare risk revealing the true nature of his bargain before them. He cannot afford so many witnesses to his treachery."

"There's no love lost between the city guard and the Legionnares," Bud said. "You can see it in their postures."

"There's that, too," Sorn agreed. "Just like in the sewer, even the smallest spark is liable to set this place aflame."

The box containing Sharee rattled a bit on the floor, and there was a muffled sound of complaint.

"Yes, we should get going," Werim said.

Bud quickly hefted Sharee, leaving Werim and Sorn to grab two other crates off of a nearby stack. They grunted under the strain. Werim wondered what was in his that it should weigh so much. He shook it gently and heard some clinking. *Wine maybe?*

"A little higher, Sorn," Marcko said. "We wouldn't want the Admiral to catch sight of your familiar face, and you *are* rather tall."

Werim peaked around the side of his own crate and watched the thief shimmy his burden up to hide behind it. Bud was having no problem with his. Fortunately, their clothes were already fairly ragged, lending a natural air of legitimacy to the ploy; they would fit right in with the dock workers. When Sorn settled, his eyes still peeked over the top edge of the box.

"It will have to do," Marcko said. "Let's get on with this madness, then."

The three of them lined up behind the politician. Werim craned his head just enough to see Sorn's heels. He hoped the thief wouldn't lose sight of Marcko. Otherwise, they might all end up walking right off the pier and into the cold water.

They started down a path between the stacks of crates. At first, Werim was worried that he might have trouble keeping up with the lankier man in front of him. Marcko, however, assumed a slow, stately pace.

Sweat began to bead on Werim's head despite the cool night. One of his footsteps dislodged a droplet, and it leaked down into his eye. It burned fiercely. He desperately wanted to wipe it away, but he dared not. There was no way he could hold the heavy crate in just one arm.

The pain worsened with each step. It was as if someone had dug a channel in his face, directing all of his sweat down into a pond that formed along the bridge of his nose. Werim's only reassurance that they were nearing the dock was the relative illumination about the edges of his burden. Yet, even that seemed an assault on his poor eyes.

"Alexzandar," Marcko called out. "I am here!"

They stopped. Werim tried to wipe his face on his shoulder. A swatch of dark cloth caught his eye, and he ducked back behind his box.

"Who be this?" The gravelly voice belonged to the High Admiral.

"Ah, hm... well." The other voice, a blubbery one, Werim assumed must be Alexzandar. "It seems as if–"

"High Admiral," Marcko interrupted. "I am Eclectic Marcko, a humble servant of the great Tasher Nation and one of many diplomatic advisers to the Archon Basileus. He has told me much about you, but I'm afraid I will have to delay proper introductions for another time. We have a schedule to keep. Isn't that right, Alexzandar?"

There was a momentary pause.

"Yes, yes, of course. As I was telling you, Lugar, I–*we* must be off," Alexzandar said.

"You be sayin' nothing about the bringin' of any advisor," Lugar growled.

"I'm sure Alexzandar just didn't want to bore you with the mundane details," Marcko replied swiftly. "He is, after all, a most practical man and cannot be expected to personally oversee every part of our great nation. It happens to be that some of my specific knowledge will be of great use to the Archon Basileus. He's asked me to be of service. Between you and me, sometimes I believe the Archon sorely underestimates his own abilities, but who am I to argue with executive orders?"

There was another pause.

"Aye," Lugar said finally. "So it be. Just remember, if I no be hearin' from you in a week, I be thinkin' you're in Tashaba with the Polemarch. An' I be havin' your city."

"My dear Admiral," Alexzandar cooed, "have I not been a gracious host? What reason have you to doubt me? As soon as I locate your Warlord, I will send a messenger with all due haste. We both wish to avoid any more bloodshed."

"Aye," Lugar said simply.

"Let's get on with it then," Marcko suggested. "Archon, after you."

"Yes, of course, Marcko," Alexzandar burbled. "We have much to discuss."

"That we do," Marcko replied.

Werim heard footsteps on wood. Shortly, Sorn's heels began moving again, and Werim followed. They stepped off of the pier and onto the treacherous incline of a gangplank. The wide board flexed slightly with their weight, and Werim fought to keep his balance. He wondered how the dock workers did this all day without falling in.

There was a sharp cracking sound, and for a moment Werim thought the gangplank was breaking beneath them. He panicked at the thought of the cold water beneath them, and nearly toppled in. The board, however, remained solid and stable beneath his feet. *What made the noise, then?*

A splash drew his eyes. Below, a crate bobbed into view, one side taking on water where a jagged hole had been punched. Slowly, it sank beneath the surface.

The next crack was closer, accompanied by the sound of shattering glass. In fact, Werim felt it in his arms. The sharp smell of vinegar stung his nostrils. He craned his head around to see what was happening. His eyes widened when he saw that a hole had been punched in the side of his crate as well. *By what?*

Whatever it was had shattered the glass inside of his box, spilling the contents to ooze on his arms.

Then, just as swiftly, the crate was pulled out of his hands. After a brief struggle, Werim let it topple down into the water. It was either him or the crate, and he had no desire to get wet for the unknown–now broken–goods.

He turned toward his assailant. It was Sorn. However, the thief's focus was beyond Werim. He was fixated on Bud's burden. Werim shimmied around to let him pass. His mind was starting to catch up. *Sharee's box is next!*

Out of the corner of his eye, originating from somewhere among the stacked crates on the dock, a fleck of black flashed toward the remaining intact box. Sorn flicked out a hand and, unbelievingly, caught the speeding object.

The night froze. The first two cracks had drawn confused attention, but it was the third item, held up for all to see in Sorn's outstretched arm, that clarified the issue. It was a black Baraban sidebow bolt. Someone was shooting at them from the dock.

Before they had time to react, a fourth shot took Sorn in the chest. He pitched over the side of the gangplank and into the water. The splash was the spark.

"They've attacked us!" Marcko yelled from the deck, the first one to find his voice. "To arms!"

Everything lurched back into motion. Werim heard himself yell, and somehow his sword was in his hand. He started to turn and survey the dock in the hopes of finding the perpetrator, but Bud was against him, forcing him up the plank with the crate still cradled in his arms. Werim backed up, losing his footing at the very top and toppling onto the deck. Bud and Sharee-in-a-box followed him in a jumbled heap on the wooden floor.

"Shove off! Shove off!" someone shouted, and the gangplank splashed down into the water.

The sound of steel on steel clanged below, and the calls of men fighting sent up a chorus into the night. Cries and curses were the refrain. The melody belonged to Death.

The solid rail of the ship provided cover for the two boys. Bud pushed the crate up against it and then leaned back, panting. Werim was seated on the other side of the box doing the same. He peeked up for a moment, wanting to survey the scene, but immediately a black speck flew at him. He dove to the deck and heard the bolt lodge into the wooden rail with a thwack. Thankfully, the boat was much stronger than the crates.

"What is it?" Bud asked.

Werim closed his eyes for a moment and tried to recall the quick glance he'd gotten before the shot. Admiral Tyniente had been surrounded by the steel-clad city guard, sword in hand and sorely outnumbered. Baraban Legionnaires rushed from between the crates toward the much smaller contingent of guards on the pier. Though the savages had numbers, the city guard held the natural chokepoints of the piers and scary water frothed on either side. It was a skirmish that would not end quickly or bloodlessly.

Though he had taken all of that in, Werim had not seen where the black speck had originated from. It appeared to have issued from the very top of one of the stacks, as if a jagged rag had ripped itself from Death's shadowy cloak to speed for Werim's head.

"I couldn't see," he admitted.

A buzz pulled Werim's head. A soft glow of light issued from around the edges of the crate. One side fell off, and Sharee tumbled out. She blinked, head swiveling side to side.

"What's going on?" she asked.

"We've been attacked," Bud replied.

"Attacked?"

"Yes, someone was shooting at you," the blond boy explained.

"Me?"

"Full of questions, that box is." Werim snickered.

Bud shot him a sour look.

The sounds of the battle faded away as they pulled out of the dock. Werim hazarded another look. This time he was not sent immediately back to the deck. They had apparently put enough distance between themselves and the dock, as no more bolts flew through the air. That, or their assailant was aiming more carefully for his next shot. Werim slid back down with a shiver.

"Anything?" Bud asked.

Werim ran a hand through curly hair. "Nothing I'd care to watch any longer."

"Those Baraban really are afraid of the water, aren't they?" Bud observed.

Werim had thought the same thing. Though their leader was surrounded, they still approached the piers with trepidation. And it didn't seem like their attention was on the small city guard.

Sharee poked her head up, and Bud yanked her immediately back down.

"Hey," she said. "I want to see."

"They were shooting at *you*," Bud reminded her.

"But, they're all fighting each other," Sharee said. "How do you know they just weren't shooting?"

"They didn't start fighting until after the shooting began," Werim said.

"Oh."

"Whoever it was knew she was in a box, but didn't know which one," Werim reasoned.

Bud nodded.

"Why would someone want to shoot me?" Sharee asked.

"They probably found out you're a freak," Werim said. "I doubt they wanted to try anything up close, not knowing what you can do. The cowards." He fingered the hilt of his blade.

"If she can do anything like the stories..." Bud trailed off.

"But I can't. I can't do anything!" Sharee insisted.

They pondered that. Bud frowned. Werim rubbed his leg.

"Poor Sorn," Werim said eventually.

Bud shot him another look. "I thought you didn't like him."

Sharee's eyes widened. "What happened to Sorn?"

"He *did* take a bolt for my sister," Werim pointed out.

"He did what?"

Bud turned saddened eyes on Sharee. "It would seem the thief was more honorable than we thought."

"Where is he? I can heal him," Sharee looked around, frantic.

Werim shook his head. "He fell over, 'Ree. And I didn't see him come up."

Sharee was back at the railing. "Then we have to go back and get him. There's still time, if only–"

Bud pulled her back down. "We can't. We can't risk losing you, too."

Werim nodded agreement. "Besides, there are far too many Baraban in that city. As soon as they find out that we didn't exactly part as friends, they'll want to stop us."

They sat in silence for a moment, no sounds but the creak of the ship and the slap of the waves beneath them. Voices drifted down from the sailors attending to the rigging. There were several men on deck, but none of them paid the group of ragged dockhands any heed. They were all focused on getting away from the city. Which was just as well, since they might have wondered why the dockhands were armed.

Finally, Bud said, "We should go check on the Eclectic."

"Is he hurt too?" Sharee asked.

"No," Werim answered. "He ran below as soon as the shooting started. Well, after making sure the city guard got involved, that is."

"I can't imagine the Archon Basileus is too happy with that bit of diplomacy," Bud said.

Werim stood first. He looked back toward the receding city. He could still just barely make out the men fighting on the dock. Torchlight glinted off of swinging blades, resembling fireflies in a lost memory of home. Unlike the fireflies though, Werim could not reach out and swat these speckles of light. Torches began to bob in other parts of the city, all converging on the docks. Werim couldn't tell which side the newcomers were on. He hoped it was the city guard, but suspected it was not.

Bud helped Sharee to her feet, bending to pick up a few of the white arrows that had tumbled loose. Werim watched as his sister removed the two darker pieces of wood from her quiver. With a quick buzz, she knit the pieces back together. She had insisted on taking the bow with her into the box.

Werim rubbed at his ear more out of habit than anything else. He had grown used to the buzzing and–though he would not admit it to his sister–he was beginning to find it not altogether unpleasant. In fact, he thought he could make out just the faintest hints of a rhythm to it, as if she were mimicking some sort of strange song of the crickets. It reminded him of his mother, and how she used to hum while carving or cooking.

He brushed the thought away. They were nearly to their father now. If what the Eclectic said was true, he was waiting for them just on the other side of this lake. He wondered how long it would take to cross.

The three of them ducked into the stairwell that the Eclectic had run down. It led below deck to a narrow corridor with doors opening off to either side. At the far end, they saw a big, gray lump with a shining bald head that could only be Marcko. He locked a door, and then turned to see his three companions headed toward him.

He held a finger to his lips and motioned them back the way they'd come. When they were as far from the locked door as possible, they slipped into one of the side rooms. It appeared to be a small cabin. A low bed ran along each wall, with a simple chest of drawers between the headboards.

The square room was cramped with four of them. Even so, Marcko shut the door. They shuffled around. Sharee and Werim sat on the beds while Bud leaned up against the chest. Marcko stood with his back to the door.

"I did not want Alexzandar to hear," he explained, cocking a thumb over his shoulder. "The man may be cowed for now, but he is wily as a mountain goat."

"What are you going to do with him?" Bud asked.

Marcko stroked his chin. "Well, I can't very well kill him unless treason is proven. Given time, I might be able to puzzle a way to force him into admitting what he has done, but time is something we're short of."

"What, exactly, has he done?" Werim asked.

"Allowed the enemy into one of our cities, for starters," Marcko said. "I also believe he may be in league with the Triumvirate, if what Sorn said was true." He frowned. "Where is the thief?"

They all looked down at the floor.

"He is no longer with us," Bud said.

Marcko's eyes widened. "Is he... dead?"

"Yes," Bud said.

"You don't know that," Sharee argued. "You said yourself that you only saw him get hit and then plunge into the water."

"It was in the chest," Bud explained. "I doubt he could have survived."

Marcko reached out a hand and settled it on Sharee's shoulder. "If there is a man that could survive such a fall, it would be the thief. It may be doing him a disservice to count him out just yet. I suspect..." he trailed off. It seemed as if there was something more to say. Instead, he continued, "No matter. We can only focus on the road ahead of us."

They all nodded. Werim had learned that looking ahead was preferable to dwelling on what was already past. It was something he might not have admitted a year ago.

"So, where are we headed?" Werim asked.

Marcko smiled. "It seems that Alexzandar intended to visit the prison as well. Likely, he wanted to meet with Warlord Vraika. I see no reason to alter our course, in this case."

"Well, that's fortunate," Bud said.

Marcko nodded, and the held up a finger. "Now, I don't wish to let it be known amongst the sailors of this vessel that Alexzandar is in my custody," Marcko began. "They will perhaps sail more swiftly if they continue to believe they are in the service of the

Archon Basileus. Unfortunately, a solitary mountain Eclectic does not command the same sort of respect."

"So you locked him in?" Werim asked. "How? Didn't he fight?"

"Looks can be deceiving. I am not as soft as your typical politician." He grinned and flexed a hand. "There's only one room that locks from the outside, and that's the storeroom." He looked the three of them over. "Forgive me if I continue the ruse that you three are my personal servants. It will make less to explain, and I can offer your service in accessing the stores, should the captain require it. Thus, we can keep his men out and blissfully unaware."

Werim nodded. "That's fine. We'll need a place to stay, though. I don't think it's a good idea for us to be wandering around with the other sailors. They might wonder about us. Besides, I could use some sleep."

"True enough," Marcko agreed. He looked around. "You can use this room. I'll tell the captain as much. It may not be large, but it beats sleeping in the hold on a hammock."

"How long until we reach the prison?" Bud asked.

"As long as we keep the sails up through the night–of which there isn't much left–we should be floating in under cover of darkness tomorrow."

"That long?" Sharee asked.

Marcko shrugged. "It's a big lake. In fact, in the very middle, you can't see land at all."

For some reason, Werim found that thought particularly disquieting. And he could swim.

"What will we do when we get there?" Bud wanted to know.

"It may be that I can, ah, *entice* Alexzandar to supply me with a writ." Marcko pulled one side of his long, gray robe away just enough to reveal the hilt of a knife. "I would make sure that it warns the warden of imminent attack, as well as secures the, ah, *transfer* of our choice of individuals."

"And if he doesn't supply the paper?" Werim asked.

"He will," Marcko replied.

Werim shrugged. He didn't see that they had another choice. They needed the men. They needed his father.

Marcko looked at Werim. "I need to go speak with the captain now, and then I will go start to work on our friend. When I require a break, I will come and ask you to relieve me. All you need do is open the door occasionally and make some noise."

"Make noise?" Werim asked.

Marcko grinned. "I don't want our friend getting too comfortable. A tired man is more pliant."

"Why me?"

"You seem to like that sword of yours an awful lot," Marcko shrugged. "I figure you could bang around inside the storeroom for a bit with it. Makes for a good threat if he thinks you may be itching for a fight."

"Don't kill him accidentally," Bud added.

Werim frowned at his friend. "You tripped getting on the boat."

"You wouldn't get out of the way."

"I *wanted* to defend us."

"Boys," Sharee said.

Werim rolled his eyes. Was it really so bad to want to stop those who wished your loved ones harm? At least he'd get a chance to see the Archon Basileus up close, even if it were only to wave a sword in his face.

"Settle in," Marcko advised, half-turning toward the door. "I think you'll find that there's not much to do on a boat at sail. Unless you're a captain." He winked.

The Eclectic squeezed out of the room, leaving the three of them alone. Werim stretched out on the bed, not even bothering to take off his belt. He rested one hand on the hilt of his sword and the other behind his head. Bud helped Sharee take off some of her gear and set it on top of the chest. The blond boy offered the other bed to her, and he took the floor.

Staring up at the ceiling, Werim felt the ship sway on a wave, and his stomach lurched. *It's only going to be a short trip*, he reminded himself. One day and they'd be there. And then Werim could perhaps find an answer to the question that had been plaguing him this entire journey.

How do I fit into all of this?

◇ Chapter Twenty-Four

Lugar Tyniente yanked his sword out of a body. It scraped along the metal of the dead man's armor, sliding out from the narrow bit of soft, unprotected flesh at the armpit. The Admiral attempted to wipe the blood off on his pants.

His dark clothes were riddled with fresh slices, some oozing blood, but none deep. His jacket hung from his muscular frame in tatters, heavily inked skin peeking through the ruined sleeves. He bent down and scooped up his triangular hat, shoving it back on his head.

When he stood, he looked off toward the horizon. The lake was a deep blue shadow, with small waves lightly touched by the moonlight. Out on the water, a good distance off and growing steadily smaller, the departing ship burned bright. It slid effortlessly across the silver surface. It was far beyond his reach, now.

"What be yer orders, Admiral?"

Lugar turned to study the captain of his bodyguard. The man at least had the decency to clothe his face in scarlet shame. He had been no help. *Lucky that heavy armor be makin' their guard slower than a Landsha*, Lugar thought. No way would he have lived had he faced a half-dozen Legionnaires.

He forced himself to tamp down on the fading ecstasy of battle. The High Admiral didn't get a whole lot of opportunity to cross swords these days, and he reveled in the life pumping exultantly through his veins. He prided himself on being a level-headed man, but oh, the excitement of a good scrum. He looked at the ring of corpses surrounding him and sighed. *There always be a price.*

"Find the other captains," Lugar said. "It be high time to be closin' up the city. We may be havin' need for somethin' to ransom."

"And if the watch no be likin' it?" the man asked.

Lugar did not respond. Instead, he looked down at his bloody blade. No simple wiping could remove all traces of red from the steel. *Sometimes steel be the only thing men understand.*

The captain recognized the implication. "Aye, sir." He saluted and hurried away.

He took most of the Legionnaires with him, but several stayed with the Admiral. They had secured the dock, but no doubt other scuffles had sprung up. There would be fighting in the streets before long. There had certainly been enough racket. Lugar sheathed his sword and left the pier.

When he was among the crates, he gestured for his men to stay put for a moment. Then, he moved deeper into the shadows. He didn't have far to go before he encountered one that was more solid than the rest.

"They be carryin' the muse girl on in a crate," his Lead Engineer said.

"The dockhands?"

"Them's that be with that fat man, yes." The shadow reached up and came back with a weapon. It was specialized, larger than a normal sidebow. The bolt issued from a long tube with a cross fixed atop it. Lugar had seen what the weapon could do; it was built to be precise over a distance. Rarely did a man caught in the sights live to see a second shot. Nonetheless, the engineers had rigged it with a quick crank and stilts to help steady the shot. It was a cumbersome device, not one Lugar would trust to a common Legionnaire on a field of battle, but it had its uses.

"There be two fat men," Lugar pointed out. "Be they together in this?"

The engineer shook his head. "Just the second. An' they no be dockhands. Plenty of crates around, there be." The engineer patted one of the boxes beside him. "They be yer prisoners that escaped."

Lugar nodded. "The tall one do be familiar. How be they gettin' on board with an Eclectic, though?"

The engineer shrugged and shouldered his weapon. Lugar sensed that he was anxious to be on his way. His engineers never stopped until a job was complete. The job was their life, even to the point that it consumed them.

"I be needin' a few from the garrison fer the ship," the engineer said. He was staring at one of the dark vessels still in port.

Lugar nodded. "Take 'em. Best be keepin' 'em in line, too. Take a few of my guard, savvy?"

"They won't be likin' the thought of travlen' on the blue death."

"Any that refuse, send 'em to me. I be toleratin' no cowards," Lugar said.

"Aye."

And then the man was gone, melding with the shadows as if he'd never been there in the first place. Lugar shuddered. Engineers were a strange breed, yet they were very good at what they did. His Legion wouldn't be half so effective without them and their creations. His Lead Engineer would get what he needed.

Lugar returned to where he'd left his bodyguard. The smell of blood tickled his nostrils. His tattered jacket flapped in the light breeze off the lake. He needed to change. Even after a fight, an Admiral should look the part. His men fell in beside him as he headed for the central part of the city.

So the muse be on the way to the Warlord, he thought. Considering how adamant Vraika had been about the child being a boy, he was likely in for a surprise. Still, surely he could handle one youngling. Who knew when it came to muses, though? He looked at the shuttered buildings around him. *At least I be havin' somethin' to bargain with, in any case.*

~ + ~

There was a soft but persistent knock at the door. Werim ignored it and rolled over. It was probably his Mom wanting him up to do chores. Hadn't he done enough lately? If Dad were home, he would let Werim sleep in. Dad always took his side.

The knock wouldn't go away. Werim groaned. Something was digging into his side. Had he forgotten to put his sword under the bed again? It was comforting to have it near him. Still, what would Mom say about her son falling asleep on top of his sword? She'd probably be afraid that he'd cut himself on accident.

If only Dad were here…

"Werim, wake up," his sister hissed.

"You can get your own pails of water," Werim growled.

He tried to push his sword away, but it wouldn't budge. He rolled onto his back and tried again. The thing was shoved down through his belt. He never fell asleep with it belted. Dad had taught him that. *Tough to draw layin' down. Best you keep it unfettered.*

"Werim, it's Marcko," Sharee said.

Marcko? Werim sat up. Slowly, reality came back to him. The knock sounded again. This time, Werim swung his feet over the side of the bed and attempted to stand.

Unfortunately, he encountered something soft and lumpy. His ankle rolled, and he fought for balance. Losing, he fell back onto the bed with a thump.

Bud, he remembered. The shadow on the ground sawed a log in response, oblivious. The knock sounded again.

Werim cursed. "I'm coming. Just a blasted minute."

He rubbed the sleep from his eyes. A thin streak of light leaked through a round portal set high on the wall. Werim didn't recall seeing the opening before nodding off, but it had been night then. Now the light assaulted his eyes, brighter than a torch.

He shimmied down to the end of the small bed and carefully checked the floor for limbs. Stepping between them, he was able to work his way to the door. He cracked it. The Eclectic hovered just on the other side of the threshold.

"It's already almost midday. I need to get a few hours of rest before we land," Marcko said.

Werim blinked several times. "Okay."

The Eclectic held a key. "Take this. Keep him uncomfortable. Also, take one of the casks of wine up and ask the captain what he needs brought up for his men."

Chores. "Fine," Werim said.

"Don't forget to lock the door behind you when you leave."

Werim frowned. "Of course."

Marcko looked him over and nodded. "I won't be long–old men do not require as much sleep as you pups–and then I will squeeze a writ out of him."

The big man turned and disappeared into the room across the hall. Werim watched for a moment before turning back to the room. Sharee had rolled over and apparently gone back to sleep, and Bud was dead wood on the floor. He thought briefly about waking one of them up for company but decided against it. The Eclectic had given the job to him, and Werim didn't need an audience. It probably wouldn't make him seem any more menacing if he brought his sister along, and he didn't think he'd be able to even wake his friend.

Perhaps if I went above and got a bucket of lake water.... He smiled at the thought. Then, he turned and eased out of the room.

He yawned and stretched his arms on his way to the end of the hall. At the door, he fit key to lock and made ready to turn the knob. He hovered for a moment, then stepped back. His tattered, travel-stained clothing was hardly impressive. There was still a large rip in the pants, accentuated by darkened blood. His boots were scuffed and nearly worn through. In that moment, Werim decided that dockhands did not look very intimidating. *I look more like I was on the wrong end of a tavern brawl.* Not that he'd been around taverns enough to have had such an experience.

At least I have my sword. The edge was still sharp, and the bronze hilt gleamed faintly in the low light from the open stairway at his back. He drew the blade, looking at his reflection in the steel. It was neither clear nor distinct, but in his mind Werim constructed the image of a determined young man, blazing hazel eyes and a hardened jaw.

He looked down at his arms. On the one gripping the sword, a raised blue line pulsed beneath his skin. He flexed it, grinding his teeth together and getting a bit worked up. He needed to look intimidating. Hastily, he removed his shirt.

He laid the dirty piece of cloth down on the floorboards. Stretching out each sleeve, he drew his blade across the right shoulder, pressing down. It was like cutting mutton back home. Very thin and tough mutton. The blade worked back and forth until it bit into wood. He pulled the liberated piece of cloth away and went to work on the other side. Once that was completed, he pulled the shirt back over his head.

His arms were now bare. He flexed them again and was satisfied with the image. Werim worked his face into a scowl such as he would expect to find on a jailor, not a manservant or dockhand. He reached out with his left arm to turn the knob, holding his sword in a white-knuckled grip on his right.

The door whooshed back, and he stood silhouetted by the light from behind. An imposing, arms-bared, sword-wielding man, grimacing in the doorway. He let loose a growl for effect.

He took one step inside, and then struggled to adjust to the relative dimness of the storeroom. There was no portal in here. The first thing his eyes made out was a snuffed lantern resting on a box in the middle of the room. He took a step toward it, looking for the man seated behind the box. There was a shadow back there.

Light exploded. And with it, pain. He stumbled, the ground all of a sudden unsteady. Behind the box, instead of a man, were several bags of grain, stacked crudely before the unused lantern.

Werim pitched forward toward the crate. He dimly heard his sword clatter against the ground as the lantern rushed toward him. It felt as if the boat had just launched over a gigantic swell. The floor was pulled from beneath his feet like a rug.

Why does the wave cause me pain, though?

The thought seemed liquid in its own right.

Unable to halt his descent, he slammed into the box. The lantern glanced off of his head and wood shattered beneath him. Renewed pain blossomed in his skull.

With a moan, Werim rolled over. Darkness crept in at the edge of his vision. He thought he might be losing consciousness.

No, there's just a large man shutting the door for me. How thoughtful. A nap would *be nice right now.*

The man tossed aside a board he'd been carrying and shut the door. The shadows enveloped Werim like a warm blanket. Whatever darkness this was–unconsciousness or otherwise–he found that he didn't care, and slipped away.

~ + ~

Sharee arched her back like a cat, pressing her face down into the thin pillow and clenching every one of her aching muscles. She slowly relaxed, relishing the feeling as she stretched back out on the bed. She felt *so* good. It had been days since she'd last gotten a good night's rest. Normally, there was any number of sounds that kept her up, her mind churning like a wine press after the harvest. She dimly recalled Marcko's knock on the door, but that was ages ago. For once, she'd been able to chase down and capture sleep.

As she relaxed, she noticed something. The room was quiet. Too quiet.

She flipped over and looked around. Her eyes immediately lit upon Bud. He was seated on the edge of the opposite bed, frozen like a man caught stealing. The boyish look of innocence on his face was at direct odds with the large sword that rested across his knees. He'd apparently been in the midst of cleaning it, because he had a cloth in his hand, halted halfway down the blade.

"I'm sorry. I didn't mean to wake you," he said.

Sharee thought of his snoring and compared it to the potential whisper of sword-cleaning. "You didn't." He still looked a bit ashamed so she added, "I'm not sure you could have. I was sleeping hard."

He nodded and continued with what he'd been doing.

Sharee sat up and watched for a moment as he rubbed cloth over the steel in slow, smooth strokes. Light reflected off the weapon and up onto his shoulder, bathing his broad shoulders in a warm glow. His dirty shirt was tight across the chest, Sharee noted. *When had he gotten so big?*

He must have felt her eyes on him, because he raised his. He smiled, and for a moment Sharee just stared into his deep, sky-blue eyes. She felt her cheeks redden, and looked down to her things at the foot of bed. She reached for the quiver and then self-consciously pulled her hand back. There was no need to be armed here. Instead, she adjusted the pack on her waist. Then, she smoothed her short, ripped dress over the pants she'd put on to cover her legs. Finally, she ran a hand through her hair, frowning as she ran afoul of tangles and twigs.

A new mission in mind, she fished in her pack and emerged with her hairbrush. As she began running it through the mess on her head, she tried not to notice that Bud's eyes were still on her. She grunted at she hit a particularly bad snarl before ripping through it. Bud chuckled, and they both froze, eyes on each other again.

"Has Werim been gone for a while?" Sharee asked, suddenly desperate for something to fill the silence.

"I didn't see him leave," Bud noted, breaking the gaze.

Of course not, Sharee thought. *He was sleeping, too.* "How close do you think we are?"

Bud glanced up at the portal. "Probably not too long until nightfall."

Sharee was startled to realize that she had slept through most of the day. *We're close, then.* "I think my brother left to go watch over Alexzandar around midday." She vaguely recalled a muffled conversation at the door while she'd been drifting back to sleep.

Bud frowned. "He has been gone for a while."

"Did you check on him?"

Bud shook his head. "No, he wouldn't want me to interrupt his act." The blond boy shrugged. "And, I didn't want to leave you alone."

Sharee scrunched her brows together. "Why not?"

"Someone *did* just try to kill you," he said without looking up. He was deeply focused on polishing his steel again.

Sharee considered that for a moment. She wasn't used to being important. Werim was the oldest and the loudest. Generally, he got all of the attention.

"Well, I'm awake now," she said. "We should probably go wake Marcko and check on my brother. Together."

Bud set his sword aside and stood. Sharee noted that his head nearly brushed the ceiling. The cabins on the ship were not very big–Sharee could almost touch the ceiling simply by raising an arm and stretching–yet she felt small next to her brother's best friend. *Why do I find that... comforting?*

Using her unstrung bow as a walking stick, Sharee followed Bud to the door. He pulled it open and was about to step aside, but something changed his mind. Instead, he positioned himself in front of her, blocking her from the dark hallway. She could only see snippets of blackness between his thick arms and legs. On her toes, she tried to get a view.

"What?" she asked. "What is it?"

"The hallway is dark," Bud said.

Sharee rolled her eyes. *Is that all?* "Darkness isn't going to kill me."

She tried to take a step around the big boy, but he wouldn't budge.

"There should be light leaking in from the stairwell," he pointed out.

Sharee paused. He was right. Even when they'd descended in the middle of the night, a bit of moonlight had trickled down to chase the shadows away. Now, the darkness was deep and unbroken.

"Maybe someone just shut the door above," Sharee suggested.

"Maybe. But why?"

A knot of fear wormed in her stomach. She buried it.

"Let's go find my brother," she said. "He'll know what's going on."

Bud pushed her back inside and shut the door.

"What are you doing?" she asked.

"Let me get my sword," he replied.

Sharee tapped her foot while Bud retrieved his blade from the bed and returned to the door. She thought about donning her quiver, but even if she strung her bow, the weapon would be useless in such close quarters. She was better off using the wood as a long cudgel. Her fingers tightened around her staff as Bud opened the door again, but her face betrayed nothing.

Warily, Bud stepped out into the hallway. He looked down toward the storage room, and then back to the stairwell. It appeared that he was trying to decide which direction posed the greatest threat. Sharee let out a sigh and stepped confidently in front of him. She had to rub against the wall in order to pass by him in the narrow hallway, but then she strode with purpose toward the storage room. He could guard her back. She wasn't completely helpless.

At the door, she paused for a moment. Bud clomped up behind her, and she turned to hold a finger against her lips. He stared at it for a moment before nodding. Sharee put her ear against the door.

Nothing.

She shrugged and stepped back. "If he's in there, he's not being very intimidating."

Bud frowned and reached for the doorknob. It turned.

"Not locked," the blond boy muttered.

They both tensed.

Bud pulled the door back slowly, and they peeked inside. More darkness greeted them.

"I wish we had a torch," Sharee whispered.

"Or a glowstick," Bud offered.

"Werim?" Sharee called from the doorway.

Something moaned in the darkness. She jumped back, and Bud raised his sword. Then, the quality of the moan struck her.

"Werim, is that you?" she asked, more concerned this time.

There was another groan. Sharee shoved Bud aside and darted into the room. She almost tripped over a loose board that had been left in the doorway. After catching herself, she paused for a moment to try and let her eyes adjust. Light from the open door to their room was doing battle with the shadows in the corridor and gaining ground. Slowly, darker and lighter forms began to separate. One roughly the shape of a body stirred on the floor.

"Werim," Sharee named it.

She tossed her bow aside and fell to her knees next to him. Bud moved into the room and off to one side, allowing the light to spill in unhindered. As her eyes grew used to the dimness, Sharee noticed a darker shade pooled around her brother's head.

"He's bleeding," she said to Bud. "Quick, go get Marcko."

"What about Alexzandar?" Bud asked.

"Who cares, Bud? Werim is hurt." She said it a bit more forcefully than intended. "Look around if you want, but I'm sure he's gone."

She turned her attention back to her brother. Gently, she cupped his head. The blood looked to be coming from there, so she probed for the source. When her fingers found the cut in his scalp, Werim's eyes fluttered open and he hissed.

"Ow! Wha... wh..." he stammered.

"Hold still. You've got a nasty gash on your head," Sharee ordered. She tried to get a sense for the wound. His hair was matted and slippery, making it difficult.

"Mom?" Werim asked.

Sharee froze, but only for a moment. It felt as if someone had stabbed her in the heart. She looked at the puddle. *There's so much blood.*

"No, Wer. It's me, Sharee," she said.

Moisture dropped from her face to her brother's lips. *Tears,* she realized. Where had those come from? She pushed the thought aside and groped for the harp in her mind. Her vision blurred.

"Water," Werim moaned, his voice thick.

"I'll get you some water. Let me heal you first, though," Sharee said. "I promise it will only be a quick buzz."

She focused on the cut. Determined, she began to play the Song of Knitting. The notes exploded in her mind. One by one, she hammered them out, and they sang with the power of a thousand voices. Sharee had never played so loud before. The sheer strength of the melody nearly swept her away, but she kept her finger on the gash; her purpose firmly ensconced in her mind. Her brother needed her.

The end of the song snuck up on her. One moment her sound was a torrent in her ears, flowing down into her brother, and then it was gone. Silence crashed back like the waves buffeting the ship below. She sank back on her knees, exhausted. Werim's skin was unbroken beneath her fingers.

"Sharee?" Werim asked.

Sharee let out the breath she'd not realized she'd been holding. "Yes, Werim. It's me."

She couldn't see much in the darkness, but she was sure he smiled. "That song was beautiful," he said. Then, his eyes fluttered closed.

◊ Chapter Twenty-Five

Vraika halts. His men continue trudging past him through the swamp, their footfalls oddly resonant on the seemingly soft ground.

"Warlord?" his commander asks.

The Warlord does not answer.

There is something, in the distance....

Destiny, a voice answers back.

Hastily, he drops the cacophony pounding in his head. Silence deafens. He twists an ear toward the stone building squatting atop a crag in the distance.

The cries of his men break his concentration. He turns to glare at them. None of them notice. They are sinking slowly into the marsh and panicking.

Cowards.

Vraika had been playing a steady level of solidity down into the sodden soil, allowing them to pass as if over dry land. Having cut off his playing, the ground returns to its former density. The men fear drowning, even in mud. Some cry out to him in distress. They show their lack of faith in their Warlord.

"Close your eyes," he bellows. "It is no different than sand."

If they hear, they do not take heed.

I should let them all drown.

He blocks out the cries and refocuses on the not-so-distant prison. A sound, just on the verge of his hearing, it buzzes. There.

The fact that it is discernible at all from this distance is nothing short of astounding. Its source must be quite strong. Strangely, Vraika finds that he cannot make out the rhythm.

It's almost as if... no.

He looks down at the tree inscribed on his wrist, and smothers the thought. There is only one person that could possibly be making such a racket. *He must have heard me. He knows I come.*

It is to be expected. From the very moment that he crossed the river, Vraika knew he would be unable to approach in complete silence. It was this or conquer a boat, and he didn't have time to find a boat.

Let him hear.

Vraika strikes his gongs, resuming his song. He starts low, allowing his men a moment to halt their sinking and clamber out. The cries die off as they help each other from the muck. Many of them look around in amazement, still trembling.

"Have the men don their goggles," Vraika orders.

Next to him, his ashen-faced commander simply nods. The order goes out among the men. Vraika adds a second rhythm to the first.

Around them and among them, the Fog of War whirls into existence. Vraika plays the appropriate pattern before his eyes so he can see. He alone resumes the march toward the prison, pulling it ever closer. He lets his sound ring out, loud as ever.

Hesitantly, his men follow. There is safety in concealment. Their Warlord will protect them. Their faith is restored. With Vraika playing again, it is as if they march along a stone road leading directly to the secluded prison, an inky black cloud scurrying over the marshlands with impunity.

I come, brother. Hear me!

Destiny, the voice repeats.

~ + ~

Marcko woke to a pounding on the door. He rolled to his feet and looked up at the portal. The sky outside was swiftly turning red.

I've overslept, was his first thought.

He tottered over to the door and cracked it. A giant shadow lunged at him. The Eclectic stumbled back and let out a cry of fear. Then, the fading evening light illuminated his guest.

"Bud?" Marcko asked. "You scared me half to death." He fluttered a hand at his face.

"Werim's been injured," the blond boy stated. "Alexzandar is gone."

Marcko's heart jumped up to mimic his hand. "Come again?"

"The man escaped. Whacked Werim over the head. I think we've been locked down here."

"How could this have happened?" Marcko asked. "The Archon is neither swift nor strong."

"Strong enough," Bud said. "Come on."

Marcko noticed that the hulking boy was carrying his sword. Did he expect there to be a need out in the hallway? Bud turned to leave. Marcko paused. *Better to bathe our foes in light.*

"Allow me to grab a lantern," Marcko suggested.

He'd gotten a pair of them from the captain. One, he'd left with Alexzandar. The other sat atop the chest of drawers in the small passenger's cabin. Marcko fished his tinderbox out of his packs. He made sure the lantern wick was wet and then struck the flint. It took him several tries, but soon the flame caught and he replaced the cover. Holding it up, he motioned for Bud to lead the way.

They stepped out into the hallway and chased the shadows down the corridor. Bud was practically running, and Marcko found it a struggle to keep up. He was puffing when they reached the far end.

He had to squeeze sideways to fit into the crowded storeroom, but fit he did and found Sharee resting back on her knees next to her brother. The boy appeared to be sleeping. Marcko did a quick sweep of the room with the lantern, satisfying himself that nothing nefarious lurked in the shadows, and then returned to the pair on the floor.

Shattered bits of wood surrounded them, the apparent remains of the crate. The other lantern he had left was among the shards, itself broken, its oil bled out on the floor. Werim looked to have gotten it in his hair, as it was matted in wet ringlets to his forehead. Otherwise, Marcko did not notice any obvious injuries.

"Is the boy all right?" Marcko asked.

Sharee looked up. Her eyes were rimmed red, though the emerald irises held a spark of triumph. She looked exhausted.

"He will be," she said confidently. "I think I've worn him out, though."

It was an odd choice of words. *Speak for yourself, dear*, he thought, but instead said, "Did he tell you anything of Alexzandar before he dozed off?"

Sharee shook her head. "I thought...." Her voice broke, and then she took a deep breath. "I thought that was all blood." She pointed to the pool of lantern oil. "I feared–"

"The Archon must have hit him with this," Bud interrupted. He was holding a short piece of wood. "He dropped it here as he left the room."

Marcko nodded. "In any case, we can assume that the crew members of this ship are no longer our allies." He bent down to examine Werim. "You say he was struck on the head?"

"Yes," Bud replied. "With this."

"But there's not a mark on him."

Sharee was staring off into the distance. Marcko was starting to worry that she may have been the one to suffer a head injury.

"I healed him," she explained. "I was scared. It was so *loud.*"

Marcko blinked. *Muses....*

"We will be at the prison soon," Bud remarked.

Marcko turned to face the boy. "Yes. And I don't suppose they're likely to just let us saunter off now, are they? Even if we had a writ, it would be useless."

"How are we going to escape?" Sharee asked, concern in her tired eyes.

They all looked down at Werim. Marcko knew what they were thinking. The boy was usually the one with the schemes. Strange that in the short time Marcko had been with them, he should share their confidence in the boy's plots. *Just like his father.*

"There should be some water in here somewhere," Marcko said. "Perhaps we can hasten his recovery?"

Sharee nodded. "Yes, he did say he was thirsty."

"One of us should check out the door," Bud suggested.

"Of course, of course," Marcko agreed, his mind beginning to wrap itself around the situation. "We have only one source of light, though."

"These were by the door as well," Bud held up some strips of cloth. "They'll soak the oil."

"Pass them here," Marcko advised.

Shreds in hand, he laid them side by side atop the oil spill, pressing down to coerce the liquid into the material.

"His sleeves!" Sharee exclaimed. "I wondered about that. Foolish boy."

Marcko looked over. The fabric did indeed appear to have come from Werim's shirt. He wondered what might have caused the boy to remove his sleeves.

A dark stain spread on the dirty pieces of cloth, and then he handed them back to Bud. The blond boy set about wrapping them around the piece of wood. When he was done, they had only to touch it to the lantern flame, and their makeshift torch was lit.

"It will not last long, I fear, but it should provide enough time for a quick review of the door," Marcko said, taking the lantern back. "Hurry now."

Bud dashed down the hallway, a thin wisp of smoke trailing him.

Marcko turned his attentions back to the boy on the floor. *Water*, he reminded himself, and then began to search the shelves that lined the walls. The heavier casks had been organized below the bottom shelf, lodged against each other and the wall so that they would not roll. Marcko bent low to examine the writing on each. A lake-faring vessel such as this would not have stocked much water, but would possess at least one or two containers. Though the crew might bathe and drink from the lake, many of the passengers preferred their water without the taste of fish and silt. Marcko was not overly fond of the musty draught himself, though he'd been subjected to far worse. He shone the lantern on several barrels of wine before he found the one he was looking for.

"Here," he pointed. "Help me."

Sharee rose, tottered for a moment, and then joined him at the shelf. Together, they slid the heavy wooden container out and set it upright. Marcko found a cup high on a shelf near the door. He took it down and dusted it off. Now he just needed something with which to open the cask.

"Quick, give me the cup."

Marcko turned back to Sharee. She was settled back next to her brother, and there was already a hole near the top that leaked water down the side. *Of course, she doesn't need an opener.*

The girl tilted the cask and filled the cup after Marcko handed it to her. Then, she held it to her brother's mouth, propping his head. His lips parted as the liquid sloshed up against them. A bit dribbled down the front and soaked into his shirt.

"Come on, Werim. We need you," Sharee urged.

He groaned in reply.

Marcko bent down and fanned the boy's face. He was hoping that the cool air would help. It didn't appear to.

Sharee sat back, and Marcko leaned in with his lantern for a closer look. He laid a hand across the boy's forehead but did not feel fever. Likely exhaustion had taken its toll. Their road had hardly been easy of late, and who knew what effect a muse might have on someone in a weakened state.

The Eclectic sat back and pondered their options while Sharee tried again with the water. They needed to get off the ship when it docked at the prison. Marcko had friends there. Friends that would listen to him. Unfortunately, Alexzandar likely knew this as well and planned to keep his captives firmly shut up below deck. No reason to risk letting anyone out before they could all return to Tashaba, and Marcko could be hauled before the Summit. The Eclectic's chances were not good in that case. He had too few friends in the capital. It didn't matter that he was in the right. This was politics; *rightness* had nothing to do with it.

A glowing ember danced back down the hallway with Bud close behind. His torch was already beginning to die. The boy put the point of his long sword against the floor and leaned on it.

"Well, they've locked us in tight," he said.

"How so?" Marcko asked.

"Long nails, driven through the door," Bud explained. "Likely they hold boards on the far side. Strange that we didn't hear the hammering."

"Ships often make many strange noises," Marcko admitted. "I'm not sure a pounding would have alerted me." His eyes strayed to the ceiling, thoughtfully. "I was quite tired in any case."

"You're not exactly a soft sleeper yourself, Bud," Sharee said, smiling wanly.

The blond boy blushed. "It gets worse," he continued. "I caught a view from the portal in our room... we're closing in on land."

Marcko sighed. "I suspected as much. The winds were favorable all night."

"Can't we just let them deliver us to the prison? You know, as prisoners?" Sharee asked.

Marcko shook his head. "I don't think Alexzandar will do that. We know too much. He cannot risk giving me the chance to speak to anyone here. His friends are all in the capital."

"We can't go anywhere without Werim," Bud noted.

"The boy is exhausted, it could be hours before—"

A splash interrupted Marcko midsentence. He turned to cast wide eyes at Sharee. She was standing over her brother, holding the dripping cask. On the floor beside her was the top that she'd removed. Werim sat up, water sluicing down to puddle on the floor.

"We're sinking!" he exclaimed.

Sharee giggled. "Welcome back."

He turned to regard her with angry eyes. "What did you do to me?"

"Fixed you," she replied, setting the cask aside and crossing her arms.

Werim raised an eyebrow. "I was broken?"

"No more than the crate and lamp you landed on."

Werim looked at the broken shards around him. His hand went to his head. The irritation leaked out of him, and he turned to the door. A sad look crossed his face.

"I screwed up, didn't I?" he asked.

Marcko waved him off. "If anyone is at fault, it's me. I should have insisted that you take someone with you. A man doesn't get to Alexzandar's station without being crafty."

The explanation didn't seem to ease any of Werim's pain.

"We need to get off the boat," Bud said. "We're landing soon."

As if to underscore the dire nature of their predicament, Marcko heard a muffled series of thumps above.

"What was that?" Werim asked.

"Must be readying the ropes," Marcko answered.

"Already?"

When both Marcko and Bud nodded soberly, Werim attempted to stand. He got about halfway up before toppling over into his sister's waiting arms. A blush crept up his neck.

"What *did* you do to me?" he asked. "I feel drained."

Sharee shrugged. "Just buzzed you. There was a nasty gash on your head. I thought you were dying."

Werim rubbed at his scalp as if searching for the cut. He wasn't having any luck.

"If it makes you feel better, it made me really tired too," Sharee added.

Werim didn't respond, and the two of them stood together. They held arms until their legs steadied. *At least they're not fighting*, Marcko noted.

Werim looked at Bud. "Is this how you felt when she buzzed you?"

"The boat," Bud replied.

Werim nodded. "Right, right. What's wrong with the door?"

"Nailed shut," Bud said.

"And the crew?"

"Alexzandar has probably turned them against us," Marcko filled in.

The brown-haired boy thought for a moment before answering. "Then it seems we have only one choice."

"And that is?" Sharee asked.

"We escape through the back door," Werim said with a smile.

"Back door?"

"There's always a back door."

They all watched as Werim walked over to the wall and rapped a fist between two shelves. It sounded like solid wood. Marcko wasn't sure what the boy was trying to prove. He wasn't the only confused one.

"That's not a door," Bud pointed out the obvious.

Werim rolled his eyes and walked out of the storeroom. His strength was returning, but his movements were still lethargic.

Marcko picked up his lantern and followed the rest of them down the hall. At the far end, they turned into the cabin that the children had shared. The sun had set, but a full moon reflected off the water and bathed the room in silvery light. There did not appear to be an additional door in here, either.

Marcko watched in puzzlement as Werim stepped first on the bed, then atop the chest of drawers and gazed out of the portal. His face blocked all of the light, and Marcko held the lantern up so that he could see what the boy was doing. Werim seemed to be angling himself for a better view. After a few moments, he climbed back down and stood before them, a satisfied look on his face.

"What?" Sharee asked. "Did your wits get scrambled?"

"No," he replied. He pointed at the portal. "There's your back door."

Marcko looked at the tiny hole. He wasn't sure he could get his meaty arm through, much less the rest of him. The Eclectic was a fan of bending the truth, but one could only go so far.

"Werim, I don't think..." Sharee started.

"You're a muse, 'Ree," Werim said, stepping up to her. "Widen it. It's wood, and you can buzz wood, right? Just like in Knucklesporte."

Sharee went over to the wall and put her hand against it. She closed her eyes for a moment, and then smiled. "It's pine," she said. "Soft wood."

"Well?" Werim urged.

Sharee climbed up where her brother had just been. She sat cross-legged before the small portal and took a deep breath, closing her eyes. Slowly, she brought her hands up and held them palms outward as if she were warming them before a fire. The wood in front of her began to glow.

Marcko couldn't help but hold his breath. For someone who had lived his entire life being told that muses were evil, that all they did was destroy, that they were outlaws, watching Sharee bend reality was amazing. He had known the poppycock and politics thrown into all the old stories for what it was, but the opportunity to see a muse in action had never presented itself.

The wood groaned faintly as the portal began to expand. It almost appeared to bubble around edges like molten metal as it grew. Marcko noticed that Werim was smiling and tapping his foot to a melody that the Ecletic could not hear, enraptured by what his sister was doing. A quick glance at Bud showed him experiencing the same sort of deaf appreciation that Marcko was, mouth agape and eyes wide.

Sharee's hands moved steadily, bouncing in time to whatever tune she heard. When they pressed out, the wood responded. As they pulled in, it was as if the wood sucked in a breath, waiting for the next note to tell it what to do. All the while, a soft glow washed back over them and the opening grew steadily larger.

When she was finished, she dropped her arms. Werim climbed up beside her for a closer look, his feet still on the bed. Marcko could still see beyond both of them easily. A wave splashed up as he watched, causing both Sharee and Werim to scramble out of the way. Water leaked in and ran down the chest. It was cold as it washed up against the Eclectic's feet.

Marcko leaned to his left so that he could see more out of the widened portal. His eyes followed the curve of the boat as it converged on the prow. Directly beyond, land loomed large. The long finger of an approaching pier thrust toward them out of the rocky fist.

"When should we jump off?" Sharee asked.

"The water is quite cold this time of year," Marcko pointed out. "I would suggest avoiding a swim if at all possible. Also, they will likely hear the splash from above."

"Let's wait until we land," Werim suggested. "Some of the crew will surely leave with Alexzandar, so there will be fewer eyes to catch us sneaking off."

"Then jump in?" Sharee asked.

"Not if we can help it," Werim replied.

They watched as a pier took form from the darkness. The boat drifted slowly toward the pier, born by its momentum and the natural current of the lake. The wooden dock slid by on the starboard side, surprising Marcko. More often than not, ships docked to port when berths were free, but it was hardly a requirement. A gangplank could be lowered just as easily from either side. The Eclectic noted that it was probably in their favor, as a large hole in the hull of the ship might be conspicuous to anyone standing on the pier.

Eventually, the ship coasted to a halt. They heard shouting above as the sailors tied off their lines, and a scraping sound as they pushed out a gangplank.

"We're here," Bud noted.

◊ Chapter Twenty-Six

The boat rocked gently. Orange balls of fire danced in the water, reflections from the torches that had been lit above. Werim poked his head out of the widened portal and studied where the long pier met land. There was a collection of several squat houses, and then the land sloped dramatically upward. Atop the hill perched a somber, blockish building, brooding over the surrounding swamp. It featured solid stone walls with patches of lichen running up the sides. Barred windows gaped at evenly spaced intervals. A battlement ran along the roof between squat towers at each of the corners. Large braziers burned in each, illuminating the yard below.

There was no coast that Werim could see. Apart from the landing, the lake just seemed to slowly and grudgingly give way to land. Pools of water were interrupted by floating vegetation and short, twisted trees whose roots had somehow found purchase in the mud. The air smelled strongly of damp decay, and any breeze coming off of the lake was quickly caught and strangled before it could so much as stir a leaf.

The prison compound was situated on the only bit of solid land for leagues. Werim understood the choice of locale. Even if a muse should escape from a cell, they would have a hard time making it to any sort of civilization.

The Archon Basileus had left a short while ago, marching up the plank with the captain and several armed men. Some men had come out to meet them at the end of the pier. Marcko had indicated one of them to be the warden. It seemed that the Baraban Warlord had yet to arrive.

"Can we go now?" Sharee asked from the bed.

Werim turned to regard his sister. She was impatient, he understood. Their father was just up there, in that fortress atop the hill. "Yes. They should be busy talking for a while, right Marcko?"

The Eclectic nodded. "I'm not sure what Alexzandar is going to give as the reason for his late visit–I'm sure he'll dream up some sort of state business–but whatever it is will surely buy us time."

"Are we going to swim?" Bud asked.

The blond boy had taken several of the Eclectic's bags and strapped them to his person. They wanted to be able to move rapidly, and Marcko was the first to admit that he would be swifter with less to carry. After their frenzied dash to the oasis, Bud was quick to offer his help.

"Can you think of a better way?" Werim answered.

"What about the noise?" Sharee asked, adjusting her own burdens.

She had already tucked the two halves of her bow into her quiver, and was in the process of sealing up the top. She didn't want to lose anything in the water. Werim did his best not to focus on the buzzing in his head. It wasn't nearly as annoying as he'd once found it. The problem now was that he wanted to simply stop and listen. The notes tickled something in the back of his head.

"Well, remember the foot- and hand-holds in the sewer?" he asked, running a hand through his hair.

"Yes."

"I think those were made by a muse. Do you think you can mimic them in wood?" Werim stuck his head out and looked at the sides of the boat.

Sharee stood on the bed and looked with her brother. After a moment, she put her hand to the side of the boat just below the portal. There was a slight glow with a short buzz, and then her hand sunk into the wood. When she pulled it out, an indentation remained.

"Easier than making a door." She shrugged.

"The noise is not the only worry," Bud pointed out. "Even if we're quiet, we may still be spotted as we swim to shore."

Werim pulled his head back in and stared at Bud. "You're right." He put a hand to his chin. "Unless, we go around the boat and use the pier to shield us."

"Swim under the pier?" Bud clarified.

"Why not?" Werim shrugged.

He looked at Bud and then Marcko. Neither had any objections ready, though they didn't appear keen on the plan, either. He thought he heard the Eclectic mutter something about "cold" but decided to let it go.

A subtle buzzing spun him around. Sharee had eased herself over the ledge and was already starting down. Werim hurried over to peer down at her. She hung with one foot wedged into the side of the ship. As he watched, she placed the other foot against the curved wood, and there was another short trill before it sunk in. Slowly, Sharee made her way down the side of the ship. Fortunately, it only took about a dozen handholds before she reached the water. She slipped in silently, and then looked back up at her brother.

"It's not so bad," she called in a whisper. She floated away from the boat, clutching the sealed quiver that bobbed beside her.

Werim nodded and began following her down. The first step was the hardest. He groped blindly below with his foot, trying to find the notch in the wood. It was only when he recalled that he was taller than his sister that he found it, up higher than he envisioned. After that, it was a simple matter of letting his boot slide down to the next notch, his hands following him down. Sharee had crafted a small lip on the front of the notches, making them easy to grip.

He first felt the water when it seeped through his boot. Its icy tendrils tickled his soles and caused him to pause a moment. A quick glance up showed Marcko starting to heave his bulk out of the portal. Werim did not want to be caught beneath the Eclectic, so he forced himself down another step. When the cold liquid lapped up past his waist with the sudden surge of a wave, he inhaled sharply.

"Not bad?" he growled at his sister.

He slipped the rest of the way in and pushed away from the boat.

Sharee was floating easily nearby. Werim immediately wished for a floating piece of wood like her quiver. His weapon, a steel sword, dragged him down like some evil lake monster clutching at his belt. He was glad it was Bud that had taken on the extra packs.

Marcko dipped into the water with surprising litheness. The big man seemed unperturbed by the cold, despite his earlier protestations. Bud was swift on the heels of the Eclectic. He plunged in the water with a small splash that elicited a hiss from Sharee. They all stared upward for a moment, watching the lip of the deck high above, hoping that no curious sailors decided to poke their head over the side to investigate.

When the moment passed, and no alarm sounded, Sharee led them around the end of the boat. She kicked easily with her quiver out in front of her, while Werim struggled just to keep his head above the water. The waves felt much larger now that they were down among them, and more than once Werim found himself unwittingly drinking the fishy liquid. It was all he could do to keep his sister in his blurred vision.

On the other side, Sharee drifted quietly across the span between the boat and pier, angling for one of the stout posts that disappeared into the murky water. Werim took a deep breath, spit out some water, and dove beneath the waves. He kicked furiously, keeping his hands stretched out in front of him. When he emerged for air, he was dismayed to see that he was only halfway from the boat to his sister, exposed. A lantern on the dock above illuminated two guards standing to either side of the extended gangplank. Fortunately, neither of them was looking down.

Werim submerged himself again and swam the rest of the way. He came up next to Sharee and she grabbed his hand, guiding it to a freshly made handhold on the post. He nodded his thanks, and used it to catch his breath. She swam ahead and across to the next post, which was only a short distance away.

Marcko popped up next, startling Werim. The man had dipped under only a moment ago and swam the whole way on one breath. The Eclectic put a hand on the post and smiled.

"Go ahead and follow your sister. I'll make sure Bud keeps up," he said.

Werim nodded. Once more, he gathered his breath and made for the next post. This time, he tried to stay mostly above water, keeping his sister in view. She saw him coming and continued on, and Werim found the handhold that she'd left. Looking back, Marcko and Bud were still at the last post, preparing to swim toward him. He turned his attention forward and swam on.

They worked from post to post, going slowly. For Werim, the effort was grueling. Fatigue began to seep into his limbs before they were even halfway to land. That was swiftly replaced with numbness from the cold. He burned for the rest each handhold provided, gulping great gales of breath before moving on. Sharee kicked easily in front of him, making him feel the fool for being so tired. He blamed his sword, but there was no way he was removing his belt and letting the lake claim it.

His strength fled fast, and he began to despair of ever reaching land. Perhaps his journey would end right here, beneath the pier, ensnared by his own clever scheme. *Mom was always saying how I had more guts than wits*, he thought.

They had left the boat and its light far behind. The moon's fingers didn't reach beneath the pier, and Werim felt swallowed by the darkness. He could never quite clear his vision. He was either under water, or the spray from the waves crashing against the posts spewed in his face. He lost sight of his sister. *Just keep swimming*, he told himself.

Halfway between yet another set of pillars, he felt a larger-than-usual wave pull back on him and rear up. He blinked his eyes, saw angry froth, and quickly sucked in a breath.

The water slammed into him, propelling him forward. He threw his arms out, hoping not to smash into anything. When they encountered something squishy and warm, he recoiled. *A body.* It was the first thought that rang through his mind.

The movement of the water carried him forward, and pushed him up against the grotesque object. It was firmly rooted, immovable. When he tried to slither around it, it grabbed at him.

Panic shot up Werim's spine. He flailed his arms and tried to push off the corpse. *The dead have come to life!* His leg lashed out and glanced off the thing's side. It stumbled, but held firm. He heard a muffled *oomf.*

"Werim, quit it," came its hissing voice.

It called me by name! It called me by name!

It called me by name?

"Sharee?"

His sister pulled up on his sore shoulder, yanking him to his feet. Werim was astonished when his feet easily found the muddy bottom. He stood and wiped his eyes. Then, he grinned sheepishly in the gloom, shivering. The water lapped at his waist.

"That hurt, you big idiot," Sharee said, rubbing her leg beneath the water.

Werim looked down. "Sorry."

They were still hidden beneath the pier. Off in the distance, the boat floated, torches and lanterns shining on its deck. Werim saw the shadowy forms of the two guards at the end of the gangplank, as well as several on the boat. He thought he could make out a pair standing where the door to the cabins was. *Would have been a rough fight,* he reflected.

"It was probably for the best that we swam," Werim admitted.

Sharee shrugged. "It worked."

Marcko and Bud emerged together from the gloom. Bud was leaning heavily against the bigger man, gasping for breath.

"Swords make for poor flotation devices," Marcko observed.

"Thank... you," Bud said as they moved to shallower water.

"I owed you one." Marcko smiled.

"You're quite a strong swimmer, Marcko," Sharee noted.

The Eclectic nodded. "I've had some practice in these waters. Also, lard is much more buoyant than muscle." He slapped his belly.

Werim wasn't sure how to take the remark. He glanced over at Bud, but his friend was bent over with his hands on his knees, still trying to get his breath back.

They waded out of the shallows and onto the muddy beach. Grass grew right up to the water, and the mud had a dank smell to it. Sharee led them to a twisted tree nearby. There, they rearranged all their gear and tried unsuccessfully to get warm. Bud handed a few packs back to Marcko. Sharee unsealed her quiver with a soft trill. Werim scowled at his sword and shivered harder.

"Now what?" Bud asked when they appeared ready.

Werim was puzzling the question when Marcko spoke up.

"We should go straight to the prison. I can still play at being an honorable Eclectic up there," he said.

"What about Alexzandar?" Sharee asked.

Marcko pointed at one of the smaller structures. Light leaked from the various doorways and windows. "He will be busy trying to set the stage for the arrival of the Baraban Warlord, I should think."

"Where is the Warlord?" Werim wanted to know. "Shouldn't he be here by now?"

"By boat is faster than over land," Marcko said. "Especially in a swamp. Still, I expect it won't be long now."

"Well, let's get on with it, then," Werim said.

"Just try and behave as if we belong," the Eclectic suggested.

Werim looked down at his soaked clothing and raised an eyebrow.

"No one sneaks into prison," Bud noted.

"Good point, sir," Marcko said, clapping the blond boy on the back and starting out from under the scraggly tree.

Werim scowled at his sister. He didn't like the idea of walking into a prison, but what choice did they have? Their father was in there. She shrugged back. They turned toward the fortress.

A wide dirt path led up away from the docks, passing between a few of the smaller buildings and curving slightly up a steep incline. The burning braziers cast an orange glow down on everything, leaving very few shadows in which to hide. Apart from the road, the other sides of the hill were sheer and rocky, eliminating approach. Werim assumed he'd find things much the same on the back. The location was definitely chosen with its purpose in mind.

Or created, he mused.

Werim had only taken a handful of steps out from under the tree when he noticed it. It was soft, far off, but distinct, familiar. *Cymbals.* He hurried to catch up to his sister.

"Do you hear that?" he asked.

Sharee cocked her head at him. "Hear what?"

"I don't think we have a lot of time." He recognized the pattern. One of them at least.

He kept his mouth shut as Marcko led them out into the light. They strode purposefully between two of the buildings, emerging onto the dirt road. Fortunately, no one was out at this hour, though the structure that Alexzandar was in leaked light at the seams.

Up the incline they climbed, one wet squish at a time. The prison reared up before them, solid and imposing. Werim counted two guards in each of the watchtowers at the corners. It was difficult to make out more than dim shapes beneath the bright fires, but Werim swore he saw one ready a bow.

By the time they reached the top, Marcko was breathing heavily. They stopped a moment, letting him catch his breath. Werim gazed to the north. The cymbals were there. Unknowingly, he drifted a few steps toward the sound, peering out from the hill.

It was all swamp for as far as he could see. Patches of vegetation were broken by the occasional stagnant pool. Insects and amphibians croaked, uninterested in the dealings of men. The moon silvered everything, making the mud glisten the same as the water.

Scudding low, hugging the land, rolling toward the prison was a dark cloud. It stuck out like a soiled rag tossed among clean clothing–something Werim used to do to annoy his sister. The black fog was where the cymbals originated. They were growing louder by the second.

"Bud, Sharee. Look," he pointed.

"It's him," Bud said.

"Do you hear it now, 'Ree? He's playing loudly enough."

Her face had taken on an ashen cast. "Yes. I hear. I–I remember."

"Marcko, we need to find our father, *now*," Werim said.

The Eclectic joined them in staring at the strange cloud. "What is it?"

"An army? A few men? We have no way of knowing," Werim said. "At the very least, the Warlord of the Baraban Legion is coming. And I doubt he's here for a simple visit."

"No. No, I do believe you're right at that." Marcko fluttered a hand in his face. Let's hurry."

They turned and scurried over to the entrance. It was a simple iron portcullis cut into the wall. Stepping up, Werim could see that there was another gate beyond the first. Between the gates a smaller doorway opened to the right. Voices could be heard inside, and the flicker of torchlight spilled out into the causeway.

A shadow rose from the ground and preceded the man who emerged from the guardroom. On his waist was a simple cudgel, and he was lightly armored in studded leather, with a tabard thrown over top of the ensemble. A craggy rock was stitched in the middle, silver thread on a brownish-green background.

"What 'er you here for?" he asked.

Marcko stepped up and spoke. "I am Eclectic Marcko, and I've come to see a prisoner. State business, my good lad."

The guard looked him up and down. "A little wet, ain't ya?" He looked at the sky. "Don't appear t' be raining."

Marcko blushed. "We had a little, ah, mishap when docking. Surely, you've seen our boat? I'm afraid I'm not accustomed to descending a gangplank in the dark. Now if you would be so good as to open this–"

"And them?"

Werim tried his best to look official as the man squinted at them. The gooseflesh on his bare arms likely didn't help. He flashed a cooked smile anyway.

"Took 'em right with me. They valiantly tried to save their Eclectic from taking an ill-advised dip, but, alas, I'm not as fit as I once was."

"No, I mean, what 'er they here for? An' armed, no less," the man said.

Marcko fidgeted. "Ah, well. They serve as both my servants and guards. One can never be too careful, you know?"

The guard considered that, and then shrugged. "It is pretty late for visitations, why don't you come back in the morning? Be far less dangerous then."

Marcko took another step forward and shook his head. "I'm sorry, but I cannot. We are here on behalf of the Archon Basileus with a very time-sensitive mission. He would be most pleased if I could return to him within the hour."

The guard raised an eyebrow. "Captain," he called back over his shoulder.

They stood in silence for a moment until another man joined them. The newcomer was obviously older, with a thick salt-and-pepper beard that covered only the lower part of his face far down onto his neck. His tunic was nicer than the other man's tabard, with slightly more ornate armor strapped on here and there, though they both displayed the same sigil. In addition, he wore a simple pin on his right breast, apparently indicating his station.

"Yeah, what do you want, Rooge?" he growled.

"Man to see you, sir. Says he's an Eclectic, but I don't like the look of 'im. Did anyone tell you about a visit from the Archon Basileus?"

"No," the man shook his head. "I've not heard anything about..." he trailed off. He was looking through the grate curiously. "Marcko? Is that you?"

"Neckbeard?" Marcko replied.

"Ha! It is you," the man said. "And it's Captain Neckbeard now. Ha!"

"It is good to see you. It's been a long time." Marcko smiled.

"Years! How is the north treating you?" Neckbeard asked.

"Well." Marcko waved a hand. "On important business, you see. Perhaps you could assist us?" Marcko urged.

"Of course. Where are my manners? Private, get this gate raised. If the good Eclectic says he has important business, then we'll do everything in our power to help him. Good man, this is."

Private Rooge disappeared back into the guardroom, scowling but obedient. After a moment, they could hear some cranking and the portcullis raised. Marcko stepped through to clasp Neckbeard's hand. They had started talking again, but Werim wasn't listening. The cymbals grew louder in his ears. They were running out of time.

"Eclectic," Werim said, interrupting.

Marcko turned.

"We don't have a lot of time," Werim noted.

Marcko shook his head. "Ah yes. Apologies, old friend. We'll have to catch up later," he said. "For now, I need to be taken to the north wing."

"Sure, sure," Neckbeard replied. "I'll do it m'self. Your servants can remain here in the guardroom until we return."

Werim heard this and was displeased. He wanted to go to his father. Now. "Marcko, we–" he started, but the Eclectic pulled him aside.

"I will find some reason to have your father brought to the gate," Marcko explained in a hushed voice. "Trust me. I must play this game for a bit before I know how to make the proper moves. I will hurry." He looked over toward Sharee and Bud. "In the meantime, you three can make sure no one else is admitted through that gate. There should only be that one guard in the room. The others will be on the wall." He pointed up, and then looked back out the entryway. "Should the Warlord attack, sound the alarm. They have ways of dealing with muses here. This is a strong facility."

Meant for keeping people in more than out, Werim thought. He didn't like it, but nodded grudgingly. It wouldn't do them any good to come so far, get so close, and mess it up now. Besides, it would be much easier to break their father out if he were already at the gate. He had no choice but to trust the Eclectic.

Werim drifted toward the guardroom, motioning Sharee and Bud inside. Marcko returned to his friend and made some remark that left the captain laughing.

"Raise the inner!" Neckbeard hollered.

"Outer down, inner up!" came a shouted reply.

Werim watched the first gate slide shut, and then the second rumbled open. Marcko turned and winked at them before disappearing around a corner and into the prison. Werim would have nodded back, but the cymbals were splitting his ears. He hurried to join his sister and Bud in the guardroom, hoping that Marcko was right. They didn't have much time.

We're going to need your help, Father.

◊ Chapter Twenty-Seven

The guard room was deceptively large. There were several circular tables spread about, with chairs strewn haphazardly around them. Along the walls hung several tabards interspaced between burning sconces, and near the door was a collection of cudgels. A heavy wheel with wood spokes protruded from one wall, but what interested Sharee the most was the glowing blue orb that sat on a pedestal near the doorway.

It drew her attention immediately, emitting a soft whine that made her want to cover her ears. She unconsciously took a step back from it and looked for the guard. The man, Rooge, was paying her no attention, having just finished turning the wheel to lower the inner portcullis. He returned to a half-eaten meal, and sat focused on his food.

Bud was wandering along one wall, looking up at the tabards, while Werim had crossed the room to a dark doorway on the other side. He peered up at what appeared to be a stairwell, trying to discern where it went. Sharee returned her attentions to the orb.

It looked simply as if water had been captured inside of it and now swirled around in a lazy spiral. Why it should glow,

Sharee had no idea. The ambience pulsed in time with a slight rise and fall in the pitch of the whine. Sharee refused to take any steps closer. Something about it made her uncomfortable.

"What is this?" she asked no one in particular.

Private Rooge looked up from his meal and fixed her with a curious eye. "Ain't never seen an Orb of the Oracle before, have ya?"

Sharee shook her head. She'd heard mention of the Oracle before, but didn't know a whole lot about it. She reached out a tentative hand toward the device.

Rooge smiled and continued. "Well that there is what keeps the muses in line," he explained. "Only got one of 'em up here, but there're lots more in the north wing where we keep 'em all."

Sharee's hand froze. "How does it work?"

Rooge shrugged. "I don't really know. What matters is just that it does."

"Does it hurt them?" Bud asked.

Sharee looked over at the blond boy. Both he and Werim were paying attention now. Concern was plain on Bud's face.

Rooge laughed. "Naw." Then, he scratched his head. "At least, I don't think so. Make's 'em uncomfortable sure enough, but I ain't never heard 'em scream in pain or anything."

"Then what does it do to keep them from escaping?" Werim asked. "Surely, walls and bars and an annoying orb wouldn't be enough to contain a muse."

Rooge turned to look at her brother. "Boy, you lot sure are full of questions. Must not get out much. Then again, for servants, you *are* pretty young." Sharee thought the private didn't seem a whole lot older, but she didn't say so. After a moment, he pursed his lips. "I suppose... being near it... it just makes them like you an' me."

"Powerless?" Werim pressed.

Rooge nodded. "Right." He fingered the cudgel at his waist. "Thing is, most of 'em ain't never been normal before. They're really quite weak when it comes right down to it. A simple smack with a club'll set 'em right."

Sharee swallowed. She looked down at the orb, pulsing just beyond her hand. In her mind, she reached for the harp. It wasn't there. No matter how hard she tried, she could not play a note. It surprised her to find that she'd grown attached to her abilities. Having them forcefully removed was a shock akin to plunging into icy water. She backed away from the odd device and went over by Bud. Most of the room was behind her before she could find her harp.

Her brother shot her a curious look and then crossed the room to examine the orb more closely. As he approached, he seemed discomfited by it as well. When he touched it, Sharee couldn't help but tense up. He removed his hand and stared at it as if looking for some sort of wound or marking. Finding none, he shrugged and walked away. Though he tried to hide it, his footsteps were slightly hurried.

"Did you hear that thing?" he asked in a low voice when he was near.

Sharee nodded. "It's awful. Like scraping a stone across metal."

"Yeah," Werim agreed, thoughtful. "It made the cymbals shut up, though,"

Sharee focused on the buzzing in the back of her head. She hadn't noticed when it had gone away. The absence of her harp and the strange orb noise had commanded her attention.

"I didn't realize that," she admitted. "Did it hurt your hand?"

Werim showed her his palm. "No. It just tingled. Like when you've slept on your arm all night." He shook his hand at the memory of the feeling.

"Weird," Bud added.

Werim turned to regard his friend sharply, as if Bud had snuck up on them discussing something particularly embarrassing. Her brother's face reddened.

"Didn't want my sister to get hurt," he explained. "And I thought we better know how this place works."

Bud nodded. Werim grunted and stalked away.

"Still doesn't like admitting it, does he?" Bud asked after Werim was gone.

Sharee looked up at Bud's clear blue eyes, and for a moment, her mind went blank. "Admitting what?"

"That he has the same abilities as you," Bud said.

Sharee sighed. Bud was right, of course. He could obviously hear things that a normal person would not. The cymbals. Her playing. Yet, though he'd become more tolerant of her, it didn't seem he was quite ready to accept the same of himself.

"Father will know how to help him," Sharee said.

Bud nodded and put a reassuring hand on her shoulder, keeping her pinned under his gaze. For some reason, Sharee felt strangely uncomfortable. It was sort of like being near the orb–she felt a bit tingly where they touched–but not as unpleasant.

After a moment, he said, "How does it feel?"

Her heart fluttered, and Sharee scrunched up her face. "How does what feel?"

Bud blushed and pulled back his hand. "Being a muse, I mean. Don't you feel... different? I mean, after all that has happened. We've been through a lot. Changed."

"I'm not sure I understand, Bud," Sharee said. "Am I so different than I've always been?"

"Well..." his eyes swept over her as he groped for the right words. Finally, he turned away. "We can't go back. The village... it's gone."

Sharee hadn't thought of that. She hadn't *let* herself think of it. And she didn't particularly want to now.

Since leaving, she'd just been drifting from one place to the next, following everyone else, but there was a whole bushel of questions that sprang to mind if only she'd allow them. Where would they go? What would they do? Would they fight? Would they run?

Why weren't her parents fighting to begin with? Why did her mother just give herself up like that? Surely, muses weren't powerless against a Warlord. Were they?

With effort, Sharee forced herself back to the here and now. It wouldn't do to get lost in the past. The buzzing in her head was growing louder.

"I don't know what we'll do, Bud," she admitted. "I just want to use my abilities to help."

Bud nodded, and silence settled between them. All of a sudden, Bud seemed very close. Awkwardly close. Her heart thudded against her chest. It was almost louder than the cymbals. A shout from above saved her the need to think of something clever. All heads in the room turned toward the stairwell as the echoes died.

Werim vaulted the stairs first, followed closely by the private, his meal still unfinished. Sharee spun away from Bud and sprinted to follow. She heard the bigger boy clomping along behind her.

The stairwell swirled around and emerged into a small room, open on both sides. Sharee followed to the left and the sky opened above her, a thousand jewels glittering in the calm night. Silver from the moon glistened off waves in the distance, and a wispy fog cloaked the shore. The first thing Sharee noticed was a second boat gliding in toward the other side of the pier. Unlike their ship, this one wore only darkness; no torch burned upon her deck. Had the moon not been so bright, it would have been nothing but a shadow on the lake.

The few men who were on guard duty lined the bulwark. Together with the private, Sharee counted a six. They all wore the tabard and carried the same cudgel at their waists. None of them had a bow, as she might have expected. *They're not here to keep people out*, she realized.

The guards gathered not too far away, staring out at the night and talking in hushed voices with the occasional pointed finger. Sharee noticed they were not pointing at the boat. *What are they looking at?*

She followed their attentions back outward. Below, where the guardhouses should have been was a thick, dark cloud that she'd seen before. At first, she'd overlooked it for simple fog. Puffs of the black smoke stirred up here and there as men moved beneath it, looking like mice under a horribly dusty rug. The cloud was everywhere. It rolled up the hill toward them and lapped at the foot of the prison walls. Where before the big braziers at the corners had lit the muddy surroundings, now the light was swallowed by the roiling darkness.

"What does it mean?" she asked, though she already knew the answer.

"The Baraban Warlord is here," Bud confirmed from just over her shoulder.

"How do you know?" Private Rooge asked, a waver in his voice.

"We've seen this before," Werim explained calmly. He was rummaging around in his pack. "They did this same thing when they invaded our village." He fished up some familiar spectacles. "I'd almost forgotten about these," he said.

There were several shouts from below, punctuated by a blood-curdling scream. The clunk of steel on wood played below. Doors were slammed and fires bloomed, dim orange glows choked by the fog.

Werim donned the spectacles and handed the other pairs to her and Bud. Sharee hastily pulled them over her head. The scene below was worse than she'd imagined. Black clad men stalked confidently among the various structures, pulling the sleeping guards out of the buildings and bunching them together.

Sharee saw one man attempt to draw his sword. Before it was even half out, he had several Baraban blades sticking through his chest. The man never even saw where they came from. The savages left the body behind to bleed out on the dirt. She watched as the guard dragged himself a short ways before finally laying still. None of the invaders gave the corpse so much as a second glance.

To resist was slaughter. This was no hard fought battle; it was a mere passage of ownership. The prison that once belonged to Tashers was simply conscripted into the Baraban Legion. It was a mostly bloodless transfer of power, frightening all the more for its brutal efficiency. Sharee wondered if this was what the assault on Kokamongo would have looked like to an outsider.

Standing in the midst of the bustle was the Baraban Warlord. He was terrible to behold, hands held high, black gaze upon his troops with a detached curiosity. Cymbal crashes radiated out from him, a deluge of sound upon Sharee's mind. She wanted to cover her ears, but knew it would do no good.

"He's rounding them up," Bud noted. "Like cattle before butchering."

Sharee shuddered.

"Where is Alexzandar?" Werim wanted to know.

"Must not have flushed him out yet," Bud said.

"How are you seeing?" Rooge sputtered next to them. He eyed Werim warily with one hand on his cudgel, taking in her brother's ripped sleeves. The other guards had adopted similar stances of mistrust. "You're one of them, ain't you? Come to inf... in-filter-ate us from the inside."

Werim peeled off his spectacles with slow movements. "Of course not. Here, see for yourself." He held them out for Rooge.

The guard looked suspiciously for a moment before snatching them. Without pulling on the strap, he held the lenses up to his eyes. Half turning from her brother, he hazarded a glance below. Slowly, his hand dropped to his side. He turned the rest of the way forward. Then, as if he had seen enough, he jerked them away and held them out to the next guard. He stood facing the fog, his back hunched over and his head drooping.

"There's no hope for them, is there?" Rooge asked.

Werim put a hand on the man's shoulder. "He won't kill them until he has what he came for." Sharee supposed he meant it to be reassuring.

"What did he come for?" Rooge wanted to know.

"Muses." Werim pointed behind them. "That down there is just one muse. Can you imagine what would happen to our nation if there were a dozen? More?"

Rooge shook his head, his face ashen.

The spectacles were passed back. The guards had all apparently viewed their fill. Their drooping postures sang of defeat. The private examined the spectacles for a moment before handing them back to Werim.

"How do they work?" he asked.

"I don't know," Werim said. "What matters is that they do." He flashed a crooked smile.

The man smiled wanly back. "So, how did you come by this sorcery?"

Werim slipped the lenses back on and looked out at the cloud. "We killed a few of those savages when they destroyed our village," he said casually.

"And they let you leave?"

Werim chuckled. "Not exactly."

"So what do we do?" One of the guards in the back asked.

Werim didn't answer. He simply stared out at the cloud. They probably assumed he was thinking, but Sharee knew her brother better than any of them. He didn't have a plan and was scared. He hid it well, but not from her.

She thought of the guards and how they looked at her brother with respect in their eyes. It was odd for her to witness. Everyone had always treated them like children. Heck, they had always *been* children. But here, for the first time, they looked to her brother as another man. A man who had experienced some success against the enemy outside their gate. It wasn't just respect in their eyes, Sharee decided, it was also hope.

She pulled her brother aside. "Werim, you need to tell these men something."

His eyebrows knitted together. "What do you mean? I'm not their captain." He looked back to the stairwell. "I sure hope he gets back soon."

"And if he doesn't? It isn't going to take the Warlord long to wrap things up down there." She pointed back over her shoulder to where the men stood, watching them expectantly. "Look at them, Wer. They're scared. We've seen this stuff before. To them, it's all black magic. Sort of like how you felt when I first started playing Songs."

She saw the idea settle on him. "But why me?" he asked.

Sharee shrugged. "Well, I'm just a girl, right? And Bud, well... he doesn't have your confidence. For better or worse, they look to you."

Her brother threw up his hands. "But, what do we do, 'Ree? I don't know how to keep someone that powerful out of this place. For all I know, he could walk right up and carve a doorway straight into the wall like you did on the boat. What do we do then? Beat them back with these clubs? They have swords, 'Ree. Real, sharp, swords."

Sharee frowned. She knew he was right, but they couldn't just give up. Could they?

"What about that orb?" she asked. "If it works on me, it should work on him, too. Warlords may be powerful muses, but they're still muses."

"Should?"

Sharee nodded. "It will, Werim. I know it." She didn't really, but she needed him to believe.

Her brother turned away and gazed back out at the battle. She could tell he was thinking it through, putting together a plan in his head. He only needed to stall the Baraban men. Once Marcko got their father freed, he would know how to repel the Warlord. Wouldn't he?

"Private Rooge." Werim turned around. He had a gleam in his eyes.

"Yes?" the man asked.

"I have an idea that may buy us some time. I suspect we will not be able to hold out forever, but we can delay them a bit. If it comes to it, do you have swords somewhere?" Werim asked.

Rooge glanced nervously back at the cloud. "The armory is down there, sir. All we have here are the clubs and a few riot shields."

Of course, Sharee thought. *Why have weapons the prisoners might get?*

"It'll have to do," her brother said. "Do I have your leave to use the orb as well? I believe it will keep the fog from blinding us, as I don't have enough lenses for everyone."

"Yeah, sure," Rooge agreed.

"Can anything destroy it? Say, fire?" Werim asked, oddly.

Rooge raised an eyebrow. "To be honest, I don't know. Ain't never seen one break, be it from impact or flame. Trust me, we've tried." He smiled sheepishly. "Don't tell the captain that, though. We was just curious, you see?"

"Of course." Werim put a hand on the man's shoulders and looked into his eyes. "I'll need just one more favor of you, then." When the man nodded, Werim continued. "Take my sister to the north wing. Find your captain and our Eclectic. They need to be warned of the danger."

"Bu–" Sharee began.

Her brother held up a hand. "Don't argue, Sharee. One of us needs to make it to father. I'd rather not have you at the gate should things go poorly. Besides, who better to rally the reinforcements than you?" He flashed a smile.

Sharee felt her face redden, but she only nodded. She wanted to stay and help fight. However, she couldn't argue with sense. *And I can make sure they hurry back with other muses to help.*

"Reinforcements, sir?" Rooge asked.

"Don't worry about that," Werim said to the private. "I'm sure our Eclectic has filled your captain in on the way. You need only take her to them."

Rooge looked puzzled but nodded.

"Go, then," Werim urged. "Go now."

Sharee let the guard usher her to the stairwell. Just before she started down, she turned and cast one last look at her brother and Bud. Werim had gathered the remaining guards around him and was passing the spectacles, pointing and explaining things. Bud caught her glance and flashed a reassuring smile. Then, he pulled out his sword.

"Hurry," Sharee called to the guard in front of her.

She turned and fled, the whisper of her footfalls chasing her down the stone stairs like ghosts.

~ + ~

Vraika bangs harder. Before him, the Fog of War roils and crashes like a giant, black wave, soundless despite its immensity. His head is awash in terrible rhythm, pounded out on his gongs. *Hear me, Rynel*, he exults.

Behind him trails the thick throng of Legionnaires. A scant handful stays behind to watch over the cowed prisoners. They are already building a pyre in anticipation of the victory feast. Bound men huddle inside the circle of wood.

Destiny, Vraika muses.

It is almost time, the voice of the shard agrees.

Vraika's dark eyes sweep the structure before him as he scales the small hill. Not so long ago, braziers had been burning in the corner towers. They burn no longer, snuffed out perhaps in anticipation of his assault. What advantage that could provide, Vriaka knows not, but it does not matter. Destiny will not be impeded.

He surveys the high stone walls as he approaches. Stone is not the easiest of elements to inspire, especially when it has been hewn and fitted by other muses. There are easier ways to storm a keep. The prison is not made to resist a siege. It does not possess the arrow slits or murder holes that Vraika might have found in another stronghold.

A glow bleeds out from the barred gate. It appears as an open mouth, screaming in agony, spewing flickering light out into the night. It is toward this that Vraika stalks.

As he nears, his black cloud swallows the light. It washes up against the stone like a terrible floodwater, swelling well above a man's height. Vraika pushes it up to the bars. Tendrils swirl around and through, searching, seeking.

The Warlord steps up to the portcullis and peers in through his darkness. It surprises him to find that the light does not come from torches, but rather from the burning remains of one of the large braziers, upended before the second gate. The coals span the entryway, flames licking and blackening the stone walls.

A minor inconvenience, Vraika admits. Flames are but another element, easily inspired for all their fickleness. Much more pliable than stone.

"Open," Vraika bellows, "and save yourselves the trouble of resistance."

From the back room, he hears a soft twang that gives him pause. *A muse?* he questions. The quiet rythmn is overshadowed by a loud clank, and the gate before him settles deeper into the ground.

Vraika frowns and gathers his strength. If they will not welcome him in, he will rip the gate from its track, and woe to them who attempted to bar his path.

As he begins to pound out another rhythm, he hears the whine. He pauses again, puzzled. *What is back there?* Where his Fog of War should have penetrated the small room to the right, it bulges out as if brushing up against a large, transparent dome.

"Sorry, I can't open the door," a voice calls from the room. "Chain's broken."

Two boys emerge. The first holds a tall, oaken shield at the ready, a longsword in his other hand. The second wields a shorter saber, but it is what is in the fourth hand that gives Vraika pause.

The blue dissonance charm pulses, emitting an unpleasant sound. Vraika steps back involuntarily as the boy nears the gate. His fog retreats with him.

It is the orb that causes him to reevaluate the boys. The first is large, well-muscled with blond hair. He wears a simple rough-spun shirt and, despite his common appearance, does not appear to be a prison guard. He poses no threat to the Warlord, and is quickly dismissed.

The second draws Vraika's eye. Curly black hair falls over the boy's ears, and his shirt has been cut at the sleeves. The boy's right hand clutches a curved sword in the Baraban style, though the guard seems of better quality than the simple devices given to Legionnaires. Still, Vraika might have mistaken the boy for a fresh conscript, had the shirt been black instead of a travel-stained brown and his bare arms displayed some markings. There is something about this boy that troubles him, and it is not simply the orb he holds.

Vraika pulls his fog back to flow from his shoulders like a cloak. "Who are you, to bar the way of the Right Hand of the Triumvirate?"

"These are free lands," the boy with the orb answers boldly. "I don't see why we should let anyone in that we don't want to."

Vraika draws himself up, eyes flashing. "You dare challenge me, boy? Perhaps you have gone too long without a proper demonstration of power in these songless lands. *This* land has been conquered."

The boy hefts the orb. "I guess I hadn't noticed."

The smile flashed at him is full of insolence. Vraika fumes. How can a mere child know of dissonance charms, especially in these lands? *Perhaps he doesn't, and is only acting on the advice of others. Where is the muse?*

"Summon your leader, boy. I'm sure he wouldn't want your wagging tongue getting him in trouble," Vraika says.

"He's busy right now. So are all the guards. Unfortunately, I'm the only one here to talk to you." There it was again, that smile.

Vraika takes a deep breath and considers for a moment. He will not allow the boy to bait him. "Commander Borach, bring... our *ally* up here. Perhaps he can assist in this situation."

He stares hard at the boy while they wait. It surprises him that the boy does not flinch. He will be the first to die, as a lesson. His men will not tolerate weakness in him. A Warlord is absolutely strong.

There is something about those eyes...

Destiny, the shard crows.

Borach steps forward out of the fog with the fat leader of the Tashers. Vraika reflects that they truly must be a soft people to have such a soft Warlord. *Or should I call him an Admiral? He is no muse.*

The leader blinks and studies the boys. His eyes widen. It is apparent that he recognizes them. Perhaps they are guards after all, simply caught out of uniform.

"Command your subjects to bring me the muse that hides in the other room," Vraika orders. "I know he is there."

"T–they are traitors, my lord. Not mine, no, not mine. And there are no muses in our guardroom. They are all safely locked up." The fearful quivering of the man's jowls sickens Vraika.

"Traitors, you say?" he glares down at the fat man. "I can't imagine why. If that is so, then what use are you as an ally?" Vraika asks.

The pudgy man turns to the boys. "If you have any love for your country, allow this man inside," he pleads. "You should not have meddled, no, but now you have a chance to atone. Please, turn away from this course, and we will be lenient. Deals have been made."

"*You* are the traitor, Alexzandar," the boy fires back. "You'd sell our nation, for what? A song?"

"You do not understand. The Grand Warlord, his yoke is light. For greater security, a few liberties must be sacrificed. It is a small price to pay, especially if you are a law-abiding citizen," the man explains.

Vraika has heard enough.

The Fates will not be denied.

"Send this man to the pyre, Commander. He is obviously of no use," the Warlord orders.

"B–but lord..." the man cries as he is pulled away.

His Commander dutifully cuffs the fat one over the head.

Vraika turns back to the gate. "Tell me, what is your name, boy?"

Something about the question causes the boy with the orb to stand up straighter. He sets his jaw and raises his blade. The fury of the flames behind reflects in familiar hazel eyes. *So like his father...* For Vraika, it all clicks into place. The eyes. The cocky smile. The curly hair. Even the posture.

"I'm Werim Swift," the boy says proudly. "Maybe you remember my mother? I think you'll find me a lot less willing to bargain after seeing what you did to her."

◊ Chapter Twenty-Eight

The whine grew louder as Sharee sprinted down the cold stone corridor. She dashed through deep shadows that stretched between the few torches lit on the walls, reemerging into the light briefly only to plunge back into darkness. The air was damp, its smell a mixture of decaying swamp and unwashed bodies that left an unpleasant taste in her mouth. Private Rooge loped beside her, glancing over occasionally as if to make sure she could keep up. *He's breathing harder than I am.*

"We're... almost there," Rooge reassured her. "The north wing... is just ahead."

"I know," Sharee replied. *If those stupid orbs get any louder, I might go deaf.*

Sharee wasn't sure which she preferred, the buzzing of the gongs or the strange drone of the orbs. At least with the gongs she could make out a variety of notes, even if they didn't seem to flow together. Still, she knew who was making the noise, and that made it somewhat less appealing. Approaching the whine meant that her father was near.

She wasn't quite sure what she was going to do when they got there. Marcko and the captain must already be at her father's cell. Hopefully, the Eclectic had already made his case, and her father would be free. Even then, they were going to need more than just one additional person, weren't they? The Baraban Warlord had a small army with him, and he was a powerful muse. Wouldn't her father need his own troops?

Sharee turned the corner and stopped dead in her tracks. Before her stretched another long hallway, though this one had no torches. Instead, it was bathed in pulsating blue light. Set high in the walls, one above each cell door, were dozens of the orbs. They throbbed in time together, making the north wing seem almost as if it had a heartbeat. A hard lump climbed up in Sharee's throat.

Far down on the left, she could see the Captain and the Eclectic in front of a cell. Rooge took a few steps into the corridor, and then looked back when he realized Sharee wasn't following. She knew she should. She just couldn't take another step. If one orb was disconcerting, then this hallway was a nightmare come to life.

"Are you coming?" Rooge asked.

Sharee gritted her teeth and nodded. She took one step forward. Then another.

Rooge frowned at her, but turned and continued. Sharee followed step by reluctant step. When she passed under the gaze of the first orb, she felt as if she'd just plunged through a mountain waterfall, cold water sheeting over her and causing a shiver. The gongs were cut off, and so was her harp. She shifted the quiver on her shoulder and the arrows rattled. She was glad she hadn't gone completely deaf.

They moved ahead at a brisk walk. Rooge appeared almost as uncomfortable as she was. He kept his head straight forward, as if he dared not peer into any of the cells they passed. His mouth was a grim line, and he was focused on the two men mumbling at the other end.

While Sharee may have shared his ill-feelings, she saw no reason to leave her curiosity unsatisfied. Her head was constantly on a swivel. She wanted to see what these other muses looked like. Were any of them young, like her?

She couldn't see much. The blue light didn't penetrate far into the gloom beyond the bars. Dim shadows moved lethargically in sparse rooms. Sharee believed she could make out a cot, a bucket, and not much else. A quick sniff of the air confirmed her guess as to what the bucket was for.

Disappointingly, all of the shadows looked the same. Sharee supposed she expected muses to be larger than life, to be up at the bars, glaring at them in defiance as they walked by. She had hoped to bring her own raucous army–newly freed–back to her brother, but the shadows she saw were thin and frightful. They cowered at the soft sound of her footfalls, wanting only to stay hidden in the darkness that was their home. *They've all been cut off for so long.* More than anything else, they all appeared lost.

In a few of the cells, she didn't see anybody, just a formless lump quivering on the cot. Those were the dirtiest. The strong smells of rotting flesh combined with the refuse in the bucket to make her wrinkle her nose and quicken her step. *Even shadows don't want to be in those cells*, Sharee reflected.

The pulsing blue light battered Sharee, pressing on her like a weight. Though they were halfway down the hallway, she felt as if they had leagues yet to go. Being in the presence of the orbs tired her in a way that running here had not, and she found herself struggling for breath. It felt like she was moving through deep water, drowning in the heavy air.

How can they force people to live in such a place? Sharee wondered. She had only been here a few moments and already felt as if she were going mad. The orbs played strange tricks on her. She thought she saw bones poking out of the lumps in the empty rooms. The skin was sloughing off of a shadow here. The faint glistening of blood ran down the side of a face there. She needed to take her mind off them and focus on the task at hand.

"How do these doors open?" Sharee asked.

Private Rooge turned sharply as if he had forgotten she was there. For a moment, he regarded her, and Sharee was worried that she'd said too much. What if he suspected her of being a muse?

Eventually, he shrugged. "Captain has a key... of sorts."

Sharee frowned. "What does that mean?"

Rooge shook his head. "You'll see it if he wants you to see it." He'd turned his head forward once more.

Sharee's frown deepened, but she held her tongue.

Their footsteps announced them–or rather, Rooge's did, Sharee's footfalls were a lot quieter–and the two men turned toward them.

"Private?" Neckbeard appeared alarmed. "What are you doing here?"

Marcko simply raised an eyebrow at Sharee.

"We're under attack," Sharee blurted. "The Warlord is at the gates. Heck, maybe he's inside now, I don't know. Bud and Werim were going to try to stall him."

Marcko's eyes widened. "I had hoped the garrison below would buy us more time. Captain, the decision must be made now, I fear."

Neckbeard frowned. "Marcko, what you ask... I could be thrown into one of these cells for this. Well, not these, but... you know what I mean."

"Sharee?"

The voice came from the cell on Sharee's left. It was raspy, yet recognizable. She turned.

"Father," she breathed, and then rushed up to the bars.

Her father's face swam out of the gloom to meet her. He was thinner than she last recalled, and his skin had a sickly cast to it. His clothes were a mess, and his beard had grown right along with his hair, both much longer than she'd ever seen them. But the hazel eyes–so like her brother's–were the same.

Sharee couldn't help it. She felt the moisture sliding down her cheeks. She tried to bite back the tears, but they were having none of it. A grunt of frustration escaped her lips as she reached up to smear her face.

"Aren't you a sight for sore eyes," her father cooed. "My baby girl. You're here, you are. But how? There, there now." He reached a grimy hand through the bars to brush at her cheek.

"M–mom," she sniffled, unable to control herself. "She's... she's d–dead."

Her father's eyes widened. "How?"

"T–the Warlord."

"Rynel..." Marcko said, stepping up.

Her father's jaw clenched. Hard. Sharee found herself taking an involuntary step backward.

"Why didn't you tell me, Marcko?"

The Eclectic spread his arms wide. "I thought we had more time. He's here, it seems."

"Of course, he is," Rynel growled. "Let me out of here."

"I'm not sure if I sho–" Neckbeard began.

"Do it, or I swear I'll break out of here myself," her father interrupted.

"You can do that?" Rooge asked, mouth agape.

"Now!" Rynel shouted.

The sound echoed off the walls. Sharee backed away, her tears dry in an instant. She had never seen her father so angry.

"What are you going to do?" She asked.

Rynel turned hard eyes on her, "Something I should have done a long time ago."

~ + ~

The darkness in the Warlord's eyes sucked at Werim. He clutched the sphere tightly in his tingling hand, sweat making the smooth orb slick. He was terrified that he'd drop it. The Warlord certainly wouldn't hesitate to kill him should it roll the wrong way.

Not after his little display of bravado, false though it may have been.

"Rynel..." the Warlord growled.

How does he know father's name?

The dark man's anger was palpable, though Werim heard none of what he was sure must be furious pounding on the gongs. Thankfully, the orb continued to work. He had been half afraid the Warlord would take one look at the device and do something to simply destroy it.

Around the man, the conjured darkness roiled and writhed, flowing back from broad shoulders. Puffs of dust fell from the walls as stones began to rattle. Werim hoped he'd covered enough of the gate with the orb to stop the Warlord from breaking through. So far, it was holding.

Several of the Baraban men stepped forward out of the fog. Their spectacles swirled with the mist, and heavily marked arms aimed sidebows at the two boys. Bud raised his shield and Werim backed behind his friend. The orb wouldn't protect them from those sharp, black bolts.

"This shield will keep us alive, but they could still hit us," Bud whispered. "I can't cover every angle."

Werim saw that his friend was right. All it would take was one well-placed shot in the arm. "He may start tearing the stone away, anyway. Who knows?"

"Retreat?" Bud suggested.

The stones rattled.

"Retreat." Werim nodded.

Together, they began to slowly edge backward. Werim wasn't exactly sure how far the coverage of the orb extended outward. He'd gotten a vague sense of it when they'd barreled into the fog, but he'd been guessing as they stepped up to the gate.

At the corner, just before they disappeared into the guardroom, Werim paused. He turned back to cast a look at the impotent, raging Warlord on the far side of the gate. Black eyes bored into him.

Well, I've not made a friend. The errant thought brought a crooked smile to Werim's face. The Right Hand of the Triumvirate saw it and fumed hotter, if that were possible. Werim knelt down, and calmly rolled the orb into the fire. He'd given it enough force to get up into the coals, where it stuck and glowed, untouched by the heat.

The gongs returned, louder than ever. Through the cacophony, a groan of twisting metal snapped Werim's head around. He'd protected the inner gate at the expense of the outer. The Warlord and his Legion were coming in. *Well, I expected that to happen eventually. Just perhaps not so soon.*

"Bring me the Swift boy alive. Kill the other," the Warlord bellowed.

Werim turned and ran. Bud was waiting at the stairwell. Together they started up, taking the steps two at a time. When they were almost at the top, the fog surged up and swallowed them. The sudden darkness caught Werim by surprise, though he'd heard it coming in a tumult of clangor. He stumbled on the next step, his hands shooting out in front of him, and tried to twist out of Bud's way.

It didn't matter. Strong arms caught him. He heard a grunt from Bud beside him. It took Werim a moment to realize that the hands had come from above their position. He heaved a sigh of relief and let himself be pulled upward.

"Got you," one of the prison guards, Crim, whispered into his ear.

Werim had given his spectacles to the man. Cram, his twin brother, had Bud's set. They were two of the bigger guards that had been on duty.

The twins led Werim and Bud the rest of the way up the stairs and out of the fog. The clear air smelled somehow sweeter as it slapped Werim in the face. He leaned over, panting, and turned his head to watch Crim and Cram move swiftly to the right. Burning brightly in the small room atop the stairwell was the second brazier they'd relocated. Muscles straining, the two men wrapped their hands with spare tabards and hefted the huge bowl. They navigated it over to the top of the stairs, and waited.

Werim could hardly make out the footsteps of the first men, but Crim and Cram, with the lenses, could see them. The Baraban troops weren't expecting to be visible. They weren't expecting a shower of hot coals, either.

Screams ripped through the fog, and it did little to cloak the stink of burning flesh as the twins dumped the brazier. When it was empty, they shoved the still smoking bowl into the doorway, wedging it from ceiling to floor. It didn't cover the whole entryway, but it would be an annoyance and too hot to touch for some time still.

Werim didn't plan on sticking around to watch. Crim and Cram removed the spectacles and handed them back. Then, the four of them took off running toward the south wing. Gongs rang angrily behind them.

We can't lead them around forever, Sharee, Werim thought. *Hurry.*

~ + ~

When her father had disappeared in a flash, only to be replaced by a crackling ball of light, Sharee had cried out in dismay. When the sparkling orb drifted through the bars, she'd nearly run in fright. And when, after a second flash, her father had reappeared, standing unharmed in front of her, she simply stood with her mouth agape.

"How did you...?" Sharee managed in a strangled whisper.

Her father grinned crookedly. "An old trick your mother taught me." The smile couldn't completely conceal the sadness in his eyes.

"But, the orbs...." She pointed upward.

"They're not all-powerful, dear." Her father chuckled and pulled her into an embrace. "Oh, how I missed you."

The comforting warmth of his arms chased her fears away, at least for a moment. Soon enough, they came crashing back as the other men shook off their own surprise. Marcko stepped up with a smile, while the captain and his junior guard were frowning and looking around as if not sure what to do when a muse squeezes himself magically through the protective bars. If this one could, why not the rest of them?

"It is good to see you, Rynel-imba," Marcko said as daughter and father separated. "I'm sorry I don't bring better news."

"We knew it was a gamble," Rynel admitted, his face serious once more. "It seems I have you to thank for bringing my daughter." He clasped the bigger man's hand.

"D–daughter?" Rooge sputtered. "Captain... what is this?"

Neckbeard shrugged. "Apparently, a family reunion."

Rynel looked over. "Where is my son?" He turned to Sharee. "Where is your brother?"

Sharee glanced at the floor. "Hopefully holding the gate. Or at least delaying the Baraban men."

Rynel nodded with a smile. "Takes after his father, then, does he?"

"More than you know," Marcko replied.

Sharee giggled.

"So, since I'm operating under the assumption that you've been pardoned," Neckbeard spoke up, "what do we do now?"

"P–pardoned?" Rooge echoed.

Rynel raised an eyebrow at the young guard. "Does this young man have a stutter?"

Neckbeard chuckled. "Muses, you know." He shrugged.

Rynel nodded. "I get that a lot." He clapped Rooge on the back. "Marcko will tell you I'm not half bad." When the Eclectic smiled, he continued, "Captain, I'll need your help to open these cells. I doubt any of the prisoners know the trick I just used, and it would be tough to teach even in the best of situations."

"All of them?" Neckbeard asked.

"Yep. That was part of the plan."

Marcko balked. "It was?"

Rynel leveled a gaze at his friend. "That's the Right Hand of the Triumvirate on his way in. How did you think I was going to fight him? I'll need support."

"B–but... they're..." Rooge managed.

"Muses? I know. Look, I overheard Marcko filling your captain in on the situation," her father explained. "It seems your Archon Basileus has been using his position... less than faithfully. I think you'll find that many of the inmates in this wing are here because of him. I should think being imprisoned by a traitor would, at the least, warrant them a second trial, if not an outright pardon."

"Say I release them, then what?" Neckbeard asked.

Rynel ran a hand through his hair. "Well, I suppose they'll fight for us. Then, perhaps, for services rendered, they will be escorted to the borders and released."

"How do you know they'll fight for us?" Marcko asked. "What's to stop them from fighting on the other side? Many of them served the Grand Warlord."

"Not as many as you'd think, Marcko. Besides, Aarik isn't here for them. You know that, and they know that. They know the price of failure. I am their only chance for freedom."

"Who is Aarik?" Sharee wanted to know.

Her father glanced over at her, fury in his eyes. "My brother."

~ + ~

The sidebow bolt caught Crim square in the neck. Blood fountained out, spattering Werim as the man fell. His brother stopped and turned to help.

"No," Werim shouted.

But it was too late. A second bolt blossomed from Cram's chest. His body draped limply over its twin.

"Here, Werim," came Bud's call.

There was another stairwell on the south side of the prison, and his friend ducked into the room atop it. Werim joined him even as another bolt glanced off the stone wall.

They didn't stop, plunging headlong down the steps. Several times Werim thought he was going to trip, fall, and break his neck. The gongs rang ominously behind them, advancing steadily. All of the bolts had come from the fog that was rolling along the prison rampart. The cloud continued to grow, and Werim envisioned that soon it would cover half of the compound. He wondered what the prisoners below them might think when the tendrils came creeping in uninvited.

While he had still been able to talk, Crim had informed them that the south side of the prison held the non-musical inmates. That, and the wing's extremity from the north, had prompted Werim's plan to lead the Baraban invaders on this wild chase. He was currently regretting his decision. *More guts than wits....*

Several more of the guards were waiting when Werim and Bud burst forth from the stairwell into the room at the bottom. Together, the men lifted one of the large wooden tables in the room, and shoved it up against the stairwell. They piled a second table and all of the chairs behind it. It wouldn't hold for long, but it was something.

Werim had sent Maron, the last of the guards from the front gate, ahead to warn his cohorts. Apparently there were four guardrooms in the prison, each at the bottom of a stairwell midway between corners. The north room was abandoned, on account of no one wanting to be near the muses. The east room was only occupied during the day, when men might be released into the large courtyard in the middle of the compound. That left their only manned room to the south, which served Werim's purposes just fine.

He looked over the men. There was one officer and four men of lesser rank. With Maron, that made six cudgel-armed guards. Werim and Bud were the only ones with steel. *Even if they had swords, they wouldn't be able to use them in that fog*, Werim reflected.

"Where are Crim and Cram?" Maron asked. His tone indicated he already knew the answer.

Werim grimaced. "They shot at us while we were running. Cram went back for his brother, but...."

Maron nodded soberly. "What now then?"

Werim turned to face the more senior man. "Captain?"

"Lieutenant," he corrected. "Verme, sir." Werim was surprised when the man saluted, striking fist to breast. "Maron here tells me you're with the Eclectic. Says you know how to fight these intruders."

Werim frowned. "I'm afraid he gives me too much credit. I'm just trying to buy us time until the reinforcements arrive."

To his credit, Verme simply nodded. "What can we do to help?"

Werim looked toward the only other exit in the room, the one that led into the prison wing. "Do you have a key for the cells?"

The man fished a small, metallic object out of his pockets. "It's not exactly a key, but it shuts them gates when we put someone in."

"And it'll open them, too?" Werim asked.

The man screwed up his eyes. "Why would we want to do that?"

Werim pointed back at the blocked door. "We need all the help we can get. In case you weren't told, there's a small army following us."

The man didn't seem convinced.

Werim sighed. "They're Tashers, right?"

The Lieutenant nodded. "Any foreigners'd be thrown in with the muses. Never know with them."

Werim smiled. "Then we'll give them a chance to prove their loyalties. Surely they'll fight for their country."

"And if they don't?" one of the other guards asked.

Werim shrugged. "Well, we'll probably die anyway. The Baraban aren't fond of taking prisoners." *Unless you have mothers willing to die for you, that is.*

A staccato of thumps hit the table. The guards looked at the makeshift blockage with wide eyes. Werim fixed the Lieutenant with a level gaze.

"Fine," the man relented. "Let's go. Now."

Wood groaned in protest behind them as they hurried out of the room.

◊ Chapter Twenty-Nine

Sharee spread her arms and tilted her head toward the ceiling. She felt like a tree spreading new leaf beneath a radiant sun. The air even smelled cleaner as she followed her father and the other men around a corner, leaving the pulsing blue light of the north wing behind.

They didn't go very far before ducking into a small room across from a burning torch. Sharee wished she could have put more distance between her and the orbs. The maddening whine still echoed in her head. The wall before them appeared riddled with pock marks. On closer inspection, Sharee saw that each of the dents was actually a perfectly formed circle carved into solid stone. Her father ran his fingers over the bumps.

"I'll need the key first," he said.

Captain Neckbeard fished into his pockets and pulled out a small, metallic disc. It was not like a normal key, but the sight of it prickled a memory in the back of Sharee's mind. The device was the exact same shape as the indentations in the wall. Sorn had used a device like this in Knucklesporte.

"An unpickable lock," she whispered.

Her father cast a questioning look at her, but apparently decided to hold his tongue. Neckbeard lifted the disc and eyed it warily. After a long moment, he handed it over to her father.

"Which cell did I call home?" Rynel asked.

Neckbeard squinted at the depressions. They appeared to be layed out in a smaller reproduction of the wing. The captain counted several cells off, pointing at them each in turn, and then left his finger on one near the right.

"This is it," the man said.

The disc fit perfectly into the wall. Sharee jumped when a little trill squawked in her ear. At any other time, she might have been annoyed, but having just left the dreary orb wing, any song was a comfort. Without thinking, she found her harp and joyously attempted to mimic the notes. A sharp look from her father cut her off mid-melody.

"Sorry," she mumbled, eyes going to the floor.

She could hear stones grating and rumbling behind the wall, evidence that something was going on, but she dared not look up. She remembered her brother's initial misgivings all too well when he found out she was a muse. She wasn't sure if she could face her father's displeasure.

His warm hand lifted her chin. Soft, hazel eyes regarded her. She thought she detected a hint of moisture in one corner. *Is he so upset at my freakishness that he's going to cry?*

"When did this happen?" he asked.

Sharee bit her lip. "Just before..." she trailed off. If she finished the sentence, she'd cry again. She had to be strong. Like her father. He didn't cry.

"Of course, dear." Her father patted her shoulder and fixed her with a stare. "I'm sorry I wasn't there, Sharee. I missed so much. I put it out of mind until just now. I am truly sorry."

She pulled back and looked up at him uncertainly. "Is it... okay?"

Relief flooded her when her father smiled. "It's *beautiful,* dear. A harp, too, it seems. Perfect, just perfect." He pulled her into another warm embrace.

"*Ahem.*" The other three men were looking at them curiously.

Marcko tipped his head toward the wall. The square that denoted Rynel's old cell was glowing with a faint blue hue, the disc glinting in the middle. "Right, right." Sharee suspected that her father's cell had been opened, but why? *Maybe he was just testing the key.*

Her father surprised her by removing the disc and handing it back to the captain. He flexed his fingers and stepped up, placing both hands flat against the stone. He favored Sharee with a quick, conspiratorial smile, took a deep breath, and then....

It was as if a hundred crickets had crowded into the small room. They were much deeper than Sharee was used to, and she knew in an instant the sound came from her father. She focused on the noise, anxious to try and discern what her father was doing.

At first, there was a smattering of unconnected notes as if he were feeling around an instrument long left unused. Then, he pulled it together. She recognized the melody from the trill, except the song was much crisper when played by her father. It thrummed through his hands and into the wall. Sharee resisted the urge to try and play along. *I'd probably mess something up*, she reasoned.

This time, the grinding of stone on stone was deafening. The floors and ceiling shook, small showers of dust raining down on them. Sharee reached out and gripped her father's arm reflexively as he stopped playing. He stepped back and smiled down at her. The entire wall was starting to glow blue, one cell at a time.

Eventually, the grinding stopped. Silence crashed back in. The wall pulsed before them, mimicking the hallway they'd left a short time ago. Sharee listened hard. The whine of the orbs was gone. She did, however, notice that the buzz of gongs crashing in the distance had resumed. She looked up at her father. He was looking off toward other parts of the prison–toward the noise–as if he could see through the stone to the battle beyond. *I hope Werim is all right.*

"Eclectic, Captain, follow me," Rynel said. "We must hurry."

Sharee let her father lead her out of the room. The other three men followed at her back. The lone torch still burned just outside of the key room, but soon they were away from its warm light. Sharee felt as if they had exited into a different hallway. It wasn't until they turned the corner that she realized why.

Deep darkness greeted them, matched by an equally deep hush in the absence of the whine. Where before the north wing had been lit with pulsing blue light, shadow and silence now reigned. They stopped on the cusp of the gloom, the thin glow from the torch following them from the left, but failing to turn the corner and shed any light on the cells before them. It was into this darkness that her father spoke.

"Fellow muses," he bellowed, his voice echoing off the stone, "you have been released by my hand. You are free to go, though I would ask that you stay and fight with me. We share the same enemy, and one of his Hands is here...."

The darkness did not answer. It could have been that the cells were all empty, that all the prisoners had already fled. That was not the case, though. Sharee could feel it. She could feel their eyes looking toward the faint light at the head of the hallway. She could feel them wondering. The unasked question hung heavy in the air: *Who is this man?*

Her father must have felt it, too. He took a step forward. "I am Rynel Velos. Likely some of you were sent here to find me. You may have heard my tale, held up by The Grand Warlord as an example of what happens to those that dare defy him. He convinced my brother to betray me, and I was exiled by my father. He took my people, and bent them to his will, breaking their honor. His Hand killed my wife. Yes, Vral has taken much from me. I mean to see that he pays for his crimes.

"I have seen none of your faces. You may leave now, and no one will hunt you. You have my word. Yet, Vral is not so forgiving, and his agents are everywhere. You know this just as you know the penalty for failure. In his eyes, your lives are already forfeit. Return to him, and you will only find death. Hide, and death will surely find you. I am living proof of the lengths he will go to solidify his power. So, I offer you another option. Join me. Fight with me. Taste revenge with me."

Still, there was no audible answer. But Sharee heard something. It was small at first. A buzzing. Joined by other buzzings. A note here, a cymbal crash there. It was the sound of muses waking up and tasting their freedom. They reached out to instruments they'd thought long gone, caressing those first tentative notes as if brushing the hair away from the face of a lost lover with a trembling hand.

Then, one by one, they turned to a song. It was a simple one, though Sharee had never heard its like before. A hundred voices took it up in the darkness. Many of the instruments were cymbals, but strings were represented as well. Sharee thought she heard a few horns, and some other instruments she couldn't put a name to.

As the song finished, tiny flames of light sprang to life out of the gloom. They hovered in the air, each above an upraised palm. Where before the hall had pulsed in eerie blue, now it glowed with the tongues of a hundred flames. Illuminated in each flame, there was a face. Each face was turned toward the head of the hallway, toward her father. Each pair of eyes burned with hunger.

Sharee found herself lifting her own hand. She placed it upward and mimicked the song she'd just heard out of a hundred throats. Her father looked down at her, a fierce pride on his face as her flame winked into existence and joined the rest.

In the distance, the sound of gongs pecked at Sharee's ears. But here, in the hallway of muses, it was the Song of Fire that echoed off of the stones and in her head, sending a shiver of warmth down into her heart.

Werim, we're coming.

~ + ~

The tiny trill caused Werim to jump. He looked at the men around him, but they didn't seem to have heard it. His eyes landed on Bud, who was staring at him pointedly.

"What?" Werim asked.

He moved the key to the next indentation. The trill played again.

"You jumped," Bud accused.

Trill.

"Did not."

"Admit it," Bud said.

Trill.

"Admit what?" Werim asked.

"You heard it."

Trill.

"You heard something?" Werim pressed, playing coy.

Bud rolled his eyes. "No, I didn't, but you did. Muse."

Trill. Trill, trill. Gong crash.

Werim pushed his friend. "You shut your mouth." He looked around him worriedly, but the guards were more interested in the walls and ceiling, which resounded with a grinding sound. That, and the solid thunk of steel on wood echoing off the stone from around the corner.

Bud fixed him with a level stare. "What do you think they're going to do, throw you in prison?"

Werim pressed the key into the last dozen holes, doing his best to ignore the annoying trilling. Bud chuckled at his obvious discomfort. Gongs crashed in the distance, and... was there something else? Werim thought he heard another song from the north.

Sharee? he wondered.

Bud followed his wandering gaze. "Are they coming?"

Werim's eyes snapped back to his friend. "How should I know?"

"You can hear them."

"It all sounds the same."

"So you admit it, then."

"Shut up."

Werim handed the key back to the Lieutenant.

"Hear what?" the man asked.

"The grinding," Werim answered, swiftly. "It's stopped."

The man nodded. "That means you should probably talk to them."

"Me?"

"They're not going to want to listen to a guard."

"He's right," Bud chimed in.

"Then why don't you do it, Bud?" Werim asked.

"You're more charismatic," he replied.

Werim furrowed his brow. "What does that mean?"

"Just do it," Bud said.

There was another crash. This one was splintering wood, and everyone could hear it. The Baraban men had broken through.

"Fine," Werim said, casting one last look at the glowing wall before leaving. He'd have to tell Sharee about it later. She'd probably want to play with it.

They darted out into the hall. Gongs echoed off the walls, banging loudly in Werim's head. Across from them, a torch sputtered. Werim went over, pulled it out, and poked his head around the corner. Halfway down the hallway, light spilled out of the guardroom. In that light, he saw shadows moving. He cursed and flung the torch. It didn't go very far, skittering against the floor and sending embers spiraling away. The flame went out.

"That's not going to slow them," Bud pointed out.

Werim frowned at his friend and pulled him back around the corner. The guards were clustered worriedly behind them. They parted for Werim as he stalked forward. A short distance ahead was another corner. This one turned in the same direction as the guard hallway, and ran between two long rows of cells. Werim hadn't realized it, but they'd been running behind the cells when they'd exited the guardroom.

Turning the corner, his breath caught in his throat. Milling in the hallway were dozens of angry-looking men. Most were shirtless, bulging muscles catching the light of the torches on the walls spaced between every few cells. Above each cell was a hole in the stone. *What are those for?* he wondered. He tried numbering them, but lost count when he reached two dozen and was only about halfway down one wall.

Their footsteps announced them, and as one, the mass of men turned. A hush fell over the crowd, but Werim heard their questions in the echoes. *Is this some sort of trick? Why have they let us out?*

Bud stood beside him with sword drawn. The torchlight glinted off the steel, and Werim caught several hungry eyes stray to the weapon. The guards huddled behind them. Gongs rang insistently in his ear, growing ever louder. *Now or never*, he thought.

"Hello?" Werim said, his voice echoing. "You're probably wondering why you've been let out. Well, I, uh, set you free. We need your help. The prison is under attack, and I was hoping you'd help us fight in exchange for your freedom."

A big man in the front ground a fist into his palm. "Who on the Composer's arse are you?" A metal loop hung between his nostrils. It swayed when he breathed.

Werim blinked.

"Answer the man," Bud whispered, prodding him with an elbow.

The gongs in his head had already annoyed him. Bud only served to flare his temper. Werim directed it at the big man. "I'm Werim Swift, you big wind bag, and this place is about to be overrun by Baraban Legionnaires. The Right Hand of the Grand Warlord leads them. He thinks he can just waltz in here and take over the Tasher Nation. He's already made quite a mess of the north." He raised his sword and took a menacing step toward the man, pointing his blade. "I need men that want to defend their land." He cocked his head back at the guards. "I need men that aren't afraid of a damned muse." He raised his eyes to sweep over the other men. "You want freedom? Fight for it. Otherwise you can get back in your cage and let 'em cook you up for dinner for all I care. Or run, and see how far that gets you." He returned hard eyes to the man that had challenged him. "So, what'll it be?"

The huge guy stared back. Werim tried not to focus on the bulging muscles, the veins on the neck that pump, pump, pumped blood to his beady little head. He kept his sword level and steady.

Eventually the man shrugged. "Sounds fair to me." He turned to look at the other prisoners. "Don't much like foreigners anyway."

"Kill 'em," someone shouted from further down the hallway.

Several of the men nearby growled. One punched the stone wall. A general din started up. Werim heard several new curse words.

"Shut up, all of you," the big guy roared. When they reluctantly obeyed, he turned back to Werim. "I don't suppose you got any more weapons?" He was staring hungrily at the sword.

Werim smiled, unwilling to let his apprehension show. "No... but they do."

To his surprise the man smiled back. "That'll do," he growled. Several of the other men chuckled.

Then, the Baraban Fog rushed up and tumbled around the corner, sweeping forward to blind them all.

~ + ~

Her father led guards and prisoners alike around the corner, down a short corridor, and out into the large, open courtyard that dominated the middle of the prison. It was hardly pretty, mostly hard-packed dirt with weeds popping up here and there.

Brooding above was a squat tower with a long window that looked over the yard. Likely that was where the guards kept an eye on things. Directly across from it, perched on a slight hill, were two large boulders. Sharee was surprised to see that seats had been crudely carved into them. With what tools, she couldln't say.

"The Swamp Throne," Neckbeard chuckled beside her, catching her gaze. "Sometimes the men fight for the right to sit on it. Who are we to discourage them?" He smiled.

"Has anyone beaten The Bull yet?" Marcko asked.

"What do you think?" Neckbeard replied.

Both men laughed.

Sharee assumed that when referring to a throne, they meant only the larger of the two boulders. "What about the smaller one?" she wondered.

"That's, ah, for the Queen," Marcko explained.

"There are women here?" Sharee asked.

The men looked at each other and laughed harder.

Sharee turned to her father and cocked her head. He coughed out a chuckle, put an arm around her shoulder, and turned back toward the mass of muses that had followed them out into the courtyard. Apparently, he wasn't going to explain the joke.

In the back of her head, Sharee suppressed the buzzing of the gongs. The Warlord would be here soon. She caught several other pairs of eyes straying to the south. *They can hear them, too. Of course!*

She studied the muses with renewed vigor. In the front, several dark-haired young men gathered. They could have been her neighbors growing up. Apart from them, though, were more exotic looks. Short men with dark hair and golden eyes. Pale men with red eyes. In the middle of the crowd, a head bobbed above the rest on a delicate neck, topped by white, wispy hair. Yet for all their diversity, one thing disappointed Sharee.

"Why are there no women?" she asked her father.

"Let's just say that Vral mistrusts women," he explained. "That, and female muses are a bit harder to come by."

"Really?" Sharee asked.

Her father nodded. Then, he put a hand on her shoulder. "There's so much to teach you," he said, "but it'll have to wait." His eyes darted off to the south.

Shouts echoed out from a second doorway leading into the courtyard. Sharee guessed that it must lead to the other wing. *Oh no... Werim.*

Her father turned to the crowd. "I don't think we have a lot of time. We'll make our stand here." He pointed up at the guard tower. "Sharee, I'm going to send some men with you... this lot, those three there, and... you." He picked all of the young men in front, another cluster of young men in the middle–these with blond hair–and an even younger muse that had been hiding in the back.

"Me, sir?" the small voice replied.

He's only a boy, Sharee thought.

"Yes, you. Go with her."

"But we don't have bows like she does," one of the men up front pointed out.

"Throw fire," her father suggested.

"You can do that?" a blond asked.

Her father shook his head. "What are they teaching kids these days?" he mumbled. Then, to the young man, "Yes, you can. Practice. On the men that are about to come out of *that* door." He pointed to the second doorway. "I'll leave another dozen or so in the stairwell leading up to the tower. This group will do," he indicated a group of bigger men to the right. "Think you can hold them in the choke point?"

"Yes, sir," one answered, resolute.

"Marcko, go with them. Don't extend yourselves, just keep them from getting the high ground on us. Use barriers if you can," her father ordered. "The rest of you, with me near the boulders. We'll have to give ourselves cover from the sidebows. Do we have any masons?"

A few men raised their hands.

"Great, get started turning those rocks into a short wall."

"M'lord, we're weavers." It was the abnormally tall man that spoke. He spread spindly arms to indicate several muses near him. "Shall I cloak us?"

Rynel shook his head. "His song will be too strong. He has a shard. We'll need to focus on playing some dissonance against it. Give our side a chance to see."

The tall man nodded.

The group began to break up heading in different directions. Her father took Captain Neckbeard aside and was talking to him animatedly, pointing toward different parts of the prison. Sharee turned and trotted off to the tower, her young group in tow. She stepped into a small room at the base of the tower, and made her way to the stairwell in back. It spiraled up into a squat room at the top. There wasn't much in it. A table, some chairs, and that was all.

She walked over to the window and looked out. A clear view of the courtyard spread out before her. Before the thrones stood a small group of men, arms outstretched. Above the great buzzing of the Warlord in the south, Sharee could just barely make out the fainter hum of the men as they worked. The stones began to glow and expand.

Behind that position, another man climbed the sheer wall. With each step, small chunks of rock fell to bounce on the hard ground, handholds in his wake. Below, the group of weavers waited impatiently for him to reach the top. Sharee wondered how he could split stone. Wood had much more give to it. It was another question for later.

Captain Neckbeard was with a small group, including Rooge, forming up in the shadow of the doorway to the north wing. It looked like several of the men had taken the two clubs they had between them and were shaving off slivers. Sharee suspected they were modifying the flimsy wood in other ways as well, but there was too much going on for her to try to make out notes.

In the midst of it all, her father stood. Pointing here. Yelling there. And casting worried looks back to the south. Sharee strung her bow, notched an arrow, and waited, marveling at the activity below.

It had been mere moments, but already the courtyard was being transformed by the collective songs of the muses. Still, they had hardly started when the first man burst out of the south wing, the shouts of battle chasing him out into the relative quiet of the courtyard. Sharee drew to her ear and would have loosed, had she not noticed the tabard. He was a guard.

The men behind didn't have the same protection. Sharee shifted her aim, and studied the new targets. They weren't wearing the dark colors of the Baraban Legion, either. She held. *Prisoners? Did Werim release the south wing, too?*

The men were blinking as if surprised by the dim light from the moon. They stood dumbfounded for a moment, staring with disbelief at the activity, until one of them toppled forward. Sharee hadn't seen the black bolt spit out of the fog, but she saw it cleanly enough between the man's shoulder blades.

She retrained her bow on the doorway. *Come on,* she urged. The first man through with marked arms was getting an arrow in the neck.

The men ran around the base of the tower to the cover of the northern doorway. No one else came out right away. *Where are you, Werim?* She was ready for something. Anything. The Warlord himself. The noise in her head certainly sounded close enough. Instead, fog spewed forth like smoke from some awful fire, billowing below, a black tide of death crashing up against all four walls. *I can't shoot fog.* In an eyeblink, Sharee lost sight of everyone below, including her father.

How am I supposed to help if I cannot see?

◇ Chapter Thirty

The fog invaded his nostrils, worming its fingers inside and slamming into his skull. Vibrations rattled down his spine and echoed in his toes, or so Werim felt. He coughed several times and groped blindly for the wall before he remembered the spectacles riding high on his head. He quickly pulled them on and pushed the fog out of his mind. A low thrum took its place.

Everything jumped into focus around him. Bud was donning his own lenses, while the guards were fumbling around for each other. Shouts rang out among the prisoners. One shoved another, and further down the hallway it appeared that a scuffle had broken out. They weren't going to resist anyone fighting amongst themselves.

"Hey," Werim yelled. "The soldiers are coming. If you fight each other, you'll all be killed."

His voice, though loud, didn't seem to faze them.

"LISTEN TO THE BOY!" a deep voice bellowed.

Everyone froze. The voice belonged to the big man from before. He was staring toward Werim–eyes unfocused–as if guided by other senses that the fog could not touch.

Werim put a reassuring hand on the nearby lieutenant's shoulder before shouting in return. "The foreigners will come from around the corner in just a few moments. They do not expect you to be released. We will hit them once, and then fall back."

"But we can't see," a man pointed out from down the hall.

"They wear lenses. Those will work for you as well. Strip them of their lenses first, and they will be as blind as you," Werim explained.

"Then, go for the weapons," the big man added. There were a few grunts of approval at the addition.

Werim turned to the man beside him. "Lieutenant, do you think you can lead the retreat?"

The man nodded. "Aye. If they'll follow me. They should know my voice well enough."

There were a few throaty chuckles from the prisoners.

"We'll fall back to the courtyard," the lieutenant said. "If I can find it in this junk. Wish we had a few more of them lenses."

"Here, take mine," Werim said. He pulled the pair off his head and passed them to the guard.

"What are you doing?" Bud whispered.

"I'm asking some of these men to die, Bud," he answered, "the least I can do is make sure someone lives to lead the survivors out. Besides, I've got you. You can be my eyes."

"This is crazy, Werim. I can't hold your hand and fight. You're the better swordsman. Here, take mine."

"What? So you can die first? Fat chance." He felt around for Bud and focused on trying to see through the fog. He flinched when his friend caught him by the arm. A nervous laugh did little to conceal his embarrassment.

Bud tried to hand him the spectacles, but Werim pushed them away. "If I am what you think I am, Bud, then I should be able to see through this fog. That Warlord doesn't need spectacles." Werim pointed vaguely toward the source of the banging.

"You're not a Warlord," Bud observed.

Werim chuckled. "Thanks for the vote of confidence, buddy."

He focused harder. *Bud is right, even if I am a muse, I'm no Warlord.* The gongs still rattled around in his head–harsher in the midst of the fog–yet Werim's attention subdued them. A pleasant thrum washed the sound out a bit, and he focused on that instead.

To his surprise, the thrum intensified. He'd experienced the phenomenon before, but had never paid it much mind. It had happened when the invaders had first shown up in his house back in the village, and again outside of Knucklesporte. He'd just assumed it was the excitement of the fight throbbing in his head. But what if it were....

He didn't have time to finish the thought. Bud jerked around and pulled him behind. Werim assumed his friend had caught sight of the Baraban. His heart leapt into his throat. *What am I doing?* he thought. *I can't see!*

He held his sword in front of him, trying his best not to imagine what it would feel like to have a similar length of steel shoved into his belly or a sidebow bolt poked into his chest. Instead of scaring him, he found himself growing strangely angry. If he were going to die, it should be in a blaze of glory, on his terms. *If these are my last moments, then they will be* mine.

He stepped to what he envisioned was his friend's side. Bud tried to hold him back, but Werim was having none of it. Behind to the left, footsteps approached along with... a snarl? There was a big presence beside him, blowing out heavily through its nostrils like a bull.

"Steady," came the lieutenant's voice through the fog.

"They're just around the corner," Bud whispered. "One stuck his head out and then stepped back. They learned from the ambush earlier. They're trying to gauge how well we can see them, and then form up for a charge. Appeared to be swordsmen."

"Then, what are we waiting for?" Werim growled back. "We don't want them to figure out we're blind, do we?"

Bud didn't respond.

"Are the men ready?" Werim asked.

"You're crazy," Bud said. "Them *and* you."

Werim took that as assent. He took a deep breath and stoked his anger at the enemy that had invaded his land. They had driven him from his home and destroyed his village. They had killed his mother. And they would keep on killing unless someone put a stop to it.

"CHARGE!" Werim yelled.

He dashed forward. The thrum in his head burst to a crescendo. Suddenly, his sword began to glow before him. The rhythm of his anger felt as if it were channelling down into the blade, causing it to glow white hot. Power pulsed through his arm.

He held his sword before him, a beacon, and the fog shied away. Radiating outward from him was a small area where the mists weren't quite so thick. With a start, Werim realized that he could see. Dim shapes and smoky shadows ran beside him... and loomed ahead.

Next to him, the shade of the giant prisoner lumbered, charging forward with his head down as if he had horns atop it. On the other side, Bud was running, sword forward and shield at the ready. The fog roiled behind him, men following in his wake, spurred onward by the glowing blade.

Before them, the Baraban Legionnaires were lumpy clouds, rotating slowly in surprise. They were clumped just around the corner, loosing weapons and milling about. Apparently, they weren't expecting the enemy to run at them blindly. What's more, they weren't expecting the light. The intense glow baffled and blinded them. They stared for a moment, dumbfounded, as their vision struggled to adjust.

And then Werim and the prisoners were upon them. To the credit of the Legionnaires, their paralysis passed quickly. Even as the two smoky fronts slammed into one another, Baraban weapons were brought to bear.

It didn't take long for the first blood to be shed. Werim felt it spatter his face as he ducked beneath the wild swing of the first Legionnaire. A wild rage surged inside of him.

"For mother!" he cried.

The shining sword dipped down and slashed upward, carving cleanly through the shoulder of an attacker. Marked skin offered no resistance to Werim's blade as he finished the swing.

He raised his sword to catch the oncoming blow of the next soldier. Baraban steel sliced through the smoke, glinting as it raced to meet the light. The enemy blade sheered off at the handle, flew over Werim's shoulder, and clattered harmlessly to the floor. Werim slashed at the stunned shadow's middle and moved on to the next. He left darker, more solid smoke pouring out behind him.

He could no longer see Bud at his side, but he heard the thwack of steel against solid oak, and Bud's grunt as he parried. The screams of the dying echoed around them, though Werim did his best to block it out and focus on the sound in his head. Above it all, the gongs clanged with fury, but Werim's thrum fought back, a palpitating orb of strength in the midst of chaos.

His men rallied around him. Werim's eyes grew used to the fog, and he found that he could differentiate between friend and foe. The giant bull of a man swung about with meaty fists, eschewing the foreign steel for what appeared to be a severed arm. Two guards were at his back, clubs at the ready. One went down in a spray of blood as a sword out of the fog chewed into his neck. Werim danced in and ended the attacker with a swift stroke.

As the battle continued, Werim felt his confidence swell. The ploy had worked. They were throwing back the enemy. Many of the prisoners had liberated spectacles from their former owners, donning them and dipping confidently into the fog in search of more Legionnaires to kill. Werim's sword grew brighter and the fog grew thinner.

For a moment, the fight swept away from him, affording him a moment to view the carnage they'd caused. Blood hung on the walls, and the floor was carpeted with bodies. Most of the carpet was marked. Perhaps they wouldn't even need to retreat, after all. Werim would face the Warlord himself and tell his father and sister about it later.

"Retreat," the lieutenant's voice rang out. "Retreat!"

No, Werim thought. *Why? We're winning.* He turned to look behind him. Had he missed something?

A black speck flew by his face from over his shoulder, dissappering into the fog. He heard a melody of grunts around him, and the staccato of more bodies toppling. His cheek burned where the object had passed. Werim reached up and felt wetness. A glance at his fingers revealed red.

He whirled. There, at the very edge of his sphere of influence, was a fresh group of Baraban soldiers–and they all had sidebows. Even as he watched, they were reloading for a second volley.

"Retreat," Werim added his own voice to the chorus.

He turned to run. The corner was too far away. There was no way he would make it before they could fire again. Between his shoulders, he felt a forboding itch. Still, he had to try. *More guts than wits....*

He had only taken three steps when the *pfft* of sidebows filled the corridor. The floor went out from under him. Corpses reached out as if to embrace him as he toppled forward. And then, his sword winked out, and the fog came crashing back in.

~ + ~

It took Sharee a moment of staring blindly before she remembered the pair of spectacles she was still carrying. She fished them out of her pack and pulled them over her head. The fog disappeared. The moonlight was a bit subdued, so the ground looked like it was overshadowed by a cloud, but she could see.

Beside her, a short buzzing was all the warning she had as one of the young muses sang a ball of fire into the air. He hefted it as if it were a stone, and then flung it heedlessly toward the ground. Sharee's heart leapt into her mouth. There weren't any enemies in the courtyard yet!

"Hold," she choked out.

She needn't have worried. The fire arced out and then dissolved before it was even halfway to the ground. She turned to face the man and found the others staring at her, flames in hand.

"Those are our friends down there," she explained.

They stared.

"So... we shouldn't throw fire at them," she continued.

The fires winked out, but they kept staring. She didn't know what else to say, so she just stared back. Finally, the young man that had thrown the first flame spoke up.

"You can see?" he asked.

She tapped lenses on her face. "I didn't put them on because they were *pretty*."

She turned back to the fog. She hadn't meant to snap at the boy. It just struck her as dumb to toss fire around as if it weren't, well, *fire*.

Sharee was contemplating an apology when several more clumps of men burst into the courtyard, joining the first. With each group, they grew progressively bloodier. The second group had only a few spatters on their clothing. The third, a couple men with cuts. Then, men started arriving with small black rods protruding from different parts of their bodies. Arms and legs at first, but then some were supported between others, blood weeping from wounds in the chest or back.

Sidebow bolts, Sharee realized.

She waited anxiously for her brother to come stumbling out, a bolt in his leg or something stupid, but he never appeared. The prisoners kept on coming–some of them being dragged now–but Werim was not among them. *Where is he?*

She tried to listen as well as watch, hoping she'd catch something that might give her a clue. She wasn't sure what she'd hear from her brother, but it hardly mattered. With the Warlord so close, all she could make out was the buzzing of the fog, which was only very slightly different from the frenzied buzzing of the young men.

She turned back to them. "Still no bad guys down there, so you can cut it out."

If she didn't focus on any one song, they all ran together in a miasma of noise. How was she going to pick out her brother in all of *that*? *He doesn't believe he's a muse anyway. He's not going to suddenly start making noise.*

"You can hear us?" one of the blond ones asked, pulling her from her worries.

"I *am* a muse," Sharee answered.

"Yes, but you're a girl," another pointed out.

Sharee raised an eyebrow. "So?"

The boys just stared at her as if they weren't sure how to explain. Sharee turned back to the courtyard in a huff. *Boys...* she thought.

On the far side, the masons had created a low barrier, complete with crenalling. Her father came out from behind it, one fist raised in the air. It began to glow. Sharee focused until she could hear the deep thrum of his notes. It wasn't clear what he was playing, but around him, the fog thinned.

She removed her spectacles. Sure enough, in the heart of the fog, clear air surrounded her father. Several other muses trotted in his wake, and the darkness shifted away from them, too. When the small group passed, though, it closed back in and roiled, as if angered by their passage.

The group made their way to wounded men in the middle. There, one guard was wearing spectacles. He saw the oncoming men and urged the prisoners toward them. Sharee panicked for a moment as she thought about where the guard might have gotten the lenses, but then she noticed that some of the bloodied prisoners were wearing them as well. *They must have faced some of the Legionnaires in the corridor and taken them away. That's all.*

When her father reached the men, he barked an order at the wall. Sharee pulled the lenses back over her eyes and saw several additional muses scurry out from cover. They hurried toward the middle. Once there, they set to knitting up the bleeding men. With the flow of blood stopped, the men retreated back to the wall, led by a muse or a prisoner that could see in the fog.

Her father stayed, staring toward the south door until only he and the guard with the spectacles were left. The man said something to her father and then pointed up at his glowing fist. A solemn nod was the reply. Then, they returned to the wall.

Sharee ground her teeth. She badly wanted something to shoot. What were the invaders waiting for? Why weren't they chasing the bloodied men? More important, where was Bud? Where was her brother? She chewed at her lip until she tasted iron.

Stillness held the courtyard. Behind her, the young muses shifted, staring at Sharee, waiting for her to turn them loose. The whisper of their boots on the stone seemed as loud as the gongs in her ears. Then, a voice shattered the night.

"Rynel," it boomed.

It was all around, issuing from the fog itself.

"I know you are there," it continued. "I can hear you."

Her father answered, yelling from behind the wall. "I've nothing to say to you."

There was a long pause.

"He has your eyes, Rynel," the voice said. Sharee recognized it; it was the dark man.

Her father stood with a pained look on his face. She knew what he was thinking: *Werim has been caught.*

"What do you want, Vraika? A parlay?" her father asked. "I cannot give you the Oracle. It is not here."

"The shard can wait, Rynel. After this, who will stop me? No, I came for *you.*" The voice was different now, both closer and further away. It no longer issued from the fog.

Sharee's eyes darted to the south doorway. The Warlord stood one step inside, black fog billowing from his shoulders. He had his sword in one hand, and his eyes swirled with darkness. On his other wrist, the stone set in his bracer flickered with a deep purple light, pulsing along with the gongs and fog.

"Just you." The dark man pointed with his sword. "I'll even give you the same deal I offered your wench."

Rynel stiffened, anger burning in his eyes. "Was that before or after you murdered her?"

Vraika smiled. An evil, mocking smile. "Before, of course. It was more than she deserved, but some of us still respect our heritage." He shrugged. "I thought I'd found your boy, too. I wanted to give him a chance to know his true family. To be raised properly and realize his full power, instead of wasting away in hiding with you. Apparently, I sent the Grand Warlord the wrong boy. I should have known by the eyes, Rynel. What are the chances of finding two muses in one small village, though?"

Her father's face was schooled once more. Sharee had never seen him look so cold. "What is the deal, Warlord?" he asked. "What do you want for my son?"

"Simple. Your life, for theirs." The dark man pointed vaguely out at the courtyard. "All of them. It be a fair trade, no? Only the best for *family*." He sneered.

Sharee was still having a hard time wrapping her mind around the fact that this... *monster* was her uncle. Yet, she'd heard it from her father's mouth. There was so much she wanted to ask him, but... *there'll be time for that later.* They had to make it through *now* first.

Rynel didn't reply right away. Instead, he looked up toward the tower, toward Sharee. She shook her head.

Don't you do it, she thought. *I will* not *lose you, too.*

When Rynel's eyes returned to meet the dark man's, he was smiling. The chilly mirth that crinkled the skin around his eyes did nothing to touch them, though. Hazel hardness bored into the black void. For a moment, the Warlord looked unsure of himself.

"What do it be, Rynel *Swift*?" Vraika asked.

Her father laughed. "You've never been able to see beyond your own feet in the sand, Brother." He spread his arms wide. "You promise what you don't have, an old trick, but transparent. You never were a good bargainer, Aarik. It seems the shard has left that unchanged."

"My name be Vraika," the dark man said sharply. "Warlord of the Baraban Legion by blood rite. You will show me respect, or there will be no parlay."

"There was never any parlay. Not with you." Rynel observed. "Not with someone who bends and warps the Code to his own design. Not with a man who murdered his own father with trickery." The green appeared to swirl in her father's eyes, and wash out until only the whites were left. She could hear her father's thrum, buffeted by the gongs on all sides. The fog began to swirl around him. "No, there'll be no parlay."

"I did what you should have done years before, had you been strong enough," Vraika spat back. The glow in the shard began to pulse erratically.

"You stabbed him in the back, Aarik" Rynel accused, calmly.

"I did what was best for our people," Vraika roared. "You ran away. You abandoned us. You abandoned *me*... for *her*." He held up his sword arm, wrist outward, displaying the tree inked on his skin and pointed to it. "She's part of me now. I am everything you should have been... but better. Stronger."

Her father shook his head sadly. "Even by the Code you are nothing but a usurper. But you are right about one thing: I left." The air around Rynel crackled with power, lightning arcing in the fog as if it were a storm cloud. "You don't know what it means to love."

"Weakness," Vraika answered.

"Aye, a weakness you shall never taste, have I my way." Rynel nodded. He held one arm behind his back, extending the other out before him. "You always were stronger, Brother. Let us see if that saves you."

"You are no brother of mine."

Vraika launched himself forward. His feet hardly seemed to touch the ground as he arrowed toward Sharee's father, fog spinning in his wake. There was a loud pop, and the air around

Rynel cleared. He stood in the middle, legs slightly bent, palm out, braced for the attack.

The Warlord slammed into an invisible barrier. He bent forward, growled, and pushed through, sword in hand. Her father produced a stone rod, pulling it from his back with his right hand. As she watched, the stone began to glow and reshape, mimicking a sword very much like Werim's. It, however, remained a flat gray, though light danced along its edges.

Stone met steel, and the courtyard reverberated with a loud, uncomfortable grating, much like a whetstone slithering across a sword's edge. Apart from the gongs and her father's songs, Sharee hadn't realized how quiet the courtyard had become; everyone had grown silent once the two men had started talking.

Immediately following the attack, though, there were shouts from up on the wall and a new batch of buzzing joined the already cluttered symphony of battle. A gale of wind rushed in from the north and pushed the fog around the courtyard. It swiftly swirled into a cyclone and sucked up toward the sky, pulling the dark cloud with it. All of a sudden, everyone–especially those without spectacles–could see. The fog continued to pour from Vraika's shoulders, but it was sucked away as quickly as it appeared, and the Warlord could hardly pay attention to it, locked as he was in battle with Rynel.

Legionnaires came charging from the south door, battle cries announcing the overture. The voices of their own men answered, swarming out from behind the barrier. Sharee was surprised to see that the men were armed with stone weaponry. They met the savages with a clash and funneled the charge to the north where Neckbeard had formed a shield wall of prisoners wielding long, thin wooden implements. The tips appeared to be razor sharp, as they easily pierced through leather armor and skewered the first Baraban men.

Sharee drew to her ear and tried to take aim at the Warlord. The dark man danced around her father in the middle of the courtyard, a thin fog shrouding the two before it could be whisked away. They were like a gray boulder sticking up out of a rushing stream as men flowed around them.

Sharee held. She was afraid she'd hit her father. Instead, she shifted her focus to the other invaders and loosed, feathering one of the black clad men as he ran. She notched another arrow, drew, and released to the same effect, catching the enemy in the chest.

Beside her, the younger muses stepped up and began trying to hurl fire. From the corner of her eye she could see that it was not going well. Each tongue of flame flew only a short way from their fingers before dissipating in the strong wind. She let several more arrows fly before she was forced to hold again. The invaders had been pushed up against the wall below her and were taking heavy losses.

The Legion had strength of numbers, though, and they continued to pour out of the hallway. They fought savagely and pressed the defenders slowly backward, swinging about with curved swords. Sharee saw several wooden spears snap and stone weapons crumble when their owners took a fatal slash. What was worse, the defenders had no one to fill the gaps in their line. Control of the situation deteriorated swiftly. Legionaires leaked in among the defenders, and unorganized scrums began to break off in clumps.

The clatter of fighting echoed up the stairwell, alerting Sharee that some of the invaders had made it into the room below. She turned and sprinted to the stairs. Looking down around the curve, she saw Marcko at the back of a knot of men. The narrow entryway allowed them to stand shoulder to shoulder, and several of the men had found tall oaken shields. For now, the brunt of the Baraban attack was focused outward, paying only token attention to Marcko's crew as there was no need to take the stairway in order to harry a single girl with a bow.

"We'll hold," he yelled up at her. "Watch for their sidebowmen."

Sharee nodded and ran back to the window. The other muses had given up on hurling fireballs, and stood gaping beside her. The carnage below frightend them.

"Why have you all stopped?" she asked.

One of the blond boys turned to her. "It's no good, the wind sweeps it away. We're not powerful enough."

"Play me the song," she demanded.

The boy raised an eyebrow.

"Just do it."

He held out his palm. Sharee focused as she heard him begin to buzz. No matter how much she strained, she couldn't seem to make out the notes. The flame burst to life in his hand and he looked at her questioningly.

"Keep playing," she said. She reached out to lay a hand on his arm. It was just a hunch, but she remembered how touching Werim had made everything louder and clearer.

When their skin touched, the boy faltered for a moment. Then, he looked up at her. Sharee had her eyes closed, though. As soon as contact was made, the song bloomed in her mind. It was still a bit fuzzy, but understandable.

The boy finished and started from the top. After a second pass, Sharee removed her arm and nodded at him. It was very similar to the Song of Fire she'd played earlier with just a bit more form.

She held up her own palm, and mimicked the notes. Sure enough, a ball of flame swirled in her hand. She glanced at the boy and they shared a smile.

After a moment, she turned and flung it toward the battle. Like with the boys, it fizzled out a long way from the ground. She could sense it dissipating from the moment she let it go. She thought about that for a moment.

"It needs an anchor," she said.

"A what?" the boy asked.

"An anchor. Er... I don't know what you call it," she tried to explain. "When I play with leaves, the song doesn't seem to fade as much when I play it *into* something instead of *onto* something."

The boy scratched his head.

"Here," she said.

She walked over and grabbed one of the wooden chairs in the room. Carefully, she sliced off a small nub. Then, she played fire into it. Just before the song finished, she flung the wood away, aiming at a clump of Baraban men. She plucked the last notes as it flew and it burst into flame. The ball of fire sped toward the ground and burst in the middle of the men, embers flying everywhere. There were hollers, and a few men had to pat out flames on their arm or chest. She tried not to look at the one that had been hit in the face with a sizeable hunk. He was writhing on the ground.

She turned back to the boys. "See?"

They stood with their mouths open. Sharee rolled her eyes and cut off another bit of wood. She handed it to the boy that had taught her.

He stared at it for a moment before buzzing. It burst into flames, and he flung it away quickly. It slammed harmlessly into a wall, extinguishing quickly in the wind. When she looked back, the boy was shaking his palm vigorously.

She giggled. "You have to throw it away *before* you finish the song. Otherwise you'll burn your hand, silly."

The boy glared at her.

She turned to the others. "Work in pairs. Half of you cut up the rest of these chairs and the table. The other half... start throwing. Try not to hit the good guys."

To her surprise, they nodded and did as she said. Sharee returned to her bow and surveyed the battle. It had progressed, but not poorly. The defenders were holding their own. They'd reformed lines at multiple points in the courtyard, one before the wall, one in the north, and–from the sound of it–one beneath the tower. When the first fireballs started slamming into Baraban men below, the swordsmen began a panicked retreat to cover. *We've got them on the run*, thought Sharee.

Her father was still locked in battle with the dark Warlord in the middle. Streaming fog shrouded them, but Sharee could make out two shadows trading blows inside. Every now and then a loud popping noise burst from the fight, the cloud bulged out, and lightning flickered around the two men. The clash of the gongs and her father's thrum both seemed muffled, locked inside the sphere. None dared approach the duel.

A second black cloud of an alarmingly different texture streaked out from the south. *The sidebowmen*, Sharee realized. This fog was more substantial than the other, though, and when it crashed into the defenders, the men toppled forward. Covering the retreat of their swordsmen, a cluster of Baraban sidebowmen were lined up in the doorway. After releasing their first volley, they reloaded while the defenders scrambled for cover.

"There," Sharee pointed. "Shoot at them."

She put action to words and nocked an arrow. Utilizing her new song, she played fire onto the arrow as she released, and it jetted out, an orange streak through the night, followed by a half dozen fireballs.

Her arrow took one enemy in the chest, and he was instantly engulfed in flame. The other flames fell short–it was a long way away–but they did cause the fleeing Baraban to rethink their headlong flight to the doorway. Caught in the middle, they turned as one and charged the tower.

Oh, now I've done it. "Marcko, they're coming," she called, and then turned back to the window only in time to yell, "Down!"

A flurry of sidebow bolts clattered through the window, most of them striking the wall. One of her fellow muses wasn't quick enough, though, and he took a bolt in the throat. His dying gurgles turned Sharee's stomach. She pushed the sound out. There was no time for it now.

Gritting her teeth, Sharee rose, arrow at the ready. She fired at the first sidebowmen in her sights, singing fire, and hitting him in the shoulder. It was enough; the man ran screaming out into the courtyard, flailing at flames as he went.

As Sharee prepared to dive for cover once more, expecting return fire, something registered in her head. *They're not aiming at us this time.* Instead, they were aiming at the tops of the walls.

"The weavers," she breathed, but it was too late to call out warning.

The bolts flew and found their targets. The muses had been so focused on the fog that they hadn't noticed the threat. The slain toppled from the wall like an avalanche of soft stones. Their bodies struck the hard ground with a dull thud. Only those on the south wall were spared, their location having afforded them cover from the attack.

Deprived of the full strength of its song, the wind lessened and the fog thickened. Darkness washed over the forms below and turned them all to shadows. Sharee could no longer make out who was who. She yanked down her spectacles.

"Hold," she called to her boys, but they'd not been preparing to throw anyway.

More Baraban Legionnaires swarmed from the south doorway, a second wave of angry men. The defenders retreated to their original positions, many stumbling blindly for the last few steps. It would be a rout before long if they didn't do something.

Sharee looked for something to shoot, but there were simply too many. She wouldn't make a dent with her few remaining arrows. And in the midst of it all, her father remained locked in battle with the Warlord, unable to help. Through the spectacles, Sharee could see the fatigue on her father's face. The Warlord didn't even seem to be tiring. A memory swam up. *Mother....*

She turned away, unwilling to watch. Unwilling to let the doubt in her mind paralyze her. The boys were clustered around their fallen brother, blood pooling around his head. Sharee hurried over, her fingers poised to knit, but she stopped as she neared. An empty stare forestalled her. The boys all looked to her with hope in their eyes.

"He's dead," she said, shaking her head. "There's nothing I can do."

The boys turned away. Cries from dying men echoed up the stairwell. It wouldn't be long now.

There's nothing I can do, Sharee repeated in her head.

◇ Chapter Thirty-One

Strong arms pulled Werim to his feet in the darkness. Fog swirled around his face, obscuring anything further away than his nose. He couldn't tell whether the arms were friend or foe. *Foe*, he suspected, and braced himself for the blow to come. *I wonder what it'll feel like, dying?*

He kept waiting for a sword or bolt, *anything*, to pierce him, but it never happened. Instead, he was pulled, stumbling over bodies, until he reached the wall. With a start, Werim realized that he was still clutching his sword. He thought about bringing it around and slashing his captor, but what if it was a friend? *A foe would have disarmed me, even blind. Wouldn't they?*

There was a low rumbling. His captor shoved him right into the wall. Except there was no wall anymore. Werim fell forward and was caught by several other arms. He heard the rumbling again, and then whatever light that had been leaking through the fog was snuffed out. The blackness was complete. Even the gongs had diminished. He was about to ask what was going on when a hand clamped over his mouth. He desperately wished he could see.

To that end, Werim attempted to reclaim the feeling he'd had when they charged, the one that had caused his sword to glow. He vividly recalled the thrum, the pulse of the power flowing through his arm, but he didn't remember how he'd started it. One moment, they'd been running, and then–

He saw it. In the back of his mind. A single cord, like on a lute. One of the Bourges had owned a lute back in the village. They used to bring it out around harvest time and play songs for everyone. But what was it doing in his head? *Is this how I made the light?*

He poked at the string. Immediately, the thrum filled him again. It vibrated from his head all the way to his toes. The feeling was strange, but... he *liked* it. There was just one problem. No glow. He wiggled the sword in his hand, but it stayed dark. *Why won't it work?*

Werim studied the string, but could find nothing special about it, other than the fact that it was there. No matter how he prodded it, the sword would not glow. Eventually, he gave up trying and just waited for his captors to reveal themselves. There seemed nothing better to do.

The silence stretched forever, made worse by the fact that Werim had no idea where he was or who he was with. He began to believe he was hearing things. The gongs outside changed in timbre, and then went away, leaving his ears humming. Or was that his thrum?

A clicking noise filled his head. No, the room. Someone was striking flint in order to light a lamp. He could see the sparks, and then the oil caught. It warmed to reveal a short, fog-free corridor. Werim blinked at the sudden light.

"Who?" was the first word out of his mouth, but then his vision cleared.

Bud stood in front of him, rips in his clothing and blood all over. Most of it seemed to belong to others, though a few shallow wounds weeped on his arms and legs. He's lost his oaken shield, though bits of it clung to his wet shirt.

Behind Bud, crammed into the small area, were a dozen other men, all former prisoners, pulling down spectacles to hang around their necks. They'd apparently found swords as well. Many displayed splotches of blood, some theirs, some not.

Bud held a finger to his lips, and pointed over Werim's shoulder. Werim raised an eyebrow before turning to look. There were two walls behind him. The first was breathing. Werim had to crane his neck to look up at the prisoner. Lamplight glinted off the metal in his nose. *He's even bigger up close.*

The giant pulled sidebow bolts out of beefy arms as if they were merely thorns from a wild blackberry bush. He snorted with each wet sound as the projectiles were removed. *He really is a bull!*

The man caught his stare and flashed a toothy smile before herding Werim away from the second wall. That one was solid stone. At least, it appeared solid, but Werim could hear muffled voices on the other side, as well as the diminished clangor of gongs. He put it together quickly. It had been the big man that pulled him from amongst the dead and shoved him to safety. Then, they had somehow passed through the stone and into this narrow hallway. Werim looked around the group and saw only more stone. The passage appeared to lead nowhere.

"What is this place?" Werim whispered.

"The back door," the Bull grunted behind him. He placed an ear to the wall, nodded, and then returned to the small group. "Sounds like they're moving on. Keep it down, though. Voices echo in here."

"Back door?" Werim asked.

"There's always a back door," Bud intoned.

Werim scowled at his friend and turned to the Bull.

The big man shrugged. "Some clever muses must have hidden it when they built this place. Most of the prisoners know about it."

"And the guards?" Werim asked.

The Bull smiled. "Well, when they hear talk about the back door, some of them think...." He paused, a chuckle rumbling quietly from his big lips. "Let's just say that Neckbeard knows. Maybe the lieutenant as well." He shrugged again.

Werim cocked his head.

A second prisoner, this one with an old scar on his face, spoke up. "They get a kick out of letting the younger guards believe what they want. And we get some fresh air from time to time. Everyone wins."

"They let you use it?" Bud asked.

Scarface nodded. "It's not like we can go anywhere. I mean, we're in the middle of a bloody *swamp*, if you hadn't noticed."

Werim shook his head. It wasn't really an issue now anyway. The important thing was that some of them had evaded being slaughtered by the Baraban sidebowmen. He turned to the Bull.

"Thank you," Werim said, "for pulling me out of there."

The Bull inclined his head. "Figured I owed you one," he rumbled.

"So, we gonna escape? Steal a boat, get back to living? I figure theys don't got a lotta people guarding the docks..." Scarface suggested.

"No," Werim answered.

"No," the Bull snorted.

"No?"

"No," Bud repeated. "Sharee is still in there."

Werim nodded at his friend. "And the rest of the prisoners. And, hopefully, my father."

"And a whole bunch of invaders," the Bull added.

"But, there are too many of them," Scarface whined. "It's suicide."

The Bull turned beady eyes on him. "Are you a coward?" He didn't even have to lean forward to loom over the smaller prisoner.

Scarface swallowed hard and shook his head.

"We've got the advantage on them now," Bud pointed out. "They don't know we're here."

Werim nodded. Bud was right. He could see it played out in his head. "They'll follow the stragglers into the courtyard. My father and the rest of the north wing should have been freed by now. If I had to guess, I'd say they'll meet there."

"The plan?" the Bull asked. He wiped bloodstained hands on his shirt, doing little to clean them. "I liked the last one well enough. Don't suppose you got another?" He grinned.

Werim thought for a moment. "I've seen the Baraban invade places before. They like to send their swordsmen in first, and then shoot unsuspecting men with sidebows."

Bud was nodding. "They did it again just now."

"Ah, but that means they'll probably do the same thing in the courtyard, and the sidebows will hang back."

"Unprotected," the Bull observed.

Werim smiled. "We'll fall on them from behind."

"They'll still have swordsmen," Scarface pointed out.

"And a Warlord," Bud added.

Werim shrugged. "Hopefully our allies from the north wing will have a handle on that. If not, then this is a lost cause, anyway. But we have to try."

"We do?" It was Scarface again.

"We do," a deep rumble answered. "Tashers aren't cowards. We've stayed out of this war for too long. It's about time we *did* something."

Werim gave the Bull an appraising look, but the man's face revealed nothing. "Well," Werim said, "can you get us back out of here, then?" Werim listened for a moment. "I'm guessing the fog is still out there, too, so someone is going to have to help me. My sword seems to have lost its glow."

Bud tossed a pair of spectacles at him. "Thought that might happen." He shrugged. "Found them on the floor." He pulled on his own pair.

The other prisoners followed suit. So did Werim. The Bull turned back to the wall and put his hand up against it. He felt along the smooth surface for something. When he found it, he pressed with a finger until he heard a click. Werim leaned in, but could only make out flat, featureless stone.

A sudden trill sent him jumping back. It was quiet, especially when compared to the cacophony that Werim could still hear on the other side, but unexpected all the same. The Bull looked back, scratched his nose, and smiled. Then, he nodded over Werim's shoulder, and one of the other men snuffed out the lamp.

They waited for a moment in the darkness before a vertical line appeared on the wall, glowing. The silhouette of the Bull put his shoulder into the wall, and pushed. There was a dull rumble, and the large stone slab swung outward, revealing the dimly lit corridor.

Torches flickered on the walls, and their light was brighter than Werim recalled. He pulled his spectacles down for a moment. The fog was still there, yet it was thinner than before, like when his sword had first started shining. He replaced the spectacles and looked down. It certainly wasn't glowing now.

Werim tried to focus on the distant gongs. They were quieter, and there were other noises, other songs. It was strange, but for some reason it seemed to Werim like the melodies were working against each other, like the strange instruments were interfering with one another. He couldn't name all of the voices, but there was one that stuck out. It reminded him of his sister's harp, except deeper, more resonant. Both it and the strong gongs of the Warlord warred in the same location.

"They're fighting in the courtyard," Werim said to his small group.

They stepped over the bodies, and tried not to slip on the blood. The back door was situated on the far wall between two hallways that ran along the front and back of the cells. At the turn where Werim had led the charge into the rear hallway, there were primarily Baraban bodies. As they moved away from the corner, however, prisoners littered the floor more heavily than Legionnaires. Many of the corpses had bolts sprouting from their backs, and others showed deep, red gashes. No matter the manner of death, each body was a knife in Werim's heart.

It's my fault they died, he thought. *If I'd not involved them....*

"They lived as prisoners and died patriots," the Bull rumbled. "A much better end than any of us had reason to expect." He favored Werim with a level gaze.

"They were shot in the back," Scarface growled. His knuckles were white on his sword. "It ain't right. Even for the likes of them."

The other men nodded.

"Let's pay them back in kind, then," Werim said.

The men grunted agreement.

They crept on silent feet past the juncture with the cell hallway. There, the bodies of prisoners lay thickest on the floor. Men facing the charge had been mowed down from behind by a second Baraban force. The prisoners hadn't even realized their fate until the Legionnaires were upon them, cloaked by the fog. It was a slaughter.

Ahead, the hallway jogged to the left before turning back north and opening into the courtyard. Werim's small force snuck to the corner and hesitated. They could hear the sounds of sidebows being loosed just around the bend. *Pfft, click click click. Pfft, click click click.*

Werim took a peek. A cluster of two dozen sidebowmen was arrayed in the doorway. Their backs were to the hall, and they were firing at will out into the fray. As Werim watched, a flaming arrow streaked from above and caught one of the men in the shoulder. He ran shrieking out into the night as the flames engulfed him.

Sharee? he thought. *Who else has a bow?*

He turned back to the men.

"There are about twenty of them," Werim whispered. "No swordsmen nearby. They must all be busy."

"Kill them before they have a chance to yell," the Bull suggested.

Werim nodded. "Let's go, then."

Unlike the last charge he led, there was no yelling this time. His group of twelve stalked around the corner like a pack of wolves, steel fangs bared and foaming at the mouth. Their steps only hastened at the last moment, as the men in the rear finally heard the approaching footfalls and turned to look.

Werim sliced the first man across the neck. Blood fountained, and the man fell with a wet gurgle. Beside him, the other Legionnaires fared much the same. Stepping over the first line of bodies, Werim buried his sword deep into the chest of the next man. By the time he had wrenched it free, there were no more sidebowmen left.

There were plenty of Baraban, though. The courtyard was full of them. Werim had a hard time locating any of the defenders. He saw a knot of fighting to his left against the wall, and another in the doorway across from him. In the middle, a crackling ball of energy pulsed. Even the spectacles failed to completely pierce the cloud surrounding it. Fog emanated from the strange storm and, as Werim stared, he could make out the shadows of two men fighting on the inside.

Father? he wondered. The deluge of gongs and underlying thrum of deep strings came from within the dark orb, even as lightning crackled across its surface. *Who else could it be?*

On the wall above him, the voices of several other instruments drew his attention. He couldn't see them, but a group of muses were making a racket. A steady breeze blew from them, but it didn't completely dispel the fog.

"This doesn't seem to be going well," Scarface pointed out.

The man was right. Marked Legionnaires held most of the yard, pressing what was left of the defenders up against the walls. It was a battle of numbers at this point–both sides having made their moves–and the Baraban had the advantage both in heads and visibility.

The sound of shouts and steel pulled Werim's eyes to the guard tower that loomed over the battle. He looked at the window just in time to glimpse a head diving back below the sill. The glimpse of auburn hair was all he needed, however.

"Sharee's in the tower, Bud," he said, turning to his friend. "Sounds like they have the Legion bottled up in the stairwell. Take these men and secure the high ground first. Then, see where else you can help."

Bud nodded. "Where are you going?" he asked.

"There." Werim pointed.

To Bud's credit, he only raised an eyebrow. "You know how to get in?"

Werim shook his head. "My dad's in there, though, so I'd better find out. And quick." He glanced around. "Otherwise, we're going to lose this battle."

He turned back to the orb. He could make out the two men a little better now, and he didn't like what he was seeing. *No one fights well tired.* It was one of the first lessons his dad had taught him. Werim had wanted to practice with his sword all day, every day, and shirk his chores. His father had set him straight with those words. *And a sound beating with a quarterstaff,* Werim remembered with a smile. Afterward, he hadn't even been able to lift his arms. Only then had his dad pulled out a sword. The sparring had lasted perhaps two cuts before Werim had been slapped by the flat blade. On the head no less.

His father was the best swordsman Werim knew, but it was easy to see that he was tiring. He barely kept up with the Warlord's swings. Whatever trick the dark man used to keep refreshed, it was working.

"Going after the head of the snake, then," the Bull rumbled, eying the tumult. "You're going to need to cut through the body first."

Werim hadn't really thought of that. They weren't likely to simply let him stride in, were they?

"I'll watch your back," the Bull suggested. He shoved a sword through his belt, and then picked up two sidebows. "They won't be too quick to charge me with these."

"You know how to work those?" Bud asked.

The Bull leveled one at a crowd of men. "Sure. Just pull the lever." The bolt streaked out and speared a Legionnaire in the back.

"Easy as pie." He tossed that sidebow aside and picked up another. "Never did like to crank 'em back though."

Werim nodded at the big man. He just hoped he wouldn't be responsible for another death. "Take that tower, Bud. When I get in, give our big friend here some cover to retreat."

Bud nodded, and picked up a sidebow of his own. Several of the prisoners armed themselves similarly. Scarface picked up a second sword.

"Let's get on with it, then," Bud said.

He put a hand on Werim's shoulder, squeezed, and then trotted off. The rest of the small group followed, leaving Werim with the Bull. The big man appeared to be gauging the flow of the battle.

"Let's get on with it, then," he said, "before they realize we're here."

And with that, they plodded off.

All of the attention was focused on the remaining clumps of resistance. They walked unmolested across the courtyard until they were about twenty steps from the warring muses. Werim could easily see his father now, trading strikes with the dark man. The blows were muffled, but the sound the two men made in his mind was almost overwhelming. Obviously, swordplay wasn't the only weapon between them. They warred with rhythm and melody just as nimbly. Werim stood rooted in awe. *It's all so complex. So intricate.*

"Just where be you wantin' to go?"

The voice cut through his musings and came from the leader of a group of three Legionnaires. He was a big man–smaller than the Bull, but not by much–with heavily marked arms. Something about him struck Werim as familiar, but he didn't know why.

The group had broken off from the melee behind the stormy orb, and approached around its side. The Bull leveled both of his sidebows at the speaker. Everyone stopped.

"This doesn't concern you," the Bull rumbled.

The big Baraban cocked his head. "I wouldn't be so sure, were I you. See, I be Borach, Commander of the Warlord's personal guard. Anything that be threatenin' him be exactly my concern, savvy?"

The Bull snorted, sidebows steady. "That's the boy's father in there. He just wants to say hello. And maybe lend him a hand." He flashed a feral grin. "I don't think you *be* in much of a position to bargain, friend."

The leader eyed the sidebows for a moment, and then laughed. "Ha. A Baraban always be of a mind for bargainin'. Family, says you? The Warlord be sufferin' no interruptions, says I. But family, well... that be a different story." He spread his arms. "Let's see him try to get in. I do be havin' my doubts that the Warlord be lettin' him pass troo that cloud. If he do, then I be lettin' him go. Fair enough?"

The Bull glanced back over his shoulder. "Get going, kid."

Werim swallowed. All eyes were on him. He turned toward the crackling storm and took a few steps forward. *How am I going to get in?*

~ + ~

Werim approached the swirling ball of fog. Behind him, a giant of a man held the Baraban at bay. For now, at least.

Sharee reached for an arrow. Her hand found an empty quiver, save for one last whitewood shaft. She pulled it out and nocked it. *Better make it count,* she thought.

She ran a finger along the bowstring as Werim stepped up to the storm. Her hand trembled as he lifted his sword. The rest of the battle faded except for her brother, the cloud, and the two men fighting inside of it. The gongs and strings were overpowering. Her father's sound was waning, fading in time to the strength of his sword blows. He needed help. If she only had a shot....

Something nipped at her ears. Her brother. It was little more than another small buzz, yet for some reason she picked it out of the cacophony. The thrum was unorganized, with no melody that she could discern, but a thrum all the same. Had he finally embraced what he was?

Werim brought his sword down. There was a crackle, and jagged bolts of lightning spiderwebbed out from where he'd struck the cloud. They jittered around like cracks in some giant glass sphere, and then dissipated. He swung again, to much the same effect. And then a third time, and a fourth. His thrum began to dwindle.

He isn't strong enough, she realized. *Especially not while he still has doubts.*

She wanted to run to him, to help him, but she knew she couldn't. The clash of swords below attested to that. And even if she could somehow sneak through, what would she tell him that she hadn't already?

Believe, Werim. We are strong.

The men in the storm turned toward her brother. His banging had apparently caused enough of a disturbance to catch their attention. They both stared at the boy on the outside. Her father smiled. Vriaka scowled.

The dark man flicked his hand. A bolt of lightning streaked out and struck her brother's wrist. Sharee heard herself scream as his sword went flying, and he was knocked to the ground.

"Werim!"

The Warlord turned to her father. Anger rushed over the barriers of fatigue and drowned good sense. She watched in horror as Rynel charged, stone sword held upright like a torch.

Vraika smiled. Out of the bracer on his arm sprung a second blade, the same shadowy steel that had claimed her mother's life. Rynel saw it at the last second, and moved to block it. The move left his middle unprotected, and the dark man took advantage.

The bracer blade met Rynel's stone sword with a resounding crash of gongs and strings. The other, normal blade ripped along her father's stomach. The flesh parted, and blood sprayed out. Just for a moment, the strings faltered, and the stone blocking the bracer shattered into a million pieces. Rynel grabbed his stomach and fell to a knee.

The Warlord could have ended it with a simple downstroke there, but he paused and looked up toward Sharee. It was then that she realized she was not only screaming, but also playing. Loudly.

Her last arrow was pulled back to her check, and it glowed with a radiant light that made her eyes water. Sharee didn't recall either drawing the bow, or playing any notes, but she had afforded her brother a few extra moments to regain his courage.

Damnit, Werim. Believe. She released the arrow.

It spun through the air, sparkles of light trailing behind it in a spiral. A painful ringing echoed in her ears in the wake of the shot, but she shook it off, intent on the flight of the arrow. It slammed into the cloud, and an ear-splitting screech caused all the muses in the courtyard to flinch.

The barrier deflected the arrow but shattered under the pressure. Lightning shot out from all around the orb, and the fog sunk to the ground, rolling away like a giant wave. It slammed into the walls and then seemed to suck into the stone, dissipating.

Suddenly, the air was clear. The fighting paused for a moment, as all eyes turned inward. Vraika stood over her bleeding father, a look of shock on his face as he stared at Sharee. She glared defiantly back.

She saw him mouth something. "Two?" she believed it was.

She hadn't killed the monster, but he was unprotected.

Get up, Werim. Save our father.

~ + ~

At first, he'd thought: *I've lost my sword. I'm helpless, powerless.*

"Weak, just like your father." That's what the dark man said as he disarmed Werim. "After I finish killing the last of your pathetic parents, I'll be showin' you what a true father be. Then, you be forgettin' all about them."

The words had stung as bad as the bolt of energy. Yet Werim was on the ground, weaponless. For once, he had no retort.

His wrist throbbed where the lightning had struck it, and his body shivered with fatigue and pain. A very large part of him wanted to roll over right there and die. He'd come so close, only to be swatted away like a fly.

His father paid the price for his failure. Blood ran through Rynel's fingers, and dripped down to darken the dirt. Werim could do *nothing*.

Then, he'd heard the harp and pushed himself out of the dust to stare in awe. It was nothing like the quiet buzzings from before, the crickets. This time, he could almost see Sharee's fingers moving across an instrument. A *huge* instrument, blaring out over the courtyard and rising even atop the gongs.

The cloud exploded, and Werim let the sound wash through him. The awful noise of the barrier shattering felt like tiny knives piercing his skull. A deep rumble followed the rolling, dispersing fog, though, and it was music to his ears. The gongs were silent, sheered off in the wake of the attack.

Werim struggled to his feet. The sounds of fighting faded; the courtyard grew eerily still. Everyone stared at the three muses in the middle.

Vraika's focus was on Sharee, eyes wide. "Two?" he wondered.

The moonlight glinted off the Warlord's blade. *I need a weapon*, Werim thought, his purpose renewed. *I need something.* He nearly tripped over the whitewood arrow sticking out of the ground. He pulled it free and held it up. *Yes.*

He took a deep breath and found the cord in his head. With a confident finger, he plucked it. A thrum filled him. He plucked it again. And again. He shaped the thrum into the same pulsation he had felt during his charge. If he could channel that into the arrow, it wouldn't matter that he faced a sword.

Durm dada-durm, durm dada-durm, he played.

The whitewood began to glow.

Vraika turned toward him, eyes black.

Durm dada-durm, durm dada-durm.

Hear me, Sharee? He played louder. *I am a muse.*

The arrow shone, a second sun. The beat pounded in his head. *Hear me, father?*

DURM DADA-DURM.

He took a step toward the Warlord. A flurry of gongs assaulted his song, but he persisted. He had lost his mother. He would not lose his father, too.

DURM DADA-DURM.

As Werim neared, the bracer on the Warlord's wrist continued to glow, the shadow-wreathed blade protruding from it. Vraika looked down as if just now remembering that it was still there. His dark eyes returned to Werim, fury smoldering at their edges. It was plain there would be no quarter offered now. No parlay.

The Warlord readied himself, sword held high, bracer blade low.

DURM DADA-DURM.

Another step. What if the bracer blade could block his attack? He would need to strike high, exposing himself. Werim's stomach tightened. He raised the shining arrow.

And the bracer fell away.

The clanging of the gongs dropped to a whisper. Vraika looked down in horror as the shard went dark and clattered to the ground. Just beneath his wrist was Rynel's outstretched hand, shaking. Werim's father was on his knees, his left hand holding his belly, but his eyes shone with triumph.

Vraika roared and brought his sword down. The blade sliced through Rynel's wrist. Blood sprayed, and his father fell on the bracer.

Werim saw his opening and struck. The arrow flared as it pierced Vraika's neck. The first beat of the Warlord's heart sent blood oozing back at Werim. He played louder. The vibration of his song flowed down into the whitewood and rattled the stones around them.

He put his weight behind it, pressing until the shaft went all the way through, its gleaming tip poking out from the other side. Only then did he step back and peer into his uncle's eyes.

Hazel eyes, Werim saw. They were clear now that life was leaving the man, pulsing out through the wound. The throb of his heart weakened, and slowed, the beats playing the coda of his requiem. With a last gurgle, he fell backward.

"Right hand, for Right Hand," Rynel croaked, bent over on the ground.

Werim knelt down next to his father. There was blood everywhere. He didn't know what to do.

"We have to heal you, father," he said. "Sharee!" he called out. "Come quick."

"Wait," his father whispered, turning his head. "There is one more thing." A mishevious smile was on his lips.

Rynel closed his eyes. Amazingly, Werim heard a thrum start up in the wounded man. What was he doing?

"AARIK HAS FALLEN," Rynel cried out, his voice supernaturally amplified. Something glowed in his throat, and in his hand. "BY BLOOD RITE, THE SHARD IS PASSED TO THE VICTOR. SURRENDER AND BE SPARED."

The glow faded, and Werim stared down at his father. "I don't understand..." he said.

Rynel still smiled. He eased himself to the ground, and rolled onto his back. Then, he held out what was clutched in his remaining hand: the fallen bracer. He pressed it to his son's chest.

When Werim took it, his father laid back. "Take care of them," he said.

"Take care of whom, Father?" Werim asked, but Rynel was fading fast.

With what little strength remained, Rynel pulled up the sleeve on his upper right arm. There, among the dirt and grime, Werim saw something. A marking. Under the skin. A huge skull atop a pile of bones.

Werim rocked back on his knees as the realization crashed into him. He'd suspected, maybe, but right there in front of him, on his father's arm was the last bit of proof. It was *their* emblem, in *their* fashion. *He's... I'm... Baraban.*

"I'm proud of you, son," Rynel whispered.

Then, his eyes fluttered closed.

~ + ~

The stairs passed in a blur. Sharee ignored the questions of the young muses as she ran. *Sharee, come quick!* Her brother's plea echoed in her head.

Carnage greeted her at the foot of the stair. She had to shove her way around Marcko and the few defenders that remained. Just beyond them, a pile of bodies stained the floor, blood pooling. A small knot of Baraban soldiers stood on the other side, ringed by more corpses.

Sharee paused for a moment, but continued on when she saw that they were laying down their blades. They didn't try to stop her as she pushed through. There was another small group of defenders in the entryway to the guardroom. These wore the spectacles of the Legion and the stained clothing of the prisoners. They, too, appeared to be laying down their blades. Both sides were heeding her father's bellowed advice, it seemed.

Father....

She had to get to him.

"Sharee," Bud called.

If she was surprised to see him among the prisoners, she did not show it.

"My father," she answered, pushing past him, her face a grim mask.

He followed on her heels, but she paid him no attention.

She stumbled when she hit the dirt. Bud tried to help, but she pushed him away and kept going. There were other men in the courtyard, all laying down their weapons. She shoved her way between them, frantic.

"Father," she called. "Werim. I'm coming."

The men had formed a ring in the middle. They stood, unarmed, gawking. She burst through and stopped. The scene froze her mind. Werim knelt next to her father, blood up to his elbows. He had removed his shirt and was pressing it into the wounds. She could hear his thrum, and his hands glowed faintly. He was playing, but it was disjointed, unorganized. It wasn't doing anything.

"Help," Werim called, his voice hoarse.

Sharee dashed forward. Werim looked up at her, dust and blood mingling in wet streaks on his face.

"Sharee," he said. "Do something. Knit him, or whatever."

Her father was still breathing. His chest jerked with small, shallow breaths. His wounds seeped.

I just need to knit them up, she told herself. *He'll be okay.*

A deep weariness sung from her soul and threatened to pull her under as she reached for her harp. Sharee shook off the dizziness. The stress and action of the fight had exacted its toll–not to mention the journey–but her father needed her.

She labored through the first few notes. It felt like the strings were a fraction of their normal size, and trying to pluck one resulted in several clanging out. She closed her eyes and focused, but it didn't seem to help.

"Renee?"

Sharee's eyes snapped open. Her father was awake, his eyes struggling to focus on her face. Several times they threatened to roll back up into his head.

"Renee?" he asked again.

He thinks I'm mom, the thought struck her like a bolt of lightning. "No, Daddy. It's Sharee," she corrected, gently.

Rynel's lips were cracked, and blood continued to ooze from his wounds. Her terrible playing had done nothing to heal them. Werim leaned in with her, both of them intent on their father's face.

"Renee, I–I heard you," Rynel continued. "Where did you go?"

Sharee pursed her lips. He was obviously delirious. She needed to stop the blood flow. She began playing again. The notes skittered. She tried again.

"What's wrong, Sharee?" Werim asked, hearing her failed attempts. "Buzz him, already."

"I–I'm trying," she stammered.

Her hands were shaking. The harp in her mind was shaking, too. For the life of her, she couldn't steady it.

"You play so beautifully, Renee," her father said. His eyes were closed and he was smiling. "You always have."

"Dad. Hey! Wake up," Sharee shouted. She fat-fingered a few more notes. "Damnit! It's not working. I can't help him."

"Take a deep breath, Sharee. You can do this," Bud said. He came up behind her and put a reassuring hand on her shoulder.

She looked up. "I can't. This has happened before. I'm too tired. The notes, they won't come," she explained. "Where are the other muses? Surely, some of them can help. Where are they? HELP!"

"They're coming, Sharee. Just do what you can. Some of them have to climb down from the wall," he said turning to point. Something up there must have spooked him, however, for he immediately went pale. "No..." he breathed.

Bud's hand shot out, pushing Sharee to the ground. Then, he grunted and toppled forward. A long sidebow bolt stuck out of his neck. Another bloody wound.

Something inside of Sharee snapped. She stood and started yelling. High atop the wall, she saw him. A lone, marked man lying on his stomach, his large weapon propped in front of him. From his side, he pulled another of the special bolts. His other hand cranked the weapon.

There was a small stone next to Bud's prone form. Filled with rage, Sharee snatched it up. She forgot about her fatigue, about the battle and all that had happened. The red stain spreading around Bud drove it all from her mind.

She played something. She wasn't sure what. And then she hurled the stone.

Her ears popped. Abruptly, the world went silent. She couldn't even hear her own screaming, but she felt it in her raw throat.

As it flew, the stone burst into a huge ball of flame, larger than a full-grown oak tree. It flew straight into the shooter atop the wall and exploded soundlessly. Stone showered them, and Sharee turned away. A wetness slid down the sides of her face, tickling beneath her numb ears. She reached up and wiped at it. Her hand came away red.

It's so quiet, she thought. Then, she slumped forward and fell on top of Bud.

◊ Chapter Thirty-Two

The cabin seemed unnecessarily cramped, though Alexzandar was the only one in it. He rocked side to side with the swaying of the ship. The wind creaked in the rigging, a sharp sound on the quiet lake. Every now and then, footsteps tapped against the floorboards overhead, though no voices wafted in from the open window of the captain's quarters. As the water sped by, Alexzandar noted that the only reflection was the moon's wan light. He had warned the makeshift crew to slip out with stealth, and he was glad to see that the dim-witted guardsmen had enough sense to heed his orders.

He looked down at his clothes and scowled. His white robes had been ruined, blackened by smoke and stained by mud. He suspected there were a few blood stains hidden in the mess as well. They had once been such magnificent robes, but now his former grandeur had been despoiled to that of a refugee.

It is a shame that the Archon Basileus of the great Tasher Nation is forced to rely on prison guards to smuggle him across his own lands. After the booming voice had confirmed the death of the Baraban Warlord, Alexzandar had sprung to action. While the few remaining Baraban were surrendering, he'd convinced the previously captive guardsmen to help him steal one of the two docked ships. It had taken some concessions on his part–not to mention some lies–to get them to trust him again. Alexzandar clenched his hand into a tight fist, but refrained from hitting anything. The last thing he needed was a broken knuckle. *Marcko will pay for his betrayal. And those mongrel village children.*

The squeal of the cabin door announced a visitor. Alexzandar turned to find one of the guards standing just beyond the threshold. If memory served, this man was the highest ranking among the riff-raff. The rest of the crew looked to him as their superior.

"Archon Basileus, sir, we are out of sight of land," the man informed.

Alexzandar nodded. "Keep us under full sail, my good man. We shall travel throughout the night." He fluttered a hand before his face. "Dear me, one can only imagine what those traitors might do to us if we are caught."

"They'll not catch what they can't see, sir."

"Or hear, Captain," Alexzandar amended. "Or hear. Who knows what those muses are capable of?"

"Yes, sir. And it's simply Lieutenant, if it please you, sir," the man said.

Alexzandar smiled. "No, I do believe I have the right of it, *Captain.*"

The man flushed. "T–thank you, sir."

Simpleton, Alexzandar thought. But he said, "Please, see to your ship. I fear the night's events have exhausted me, and I require a bit of rest."

"Of course, sir."

The door clicked shut behind him. Alexzandar took out his fan and splayed it on the desk. He stared at it for a long while before working up his courage. Finally, he picked it up, closed it, and tapped it twice. Turning it on its side, he had to shake it for a moment before the charm finally won free of the tiny compartment.

It clattered on the wooden surface, the crimson jewel glinting in the fluttering lamplight.

Alexzandar fished a tallow candle from one of the drawers. He walked over to the lamp, opened it, and lit the wick. Carrying the flame back to the desk, he paused over the charm once again.

With a deep breath, he touched the flame to the jewel. The orange tongue flared for a moment, and then appeared to be sucked into the charm. What appeared to be a small ember glowed in its heart. It began to pulse. After several long moments, the light steadied. A voice emanated from it.

"You have news for me, my servant?" it rasped.

"Yes, Grand Warlord," he said, fanning himself. "It seems that your Right Hand has, well, been severed. I've been told that a young boy–named Swift–was the one that struck the fatal blow. It was blind luck, no doubt."

There was a long silence. That made Alexzandar nervous. For all he knew, Vral could use the charm to set the entire boat on fire, stranding them out in the middle of the lake, at best. At worst... he shuddered. *Does he even know where we are?* He fanned himself again.

"A boy, you say?" Vral finally answered.

"Y-yes, Lord."

"How... illogical. And what of this boy's father?"

"He was badly wounded. When I left, I heard it whispered that he might not live through the night," Alexzandar reported.

There was a strange hissing sound, like wet bones being dropped onto hot coals. "Left? Why would you leave?" the voice wanted to know.

"I-I had to, Lord. There are those that know of our... alliance." The fat man swallowed. "I must return to the capital before they do. To forstall any... unpleasantness, you see?"

"Hmm..." Vral hummed, his voice–as always–devoid of emotion.

It made Alexzandar's blood cold. He knew the price of failure. Yet in this case, surely, it had already been paid. It was not the Archon's fault that Vraika had died.

"So be it," Vral said. "Our other agreement is still in effect, however. Another servant will contact you in due time. Do not fail me in this, Alexzandar."

"I wo–," he started to reply, but the light in the stone snuffed out. The Grand Warlord was gone.

Alexzandar leaned back and heaved a sigh of relief. Had he waited for Vral to contact him, to learn of tonight's events through another, things might have gone worse. Much worse. Yes, he did the right thing. He waddled over to the bed, already feeling better about himself.

Once I reach Tashaba, these... rebels will not be able to touch me. Then, I'll send the army after them. Such a battle could even serve to see me re-elected. He smiled. *A good politician finds the benefit in any situation.*

~ + ~

The soft sound of waves swishing against the shore woke Sharee. She heard the crackling of a fire nearby, and a gentle breeze sent a chill through her. The small room swam into view around her. She lay on a cot. A desk sat near the wall, and all the windows were thrown open. Fading daylight spilled in, spearing at her sensitive eyes. She blinked several times and tried to sit up.

A wave of dizziness assaulted her, pressing her back down. Her head throbbed painfully, and her ears felt as if someone had stuffed cotton in them. *At least I can hear.* She'd been afraid that she'd gone deaf.

Sharee took several deep breaths and heaved herself into a seated position. She threw her legs over the side of the cot, and sat for a moment. Her vision swam. She could feel each beat of her heart reverberate through her entire body.

"Oww," she moaned.

When the pain ebbed a bit, she took stock of herself. There were a couple large bruises on her arms and legs, and her face felt a bit tender, but otherwise she was a lot more whole than she had any right to be. Vivid memories of battle replayed in her head. A few bruises were a small price to pay to have escaped with her life.

Her things rested on a table nearby. The bow was still strung, and the quiver empty, though a few arrows lay alongside it. Their tips were stained red. Next to the weapons was her satchel. She could see the sharp corners of the carved box pressing against the fabric, and the handle of her hairbrush poked out. *At least I haven't lost anything, then.*

Eventually, when she could forestall it no longer, she reached for the harp in the back of her mind. She'd been afraid of what she might find. What if she had somehow wrecked her instrument and would never be able to play again?

Fortunately, it was there. The instrument didn't seem injured in any way. Tentatively, she reached out and pucked a string.

She immediately regretted the decision. The note brought on a wave of pain much worse than sitting up had. Sharee leaned forward and fought against the urge to throw up.

She gulped down a few more deep breaths, and the nausea passed. Then, the door slammed open. Her brother posed, framed by the setting sun so that he appeared outlined by a radiance. His face and hands were cleaner than she remembered, though soot clung to his clothes. She saw with a start that he had donned the leather armor of a prison guard captain, though a dark handprint covered the sigil.

When Werim saw she was awake, he smiled and came further into the room. "I thought that was you," he said.

It took her a moment to connect the dots. "You... you heard that?" she asked.

He grinned sheepishly. "Well, I wasn't far away. Just talking to some of the guys in the cabin next door."

She glanced toward the open doorway, hoping to see a blond head, but instead finding only a red shirt. "Is that Rooge?" she asked.

Werim nodded. "Yep."

"What's he doing outside of my door?"

Werim chuckled. "Seems he was tickled pink to live through that battle. For whatever reason, he blames you for that." Werim flashed his crooked smile. "As payback, he's sworn himself to be your personal protector."

Sharee put a hand to her head, shaking. "Great."

"It gets better," her brother promised.

Rooge moved aside for the next person to enter the room. Sharee tried to shield her eyes from the sun, but all she could make out was a large, male form. *Who is Werim pawning off on me, now?*

Her heart skipped a beat as the door closed behind him. Bud hesitated awkwardly, spying her with worried eyes. He walked slowly to her side, and then stopped a hand's span away and just looked at her. One moment he appeared about to lean in and hug her, and then the next he looked about ready to run away.

Sharee reached for his hand. A cloth bandage had been wrapped around his neck, but it appeared clean.

"You're all right," they both said simultaneously.

His voice was different, quiet and coarse on her sensitive ears. Even so, she felt the heat rise into her cheeks. His blush mirrored hers as they simply stared at each other.

Werim rolled his eyes. "Bud's been worried sick ever since he got you out of that courtyard."

"Got me out?" Sharee asked.

"Yeah, after you destroyed the entire east side of the building, you passed out on top of the poor guy," Werim explained.

Bud squeezed her hand, "It was fine. You needed a soft place to land, and I was down there anyway." It was hardly more than a whisper, gravelly like an old man.

"But you were shot," Sharee said. It hadn't seemed the kind of injury one ever got up from, yet he appeared healthier than she felt, apart from the voice.

The blond boy shrugged. "It wasn't that bad."

"You should have seen when they yanked it out." Werim grinned. "Sounded like a drowning goat. He's lucky the other muses came quickly. Even then he wouldn't let them heal him up properly. Kept saying he had to get you out. I thought he'd lost his wits."

Bud glared at his friend.

"Anyway, the big oaf was halfway through the rubble with you on his shoulder before I reminded him about the back door," Werim continued.

Sharee raised an eyebrow. "Back door?"

"There's always a back door," Bud grated out, waving a hand.

"Of course." She smiled at him. "Why not?"

Werim scowled. "Well, we couldn't really go out the front. Not after you blew it up, 'Ree."

Bud squeezed her hand. "You got the guy, that's what matters."

"At least, we think," Werim said. "There wasn't really a body left. The other Baraban said that the man wasn't with their group. They say he was something called the Lead Engineer. I suppose I'm going to have to learn what that is. In any case, that was pretty freakish, 'Ree," Werim added, playfully. "You'll have to show me how you did it sometime."

Sharee looked down at the ground. "I'm not sure I can, Werim. I... I think I may have hurt myself, though I don't know exactly how."

"You mean the bloody ears?" Werim asked. "Don't worry too much about it. I mean, it's not good, but I talked to some of the other muses, and they said that it happens. Basically, when a muse pushes themselves too far, well, their ears bleed. Another thing I'm probably going to have to learn." He looked at her wan face, and his own eyes softened. "The way they explained it, it's sort of like the morning after you get really drunk, which is pretty awful." Bud nodded at that. "But don't worry, because it will go away. Just takes some time to smooth out."

"And until then, you should be very careful about what you play, and how loud you play it," Bud added. "They said you passed out before you could do any real damage, but you're going to be weaker for some time. It'll probably be painful to... do whatever it is you do."

Sharee nodded. "You could say that again." She met his blue eyes and got the message. "Don't worry. I'll take it easy."

They paused and listened to the water outside for a few moments. Finally, Sharee worked up the courage to ask the one question she feared to know the answer to. She looked at her brother.

"How's Father?" she asked.

Werim shifted from one foot to the other. He looked down at his boots, and fingered a new pouch that hung at his waist. "Well, he's not dead," was the answer she got.

Sharee frowned. "What does that mean? Was I too late? Did I screw it up by passing out?"

Werim shook his head. "No, no. Your fireball actually scared a lot of Baraban. Those that hadn't already been laying their weapons down dropped them immediately. Then, the other muses came out from behind the wall. There were a couple healers, and they got Dad knitted up quickly enough. It's just..."

"What?" she asked, heart beating painfully against her chest.

"He won't wake up," Bud finished for Werim.

"Won't wake up?"

"Yeah. It's like he's sleeping," Werim explained. "One of the weavers tried to tell me something about how the body listens to the song played by the spirit, and that he thinks there are ways to make one deaf, or something. I don't know. It didn't make a lot of sense to me, and apparently all of the muses held here–with the exception of Dad–were either weak, or untrained anyway. They say we need a Warlord to help him. A *real* Warlord."

"We'll figure it out," Bud said. "What matters is that he–and you–are safe."

"For now," Werim amended. "I've been talking to some of these Baraban guys, and–"

"You've been what?" Sharee asked. "Why haven't you sent them off, walking back through the swamp?"

Werim's hand brushed against the pouch again. "It's not that simple, 'Ree. They have a Code, and honor, and stuff like that."

"What he's trying to say is that he's their new leader," Bud filled in.

"What?!"

Werim stared hard at his boots. "Apparently, the person who kills the old Warlord takes his place as the new one. They call it the Blood Rite. So, um, that's me."

"Forget their Code, Werim," Sharee argued, wincing as she raised her voice. "Just because they have some stupid rules, or whatever, doesn't mean you have to follow them."

Werim caught her with his hazel eyes and held on. "Sharee, Dad was one of them. I think, well… I think Dad wanted me to do this."

"Why?" she asked. It was all she could think of as the revelation settled in.

"The old Warlord was our uncle, Sharee. Father's brother. There are more than a few among the Baraban men that seem to think our father should have been the Warlord instead. These are his people, 'Ree. In a way, *our* people. Or at least mine. I'll understand if you don't feel the same." He looked away.

Sharee let it sink in for a moment. "Fine," she said, sighing. "I guess they could do worse… not much, though." She giggled.

Werim grinned back.

Bud helped Sharee get to her feet, and then the three of them left the cabin. Rooge followed them at a respectful distance, eyes darting as if he still expected some attack. She caught Bud frowning at the young man.

Outside, the setting sun dipped its toes into the watery horizon, glinting off the calm surface. A fire burned in a big pit that had been dug on the beach before the dock. A single ship sat at anchor, and men milled about. She saw prisoners, guards, and Baraban mixed together, talking, cooking, or working at some small task. Eclectic Marcko sat with two giant men—one a prisoner with a ring through his nose, the other a huge Legionnaire—and they were pouring mugs and cups of beverages from several casks. Captain Neckbeard stood nearby, directing men to a giant pot of stew. For the moment, things appeared harmonious.

"So, what now?" Bud asked.

Sharee looked to her brother.

He took a deep breath, not wanting to spoil the scene. "Well, if there's one thing they all agree on, it's that Vral's not going to just leave us alone once he hears of what we've done here. A muse army against him—even a small one—is something he won't let happen. We've been forced into war with the Triumvirate, and we're going to need allies."

Bud nodded. "Besides, we can hardly go home."

"So, we'll fight," Werim said. "It's what Mom and Dad would want, I think. And hopefully we'll be able to find another Warlord along the way. A friendly one, this time."

The wind drifted by and, just for a moment, she could have sworn it carried notes from a set of pipes. A familiar tune filled her head and soothed her, as only that tune could. *Listen to your spirit, play your song,* she heard.

Yes, Mother. Always. Sharee nodded.

"We fight," she repeated.

◆ Epilogue

Crickets and bullfrogs played late into the night, Lugar Tyniente's only company as he sat next to a sputtering flame. The fickle orange light revealed a map of Kinnsley and the surrounding area spread out on a heavy oak desk. The lamp was running low on oil. He opened the door, looking for one of his guards to go and fetch him some more.

I should be askin' them to bring me sleep instead, he thought. But the Warlord would soon return, and Lugar needed to be prepared for his arrival. They would need to move swiftly. The Tasher army was surely making preparations of its own.

"Admiral?" one of the guards asked.

"I be needin' a fresh lamp," he said, voice roughened by fatigue. "P'raps some rum as well."

"Aye aye," the man responded, striking fist to breast.

He hurried off. Lugar shut the door and crossed the room. A window admitted the cool air along with wan moonlight. High in the central keep, he had a good view of the occupied city's rooftops. Thin tendrils of smoke rose out of many a chimney, drifting up to be brushed away by the breeze off the lake.

The night was quiet, like every night since the Admiral had ordered the city guard locked inside their barracks. The cityfolk remained indoors for the most part. They were afraid of the

Legionaires. *They be havin' good reason, too.* His men were restless. They wanted to move, to fight. They had not come to this land to turn soft in a city.

His eyes were drawn to the port and the dark blue beyond. Waves sparkled where kissed by the moon. It was a serene scene, but Lugar didn't care for it. He'd much rather be out on the sands, atop a Landsha. Or in the heart of an oasis, lying in the arms of wenches. There was one in particular he dreamt of often. Dark hair and smoky eyes, the kind that makes a man forget what he is for a time, and live only in the moment.

He brushed the memory away. It was not the first time he'd felt homesick. He served his people, and his people served the Warlord. The Warlord wanted them here, holding this city. It was simple.

A soft knock at the door spun him around. He went over and opened it. The guard had returned. Lugar accepted a fresh lamp, along with an earthenware jug. He closed the door, returned to his desk, and set both items down.

The first lamp had sputtered out in the midst of his musings. He was about to go ask the guard for some tinder when a purple glow pulsed from his waist. He looked down at the hilt of his sword. In it, a small stone warmed and faded, warmed and faded, warmed and faded. *Three beats.* It paused before repeating the pattern.

Lugar's knife lay on the table. He'd been using it to slice off hunks of cheese earlier, though only crumbs remained now. He picked up the blade and looked at his palm. There, marked in an ink much different than most other markings, was a prism. The symbol had been etched into him with muse blood on the day he'd been raised to Admiral, same as it had been etched on every previous Admiral's palm.

Lugar traced the symbol with the blade of his knife. The borders turned red. The sword was starting another round of pulses when he covered the gem with his bloody palm. When he removed his hand, it stopped. A few seconds passed, and it did not start again. Satsified, the High Admiral of the Baraban Legion set the knife down.

A sharp knock at the door startled him. *What be it now?*

"Come in," he called.

A young Legionnaire entered. An engineer by the marks on his arms. The man moved so that he stood on the far side of the desk, and saluted. He waited obediently for the Admiral to address him.

"You have news?" Lugar asked.

"Aye. We've found how the Eclectic and his group entered the city," the man reported. "Seems there be an entrance to the sewer about a league to the north along the edge of the smotherin' blue."

"The sewers?"

"Aye, sir. They be leavin' a horse behind," he said.

"So you have the horse?"

The man shifted. "Well, no."

The Admiral raised an eyebrow. "Then how be you knowin' they left a horse?"

"Tracks, sir. And we found these stuffed in a discarded saddlebag."

The engineer held up a bundle of clothing.

"Let me see them." He waved the man to set them on the desk.

"Your hand, sir. It be bleeding," the Legionnaire observed.

"Aye," Lugar replied.

"Do you want me to find a healer?" he asked.

Lugar ignored that and spread out the clothes. Interestingly, they were still damp. The shirt had a hole in the shoulder, and a blood stain surrounded it. Lugar held it up and stuck his finger through. *It be the right size for a sidebow bolt.*

"There be tracks," the engineer said. "Do you want us to follow them?" The young man was still staring at his Admiral's blood.

"Huh?" Lugar grunted. He'd been focused on the clothing. *They be damp, but left outside of the sewer....*

"The tracks, sir. Follow the tracks?"

Lugar thought about it for a moment. He adjusted the sword at his waist. Then, he looked at his bloody palm.

"No," he said, finally. "Let it be, for now." He waved. "Leave me."

The man saluted, turned, and left, closing the door behind him.

Lugar stared at the jug on his desk. With a sigh, he picked it up. He walked back to the window.

"Twice," he mumbled, staring out into the night once more. "I be the only Admiral that could be claimin' that, I reckon."

His eyes searched the horizon, wondering when the great blue beast might deliver up its burden. Surely, he had a few days yet. Still, his mind was already cast ahead, wondering what service his new Warlord might require.

He lifted the jug to his mouth, and drank deeply.

~ + ~ THE END ~ + ~

About the Author

Electrical engineer by day. Aspiring author by night. Matt Hofferth hopes to one day realize his dream of becoming a full time writer, but until then, he still plays the part of mild-mannered professional as he must. His hobbies, apart from writing on his lunch break or whenever time finds him, include helping out as an assistant football coach at local Westfield High and being an avid video gamer. He lives in Noblesville, Indiana.

For information on his latest adventures and projects, please visit his website at:

www.hofferthbooks.com

A List of Works by Matt Hofferth

Urban Fantasy

- The Binder's Daughter

Epic Fantasy
A Symphony of Two Keys

1. Melody of the Fates

Shorter Works

- The Only Sparkle On A Vampire Should Be The Zipper

Acknowledgements

Compositions such as this rarely play to completion without the help of many instrumentalists. On drums, my alpha reader and muse theorist, Kris Boultbee. Dropping the bass, my solid and steady beta reader, Andy Betts. Wielding the scarlet jazz flutes (sort of look like red pens, right?), my editors, Julie Talley and Molly Joll. Belting out the soulful sax, my mother, Karin Hinton. I'm the guy with the guitar. We are Hofferth Books. Good night!

Legal Notes

www.hofferthbooks.com

Thank You!